Lady Charlotte Always Gets Her Man

Lady Charlotte Always Gets Her Man

VIOLET MARSH

FOREVER

New York   Boston

Forever
Hachette Book Group
1290 Avenue of the Americas, New York, NY 10104
read-forever.com
twitter.com/readforeverpub

First Edition: March 2024

Forever is an imprint of Grand Central Publishing. The Forever name and logo are trademarks of Hachette Book Group, Inc.

The publisher is not responsible for websites (or their content) that are not owned by the publisher.

Forever books may be purchased in bulk for business, educational, or promotional use. For information, please contact your local bookseller or the Hachette Book Group Special Markets Department at special.markets@hbgusa.com.

Print book interior design by Taylor Navis

Library of Congress Cataloging-in-Publication Data

Names: Marsh, Violet, author.
Title: Lady Charlotte always gets her man / Violet Marsh.
Description: First edition. | New York : Forever, 2024.
Identifiers: LCCN 2023040984 | ISBN 9781538739693 (trade paperback) | ISBN 9781538739716 (ebook)
Subjects: LCSH: Coffeehouses—Fiction. | London (England)—Social life and customs—18th century—Fiction. | LCGFT: Historical fiction. | Romance fiction. | Novels.
Classification: LCC PS3613.A76993 L33 2024 | DDC 813/.6—dc23/eng /20230920
LC record available at https://lccn.loc.gov/2023040984

ISBN: 9781538739693 (trade paperback), 9781538739716 (ebook)

Printed in the United States of America

LSC

Printing 2, 2024

This book is dedicated to Mrs. Spudy and her daughter, Beth. Thank you both for all the romance books you've shared with me throughout the years, which helped turn me into the writer that I am today.

Chapter One

❧

T his gown will be perfect for the betrothal ball."

Panic and horror flooded Lady Charlotte Lovett at her mother's offhand statement. The two of them were standing in front of an ornate mirror at their favorite modiste's shop and surrounded by sinfully soft silks, delicate laces, and finely woven woolen cloth. It was not the setting for dramatic, life-changing announcements. Yet Charlotte could not escape the feeling that her mother's seemingly innocent observation was actually a harbinger of doom.

"Whose betrothal ball?" Charlotte's heart pounded desperately against her stays as she prayed her suspicions were unfounded.

"Yours," her mother replied crisply. She circled around Charlotte as she checked the new dress for any flaws. Pursing her lips, Mother yanked the stomacher downward. Turning sharply to the dressmaker, she instructed in a clipped tone, "The bodice is not framing Charlotte's décolletage. She must be turned out absolutely perfectly."

"I…I am engaged?" The words flew from Charlotte's lips even though she had suspected the truth. Her gut clenched so violently that she nearly flinched.

"Do not act so surprised," Mother said absently as she continued to arrange the front piece of the gown. "You should have been married ages ago. Your father and I decided it was past time to stop humoring your missish qualms and conduct the arrangements entirely ourselves."

Missish qualms? Every last one of their candidates had possessed the hallmarks of a tyrant—a rich, connected tyrant, but a tyrant all the same. It was why Charlotte was still unmarried at the grand age of five-and-twenty. She had tried offering her own suggestions, but her father would not hear of it. He wished to create a dynasty, and her opinions were obviously inconsequential.

"Who is the groom?" Lady Charlotte managed to ask. Nausea sloshed through her. She squeezed her eyes closed as if she could stop not just the queasiness but the entire farce.

Please let it not be the ancient Lord Paltham, who inquired after the natural shape of my hips beneath my petticoats. He is much too obsessed over whether I could bear him Paltham heirs, who he claims are always brawny babes.

"This is hardly the place, Charlotte." Her mother's lips tightened ever so slightly as she nodded with her chin toward the modiste. The dressmaker was doing a commendable job of pretending to be too absorbed in her work of stretching the silk skirts over the pannier to overhear the conversation.

"Madame Vernier, could you please give us a moment?" Charlotte asked, refusing to allow her mother any excuse to prevaricate.

"Why, of course, mademoiselle." Madame Vernier bobbed her head as she made a hasty retreat.

As soon as the woman shut the heavy door behind her, Charlotte turned from the mirror to stare directly into her mother's eyes. Observing her parent's detached expression, Charlotte wondered with a pang of frustration why she'd even bothered. She would find no empathy there.

"Who is the groom?" Charlotte demanded, not even bothering to temper her voice.

Her mother arched one of her exceedingly thin eyebrows, but

she did not otherwise scold Charlotte for her tone. "William Talbot, Viscount Hawley."

Every fiber within Charlotte shrieked in silent horror, but she, herself, made no sound. Anyone—even the uncouth Lord Paltham—would be preferable to the monstrous Hawley. An image of the smirking, handsome man rose in Charlotte's mind. The fiend's chiseled beauty could not distract from the cold, hard meanness that lurked in his crystalline eyes.

"Hawley shall make you a duchess when his father, the Duke of Lansberry, passes," her mother continued, as if the title were all that mattered. But then, from the perspective of Charlotte's parents, social standing was paramount to everything, especially after the taint that her aunt's marriage had left upon the family.

"At least something good has come from your brother's association with Lansberry's youngest son, Matthew," Mother continued. "Why Alexander chose to be friends with the third in line rather than Lord Hawley, I shall never understand. But Alexander's relationship with the family expanded our sphere of influence to include the duke, which in turn has ultimately resulted in this betrothal."

Charlotte ignored her mother's musings about Matthew Talbot, a physician and naturalist, who was nothing like the rest of his brutish relatives. What mattered at the moment was the elder brother.

"Lord Hawley is not even nine-and-twenty, yet he has twice been widowed within a span of three years. The mourning period for his second wife hasn't even ended. If he were a woman, he would be in seclusion and couldn't remarry for another six months." Charlotte couldn't keep an edge of desperation from her voice.

"As the heir apparent, the viscount has a duty to quickly remarry and produce male issue," her mother continued in her usual clipped tone. "Both wives died in tragic accidents, the poor man. But there is no reason to think you would succumb to the same fate. It is not as if a curse is upon the family."

No, it wasn't bad luck that had befallen Hawley's young brides but, according to whispers, something much more suspicious and sinister. Fear pumped through Charlotte as she scrambled for a way to make her mother see beyond the man's title to his dangerous character. "People who cross the viscount have a tendency to end up dead."

Her mother sniffed. "Do not be melodramatic, dear. It doesn't suit you."

"When Mr. Monroe beat Lord Hawley at whist, he was found with his throat slit—only the winnings had been taken and no other valuables."

Her mother shrugged. "It was in an extremely seedy section of London. What do you expect?"

"After Lord Hawley's mistress threw him over for another man, both she and her new lover burned to death in a house fire." Charlotte grabbed her mother's arm as if the gesture would somehow make her words miraculously heeded.

"You listen too much to prurient gossip, darling. It is not an admirable trait, especially for an unmarried miss, who is fast becoming an old maid." Her mother deliberately lifted Charlotte's fingers from her silk-clad arm. "Do you really imagine that an heir apparent to a dukedom is lurking about dark alleys attacking people and torching buildings?"

"He would not need to personally. I have heard that he associates with questionable..." Even Charlotte could hear how frantic her normally even-toned voice had become, but she could do nothing to staunch the fear seeping from her.

Her mother held up a gloved hand, her facial features set in elegant, yet unyielding lines. "That is enough, Charlotte. I will not listen to more of this drivel. Your father and I spoke with the Duke of

Lansberry before he left to address an urgent matter on his Scottish estate. All of the details have not only been finalized but agreed to. We would announce immediately, but the duke wished for us to wait until he returned from the Highlands in two months' time. At least that will give us ample opportunity to prepare for the betrothal ball and the wedding. Both events must be grand enough to be discussed in drawing rooms, not for just this Season but for decades to come. Our families do have reputations in Society to uphold."

Two months. Two damnable short months. That was all Charlotte had to extricate herself from a marriage to a young man who had already buried two wives.

"The bodice of this dress is just not right." Charlotte's mother had turned her attention back to the gown and was staring at Charlotte's stomacher as if she could glare the fabric into submission like she did to everything and everyone else.

"Perhaps you should review fashion plates with Madame Vernier," Charlotte suggested, desperate to escape her mother, her current situation, and her whole bloody cosseted life.

Her mother nodded. "I am glad you have returned to being reasonable."

"Of course, Mother," Charlotte lied. She had no doubt that her mother detected the falsehood, but that would not bother the Society matron. Charlotte had stopped arguing and acquiesced as she always did. It was of no import how she actually felt. It never was, as long as she acted outwardly demure and pleasant.

Mother strode to the door and opened it, but she paused before crossing the threshold. "Are you not accompanying me to review the samples?"

"I need a few moments to compose myself." Charlotte pressed her lips into a sweet smile.

Her mother's expression turned impenetrable. "Do not dawdle too long, darling. Women of our breeding do not sulk."

"Understood, Mother," Charlotte said.

With regal grace, her mother swept into the hallway, not even bothering to shut the oak door behind her. Charlotte walked across the room and gently closed it, wishing she could shut out her parents' ambitions just as easily.

Sinking back against the wood, Charlotte found herself staring at the French doors opposite her that Madame Vernier had installed years before to inject a bit of the Continent into her London shop. The early spring day was unseasonably warm, and Madame Vernier's staff had left the massive glass slightly ajar— enough to let in air but not enough for people passing by on the street to catch glimpses of the clients. The drawn drapes fluttered in the breeze, beckoning to Charlotte.

An unholy energy, fueled by panic, buzzed through her. When pulled back, the French doors would present an opening large and grand enough even to accommodate Charlotte's ridiculously large skirts. Moreover, the room was on the first floor.

Consumed by the urge to flee, Charlotte grabbed a swatch of gauzy material that Madame Vernier had been using as a make-shift neckerchief for Charlotte. Luckily the material had not been cut and served as a perfect veil. Pulling the sheer material over her head, Charlotte crossed over to the French doors. Parting them, she stepped through and onto the street.

Then she ran.

Chapter Two

At first, Charlotte did not have a direction in mind as she dashed through London. Instinctively, she headed away from the crowded streets frequented by the upper classes. She barely registered the shocked expressions of passers-by at the sight of a lady dressed in court attire dashing pell-mell along the cobblestones. Several times, she had to move her body at odd angles to avoid whacking someone with her pannier. Yet she did not slack her pace, not even when the buildings became older and less meticulously maintained. Fine ladies and their maids no longer populated the thoroughfare.

A painful stitch in Charlotte's side finally caused her to pause. As she leaned against the rough brick facade of a nearby building, surprise shot through her. She'd traveled all the way to Covent Garden—and not a very savory part of it. Scooching into a side alley, she tried to gather her frenetic thoughts and emotions and put her intelligence to use.

Running from the modiste had accomplished nothing. Although Charlotte possessed a small inheritance from a great-aunt, it would not be enough to live on for the rest of her life. She had no choice but to return to her parents and their machinations. All she had done was gotten herself woefully lost in an unfamiliar and likely dangerous section of the city.

Forcing herself to breathe in and out, Charlotte focused on

the most urgent problem: finding her way through the warren of streets she'd blundered into. Her only incursions into Covent Garden had been strictly limited to attending the Theatre Royal. This part of the city was more the realm of her twin brother.

Peeking around the corner, she scanned the larger street for any landmark that Alexander might have mentioned. Everything looked drab and unremarkable. Coffeehouses blended into alehouses and perhaps even a bordello or two, and then back into coffeehouses. An incongruous laugh rose inside Charlotte, who for the first time in her life found herself on the verge of having the vapors.

To think, she had yearned to accompany her brother to this section of London! Although she had no interest in the drinking establishments or the brothels, she'd long wanted to visit a coffeehouse, choke down some of the bitter brew, and engage in a debate unfettered by the rules of polite society. She and her friends had secretly fantasized about visiting the noisy spaces instead of enduring the suffocating atmosphere of her mother's especially strict salon and its endless decorum. But coffeehouses were barred to women, except for the proprietresses.

Stifling another inappropriate giggle, Charlotte tried to soberly take an accounting of the street. Richly clad aristocratic young rogues mixed with laborers. Not all the better-dressed men, however, had the bearing of the peerage or gentry. Instead, their demeanor seemed hard, coarse, and most assuredly deadly. A chill slithered over Charlotte as she wondered if she was espying some of the fabled highwaymen who dressed like fops; or perhaps these hardened fellows were smugglers or river pirates. This, Charlotte realized, was a world that Lord Hawley would frequent as he discarded his Society trappings and donned his true persona. The truth of the villain could be found in places like Covent Garden, not at the balls, soirees, and musicales that Charlotte attended.

But there was one coffeehouse where she might at least be able to seek temporary shelter and arrange for a hackney carriage: the Black Sheep. Not only was it her twin's favorite haunt, but one of the proprietresses was Charlotte's cousin—estranged, but still family. And Alexander told such stories about the establishment.

The Black Sheep—even the name called to something inside Charlotte, not just to her current panic but to the misfit part of her that wanted to debate and maybe even defy the rules prescribed to ladies. What would it be like to live as her cousin did—freed from Society, owning a place that was a hotbed for revolutionary ideas? Would it be similar to how she imagined her grandmother and great-aunt's salon? Mother had stifled its daring philosophical atmosphere after Charlotte's aunt had run away with a pirate, but how magnificent it must have been in its heyday.

Just a few weeks ago, her cousin and product of that shocking union, Hannah Wick, had approached Alexander about investing in an expansion of her coffeehouse. The space adjacent to the Black Sheep had recently become available for rent, and Hannah had wished for help in paying the lease. The sum was not a grand one, but Charlotte's brother didn't have the funds.

Suddenly, a brilliant plan ripped through the doom encasing Charlotte. She had the money—her inheritance! What if she transformed her dreams of a coffeehouse where women could attend into reality? She knew such a place would attract scores of customers, and customers meant blunt, and blunt meant she would have an income separate from her parents. If she was a co-owner of the Black Sheep, she would have access to all its customers, including those with criminal connections who might know of Hawley's misdeeds.

Good lord, perhaps Charlotte had been running somewhere after all. An almost giddy excitement collided with her anxiousness. A part of Charlotte warned her that she should not plunge into murky, unknown waters, but she ruthlessly silenced the doubts. If she wanted freedom, she had to be bold.

Afraid that further consideration would sway her into dismissing the scheme, Charlotte burst into the larger street. A flower seller pushing her cart seemed the most approachable person. After hurrying to catch up to the woman, Charlotte blurted out, "Miss. Please. Can you tell me where to find the Black Sheep coffeehouse?"

The female peddler blinked, likely in shock over Charlotte's formal appearance and polished accent. Too startled and confused to protest or even to ask for coin, she jabbed her finger to the right. "Four streets that way, milady, then toward the south."

"Thank you!" Charlotte wished she could pay the flower seller, but she had left her reticule at the modiste's. Instead, she gave a friendly salute before she wove through the crowd in the direction indicated.

Within three minutes, her breath coming in gasps both from anticipation and exertion, Charlotte stood before the famed Black Sheep. At this hour, it was not open to the public, which meant she could talk to the proprietresses alone.

Charlotte raised her gloved hand to rap at the sturdy wooden door, but her heart seemed to knock instead. Before nerves could stop her, Charlotte let her knuckles fall against the oak. Once. Twice. Thrice.

The door opened to show Charlotte's cousin. Until now, Charlotte had only spied Hannah in passing, but she had no trouble recognizing her. After all, it was a bit like peering into her own looking glass. They had the same Titian red hair and pale white skin with a light smattering of freckles over the bridge of their noses. Unlike Charlotte, however, Hannah did not hide the brown flecks with powder. Since their mothers had been identical twins, it was no wonder they looked similar, despite the widely divergent paths their immediate families had taken.

"Hello, Hannah Wick," Charlotte said rather clumsily as her throat unexpectedly tightened. She was rather at a loss about exactly how to greet this relative to whom she'd never spoken. Charlotte briefly pulled back her veil, and Hannah's green eyes widened. Within mere moments, the young woman regained her composure—an asset for the owner of a rowdy coffeehouse.

"Come in straight away, Cousin. You'll be set upon by every cut-purse and filching thief in Covent Garden dressed in that finery."

At Hannah's hastily spoken command, Charlotte attempted to slip through the opening between the coffeehouse's heavy wooden door and its half-timber exterior. Unfortunately, she had entirely forgotten about her massive hoop petticoat. The stiff pannier collided with the wattle and daub. Charlotte found herself bouncing backward into a gaggle of smartly dressed gentlemen walking down the street.

Swerving en masse like a herd of disgruntled sheep, the fops murmured something about slatternly morts. One even rudely elbowed her with his brightly clad arm. Charlotte was accustomed to receiving vastly different treatment from the opposite sex, but given the circumstances, their crude responses actually soothed her.

The young bucks hadn't recognized her as they continued to gambol south along the thoroughfare. Thank goodness Charlotte had grabbed that veil. But even if the gauzy fabric had shielded her this time, it might prove less effective in another close encounter with the peerage.

Wasting no more time in reaching safety, Charlotte turned sideways and pushed. The delicate silk of her dress caught on a splinter in the wooden doorjamb. Ignoring both the tug and the sound of ripping fabric, she continued to shove her body and massive skirt forward. As much as she loved a pretty gown, she did not appreciate this one.

"Gadso! What is she wearing?"

Still wedged in the door like an entire loaf of bread, Charlotte could not spy the second female speaker as she peered into the long, narrow building with its white daub walls. But even if she didn't know the identity of the other occupant, she really had no other choice but to continue trying to enter the Black Sheep.

"A gown for my betrothal ball." Charlotte could not help but spit out the last two words as she finally burst into the building. Sour panic churned, and her innards twisted again. Right now she would eagerly trade her ridiculous, delicate attire for the service-able linsey-woolsey short dress and practical skirts that her cousin wore.

"Why are you here? It is not as if our families are on speaking terms." Hannah regarded Charlotte with wary intensity. Since it was a look that Charlotte's own mother often employed, Charlotte was well-accustomed to such scrutiny. In fact, it ironically rebal-anced her. An examination was something Charlotte could handle with aplomb.

"My brother does frequent your establishment." Charlotte straightened her shoulders and smoothed down the ripped silk in an attempt to hide a glimpse of her linen undergarments. She wished, however, that her hands did not have a slight tremor.

"Coffeehouses do not serve women, so you cannot be here for the brew. If you're a runaway bride seeking shelter, I suggest you try a more hospitable host. Since my mother was cut off by yours for following her heart, do not expect sympathy."

"I am not a runaway bride." *Not precisely, at least,* Charlotte thought as she removed the veil. "I only fled a dress fitting."

"Where the word 'betrothal' was bandied about? You're quib-bling." The second speaker's voice again came from the back of the narrow room. Charlotte scanned past the long, empty tables. Finally, her gaze lit on who she assumed was, from her brother's description of the other proprietress, Miss Sophia Wick, Hannah's paternal cousin. Like Hannah, she wore a white linen cap and clothes of linsey-woolsey. The hard edge of Sophia's London accent was softened with hints of the Caribbean, but her golden-brown eyes held an unmistakable challenge. Neither of the mistresses Wick were pleased with Charlotte's unexpected appearance.

An anxious flutter beat against Charlotte's breast. Normally, she could address any social situation, but this wasn't the type of gathering she'd been bred to navigate.

"I have come with a business proposition." When Charlotte heard the words burst from her own lips, she should have felt absurd. But she didn't. Instead, a wellspring of hope flooded her, and with it, her old confidence.

The Wick cousins exchanged a glance before they both doubled over in laughter. The guffaws pricked at Charlotte's rediscovered poise but didn't pop it entirely.

Sophia recovered first. "You expect us to believe that the daughter of a duke wishes to do business with the children of pirates?"

Charlotte smiled warmly just as she did when greeting guests at the literary salon. "You're not the offspring of any old buccaneer, though, are you? Your mother is royalty in that world." Sophia was the daughter of a pirate princess with African, Dutch, and Taíno ancestry. According to legend, Sophia's mother had rescued and then fallen in love with Sophia's father, a white English ragamuffin who'd been deported with his brother to the New World.

"Aye," Sophia acknowledged, her lips tilting upward with pride. "She is. I'll give you credit for a honeyed tongue, but that is not enough for me to entertain whatever foolish scheme you've devised."

"It's not only my plan. It is both of yours as well." Charlotte kept her voice amiable. "My brother said you have a desire to expand the Black Sheep, is that not true?"

Once again, the cousins glanced in each other's direction. This time neither laughed.

Good. Charlotte would sway them.

"Your brother declined." Hannah's red brows drew downward. "Why are you keen when he was not?"

Because Alexander receives a paltry allowance from our father.

But even though the duke's disdain for his heir apparent was an open secret among the upper echelons of Society, and likely much of the lower rungs as well, Charlotte would not embarrass her brother by saying so. Instead, she ignored the question entirely.

"I received a small bequest a year ago," Charlotte explained, the words tumbling out quickly as she prayed these women would give her more credence than her own mother did. "From what you told my brother, it will be just enough to cover the lease for half a year. By then, the profits from the expansion will be enough to pay rent."

"Why sully your hands with trade? You are a lady. You would have no social standing left if it were discovered that you were the co-owner of a coffeehouse known for attracting eccentrics, including those of the criminal variety." Sophia moved closer, and the light from one of the narrow windows washed over her light brown skin. She looked striking in the sunbeam, and it was not hard to imagine her commanding a ship like her mother.

"Perhaps in certain circles I would lose my status. In some though, such notoriety would bring me renown." Charlotte spoke bluntly, even as her chest constricted with the enormity of her proposal. If she were found out, the flawless reputation she had worked so hard to create would unravel, yet perhaps that unspooling would also loosen the bonds immobilizing her.

"So this is a scheme to make yourself appear daring?" Hannah's green eyes sparked with rage. "Some sort of lark? A wager?"

"No." Charlotte spoke with a coolness that belied the fiery

tempest inside her. "It is a bid for independence. My inheritance is not enough to sustain me over the years without another source."

Hannah snorted, sending tendrils of red hair flying against her mobcap. "How much do you think we earn? It is hardly ample enough to keep the likes of you satisfied. Marry an indulgent man instead."

"My parents insist upon selecting my bridegroom. I assure you, indulgent is not a quality they seek out. Rather the opposite," Charlotte said as she battled back the clawing dread that had chased her through the streets of London.

"I find it hard to dredge up sympathy for a noble," Hannah said drily.

"Your mother was one originally," Charlotte pointed out, careful not to allow a single ripple of frustration or panic to disrupt her calm tone. After all, she needed the Wick cousins much more than they required her. She could not run a coffeehouse herself. "I do not need to live in high style." *Just not in a gilt prison.*

And Charlotte wanted more than financial security. If she was to unearth evidence of Hawley's perfidy and stop the wedding, this was her best chance, really her only chance, to do it.

"Silly ol' bird." The dreadful squawk seemed to bounce off the spartan interior as a lime-green parrot flapped into the room from a doorway Charlotte had overlooked. The palpable disdain in the creature's voice was matched by the pure malevolence in its single eye. Staring at her the entire time, it landed on Hannah's shoulder.

Normally, Charlotte would have laughed at the absurdity of a glorified bag of feathers calling her foolish. She didn't, due to a couple reasons.

For one, the avian creature had twisted its head so dramatically that its beak now pointed toward the timbered ceiling. It made for a rather intimidating stance, especially coupled with the dastardly gleam in its amber iris. The winged beast seemed more than capable of not only taking offense but enacting revenge.

Even more salient, however, Charlotte half feared that she agreed with the parrot's harsh assessment. Her plan to save herself and learn Viscount Hawley's secrets was flimsy at best…dangerous at worst. It was a half-formed scheme built on unrealized dreams and desperation.

"I believe our pet Pan said it very aptly." Sophia Wick clasped her elegant fingers together. "Any business started as a ploy to escape an aristocratic marriage is doomed to fail."

Even more doubts began to press upon Charlotte's precious bubble of hope, threatening to puncture it entirely this time. But she earnestly clung to her optimism and to her composure. Her plan would work. It had to.

"My cousin is right. I see no reason to assume the risks that you are presenting." Hannah reached up to scratch Pan on his feathery chest. The bird looked exceedingly smug.

"I promise that enlarging the coffeehouse will benefit all of us." Charlotte stepped forward toward the Wick cousins, trying to make them understand that she did not view this as a game or even as only an escape. Yes, her ideas partially sprang from her daydreams with her friends, but that made her proposal no less earnest. "This is not mere whimsy. I'm not just offering to help pay the lease. I have an idea to expand your clientage."

"Truly?" Sophia lifted one dark eyebrow, her voice dripping with skepticism. "What would that entail, precisely?"

Charlotte drew in a breath, and her chest pressed against her stays. The rigid structure gave her strength. "I have many connections to literary salons. My mother runs one, and I assist with her hosting duties."

Hannah snorted. "I hardly see how that genteel activity has anything to do with our coffeehouse. From what I've heard, your mother has ruthlessly stamped out any whiff of revolutionary thought that our grandmother and great-aunt previously cultivated. We cater to people who eschew social strictures and whose ideas are considered uncomfortably radical, not fashionably 'enlightened.' It is rough-and-tumble, not silks and divans."

"Would women daring enough to attend a secret mixed-company coffeehouse be unconventional enough for you?"

"What exactly are you envisioning?" Sophia asked. When she stepped toward Charlotte, Pan flew from Hannah's shoulder to Sophia's. As Sophia continued to advance, the avian nightmare turned his head in intimidating circles.

Ignoring the bird's gyrating eye, Charlotte focused entirely on Sophia. "A new type of coffeehouse—one that people will be clamoring to obtain access to."

"Are you suggesting a private venue where we host tête-à-têtes for you and your high society friends who want the facade of adventure?" Hannah scoffed.

"No. There is clandestine, and there is *clandestine*," Charlotte said. "It is not as if the Black Sheep does not already deal in confidences."

It did not surprise her when the Wick cousins once again turned toward each other. They were clearly close. Charlotte understood. She and Alexander communicated in the same wordless way. Pan, however, must not have appreciated the tension. With a flutter of lime wings, he circled the room.

"What secrets are you referring to?" Sophia asked finally, her melodic voice hardening into a decided edge.

Just then, Pan decided to settle. On Charlotte's head.

Only years of social training to be calm prevented her from screaming. Luckily, the misbegotten bird did not dig his claws into her scalp...much. But he did bend his body over Charlotte's face to stick his eye directly in her field of vision.

"The Black Sheep's code of conduct states that no debates shall touch upon religion and politics, but according to my brother, that is most definitely not the case." Charlotte tried to peer around the parrot. It proved impossible as the creature bobbed its head in any direction that she turned.

"No member is supposed to discuss what happens within these walls." Hannah's mouth twisted, and her already pink cheeks darkened in patent agitation.

"Blackguard! Villain! Filching cove!" Pan flew toward one of the ceiling beams and perched there as if watching for dragoons to ram down the door.

"My brother knew I would keep his confidence." Charlotte spoke hastily to allay Hannah and Sophia's concerns. "The truth of the matter is that covert activities have a way of reaching the ears of those eager to participate. My friends and I often talk about how we wish we could sit in a coffeehouse and have a good spate without worrying a whit about manners."

Sophia appeared more receptive to Charlotte's ideas than her fellow proprietress. She, however, did not seem entirely convinced either. "Do you really think a group of ladies with their wide skirts and powdered hair will wish to sit around long tables and rub elbows with shopkeepers?"

"Not at long tables—no." Charlotte shook her head, trying to remain calm despite the hope and gloom warring inside her. "I was thinking of something a bit more comfortable and welcoming, relaxing even."

Hannah opened her mouth, presumably to utter another protest, but Sophia waved her cousin into silence. "Please elaborate, Lady Charlotte."

"We will install a disguised door between your current shop and the new addition," Charlotte spoke quickly as the half-formed vision began to crystalize. Her years of organizing Society events were serving her well despite the emotions clanging through her. "That shall be the only entrance. We fill the room with sofas and chairs, all elegantly appointed, but more comfortable than fashionable."

"Like a parlor?" Sophia pressed.

Hannah made a moue of disgust. "We are not some lady's drawing room."

"This would be snugger than those formal rooms. I envision an exceedingly inviting sanctuary with cushions that make you want to sink down and stay awhile." Charlotte barely managed to keep the tempo of her voice steady with all the excitement and panic.

"How would this not just be a meeting place for your acquaintances?" Sophia asked suspiciously. "Do you expect to attract females outside your inner circle?"

"It would not just be ladies, but a mixed group, similar to a salon."

"How mixed?" Hannah asked, her voice not quite as sharp as before but still probing. "We do not just serve the gentry."

"The appeal of the coffeehouse is its egalitarian exchange of ideas untrammeled by subtleties and tact." As Charlotte spoke, her hope transformed into a fire of want. Oh, how tired she was of being nice. She did not want to politely converse with charming smiles and coquettish winks. She wanted to debate. Boldly. Fiercely. Without restraint. Without worrying what a man, especially a prospective husband, might think.

"Are you sure you are not romanticizing the idea of the penny university?" Sophia asked, using the popular nickname for coffeehouses. For a single copper, a man could gain admittance to one of the establishments where he could have his cup refilled as he nattered with gentlemen of all ranks, including leading luminaries in any variety of disciplines.

"Perhaps I am aiming for an ideal. But is that so wrong? Establishments are about appearances, are they not? We will be offering an atmosphere that no one else does. Its concealed nature will only enhance the appeal. You could charge higher prices for coffee, even offer different recipes that add unexpected flavors. It will be a place to indulge the body and the mind—a retreat, an escape from all strictures." Charlotte knew she sounded effusive. She couldn't help it. She'd heard so many tales from her brother about the Black Sheep.

"You are fine with consorting with beau-takers?" Hannah pushed again, using the term for criminals who defrauded the gentry. "And illegal gin producers? How about highwaymen? Smugglers? A river pirate or two?"

"Isn't that the point of a coffeehouse? To mingle with all?" Charlotte spoke lightly, but her heart began to thump so dramatically that she could only pray the women did not detect its thundering. The bubble of hope had swelled to almost painful proportions.

"You are actually serious about joining our venture." Sophia's observation was a statement, not a question, but Charlotte nodded all the same.

Sophia turned toward Hannah. "We have talked about wanting to experiment with the coffee—maybe even serve light refreshments. Lady Charlotte is right. Most of her suggestions mirror what we've already been planning."

Hannah rubbed her brow, the movement causing her mobcap to rustle. Then she heaved out a breath, and Charlotte barely stopped her own sigh. In Hannah's exhalation, Charlotte detected a relenting note. For the first time since her mother's pronouncement, the fear inside Charlotte began to ebb a fraction.

"We do truly want to expand," Hannah admitted, "but this is our livelihood, Charlotte—not some pretty bauble that can be replaced if dropped and shattered."

"I will not treat the Black Sheep as such," Charlotte promised, coming near to choking on her welling emotion.

"We will be in charge," Sophia said sternly. "This is our domain, not yours."

"Understood," Charlotte said, before adding very carefully, "although I would like the ability to propose ideas."

"It sounds as if we need an agreement drawn up—a charter, if you will." Sophia gestured toward one of the long-scarred tables. "Take a seat. It will be a long discussion."

Relief thundering through her, Charlotte started to arrange her skirts. Although the petticoat did fold up to allow her to sit, the chairs were not just narrow but closely placed. Eager to document the deal that could not just save but transform her, Charlotte pulled out several seats to make room. Unfortunately, her pannier still knocked one down and caused another to wobble.

To Charlotte's surprise, the Wick cousins did not laugh at her predicament. Instead, Hannah crossed over to one of the windows and emphatically closed the shutter. "You might as well step out of that ridiculous gown. This isn't the king's court, and you'll find we're not given to ceremony here."

Near giddy from the maelstrom of relief, Charlotte wondered if she had ever heard a better suggestion. With an alacrity that should have mortified her, she removed the offending dress and panniers and then stood in nothing but her chemise, stays, and a single petticoat. She would have expected to feel scandalous. She did not. She felt wonderfully, utterly liberated. Without a backward glance at the discarded betrothal gown, she slid onto a chair and prepared to discuss her future.

Chapter Three

Y ou're looking unfashionably hale and healthy. Pale is still the vogue here in London."

Matthew Talbot felt his mouth stretch into a smile at the familiar voice of his best friend, Alexander Lovett, Marquess of Heathford. It felt surprisingly good to be back on the streets of the capital city after a year abroad.

Normally, Matthew didn't mind long sea voyages, but this one had seemed interminable for some blighted reason. It wasn't even as if Matthew particularly liked Britain, although he supposed he didn't mind the foggy place of his birth. The isle offered enough flora and fauna to keep a chap like him busy sketching and categorizing, especially in the Scottish Highlands where he'd spent most of his early childhood.

It wasn't precisely home, but then again, no place was. Matthew did not fit anywhere, especially not with his family. His father, the Duke of Lansberry, had never understood how a son of his could be more interested in studying a pheasant than shooting it. And his older brothers, especially Hawley...well that didn't bear thinking about, not when the day was sunny and he was in the company of his best friend on the thoroughfare leading to his favorite place in all of London—the Black Sheep.

"Jolly Old England never changes much, I am afraid," Matthew said as he waited for Alexander to catch up to him. Despite using a cane for balance rather than fashion, Alexander moved quickly over the cobblestones. Matthew had tried to employ his skills as a surgeon to help straighten his mate's clubfoot, but too many quacks had tried before him and had caused irreparable harm. But despite the twinges of pain Alexander's leg gave him and his uneven gait, he was an athletic sort, engaging in sports from horseback riding to fowling. Yet somehow, despite Matthew's preference for observing wildlife rather than chasing after it, they'd been fast friends for nearly two decades, bonded by their mutual outsider status at their boarding school.

"Oh, but there have been some developments in your absence. A new boxing arena opened, a veritable plague of highwaymen has beset London's thoroughfares, and Mr. Powys has penned the most hilarious, scandal-ridden play," Alexander said with mock theatrical drama as he reached Matthew's side. "And you will soon discover the most interesting news and transformation when we reach our destination."

"Do you mean something has changed at the Black Sheep?" Concern rippled through Matthew. The establishment was a safe haven. Where else could a man discuss the minutiae of Hooke's and Leeuwenhoek's theories on cells and the validity of immunization one moment, Pope and Swift the next, reform and the latest debates in Parliament the third, and finally the plants and animals of the Old and New World? It was at once radical and pedantic, and Matthew loved it.

"The very place." Alexander winked. "The changes might leave you tongue-tied at first, but the place has become so deuced comfortable, I daresay that even you'll unbend in due course."

Although Matthew had become accustomed to giving large lectures at colleges or in front of learned societies, he was horribly awkward in social situations, especially new ones. If he kept the matters limited to science, he could muddle along until he lost himself in the facts. The more rigid things were, the more at ease Matthew paradoxically felt. He rather liked the Black Sheep's spartan interior and high-backed wooden chairs. There was nothing to distract from the debate at hand.

"Have they redecorated?" Matthew asked, unable to hide his hesitancy. It was absurd, his reluctance to learn about the alterations.

Alexander paused, his hazel gaze sweeping up and down the street. No one was close to them, but Alexander still leaned in a fraction toward Matthew as he spoke. "Not exactly. They've opened a new room, a secret one."

Alexander spoke the last two words with a flourish, but Matthew could muster no enthusiasm at the idea of a clandestine addition to his favorite retreat. He had enough covert activities to contend with already. He did not need to add more.

"At the Black Sheep?" Matthew asked cautiously.

Alexander laughed. "You needn't sound as if I'd asked you to step into a pit of vipers."

"I wouldn't mind a snake den, as long as we're talking about actual reptiles, not metaphorical ones. Serpents are rather fascinating creatures and deeply misunderstood."

"Silly me for making such a comparison," Alexander said jovially as they turned onto the street that led to the coffeehouse. "You probably would have preferred it if the Black Sheep left the cobwebs in the new space. You could write another paper on spiders."

"'On the Web-Weaving Mating Habits of the Black Lace-Weaver Spider' was very well received," Matthew protested, more out of reflex than in any real defense. Alexander had been the one person who had always supported Matthew's academic pursuits, even the most outwardly prosaic ones.

"There is other news as well."

At Alexander's uncharacteristically somber tone, Matthew swung his head to study his friend. Alexander preferred to regard the world through a lens of perennial amusement. When he sobered, the circumstances were always serious.

"What is it?" Matthew asked, keeping his voice low.

"Hawley's second wife died about six months ago. Carriage wreck."

Shards of icy horror met with flames of guilt. As the unholy mess churned in Matthew's gullet, he remained outwardly calm. "I assume it was found to be an accident like his first wife's fall from Hawley's prized stallion?"

The viscountess had broken her neck after being thrown...even though she'd always been afraid of riding and refused to enter the stables. Yet no one openly questioned Hawley, as he liberally sobbed in public and waxed on poetically about losing a lovely bride still in the bloom of youth.

Alexander's jaw tightened as he nodded. "This latest inquest was a farce just like the one for the first Lady Hawley, but I did attend. I took notes for you, especially when the surgeon who examined the body testified."

"I shouldn't have left on another voyage," Matthew said grimly. "I should have stayed and found proof of my brother's perfidy."

But he'd also had duties to pursue in the New World— responsibilities that couldn't wait either. If he had stayed, he would have condemned others to suffering. There had been no easy path.

"You spent a year trying to prove Hawley's guilt." Alexander stopped walking and clasped Matthew's shoulder with the hand not gripping his cane. "You needn't blame yourself when everyone considers Hawley's wilder side a charming affectation."

"He's my brother. I should be the one to stop him."

Alexander gave Matthew a squeeze before releasing him. "And you will, with my help. We must succeed this time. Your father and mine are discussing a union between Hawley and my twin. I can't—won't—let him marry her."

"Your sister?" A sick sensation chilled every identifiable organ in Matthew's body. Not Lady Charlotte. Surely, his father wouldn't be so mad as to shackle such a bright, kindhearted soul to a villainous blackguard. Although the old duke was blind to his heir apparent's murderous nature, he wasn't completely unaware of the darkness in Hawley's soul. After all, he'd helped cultivate it.

"Unfortunately, yes." Matthew slammed his cane against the ground in a rare outward expression of anger. But then his expression smoothed as it always did. "But Lottie isn't allowing herself to be cowed. In fact, she's embarked on her own grand escapade."

Lady Charlotte. She'd been a whirl of skirts the first time twelve-year-old Matthew had seen her as she'd nearly tackled her brother with her exuberant embrace. She'd summarily grabbed her sibling's hand, chattering away about all the happenings Alexander had missed while he'd been away at school, from the vicar's new baby stealing everyone's attention at the Sunday sermon to her thoughts on *Robinson Crusoe*, to the growing hedgehog family in the home garden. When Lady Charlotte had finally noticed Matthew standing utterly still in the darkest corner of the foyer, her smile hadn't dimmed a whit. He, of course, had only managed a faint grin.

"What do you mean Charlotte is undertaking her own adventure?" Matthew asked as a fierce protectiveness billowed through him. He couldn't allow Hawley's blackness to seep into Charlotte's life. With the joy she gave to others, she deserved happiness.

Alexander's perennial grin returned along with a decidedly enigmatic twist to his lips. "Once we're ensconced in the Black Sheep, I'll tell you more." Alexander waited a beat and waggled his brows. "In the clandestine room, of course."

Matthew didn't even try to suppress a groan. He was accustomed to Alexander's mercurial moods and knew his friend hid his worries and pain behind jokes and grins, but Matthew didn't wish to be reminded of the changes to his preferred establishment. He just wanted to head inside the familiar coffeehouse and sip on bitter brew while he and Alexander plotted to reveal Hawley's true nature.

"You'll appreciate the changes. I promise." Alexander started walking again, his cane clicking merrily along the cobblestones.

With a start, Matthew realized they'd stopped only a few feet away from the Black Sheep. Hurrying after his friend, Matthew caught up to Alexander just as he was opening the heavy front door. Falling silent, Matthew stepped inside after Alexander and surveyed the familiar space. It was curiously less crowded than normal for that time of day, and definitely less noisy. Although many of the regulars were still clustered around the tables and were speaking passionately, the energy didn't feel the same. It didn't appear gutted…just a wee bit duller. Matthew wasn't sure though, if it was an actual shift in atmosphere or just that everything felt darker after learning of Hawley's impending betrothal to Lady Charlotte.

Miss Hannah Wick drifted over, giving them a wink. "Why, aren't you a sight for sore eyes, Dr. Talbot! I do hope your journey went well. Has Lord Heathford told you about the alteration to our brew?"

"The coffee has changed too?" Matthew asked. Swounds, had they made the swill worse? The Black Sheep did offer a better drink than most of the establishments, but it still wasn't exactly an appealing beverage. The refreshing jolt it gave a man, however, more than made up for its flavor.

"I haven't told him all of it. I thought I'd let him get a taste for himself," Alexander explained.

"You won't share our recipe, Dr. Talbot?"

Hannah's green gaze bored into Matthew, and he realized her question carried hidden meaning. Although he still didn't possess any clue as to what they were actually talking about, he nodded. He might not particularly like secrets, but he damn well knew how to keep them. He wouldn't have survived these past few years if he didn't.

"He wouldn't dream of revealing your most unusual ingredients," Alexander promised Hannah.

"Come along then." Sending her mobcap bouncing, Hannah set off briskly toward the back of the shop. Pushing open a door, she led them into a narrow passage that had always been off-limits to customers. Once the door shut behind them, she pressed on an inconspicuous piece of paneling in the wall.

It swung wide to reveal a boisterous gathering that looked more like a sartorial print from William Hogarth's A Rake's Progress series than a real-life tableau. The cushions on the rather plainly carved furniture were stuffed near to bursting; they were so sinfully plump. It appeared nigh impossible for a human being to maintain good posture on them. They were clearly designed for lounging...and for pleasing the body rather than the eye. The white daub walls had been covered with a coat of powder blue, and the ceiling had even been painted with a few clouds in Continental fashion. Conversation burbled around like a series of fountains in a French-style formal garden. Lighter feminine voices mixed with the deeper tones of masculine ones. Between the potent mix of colognes and the bright silk clothing of the men and women, the hidden space brought to mind a glasshouse—full of blooms gathered from all corners of the world that would ne'er grow together in nature.

Despite the perfumed assault on the entirety of Matthew's senses, what immobilized him faster than the venom of a cobra de capello was the sight of Lady Charlotte seated at the very center point of the gathering. He swore her unpowdered auburn hair glowed with its own light.

At the unexpected sight of her, the air whooshed from his body. Matthew had not laid eyes on Alexander's twin sister for years. He'd been ousted from polite society after he'd scandalously decided to earn a living as a physician and professor rather than become a vicar or a military officer. His decision to learn the skills of surgeons, an uneducated profession associated with barbers, had earned him only more derision. But his most unforgiveable transgression was his choice to eschew his right as a son of a duke to be called Lord Matthew Talbot and instead select to be addressed as a doctor, a title he'd earned through his formal education.

Lady Charlotte tipped back her head and laughed, her painted lips parted in the most inviting manner. The melodic sound found its way into Matthew's heart and then curled up there. Lady Charlotte had always had this effect on him, ever since he'd first laid eyes on her all those years ago at her family's country seat. At Falcondale Hall, Matthew had discovered more than a respite from his siblings' merciless pranks and his father's disdain...He'd found Lady Charlotte.

"Dr. Matthew Talbot!" Lady Charlotte's voice had gained a rich flavor since their childhood days, and it dumbfounded him as much as a bee confronted with a smoker. But unlike an apis mellifera, he was not lulled into a stupor but rather besieged by too much vigor. His heart pounded, his chest contracted, his throat tightened, and his intellect...well his intellect struggled under the heft of his physical reactions.

"Milady." He had to force the single word through tightly bound muscles.

When he and Alexander reached Lady Charlotte's side, Matthew bobbed slightly. Some of his unfashionably short hair slipped from its binding. Hastily, Matthew tucked the wayward chunk behind his ear.

Lady Charlotte, in contrast, was perfection personified. Not one

Titian red strand dared to spring loose from the tight curls of her elegant coiffure. Gone was the wild hoyden who would climb down a tree from her window to join her brother and Matthew for a romp through the woods or a lazy afternoon at the fishing pond. In her place stood an elegant lady who embodied every beauty ideal, from her flawless porcelain complexion touched with a rosy hint of rouge to her well-shaped bosom lifted high by her stays.

Matthew felt like a doomed dodo standing before a bird of paradise. He had always dressed practically, avoiding the flamboyant colors preferred by other aristocratic men. He couldn't hide his tall, narrow frame though. His brothers had always quipped that he was a stick masquerading as a sapling. Although he was not as rawboned as he had been as a lad, he possessed an unfashionable lankiness made worse by his refusal to engage in the practice of padding his legs to appear more muscular. It also did not help that he was constantly bonking his head on doorframes or ducking to enter rooms. *Jester.* His siblings' old nickname for Matthew burned inside him.

"Alexander said that you have just returned from a voyage to the Colonies." Lady Charlotte smiled gracefully as she patted a seat next to her.

Matthew's heart flopped. Somehow, he managed to nod his head and sit down beside her without tripping over his feet. Alexander reclined in an armchair across from them.

"It has been forever since I last saw you." Lady Charlotte kept talking to Matthew as if the present discourse had not been virtually one-sided.

It had been approximately three years and two months since their last ill-fated encounter. Alexander had persuaded Matthew to attend the legendary salon that Lady Charlotte and her mother held. Although Matthew prized nothing more than a good book, he preferred treatises to novels. In a scientific setting, he could debate all manner of topics, but when it came to discussing satire of modern sensibilities or, even worse, the emotions of the characters, he failed miserably. Due to his position as a university lecturer, the other guests had expected him to say something brilliant at every turn of the conversation. Instead, he had muttered some incoherent sounds and prayed someone else would speak. More than once, it had been Lady Charlotte who'd rescued him by proffering her own opinions.

Desperate not to repeat his prior abysmal performance, Matthew scrambled to construct a full sentence. Unfortunately, he blurted out, "What the devil are you doing here, Lady Charlotte?"

Matthew winced at his clumsy words. Lady Charlotte, however, did not appear taken aback.

"Didn't Alexander tell you?" She glanced at her brother, whose presence Matthew had damn near forgotten.

Alexander shrugged. "I wanted to surprise him."

Lady Charlotte rolled her eyes at her twin before she leaned close to Matthew. Once again, his blasted heart refused to act in the normal manner. Although he knew it was physiologically impossible, he swore it jumped around inside him. When a warm puff of Charlotte's breath touched his ear, his *cor meum* slammed against his sternum with the force of a battering ram.

"The mistresses Wick have established this room for debate between sexes. I have been recruiting female patrons for several weeks now. It is a veritable success, wouldn't you say?"

Rather dazedly, Matthew scanned the alien addition to his formerly familiar coffeehouse. It reminded him of an elegant salon, infused with all the rules of social etiquette that he would never absorb. He had devoted his life to understanding the physical workings of the human body and of the natural world—but the human psyche would never be something he could comprehend.

"I've secretly started coming to the Black Sheep. Mother thinks

I've been visiting my friend, Calliope, instead. I swear I can feel my grandmother and great-aunt's presence in this place. It is how I imagine the salon when they hosted it. No wonder men are always disappearing into coffeehouses." Lady Charlotte's lips were so close to Matthew's flesh that he could detect her body heat. His skin prickled, and a shiver threatened to rise up. Lady Charlotte's presence was not just a fantasy or even an anomaly but a new reality.

Matthew's favorite haunt, his former escape from the pressures of city existence, had just become his Hades . . . and his Elysium.

Chapter Four

Matthew Talbot was both exactly how Charlotte remembered him and intriguingly different. She recalled him as a quiet but good-natured sort who had never begrudged his friend's sister tagging along during the boys' holidays from school. Despite years of spending weeks in Matthew's company, Charlotte knew little about him other than that he possessed a singular habit of fading into the scenery and that he'd spent a large portion of his childhood on his father's remote Scottish estate.

Although Charlotte had been endlessly coached by her nurse, governess, and her mother on the art of conversation, she had never succeeded in coaxing Matthew from his veritable fortress of silence. Although, truth be told, she had not put her full efforts into it. She had always been so thrilled to have her beloved brother home that she rather enjoyed not having to share their chats with an interloper.

At this precise moment, Matthew seemed to be doing his best to scrunch his tall frame in half and disappear into the fabric of the couch. Despite his great height, he'd managed the trick countless times before. But right now, Charlotte had no intention of allowing him to vanish into the background.

She needed him. Desperately.

The clandestine room of the Black Sheep had been open for two weeks, and Charlotte was frustratingly nowhere near gathering any truths about Viscount Hawley, and the dread over her impending engagement burgeoned each day. The more colorful customers had not yet deigned to venture into the "women's lair" as they'd labeled the new back room. Charlotte had no more knowledge of the nefarious parts of London than she'd previously possessed.

Without other options, she had tried to gather gossip about Lord Hawley from the aristocratic women who'd already discovered the Black Sheep through a network of whispers. Charlotte had hoped that the ladies would talk more freely at the coffeehouse than in their parents' or husbands' drawing rooms. Although she hadn't been wrong, there had been no useful tittle-tattle. The only notable tidbit was about Lady Greenvale, the sister of Hawley's second wife. Ever since her sibling's death, Countess Greenvale had been discretely espousing radical ideas about divorce. Charlotte longed to speak to the woman at the Black Sheep, where they could converse without restraint, but she couldn't simply send her a written invitation. Instead, she'd asked the countess's acquaintances to inform her about their clandestine establishment.

But Lady Greenvale hadn't visited yet, and even if she did, she might not know anything of import. Right now, Charlotte's best chance of learning about Viscount Hawley's misdeeds was through his brother.

Unfortunately, Alexander positively refused to question Matthew on Charlotte's behalf. He insisted that if his best friend had proof of Hawley committing murder, then the honorable physician would have already reported the crime. Alexander made it abundantly clear that he didn't want Charlotte attempting to unearth Hawley's misdeeds. He promised that he was investigating on his own, and he refused to give Charlotte any details.

But she had enough of others dictating her fate, and she refused to wait demurely. Every tick of the clock was a moment closer to the return of the Duke of Lansberry and the finalization of her engagement. There was a chance that Matthew had observed something but didn't realize its significance…or perhaps the good doctor wasn't as upstanding as Alexander believed. Hawley was Matthew's sibling after all, even if, by Alexander's account, the viscount had been an awful one. People often possessed an illogical and undying instinct to protect family members.

Since Alexander had just excused himself to fetch coffee, Charlotte had an opportunity to question the reserved Matthew. Yet even as he tried to make himself inconspicuous, he didn't actually succeed. Charlotte found herself acutely aware of Matthew, although she wasn't exactly sure why. As soon as he'd sat down, an odd, prickly heat had rushed over her. Until now, she had never considered that the perfectly pleasant Matthew could be the type who could make a person flush, for any reason. Yet a giddy sort of anticipation spiraled through her, pushing away some of the constant doom.

"Traveling agrees with you," Charlotte said, trying to categorize for herself the subtle ways in which Matthew had transformed during the intervening years.

Matthew's rather surprisingly broad shoulders jerked. His gray eyes widened as he swiveled to glance at her directly. "It does?"

Charlotte tapped her finger against her chin as she took the opportunity to study more than just his profile. Matthew's formerly pale skin now possessed a golden glow. His complexion made her think of lazy days in the gardens at Falcondale Hall, when the chill of spring had just given way to the deeper, truer warmth of summer.

"Do you spend a great deal of time outdoors?" Charlotte asked.

"Yes. A good bit." Matthew visibly swallowed, and Charlotte watched as the corded tendons in his neck moved and flexed. He'd lost his gangly appearance. Muscles smoothed over places where bones and joints used to protrude, and his limbs no longer seemed too lengthy for the rest of him. His body wasn't all bulging power though. Instead, his form possessed a refined strength that made Charlotte scandalously curious as to what he had hidden under his layers of coat, waistcoat, and shirt.

"Dr. Matthew Talbot!"

Charlotte turned to see Sophia standing in front of them with Pan perched on her shoulder. The parrot twisted his lime-green body in the perfect position to stare Charlotte down with his unblinking reddish-brown eye.

A smile blossomed over Sophia's face. Although she was welcoming to all guests, Charlotte detected an extra hint of warmth in the woman's eyes.

"Miss Wick. A pleasure as always." Matthew rose and dipped his chin in greeting, the movement quick and economical. He still seemed stiff, but Charlotte swore that his muscles uncoiled just a fraction. For a man who constantly held himself as tightly as Matthew did, it was telling—but of comradeship or something more, Charlotte could not entirely determine.

"It's wonderful to see your face again. Hannah and I were just mentioning the other day that your vessel should be arriving back in England soon."

The left side of Matthew's mouth tilted up ever so slightly, which for him was the equivalent of a broad smile. "Your cousin greeted me when Alexander and I walked through the door. I've missed the Black Sheep. It's good to be back among friends."

Friends. He spoke the word casually—well, as casually as possible for Matthew. There was no stress, no hidden meaning. Relief burst through Charlotte. Matthew's lack of entanglements made her plans easier...yet, oddly, her reaction seemed more complex than that.

"Did you bring Pan back a companion?" Sophia asked.

At the mention of his name, the parrot fluffed out his chest feathers. He didn't make a single sound but ominously began stretching and scrunching his neck in patent offense to the suggestion that he required a comrade. During the entire display, he did not break his gaze from Charlotte, as if he blamed her personally for the perceived indignity.

"I was in the northern part of the Americas, not the southern, so I did not come across another parrot," Matthew said. The single sentence caused Pan to freeze, and the bird returned to mimicking a stuffed one.

"I was hoping you might run into a sailor willing to sell his pet," Sophia sighed. "Pan always seems to be in his doldrums. Another bird would be good for him."

She reached up and scratched Pan's chest. She only managed a few scritches, however, before Pan clicked his beak in warning. Hastily, Sophia withdrew, and smug satisfaction gleamed in the parrot's eye as he continued to glare at Charlotte.

Trying her best to ignore the malevolent bag of feathers, Charlotte instead focused on the human conversation buzzing about her. The Wicks definitely had connections to pirates, and Matthew had just returned from a long sea voyage. Could he be involved in his older brother's nefarious dealings? Did those transactions involve marauders on the high seas? Charlotte's heart set off on a gallop.

"Your latest journey was one of many then, Dr. Talbot?" Charlotte inquired, forcing her voice to remain neutral despite the intense anticipation swirling through her.

"Aye." Matthew jerked his chin again. His slight Scottish brogue was a testament to both his Highland childhood and his university days in Edinburgh.

"Dr. Talbot, here, is a true swashbuckler." Sophia bumped Matthew's shoulder lightly, but the gesture was patently friendly without a hint of flirtation. Still, red stained Matthew's cheeks, the color apparent even beneath his sun-kissed complexion. The movement freed the chunk of dark brown hair that he'd earlier tucked behind his ear.

He should have appeared silly between the unkempt strands and his neck as red as a hawthorn berry. But he didn't. Instead, he seemed...oddly tempting. Charlotte wanted to smooth the errant locks...or undo the rest of his clubbed-back hair and run her fingers through his silky, unfashionably short mane. Then she'd explore how deep his flush went, first by unloosening his cravat, and next the buttons of his...

"I would not go so far as to say I am an adventurer. I have seen bits of the world. That's all," Matthew said as he fixed his hair.

"That's more than most folks ever do," Sophia pointed out and sat down in the chair across from the sofa, clearly now invested in the chat. Both Hannah and Sophia employed additional workers, which freed them to join whatever animated discussion intrigued them.

Matthew resumed his seat as well, but Sophia turned to Charlotte when she spoke. "I've never met a more modest man than Dr. Talbot. Most gents are braggarts, but this fellow is the opposite."

That fit with the boy Charlotte remembered, but for the first time, she began to wonder why. Perhaps humbleness was an intrinsic part of Matthew. Or, just as likely, his past may have instilled self-effacement into his soul. But what if he had more sinister reasons not to draw attention to himself—a trick rather than a trait?

Suddenly, some of the burgeoning attraction inside Charlotte shifted into suspicion. She had no time to disentangle the conflicting sensations. She had to dig for any clue, no matter how unlikely, and she would employ all means necessary.

"What is the cause of your trips away from our foggy shores?" Charlotte leaned her body ever so slightly in Matthew's direction. The maneuver worked well to set salon guests at ease or subtly flatter intellectuals who needed their egos stroked. It also drew out secrets. Intimacy—fabricated or earnest—always did. Her heart beat faster, but whether from danger, increased nearness to Matthew, or both, she did not know.

"My benefactor is the reason for my travels," Matthew said as he rather quickly reached for the cup of coffee that Sophia had brought him. "Mr. Tavish Stewart."

Charlotte had precisely two social circles—that of the highest echelons of Society and that of the luminaries of the literary community. Even she, though, had heard of Mr. Tavish Stewart, the mysterious Scotsman who had amassed a fortune from shipping. Her mother's friends generally would not sully themselves with gossip about those whose wealth originated from trade, no matter how large or impressive the riches. Mr. Stewart, however, offered wagging tongues a temptation too sweet to ignore—a delicious enigma. No one, no matter how well connected, could learn anything of his past. It was as if he had appeared like the legendary Athena, fully formed from mere sea-foam.

"Truly?" Charlotte inched her body even closer to Matthew's, sensing their nearness unsettled him even more than it did her. "How ever did you become acquainted with Mr. Stewart?"

"In Edinburgh. When I was a student. He'd read one of the papers that I'd written for the Amica Fauna Society and then attended a lecture that I gave on the subject of the wildcat. He was impressed with the efforts I took to track and sketch the elusive animal, rather than rely on the myriad of myths. He offered me a position as surgeon on the flagship of his fleet and the chance to study wildlife at the ports of call."

Charlotte vaguely remembered Alexander telling her that Matthew worked as a surgeon on a seafaring vessel, but she had assumed he served the Royal Navy in some capacity.

"Is it common for a merchant ship to employ a physician?" Charlotte asked, her mind working quickly as she tried to organize the collection of new information into some semblance of order.

"Mr. Stewart and his commercial practices are anything but common," Sophia said.

"In what manner?" Charlotte asked, trying to keep her voice casual despite the chill skittering up and down her spine. Half-formed images sprouted in her mind—pirates holding cutlasses above their heads, smugglers slipping unseen into a sea cave, privateers swooping down upon a foreign vessel. This was her very first hint of criminal activity, and she wanted to pounce on it like a foolish pup. But any display of eagerness might scare away her quarry.

"In the best way," Sophia answered rather mysteriously. Charlotte had learned it was difficult to extract any information from the Wick cousins, no matter how innocuous.

"What is in the best way?" Alexander asked cheerfully as he rejoined their little group, his cup of coffee gripped in his free hand.

"The manner in which Mr. Stewart operates his business," Sophia answered.

"Which one?" Alexander inquired.

"He has more than one?" Charlotte asked, even more intrigued.

"He also owns a printing business. It is more of an amusement than a serious endeavor," Matthew quickly interjected. Given that the man rarely volunteered much, Charlotte turned sharply in his direction. His face looked…stern, as if he was offering Sophia some sort of warning. But about what? The suspicions already thrumming through Charlotte grew stronger.

"An 'amusement' that garners him a hefty income each year." Alexander snorted before he took a sip of his coffee. Putting it down on a low table in front of him, he smiled at Sophia. "I say, you and your cousin are veritable geniuses at creating these novelty coffee drinks. I never thought the brew could taste so divine. I would drink this even without its invigorating effects."

"Thank you." Sophia beamed.

Charlotte, however, was less than pleased with her brother's non sequitur. Normally, she loved how his always active mind flitted from subject to subject with abandon, but right now, she wanted nothing to divert the flow of conversation.

"Why is Mr. Stewart's pastime so profitable?" Charlotte asked.

"He is known for producing detailed prints of the natural world," Sophia explained. "They've become very popular in the homes of the middling class—a sign of an owner's sophistication."

"Also their wealth, given the hefty price Stewart demands. The designs are not easy to forge," Alexander added.

"The printing house also produces important medical and naturalist texts that are used by universities," Matthew added, his voice a quiet rumble compared to Alexander's jovial one.

"And purchased by cits who are eager for private libraries that declare them to be learned members of society." Sophia gave a knowing wink, clearly not impressed with superficial trappings of enlightenment.

"The books are invaluable to universities, and Mr. Stewart does not charge them an exorbitant rate," Matthew said, his voice still low in volume but with a surprisingly unyielding edge. Charlotte studied him even more closely, her senses heightened. Clearly, Matthew was made of sterner stuff than his quiet demeanor portended.

This additional unexpected complexity fascinated her...for reasons, concerningly, that went beyond her investigation. For the second time that hour, Charlotte found herself wanting to peel back Matthew's layers, but this time not just the corporeal ones but the metaphysical as well. He reminded her of a seemingly simple bucolic novel that in reality was rife with underlying meaning and tension.

"What my dear chum is failing to tell you is that Matthew himself is responsible for many of the drawings and much of the text." Alexander tipped back his coffee mug after he spoke, drained it, and then plopped it down on the table. "That was delicious. I think I shall have another."

"We now charge separately for those drinks," Sophia reminded him.

Alexander sighed as he stood up. He patted his pocket ruefully. "My purse is exceedingly aware. Highway robbery, I tell you."

Sophia laughed as she rose too. "You need to talk to one of our customers who is an actual highwayman. There is a distinct difference between the two."

"It is true then—what you and Hannah have said before. You really do have highwaymen as patrons?" Charlotte asked, straightening as a thrill burst through her. This potential lead into discovering Hawley's misdoings was blessedly not burdened with the complications of her odd reaction to Matthew.

Sophia responded with an enigmatic smile, and Charlotte sank back into the settee. She could not tell whether the coffeehouse owner was serious or jesting.

"I do not see a difference between a highwayman and you, Miss Wick," Alexander joked. "Coffee, that glorious restorative, is my lifeblood. Threatening to deprive me of its vigor is akin to leveling a pistol at my poor, exposed chest."

"You're forever the dramatic one, Lord Heathford." Sophia gave an exasperated shake of her head as she followed him in his pursuit of more coffee.

"You wound me," Alexander teased as the two of them disappeared among the crowd, leaving Charlotte and Matthew alone once more on the settee.

While Matthew visibly stiffened at the retreat of his familiar friends, Charlotte was glad for the return of their previous intimacy. Settling back against the soft cushions, Charlotte fixed Matthew with one of her warmest, most gracious smiles.

He blinked. Twice.

It was time to start stripping away Dr. Matthew Talbot's various layers.

Chapter Five

❧

As Matthew mounted the front stairs to the Lovett town house, he wondered how Lady Charlotte had ever convinced him to return to her mother's salon. Even more astonishing, he'd actually consented to leading the discussion about his first natural science publication, *Ferus Cattus of Caledonia*. Nervously, he clutched the thin volume in his left hand. He was perspiring so profusely it was a wonder that his sweat didn't seep past the cover and cause the ink on the pages to bleed. His sophomoric effort had not been printed by Tavish's publishing house and was of poor quality.

Swallowing, Matthew glanced up at the Doric columns. He felt rather like a supplicant—or perhaps more accurately the sacrificial calf—dragged before the oracles to be dissected.

His dry, scientific knowledge was not what the salon members sought. They wished to discuss the vagaries of the human spirit and mind, but he only understood the banal functions of corporeal bodies.

A tall butler with a solemn, refined face opened the door, took Matthew's card, and intoned a polite but not overly warm greeting. The servant, with his symmetrical features and cool, almost regal bearing, matched the Palladian structure soaring above Matthew's head. It was grandeur—simultaneously understated and overstated.

The large halls that Matthew normally entered were those of

universities. Although he did frequent the residences of his bene-factor, Tavish didn't believe in formality. But the atmosphere in the Lovett town house was as stiff as the horsehair-stuffed skirt of the butler's impeccably tailored coat.

"Tell me again why I am attending my mother's salon rather than enjoying today's perfect curricle-racing weather?" Alexander's wry voice broke into Matthew's reverie.

Matthew turned to find his best friend leaning on an ornate cane as Alexander stood in one of the arched doorways lining the massive foyer.

"Damned if I know myself," Matthew admitted with a rueful smile.

"You are the one who accepted Lottie's invitation." Alexander made his way to Matthew's side, and they began to move in unison to the deeper recesses of the house. Matthew could hear a mixture of polished male and female voices drifting into the hallway from another set of open doors. Obviously, Alexander had been waiting for Matthew before entering the domain of his mother, the formi-dable Duchess of Falcondale.

"I am still not entirely sure how it happened. One minute, I was sitting next to your sister at the Black Sheep, and the next, I was pledging to come this Wednesday," Matthew explained.

"And you oh-so-kindly invited me along." Alexander sighed, patently making the sound as laborious as possible. He winked at Matthew to demonstrate no actual ill will, but Matthew felt a trickle of guilt. He wasn't the only one who'd grown up as an out-sider in his own home.

"I do thank you for the support. I know you're not fond of these events either."

Alexander shrugged and straightened the right cuff of his coat as he paused before the threshold of the parlor. "When Lottie plays hostess, the salons aren't so awful. If Mother is not chiefly in charge of managing the flow of conversation, she is much less inclined to shoot daggers in my direction when the thumping of my cane interrupts the discourse."

Before Matthew could respond, Alexander resumed his uneven stride and burst into the drawing room like a conquering Julius Caesar entering Gaul. Matthew followed quietly, preferring not to draw any attention to his own arrival.

The semicircular room reminded Matthew of the famous Raphael fresco of Aristotle and Plato at the School of Athens, a resemblance that he assumed was intentional on the part of the Duchess of Falcondale. The large central back window was deeply recessed, giving the appearance of an impressive arch. A raised section of flooring by the outer wall formed a dais reached by broad, terraced steps. Bathed in light, both natural and that of her own making, Lady Charlotte sat in the middle of the Grecian backdrop where her mother usually held court.

Matthew felt not just blinded but seared from the inside out. Swallowing, he realized he'd been wrong earlier to compare Lady Charlotte to a mere oracle. She was the very goddess of knowledge. Even her ethereal white gown seemed inspired by the togas of old, the silk flowing around her like a waterfall frozen in time.

Perfection. Both the Duke of Falcondale and his duchess demanded it. Matthew knew all too well what that quest had cost Alexander—still cost his friend. But he had never considered what toll it eked from Lady Charlotte to become this radiant deity. Because now Matthew had seen her shine on her own terms in the back room of the Black Sheep—a realm she, not her parents, had shaped.

Looking at her, he could observe the faintest differences. Her pink lips were pressed just a hair or two against each other, while the skin around her emerald-green eyes appeared ever so slightly pinched. Most people wouldn't notice, but Matthew had always been observant…a fact that had both saved him and rained trouble down upon his head.

Taking a fortifying breath, Matthew began walking toward Lady Charlotte, who had just been joined by Alexander. But before he'd managed two steps, a crawling sensation slithered up and down his neck at the sound of an all-too familiar drawl.

"Be glad you moved forward or I wouldn't have seen you. Wouldn't want to accidently step on you, now would I, Mat?"

Old, arctic emotions crashed down upon Matthew, but he wouldn't let them drown—or freeze—him this time. He was no longer a scrawny, scared child, but a man, one who hadn't just traveled the world but explored it. He'd stalked wolves and bears in the Colonies just to learn the fearsome beasts' secrets.

"Hawley," Matthew said stiffly as he turned to face his eldest brother. During their months apart, the viscount hadn't changed. Despite his life of dissolution, Hawley looked remarkably hale and still miraculously free of the pox. The viscount might enjoy an overabundance of drink washed down with an imprudent amount of laudanum, but he also relished the sporting life, especially anything involving his fists.

"Mat." Hawley's aristocratic lips quirked into a smirk as he finished speaking.

Against Matthew's will, he flinched at the old epithet. It had little to do with it being a diminutive of his given name and everything to do with how his siblings had viewed him: a doormat.

"I didn't think literary salons were to your liking." Matthew smiled ever so politely as he stiffened his shoulders, knowing Hawley expected a quivering retreat, not poise. But his older brother wouldn't find Matthew to be the lad he'd run roughshod over. Matthew was determined to protect not just Lady Charlotte, but anyone who became Hawley's prey.

"They're not," Hawley said shortly, his gray eyes burning like the center of a hot flame, "but it's been ages since I've watched you play the court jester."

"I'm afraid I've left my cap and bells at home," Matthew said pleasantly, wishing the schoolboy taunt didn't cause his already twisting insides to knot upon themselves. At least this time, he wasn't displaying his emotions for Hawley to feast upon.

"You don't need a fool's hat to be my marionette, little brother." Hawley leaned close to Matthew, but took no care to lower his voice. "I know how to pull your strings."

"Did you come here just to insult me with mixed metaphors? You must lead a rather dull life then," Matthew said, keeping his voice light, although he was purposely prodding Hawley. Matthew wanted to learn his brother's exact intentions toward Lady Charlotte. Did he want the union as much as their father did? The more interest Hawley had in the lady, the more peril she faced.

Hawley smiled. It was not a kind one, not that the reprobate possessed one of those. "Hardly, Mat. You're like a half-forgotten ball from childhood. Amusing to bat about from time to time but not that interesting. Lady Charlotte is the true reason that I roused myself from bed rather than enjoying a long lie-in."

Matthew preferred to avoid direct conflict, but his fingers involuntarily clenched into a fist. An old sense of guilt settled in Matthew's gut. He may have escaped his brother's abuse, but others still suffered his cruelty. He'd tried so hard to find proof of Hawley's murderous tendencies, but the monster had both the means and the cunning to erase his villainy.

Hawley clearly noticed Matthew's balled hand and gave a laugh. The ugly sound of it skittered along Matthew's flesh as old memories flooded him. The viscount had made that same guffaw when he'd torn off the wings of butterflies that Matthew had been peacefully observing. Their middle brother had held Matthew down and forced him to watch.

Hawley was always attracted to pretty things...and he also enjoyed destroying them.

"I suppose our sire hasn't explained his plans to you yet." Hawley had sped up the unnaturally slow cadence of his voice, and Matthew could hear the sizzle of unholy excitement in the less-measured tempo. Hawley waited a beat or two, and when Matthew did not speak, the viscount chuckled again. "Oh, that's right. Father tells you nothing. He's always considered you odd. Whenever he is in his cups, he blathers about how you are a fairy changeling."

Matthew refused to clench his jaw. "Father is often soused, and his otherworldly theory is hardly a safely guarded secret, even if it has no basis in the actual natural order."

"I agree that Father's beliefs belong in a time long past. He is hardly the example of modern enlightenment, but occasionally his old-fashioned ideas have their merits."

Hawley using the words *modern* and *enlightenment* might have amused Matthew, if he didn't realize that his brother was alluding to his upcoming arranged marriage. Matthew could feel nothing but an intense—almost rage-like—need to stop Hawley once and for all.

"I wouldn't know, as the duke is not keen on sharing his insights with me, which you were quick to point out only a moment ago." Matthew shoved his emotions deep inside and kept an outward calm as he pretended ignorance. It would do Lady Charlotte no good if Hawley realized that Matthew had any connection to her beyond being friends with her twin.

"Father has arranged a marriage for me. The Duke of Falcondale is very pleased to soon have another ducal heir in the family. Given the sorry state of Falcondale's own successor, it is hardly surprising that he wishes to secure his family legacy through the female line instead of only through the male."

Matthew swung toward his brother, hoping that his expression only showed feigned shock and not the horror that churned inside him every time he thought of Charlotte married to this brute. Hawley, who always dressed like a deuced strutting peacock, rose up in his buckle-festooned shoes and clicked them down on the polished parquet, his broad chest puffed out.

"She will be my most beautiful wife yet, don't you think?" Hawley lazily moved his gaze from Matthew to focus on Lady Charlotte. He slowly traced her form, his mouth quirking slightly upward with each inch that his eyes traversed.

Matthew studied Lady Charlotte alongside his brother but with the eyes of an observer, not a manipulator. The stress around her eyes had increased, and the pressure against her lips had caused her smile to flatten several degrees. She was watching Hawley, her green eyes alert, her body tense. She reminded Matthew of a panther that he'd spied in the woods of America. Silent, on guard, ready to attack or flee as the situation demanded. She was fierce, Lady Charlotte, and intelligent enough to recognize when she was being hunted.

"I haven't read a betrothal notice," Matthew said with a casualness he certainly didn't feel.

"We are waiting until Father returns from Scotland," Hawley said, "but that is just a formality. Everything has been agreed upon."

"Has the lady consented?" Matthew asked, the words slipping from him before he thought better. Hawley would inevitably view the question as a challenge, and the last thing Matthew wanted was to provoke more interest in Lady Charlotte.

Hawley's head snapped in Matthew's direction. "You never mentioned how lovely Alexander the Galling's sister was. I can see why you'd want to hide such a gem for yourself, not that she'd ever pay you any attention."

"I would never be so foolish as to think she would cast her eyes in my direction," Matthew said quietly. It was the truth—even if Lady Charlotte had been showing a curious interest in him since he encountered her in the Black Sheep a few days ago. But he would have said the words anyway. Hawley had always taken pleasure in decimating the things Matthew cared about, and the less of a competition this seemed, the better.

As much as Matthew hated this conversation, Hawley was giving him an unexpected opportunity to probe into his brother's first marriages. Although Hawley likely wouldn't divulge much, he might let the barest of facts slip.

"The identity of your intended aside, don't you think it is a might too early to be looking for another bride? The latest Lady Hawley was only buried a scant six months ago." Matthew kept his voice relaxed, but he studied his brother closely.

The faintest flicker of something ugly flashed deep in Hawley's eyes. Matthew probably wouldn't have recognized it if he hadn't endured the full blast of his brother's cruelty in the past. Within an instant, Hawley hid his true emotions under an outpouring of sadness. He even managed to manufacture a sheen of tears.

"Although misfortune has plagued my marriages, I must fulfill my duty of begetting an heir." Hawley infused his voice with the perfect mix of resolve and remorse. He'd used the same tone to escape punishment from the schoolmaster for his pranks.

"It is indeed tragic coincidence, both your wives dead from broken necks in two very different accidents." Matthew kept all accusation from his voice, but Hawley's eyes still narrowed before the viscount masked his initial reaction with affront.

"I am a grieving widower." Hawley pressed his palm against his sternum as if staunching a bleeding heart. "How could you accuse me of evildoing?"

"Did I?" Matthew asked. "I merely mentioned the unfortunate

repetition of the cause of death. You are the one who alluded to a crime."

Hawley glanced about the room before taking a menacing step forward. "Do not attempt to be clever, Mat. You haven't the nerve for it."

A grim certainty bled through Matthew. He had no doubt about his brother's guilt, but he had no way of proving it. Perhaps by making himself a target, he could obtain evidence when Hawley inevitably attacked him.

"That is true. If I were actually brave, I'd mention that both your wives had the u-shaped bone in their necks snapped. That particular injury typically comes from strangulation. I've served as a surgeon on enough inquests to know." Matthew lifted his eyes to stare down his brother. Even now, after all these years, it was hard to look directly at Hawley without flinching. But Matthew needed to gauge every aspect of Hawley's reaction.

A slight flush touched the viscount's skin as he began to step forward. For a moment, Matthew thought his brother might publicly strike him. But the viscount had learned to hide his temper better than he had as a lad. Instead of hitting Matthew, he merely pretended to pick off a piece of lint from his coat. Using the action as an excuse, he leaned close to Matthew's ear.

"You're nothing more than a bloody barbershop surgeon. You've forgotten your place, Mat," Hawley said softly. "You best remember it before I show you exactly where it is."

Once more, those old memories shivered through Matthew, and he did his utmost to battle them back again. Lady Charlotte couldn't afford for him to be the weak, younger sibling.

"What are you doing here, Hawley?" Alexander stood before them now, his knuckles white against the ornate handle of his cane.

"Why, to see your incomparable sister, Galling. I would have never guessed that you would be related to such a perfect specimen of womanhood."

"Still using childishly cruel nicknames, Hawley?" Alexander raised a single auburn brow. "You haven't changed."

"Neither have you." The viscount stared pointedly at Alexander's walking stick.

"I have actually," Alexander said with a nonchalance that somehow only heightened the seriousness of his words. "If you hurt my sister in any way, you will find out exactly how much."

"You do realize it was the lady in question who sent me an invitation to this event, not the Duchess of Falcondale? It is clear that Lady Charlotte and her parents find me a suitable match."

"Shite," Alexander murmured, glancing back at his twin.

Hawley smirked as if certain he'd scored a point. Matthew, however, wasn't so sure. Alexander shared a close bond with his sister. If Matthew could detect her real feelings toward the viscount, Alexander would be able to do so easily. Alexander couldn't be fretting about Lady Charlotte succumbing to Hawley's outward charms.

No, something else was worrying him.

Matthew looked back in the lady's direction only to find her strolling toward them. Her emerald eyes glistened. She was on the offensive.

"I apologize for interrupting, but I am afraid I am in need of Dr. Talbot. We will shortly begin the discussion of his book." Lady Charlotte lightly brushed her gloved hand against Matthew's arm, and he swore heat sizzled along his muscles and traveled straight to his spine. How could a simple touch cause such a reaction, especially under the circumstances? What extraordinary vessels in the human body were the conduits of the powerful sparks?

"I was surprised when the invitation mentioned what drivel

we'd be discussing," Hawley said silkily. "Are we really going to converse about kittens?"

"Only those with exceedingly sharp claws, my lord," Lady Charlotte answered with a light, airy smile.

Hawley turned his full attention on her, and Matthew had to dig his nails into the palms of his hands to stop himself from jumping in front of Lady Charlotte. Such an action would only provoke Hawley more.

"I prefer kittens that are soft and biddable." Hawley turned his voice into a smooth caress. "Even if they try to scratch me, I know how to make them purr."

"I didn't know you had so much experience with wildcats, my lord." Lady Charlotte spoke with bright innocence, but Matthew knew a woman as clever as she couldn't have missed Hawley's double entendre.

For the briefest of moments, the skin around Hawley's eyes tensed, and Matthew once again saw a hint of his buried rage. He obviously hadn't appreciated how handily Lady Charlotte had parried his innuendo.

"I am exceedingly good at taming all manner of creatures." The words were a threat, but Hawley made them sound like a naughty, but clever, quip—the kind that earned him the reputation as a charming, incorrigible rogue.

"Well, now I know who to summon if any beasts escape the Tower and find their way to my parents' garden," Lady Charlotte said as she gently gave Matthew's arm a tug. "But as much as I am enjoying our conversation about animals, Dr. Talbot must come to the front of the room."

Hawley started to move his mouth, most likely in protest, but Matthew and Lady Charlotte were quicker. Together, they whirled away, and Alexander hurriedly took his own leave from Hawley.

As Matthew walked to the dais with Lady Charlotte, he yearned to warn her about the dangers of provoking his brother, but it wasn't his place. Moreover, he was fairly certain the woman was well aware of exactly what kind of lion she was attempting to beard.

Any hint of relief Matthew felt at being removed from the barbed conversation with Hawley was extremely short lived. As soon as he turned to face the crowd slowly assuming their seats, a new queasy feeling merged with his other unpleasant emotions. These weren't young male students or even his colleagues at the Amica Fauna Society or the Hippocrates League. They were the top echelon of the upper class and the esteemed artists and writers who were allowed temporary entrance into these rarefied circles.

Why had Matthew ever agreed to such an obvious farce? These people had no interest in discussing an animal that they all considered vermin, which destroyed their pheasants and other game birds.

Alexander shot him an encouraging look as he found a chair near the back row, far from the Duchess of Falcondale, who sat in regal stiffness. Although Matthew appreciated his friend's attempt to calm him, the booming inside his chest only grew stronger. He tried drawing in air to regulate his erratic breathing, but he only succeeded in making a huffing sound.

Lady Charlotte indicated with her eyes for him to step into a small alcove by the window that was hidden from the audience. He immediately complied, although he doubted a moment alone would be enough to fortify him. He'd just have to blunder along as he had during his first few lectures.

To his shock, Lady Charlotte reached for him as she used a Doric pillar to obscure her movements from the assembly. As her pink lips drew closer and closer, Matthew's already quickened breath turned jagged. An almost painful but utterly delightful anticipation gripped his heart. The organ seemed to squeeze tight as fissures of something bright and hot cascaded through him.

Before his frazzled mind could comprehend what was happening, her pale, delicate fingers reached up and tucked a wayward strand of hair behind his ear. She stepped back, her mouth drawn into the most wonderfully welcoming smile. Despite the small twang of disappointment, Matthew's body vibrated with an energy he had not known humans could generate.

"Your forelock was dangling over your eyes."

It wasn't just his hair that was askew now. Matthew swallowed, and after years of saying as little as possible in her presence, words tumbled from his mouth. "It is always doing that. My fault, I suppose. I don't grow my hair long enough to stay properly tied back—consequence of being in the wilderness for long stretches. Too much combing. Then there's, of course, all the time I spend looking through microscopes. An abundance of tiny creatures live in fur and hair. The louse, of course. Fleas. And mites too. And…"

Shite! Was he talking to Lady Charlotte about head lice? Not just talking but babbling.

The excess heat in Matthew's body transformed into an embarrassed flush. Yet to his surprise, Lady Charlotte did not look disgusted but amused. Even more astonishing, her mirth did not appear at his expense but rather had a…dare he say…fond tinge to it.

"Don't change anything about your coiffure." Lady Charlotte winked. "I like fixing it too much."

A brilliant grin still on her face, she jerked her neck to indicate for him to follow her back out onto the dais. More than a bit stunned, he complied. Dimly, he heard her introduce him and his book to the gathered throng. This time, when he looked upon the faces, he only saw a blur, while heady excitement filled him.

By smoothing back his errant lock, Lady Charlotte had

miraculously quieted the jumble of anxiety spiraling through Matthew. He grasped his copy of *Ferus Cattus of Caledonia* in his hand and offered the audience a hint of a smile.

Lady Charlotte Lovett enjoyed straightening his hair, and she hadn't minded him jawing on about lice.

Matthew's grin grew just a wee bit broader.

Chapter Six

Matthew proved to be an unforeseen delight as a speaker. Charlotte had not expected the reticent man to be so animated, especially talking about the secret life of a woodland creature. Yet his affection for the wildcat added a surprising charm to his speech. Unlike when he had attended the salon years ago, he did not stumble over his words.

He possessed a wonderful speaking voice, Charlotte realized. It was not a deep bass but a warm baritone, like a friendly crackling fire that invited the listener to sit and stay awhile. When Matthew started discussing dung, however, Charlotte noticed a few women and even some men paled. Charlotte's mother sent her a meaningful look to change the direction of his speech, but Charlotte made no effort to interrupt. It was too fascinating watching how Matthew's entire countenance lit as he discussed how he determined the primary food sources of the elusive beast. His joy infected her, buoying her with the confidence to disobey her mother's command.

"It would appear their diet consists mostly of rabbits and voles..." Matthew continued, his rich voice brimming with enthusiasm.

"And good pheasants meant for my hunting amusement and stomach, not a blasted cat's," Hawley interrupted, speaking with a bored drawl that matched his insolent slouch as he regarded his brother with half-lidded eyes. "I am not sure why you are so eager to champion an annoying creature that any sane person would regard as vermin."

The entire audience straightened in almost perfect unison. Charlotte caught a few whispers about the lecturer being the viscount's seldom-seen youngest brother. Faces that had crumpled into lines of boredom suddenly became reanimated. Everyone relished tittle-tattle, especially any connected to an eligible heir apparent to a dukedom.

Hawley chortled, triggering an echoing chorus of equally mean chuckles from the crowd. A clang of guilt resounded inside Charlotte as she realized she'd literally set the stage for this mockery. She'd only wanted to use the salon as an opportunity to learn more about the two brothers and their relationship, not to bring about Matthew's humiliation.

She opened her mouth for some witty repartee, but Matthew responded more quickly. He did not bluster like his older sibling but calmly said, "The fact that the cat is viewed as a nuisance is the very reason that I decided to study the creature."

The salon's attendees slid even closer to the edges of their chairs, while respect sparked inside Charlotte. Hawley was not a man to cross, and no one did so casually. Yet Matthew spoke with an unswaying matter-of-factness that had more power than an angry retort. Charlotte had overheard Hawley call his younger brother a marionette, but perhaps Matthew did not obey all his sibling's commands... or maybe he was chaffing at whatever control the viscount, as the next familial patriarch, wielded over him.

"Ah." Hawley placed one arm on the back of his chair and reclined even more. "I see now. You have an affinity for the outcast."

A few titters arose from the audience at the thinly veiled insult, but Matthew appeared unruffled. "When observing the natural world, one should use all available insight—personal or otherwise—while taking precautions not to allow one's sentiments to be mistaken for facts."

"What earthly benefit—or even heavenly—can derive from following about a noxious creature and recording its habits?" Hawley had stiffened, his arms now crossed. Clearly, he had not expected this calm but persistent resistance.

"A better understanding of one of God's creatures? A greater appreciation for nature? A satisfaction of curiosity? We are so inquisitive about the wonders of the greater world, why should we not show equal fascination for the living things on our own isles?"

The mixture of caring and passion in Matthew's deep, warm voice washed over Charlotte, seeping into places she hadn't realized had been parched for just such an elixir. She wanted, needed to experience more of such powerful kindness.

"You do realize you are speaking of an animal that possesses scant differences from a common tabby?" Hawley sneered. "No one would notice if the wildcat vanished from the earth."

"Which is why I write about them, so that we do care about their survival. They have already disappeared from most of England. If we do not arrive at a way to live in better harmony with them, they will become a mere memory, like the dodo." Matthew's shoulders were slightly back, his chest extended. He looked like a warrior of old, ready to engage in combat for a creature most people simply dismissed.

Charlotte cocked her head as she studied Matthew. She knew she could not afford to be intrigued. Yet oh, how she suddenly craved to learn more about this man who she had been friends with so long ago but had never really known.

"The what?" Hawley chuckled, the sound cruel. "Now you are making up words. Dodo, indeed."

"The epithet is derived from Portuguese, and it is the name for a large, flightless bird from islands in the Indian Ocean. The dodo was annihilated over sixty years ago."

"Do you expect us to shed a tear over an absurd avian who has been gone for more than half a century? From how you describe it, the thing couldn't even act like a proper bird. Good riddance to the misfit, I say. The weak do not deserve to survive."

"What a frightening sphere we would inhabit if we did not look out for the defenseless. We do not need to fear and destroy what we do not fully comprehend; instead, we need to approach it with inquisitiveness and discover the wonders its unusualness may initially obscure," Matthew said.

Hawley opened his mouth, his handsome face ruddy with barely suppressed ire. Before the belligerent oaf could utter another cutting remark, Charlotte shifted. She was in charge of hosting this salon, and she was exceedingly tired of Hawley's endless bluster.

Summoning forth her most brilliant smile, she turned fully toward Matthew and partially lifted her hands. He blinked rapidly, appearing startled by her sudden attention. It was as if he'd forgotten all about her and the rest of the audience.

"Hear, hear!" Charlotte cried, keeping her voice as bright as the North Star. "Studying nature is not so different from poring over the pages of the latest novel. It is all a pursuit of greater meaning, is it not?"

The dumbfounded shock in Matthew's countenance transformed into wonderous astonishment. Then his light gray eyes darkened, and all his passion came storming back. The silvery hue should have felt cold and mysterious, but it didn't. It ignited a hot, dangerous swell inside Charlotte that seemed to rise up, taking her heart with it.

Her comment had spurred observations from the audience. Soon questions for Matthew peppered the air. He turned from her to answer, and she felt as if she'd stepped from a heated fire into a cool spring air. How had the reserved Matthew Talbot—the quiet boy who'd faded into the background of her childhood—become such a force?

Chapter Seven

For the first time in his life, Matthew found himself surrounded by a gaggle of giggling debutantes. Their excited conversation buzzed about him with such fervor he could barely follow it. He had no idea why they were standing in such a tight circle around him, especially since the salon was held in a spacious room, and many of the guests had already departed. Thank goodness, Lady Charlotte was at his side serving as an anchor. Without her, he'd feel hopelessly adrift in satin and perfumes.

"I've never heard a man, especially the son of a duke, speak so compassionately about a creature other than his horse or his dog. Your lecture was so utterly refreshing." A blonde young lady glanced over the lip of her fan, and Matthew was worried that she'd accidentally poked herself in the eye. She was blinking in the most peculiar manner.

"It was a revelation to me," another chimed in as she pushed ahead of the first speaker. "I'm Lady Fiona Sutherland. Until now, I've always found the wildcat on our clan crest to be dreadfully dull. I thought we should have had a more suitable animal like a leopard or a lion. But after your talk, I'm utterly thrilled it is a wildcat."

"I...I am a Keith." A shyer miss from the outer edge of the throng spoke in a hesitant voice and then quickly clarified, "Not the Keiths who were Jacobites. Our clan symbol is a roe deer, but our family has a deep connection with wildcats. According to an old family story, one of the beasts led an ancient Chatti ancestor to a cave when he was being pursued by an enemy."

Matthew smiled at the clearly nervous girl. "I have heard similar stories about how the Chatti tribe were impressed by the ferocity of the felines when they arrived in Scotland."

The girl beamed proudly before bashfully ducking her head. "I must go now. Mother is waiting."

As the lass slipped away, the blonde with the fan chimed in. "Poor Lady Margaret. She seems so lost this Season since she couldn't participate in last year's, when she was in mourning for her grandmother."

"Wasn't Lady Chattiglen killed by a highwayman?" Lady Fiona asked in a mock whisper.

Lady Charlotte instantly sent the group a quelling look. It didn't work.

"Oh yes! It was dreadful. I was afraid to travel at night for weeks. I missed so many wonderful balls." One of the other young ladies sighed with such misplaced sorrow that Matthew could only stare in disbelief.

"I'm still frightened as soon as the sun sets when we're in my family's coach," a different lass said with an exaggerated shiver. "There have been so many robberies on the road as of late."

"Personally, I wouldn't mind being stopped by that handsome robber who has everyone gossiping." The blonde giggled. "I heard it from Miss Upton, who heard it from Lady Anne, who heard it from Miss Lewis, that he is most dashing. The scoundrel possesses an exceedingly comely face—at least what can be seen of it below his half mask."

"Highwaymen should not be romanticized," Lady Charlotte said, her voice stern. "Did this conversation not begin with the tragedy that befell poor Lady Chattiglen?"

The blonde tapped her fan quizzically against her lips. "Well, yes, but isn't there simply something compelling about a man who courts danger in such a swashbuckling fashion? I can understand why your aun—"

"Girls, I believe your mothers are waiting for you." The Duchess of Falcondale's voice cut into the conversation. The effect was as sharp as a razor despite her otherwise pleasant, dulcet tone. "Also, please remember to mind the rules of my salon. We do not engage in discussions of such unpleasantries, nor do we exalt criminality."

A chorus of, "Yes, Your Grace," and, "We do apologize, Your Grace," arose from the throng of lasses. Then they quickly dispersed.

The Duchess of Falcondale seized Charlotte's arm. Although she did so gracefully, Matthew didn't like how the fabric of Charlotte's sleeve bunched under her mother's fingers. How hard was the woman gripping her daughter?

Matthew started to move forward, wondering how to extricate Lady Charlotte without embarrassing her. He had no finesse to handle a situation like this. Instinct told him to just grab her and stroll from the room, but he knew that would cause irreparable social harm.

Fortunately, before he took two steps, the duchess released her hold. No longer needed, Matthew tried to fade into the shadows as mother and daughter bid farewell to their final few guests. Hawley had thankfully long since left. Alexander remained though, and he took up a position beside Matthew next to the potted plant.

"We best stay and rescue Lottie," Alexander told him softly. "Otherwise, Mother will give her a scolding."

"Because of those silly lasses waxing on about highwaymen?" Matthew asked as concern whipped through him. "Lady Charlotte is hardly responsible for their foolishness. She even tried to stop the conversation."

"That wouldn't matter to Mother." Alexander sighed as he ran his fingers over the head of his cane where a bronzed Hercules battled the Nemean lion. "She always lectures Lottie at length every time my sister hosts a salon. It is the same with every ball. The few times I have traveled home with them, my mother has used the entire ride to pick apart every single action my sister took. The woman delights in enumerating flaws."

Matthew clenched his jaw as he watched Lady Charlotte with the duchess. He'd always known that Alexander's parents had constantly criticized his friend, but he hadn't realized that his sister had received similar treatment. Frustration and a sense of injustice roared through Matthew. The twins were two of the most wonderful people he'd ever chanced to meet. It was Falcondale and his wife who deserved the dressing-downs.

As soon as the last guest departed, the duchess slowly pivoted to her daughter, the movement graceful yet oddly threatening. When the Duchess of Falcondale spoke, Matthew realized she was under the misconception that she was alone with Charlotte.

"How could you let the situation devolve in such a manner? Do you have any idea how your father would react if he discovered what those wanton strumpets were discussing in his house? Must we remind him of the taint that my sister brought upon our family when she ran off with that pirate? And the subject matter of today's session? Excrement was discussed. Excrement, Charlotte, excrement. Do you think you're still a hoyden running about the countryside? I thought I was doing the right thing keeping you away from the influences of London during your childhood, but you cannot seem to shed your country bumpkin ways. Dung is not appropriate in the city." Despite the waspish choice of words, the Duchess of Falcondale's voice remained sweet and surprisingly measured, barely rising and falling. Her face stayed eerily serene, like a Madonna in a Renaissance painting.

Guilt stabbed Matthew. Desperate to help Lady Charlotte, he cleared his throat. "Your grace, it is my fault—"

But just as Matthew began his apology, Alexander smashed the ferrule of his cane against the polished floorboards. "Mother, you clearly do not understand how horses function if you think manure is limited to rural life. Have you seen the condition of a London street?"

A very soft, startled sound escaped from the duchess's barely parted lips. With her usual elegance, she slowly turned. Her gaze flickered over her son, dismissing him, but it lingered on Matthew. She did not allow much emotion to creep into her grass-green eyes, so similar in color to her daughter's but fundamentally different in every other way. Matthew sensed that she was mentally calculating how important he was and whether his presence was worth fretting over.

"I will not speak of this to anyone," Matthew said, hoping to forestall any retaliation against Lady Charlotte.

"While I thank you for your discretion, I was simply ensuring that my daughter and the salon display proper decorum." The duchess allowed her lips to curve ever so slightly into a faint, benevolent smile. "Now if you both will excuse us, Lady Charlotte and I must depart. We have an appointment at the modiste. We are very busy preparing for her imminent engagement and marriage to your elder brother."

Matthew bowed his head and took his leave with Alexander, even though everything inside him rebelled at abandoning Lady Charlotte. But he had no choice. He was simply a third son. If he tried to defend Lady Charlotte, it would further aggravate her mother.

"I brought along my curricle," Alexander announced with false cheer that Matthew knew his friend was using to hide his own frustrations. "Would you like to ride with me to the Black Sheep?"

"Aye," Matthew said, not able to inject as much enthusiasm into his voice as Alexander. But he did like the idea of escaping to the coffeehouse. After today, he wanted nothing more than the comforts of his familiar haunt followed by a relaxing evening at home by the fire.

Matthew's day did not proceed as planned. Instead of reading by a cheerful blaze, he was lurking in the fog—a very chilly, exceedingly thick fog. It was the kind of wretched spring night that felt more like unforgiving winter, where the glow from the windows barely managed to seep a foot or two from the glass panes.

It was the perfect atmosphere for skulking though. Matthew supposed he should be thankful for the inky cover. Bright moonlit nights could be dangerous for a man like him.

"Filching thief!" Pan suddenly screeched and then began to bob on Matthew's shoulder. "Filching thief!"

"Shhh," Matthew hissed, wondering not for the first time if he should have left the parrot at the Black Sheep. Pan was well trained for their normal nocturnal adventures, but this was a different type of job. Hannah and Sophia had been very generous to lend him the bird, even though this undertaking was personal.

Pan stuck his eye in front of Matthew's left one. "Filching. Thief."

Matthew glared at the parrot, although it wouldn't do any good. It wasn't so much that Pan didn't understand human facial expressions. He just blithely ignored them.

"I didn't give you the signal to create a distraction," Matthew said. "This is the silent part."

"Filching thief."

Matthew sighed. "Do you wish for me to leave you behind? Once we go over that wall, you can't keep squawking."

Pan retreated back to Matthew's shoulder. The bird didn't open his beak, but he did rustle his feathers directly in Matthew's ear.

Matthew hid a smile. Pan might act long-suffering on their midnight jaunts, but Matthew suspected that the old bird loved every moment—the more perilous the better.

A stillness descended, and Matthew's training told him it was time to make his move. "Go. Be a lookout. Report back."

Pan muttered one more "filching thief" before flying off. As Matthew waited, he refrained from pacing. Although he doubted anyone could see him, he didn't want any movement or sound to betray his presence, especially to the Night Watch. Instead, he dealt with his nervous energy as he always did, by regulating his breathing. Easy in. Easy out.

Finally, Pan returned in a flutter of feathers that could be mistaken for pigeon wings. "No souls. No souls."

Matthew reached into his bag and withdrew a grappling hook. Normally when he did this kind of exercise, there were already ropes aplenty to climb. This time, he needed to provide his own.

He threw the device easily over the bricked garden wall, the spikes catching in the soft mortar. Of course, his target would live in a house with a fortress-like gate. At least Matthew didn't have to climb onto a rooftop...yet.

Climbing up a sturdy, stationary wall was elementary. It was almost as easy as taking a stroll through a manicured park. Matthew was perched on top of the ten-foot structure within moments, his breathing not belabored in the least. He scanned the misty garden, even though Pan had already scouted the area. The little rascal might be an exceedingly intelligent bird, but that was part of the problem. He was both (a) a rascal and (b) a bird.

Matthew couldn't see anything in the fog, but more importantly, he didn't hear anything. Adjusting the hook, he quickly rappelled to the ground. He was adept at using shadows as cover, but tonight everything was the shade of pitch. Matthew possessed a dark lantern that he could adjust to allow only slivers of light, but he did not want to risk using it in the open. Instead, he moved slowly through the garden with Pan flapping circles above him. Although the bird made no other sound, Matthew was convinced the feathered fiend was laughing at him. The sensation of being mocked only intensified when Matthew accidently blundered into an ornamental tree and a few twigs slapped his face. Thankfully, he traversed the rest of the yard without incident.

When he spied a set of French doors, he allowed a triumphant smile to blossom over his face. He'd guessed correctly that the owner of this particular home would have insisted on installing the fashionable architectural feature. It didn't take Matthew long to pick the lock, as he was accustomed to much more substantial ones.

Leaving Pan outside, Matthew slipped into the town house. As soon as he inched away from the doors with their multiple panes of glass, he pulled the dark lantern from his sack and lit it. Cautiously, he lifted a panel, and the faint glow illuminated a luxurious rug. Matthew grinned. No creaking boards tonight. He had a cushioned path to follow. Breaking into an aristocrat's mansion was child's play.

Matthew drifted through the house like a wraith. Although he did not know the layout, he had a good idea that the owner would choose the room with the best vantage point over London as his private study. Matthew had earlier selected a location to try first by studying the windows as he'd waited on the foggy street for nightfall.

Matthew headed that direction now, making sure to tread lightly. His heart pounded, but he'd long ago learned to ignore it. Moving deliberately, he reached his destination. As he carefully eased the door open, relief flooded him. It was indeed the private study of his quarry.

Carefully shutting himself in the room, Matthew walked over to the window and drew the curtains closed. Only then did he pull up all the shutters on his lantern. Lifting the light high, he scanned the space. He paused when he spied a bust of the homeowner situated on a round table. Matthew followed the head's gaze. It was looking at a watercolor of a familiar Scottish estate. Matthew frowned. His target might feign family fealty, but he doubted the man would position his statue in that direction. Quickly, Matthew scanned the study's paintings. One of them showed Zeus on his throne at Mount Olympus surrounded by demigoddesses and cavorting nymphs. On the plains below, mortal men battled in a brutal, bloody contest to entertain the immortals.

Matthew walked over to the bust and turned it to face the tableau of deviant excess. As he'd hoped, he heard a snick. Crouching down, he felt under the desk, his hand brushing against an open secret compartment. Matthew reached inside, and his fingers grazed the softness of a kid leather bag. He withdrew that small satchel and dumped its contents into his hand. Cool metal poured into his palm. When he brought the object into the beam of light, gold glinted and pearls glistened.

Matthew had little interest in jewelry, but the piece called to something inside him. Pearls clustered around small bloodred rubies to form a repeating chain of flowers. A delicate clasp that looked like two hands clutching each other held the choker in a tight circle. From the center hung an onyx cameo nestled in a bed of delicate gold leaves. An indeterminant animal was carved in relief in the white portion of the semiprecious stone. It seemed crude compared to the rest of the piece—or perhaps it was intentionally stylized.

Yet as much as the necklace unexpectedly captivated Matthew, it didn't give him the answers that he sought. He flipped it over, looking for an inscription or some clue. Frustratingly, there was nothing.

The tread of footsteps in the hall caused Matthew to freeze. Quickly, he shoved the jewelry into his pocket. He glanced around the room, wondering if he should return the bust to its proper position, but the creaks drew perilously close. Matthew dashed to the window and quickly opened it. There wasn't much of a ledge, but it would have to do. Extinguishing his lantern, Matthew shoved it into his knapsack. Next, he ripped off his shoes and stockings, knowing they would only hamper his movements, and tossed them into the bag too. He threw the now-heavy load over his shoulder. Luckily, he was accustomed to balancing himself with the uneven weight while he scampered across narrow beams and other obstacles. But the four-inch outcropping of ornamental brick might prove to be a challenge.

Matthew didn't have a choice though. Without hesitation, he slipped outside, pressing his back against the building. He didn't look down but instead scanned the edifice for helpful architectural flourishes. Instead of simple brick, the vertical sides of the mansion were capped in blocks of limestone. The white rock formed a pattern that looked a bit like capital *E*s stacked upon each other, or a wide-tooth comb. Matthew just hoped that the slabs weren't flush with the rest of the outside wall as he slowly inched his way toward them.

Movement echoed from the room that Matthew had just vacated. Ignoring the sweat dripping into his eyes and the scrape of the bricks against his palms, Matthew scooched his body even faster. He'd just reached the squares of limestone when he heard the first bellow. The empty secret compartment must have been discovered.

Matthew grasped the stone embellishments. Relief flooded him when he found that the rock stuck out almost two inches. It was enough for Matthew to grab and give his feet a toehold, and thankfully the night air had made the rough surface cool, making it easier to grip. Years of unorthodox exercise had made Matthew exceedingly nimble. Ignoring his burning muscles and his abraded fingertips, he controlled his breathing and managed to descend quickly.

His feet hit solid ground. From the open window above Matthew, he could hear the crash of thrown figurines and the accompanying roars of outrage. Matthew padded quietly and quickly to the garden wall. Pan alighted from his perch in a tree, his rhythmic flapping wings setting an almost soothing beat. The locale might be different, but the mad dash to safety was familiar.

Matthew swung his grappling hook at the brick garden wall, his first throw thankfully accurate. He scaled the structure even faster than he had the first time. When he reached the top, he stopped. As he slipped on his shoes, he glanced back through the dissipating fog at the lighted window. In the warm glow stood a broad-shouldered man, angrily scanning the darkness. Although Matthew could just make out the fellow's enraged features through the fading mist, the owner of the mansion wouldn't be able to detect Matthew, especially at this distance. Still, old fear coursed through him, almost making him fumble his grappling hook as he repositioned it.

"You haven't changed a whit since childhood," Matthew said under his breath, as he took one last look at his brother's furious face. But the real question was: Had Matthew transformed enough since then? Did he have the strength to defeat his old tormentor?

Chapter Eight

You're running off to Estbrook House to visit Lady Calliope again?" Charlotte's mother did not twitch a single facial muscle and her tone remained cool, yet she managed to give the distinct impression of someone raising their eyebrow.

Charlotte tried to summon her most gracious smile. How she longed for the days of her youth when she'd been left alone in the countryside for months on end without a glimpse of either parent. She'd felt so secluded each time Alexander left for school, but Charlotte preferred even that gnawing loneliness to her mother's current obsession with dictating the minute details of Charlotte's existence. Since her debut over eight years ago, she'd become nothing but an automaton controlled by her mother's edicts.

"The Season is almost in full swing, and Lady Calliope and I have been discussing all the events we have already attended," Charlotte lied. Even Charlotte's lady's maid, Alice, who had been hired by Mother, wasn't wise to Charlotte's true activities. Calliope's loyal servants whisked Alice away and kept her occupied below stairs while Charlotte escaped to the Black Sheep. She'd don widow's garb and take one of the unmarked coaches that Calliope's family owned.

"Sometimes I worry that Lady Calliope is the one responsible for your unwed status." The duchess did not frown, as that could increase her chances of developing wrinkles. Down-turned lips, however, were heavily implied by the slight deepening of her tone. "It is true Lady Calliope is both the daughter of a living duke and the maternal half-sister to another one, but there are rumors. I heard that the Duke and Duchess of Estbrook permit their children, even the girls, to attend those scandalous masquerades their half-sibling hosts."

The Estbrooks had named their four girls after the Greek muses, and each had become legendary artists whether by pen, brush, instrument, or dance. Likewise, Lady Calliope's two sportsmen brothers easily wore the mantle of their impressive Greek hero appellations. Only Lady Calliope's older half brother, the Duke of Blackglen, didn't possess the family's glittering sheen since he rejected polite society for bacchanalian entertainment.

"Mother, Calliope's father is highly esteemed and exceedingly powerful in the House of Lords. Her mother is an incomparable hostess. You were so pleased when Calliope and I became fast friends during my introduction to Society. Don't you always tell me that she is charm personified?" Charlotte might have learned a thing or two about manipulation after all the years of being controlled.

It was a good thing too, especially since she had to convince her mother to let her leave. Yesterday, Calliope had sent a missive to Charlotte that Lady Greenvale, the sister of the late Lady Hawley, had finally made an appearance at the Black Sheep. Unfortunately, Charlotte had been trapped with her mother and her grievances about Matthew's lecture. Calliope had urged Lady Greenvale to return to the coffeehouse today, and Charlotte desperately needed to be there.

Barely parting her lips, Mother issued a small sigh. "I supposed you are right. If anyone is to blame for your peculiar views on marriage, or life in general, it is Aunt Abigail. I never should have allowed her to visit you so much in the countryside, especially when neither your father nor I were around to supervise."

Every winter—just when Charlotte thought she'd go mad from missing Alexander—Great-Aunt Abigail had appeared with her trunk full of books and her ever-sharp mind brimming with old, wonderful memories. It wasn't so much that her parents had permitted Great-Aunt Abigail's visits. They just hadn't thought to tell the servants to prevent the eccentric spinster from staying at the far-flung property. Moreover, her mother enjoyed when her aunt was away from London and not popping by the salon to try to wrest back control.

"Great-Aunt Abigail was always careful to remind me of proper etiquette. She did not speak of the days when she was hostess. She knew you didn't like it," Charlotte fibbed again. It had been her secret with her great-aunt, those days closeted in the library by a cheerful fire as they read Swift's *Gulliver's Travels* and *A Modest Proposal* and discussed his cutting satire. Great-Aunt Abigail had never married, valuing her liberty over all else. She had been much happier than Mother. Charlotte's mother was always trying to prove to her husband that her twin sister's elopement hadn't tainted his family's honor and that the sinful union hadn't cursed Alexander to be born with a clubfoot.

"Hmm," the duchess said, as if she didn't entirely believe Charlotte's last claim. "Well, if you are to go to Lady Calliope's again, please stand up and let me see how you look. We cannot have you going to the Duke of Estbrook's abode looking affright."

Charlotte hid her frustration behind a charming upturn of her lips. Mother never approved of her choices in attire.

Sure enough, a barrage of dissatisfied tongue clicks filled the room. "This won't do, Charlotte. This won't do at all. Your green gown is much too plain, and worse, it makes you look sallow or perhaps even a little tan. You should wear the striped yellow robe à la française that we just brought home from the modiste's. Are you certain, though, that you are taking the proper precautions to avoid the sun?"

"Yes, ma'am." Charlotte avoided clenching her fists. If she did, her mother would claim Charlotte was ruining her posture by tensing her muscles. There was nothing Charlotte could do to outwardly staunch her frustration. She just had to shove it deep inside.

"Also, have your maid fix your coiffure. Your curls are not perfectly formed, and I spy frizz. Your hair is determined to be unruly. It is bad enough that you and I must suffer the startling hue, but at least we can cover the garishness with powder. Wear your shepherdess hat today. Its large brim will hide your hair and protect your complexion." When her mother finished, she gave a slight flick of her wrist, effectively dismissing Charlotte. As an adolescent yanked from the countryside, Charlotte would have dashed from the room and fallen onto her bed in tears. Of course, those crying fits had only prompted more lectures about how one should walk properly at all times and how red, swollen eyes did not compliment one's face.

Keeping her steps dainty, Charlotte left the parlor. When she reached her quarters, she quietly conveyed her mother's instructions to Alice. Standing as still as a wooden doll, she allowed Alice to dress her in the prescribed gown with the alternating daffodil and cream vertical bands. But as Charlotte picked up the bundle secretly containing her widow's weeds, a whisper of freedom swept through her.

The first time Charlotte had donned the black gown, she'd felt a confluence of emotions. The somber attire was meant to convey sorrow and loss. Women wore these clothes when their world had been shrunk by pain, until it became a tight circle bounded by grief. Yet for Charlotte, the darkly dyed skirts and veil meant liberty. Not only did they hide her identity, but they gave her a status that was relatively unfettered for a noblewoman. An unwed miss was governed by her parents, a married woman by her husband, but a widow was her own person. It was a painful irony that only by losing her domestic sphere could a woman gain the greater world.

But Charlotte wondered if there could be another way. If there was, she was determined to find it, even if she had to hew it herself out of unforgiving granite.

—◈—

"Oh good! Lady Greenvale is back!" Calliope gracefully craned her neck toward the entrance to the back room of the Black Sheep. Unlike Charlotte's mother's stiff elegance, Calliope possessed a natural, almost lyrical way of moving that matched her name.

"She is!" Charlotte scrambled to her feet, forgetting all her training in etiquette. She barely stopped herself from barging toward the tall, elegantly dressed woman in the powder-blue sack-back gown. Instead, she waited until the countess had settled into a chair and had been served a piping hot cup of Sophia's latest concoction.

Taking a deep breath, Charlotte finally headed in Lady Greenvale's direction. As she weaved through the other patrons lounging on the comfortable chairs she'd had specially made, Charlotte summoned her hostess skills. She couldn't just plop herself down and subject this woman to a barrage of questions. She needed to delicately massage the conversation, molding it to take the course she wanted. Lady Greenvale had lost her sister a mere six months ago. Charlotte couldn't begin with a direct quest—

"You must be the woman who is rumored to be Lord Hawley's next bride." Lady Greenvale's voice was as sharp as her assessing brown eyes. "I would warn you away from the viscount, but given the number of my friends who hinted for me to visit you here, I suspect you already have suspicions."

Charlotte faltered, unsure how to proceed. She'd been so ready to employ finesse that she wasn't prepared for a straightforward discussion. "I—I hope I did not badger you. That was not my intent."

Lady Greenvale inclined her chin, indicating for Charlotte to sit. "I should be thanking you. Due to your persistence, I have discovered a wonderful place."

"I do beg your pardon if my presence is bringing up painful memories," Charlotte said as she perched on one of the plush chairs.

"Oh, do stop apologizing." Lady Greenvale reached forward to give Charlotte's hand a quick pat. "It is Hawley and males of his ilk who should be on their knees begging us for forgiveness, but instead they force contrition upon womenfolk."

Charlotte's surprise at Lady Greenvale's boldness must have registered on her face for Lady Greenvale continued. "My younger sister's suspicious passing has made me inclined to speak my mind for the first time in my two-and-thirty years. Perhaps, if I had not kept quiet about my worries when she was alive, she would be here today."

Charlotte straightened, wondering how to phrase her questions. The countess was certainly not shy about expressing her opinion, but that didn't mean that the topic of conversation wasn't painful.

"Do—" Charlotte paused, moistening her lips as her heart thudded in quick, almost painful beats. "Do you have reason to question the circumstances of Lady Hawley's death?"

Lady Greenvale's mouth twisted, and for a moment, her bravado cracked. Charlotte saw a glimpse of her sorrow before the countess used fierceness to sweep away grief. "Nothing that wouldn't be dismissed as either the rights of a husband, private matters between spouses, or the fantasies of a hysterical, grieving woman."

"Oh," Charlotte said, trying hard to keep her disappointment from her voice. Lady Greenvale did not need Charlotte's worries adding to her own pain.

Lady Greenvale suddenly looked around the room. Then she leaned over the small wooden table separating them. When she spoke again, her voice was low. "There is one thing. I am not certain of its significance, but it is linked to something tangible."

"What is it?" Charlotte asked, gripping the arms of her chair so hard that her fingers almost cramped around the wood.

"I am debating whether I should tell you." Lady Greenvale's fawn-colored eyes searched Charlotte's. "My own inquiries about it have yielded nothing, and it might bring you danger."

"I am about to be engaged to Lord Hawley against my will. We both know that I am already in peril. Is that not why you are speaking to me so openly?" Charlotte dropped all pretense. She sensed that Lady Greenvale would confide in her only if she truly believed Charlotte had enough strength and courage to make use of the clue.

A sad smile drifted across Lady Greenvale's face. "You are not like my sister. She was so blinded by Lord Hawley's handsomeness and wealth. You see the trueness of the man."

"My own brother was tormented by the viscount when they attended school together," Charlotte admitted. "But my parents do not care about Hawley's past. They only see his future as a duke."

"I will tell you what I know, but I am afraid it is not much." Lady Greenvale sighed, and this time she didn't hide her pain. "My sister grew to be afraid of the viscount and then to loathe him, but she did not trust me with her secrets. She was too afraid, I think, that I would confront Hawley and be hurt in the process."

Charlotte was the one who reached out now to press her fingers against Lady Greenvale's. She did not offer an apology for she understood now that the countess didn't want any of those. She desired answers, not platitudes.

"I visited my sister a few days before her death, and she bustled into the drawing room all flushed and excited. I noticed what appeared to be old-fashioned jewelry dangling from the slit in her skirts. My sister loved the newest designs, especially delicate, finely wrought pieces. What I'd glimpsed, though, was a thick choker with pearl flowers forming a daisy-like chain. I was afraid her husband was dictating the smallest minutiae of her life, so I questioned her. She shoved the gems out of sight and tried to change the subject. When I pressed her, she promised that very soon she would be able to tell me everything. I wasn't satisfied with that answer, but she would only say that the necklace was a key to unlock the shackles keeping her prisoner."

"What happened to the choker?" Charlotte asked. Energy flickered through her, like a thousand wildfires igniting at once.

"I do not know," Lady Greenvale said. "I mentioned it to Lord Hawley, but he told me that he knew nothing about it. I have asked her friends if they ever saw it, but they had not."

"Could you sketch it?" Charlotte asked, her words tumbling out excitedly as she imagined using the drawing to question the other patrons of the Black Sheep, especially the unsavory sorts.

Lady Greenvale regretfully shook her head. "I am not an artist, and I barely saw the jewels. But it might be for the best. Showing a picture of the accessory or even inquiring about it may put your life at risk. In fact, only yesterday, I was warned to stop talking about the pearls."

"By Lord Hawley?" Charlotte asked as shivers of anticipation skittered up and down her spine. If the viscount was issuing threats, then perhaps the necklace was indeed proof of some misdeed.

The left side of Lady Greenvale's mouth twisted downward as she seemed to be mulling how to answer. "No. It was his brother. The youngest one who became a physician and scientist. I am not sure if it was well-intentioned advice or an attempt at intimidation. He was exceedingly urgent in his instructions for secrecy though."

"Dr. Talbot told you not to discuss the choker?" Charlotte's heart felt as if someone had struck her chest, it convulsed so violently. Could Matthew truly be involved? Although Charlotte had not discounted him as a suspect, part of her had never truly considered him to be a villain. But now uncertainty crept in.

"Yes. As I said, he very emphatically told me to never again discuss it with others."

"Why did you mention it to him in the first place?" Charlotte's mind scrambled to understand this new information, desperate to put it into a pattern that both made sense and didn't categorize Matthew as a lackey for his brother.

"After I arrived at the Black Sheep yesterday, Dr. Talbot approached me—very politely I might add. He introduced himself and expressed his condolences. Although he did not outright say that he suspected his brother of harming my sister, his words skirted close to such a confession."

"Dr. Talbot was investigating Hawley then? Not seeking to protect him?" Charlotte asked hopefully.

"Of that I am not clear." Lady Greenvale continued to twist her lips as she clearly wrestled with Charlotte's question. "He may be seeking to unmask his brother's perfidy or he could be keen to cover up what others know. I trust no one of the Lansberry line. They can charm and kill at the same time."

But Matthew was different. Wasn't he? How could the man who talked so passionately about saving an unloved pest like the wildcat be on the side of his vicious brother? But hadn't Charlotte herself considered it, knowing how much blood ties can bind a person?

Betrayal and pain engulfed her. Although Matthew had made her no promises, the idea of him working to hide his brother's crimes felt like a crippling, personal blow.

"Why did you confide in me?" Charlotte asked, her voice dropping to a faint whisper, and not because she was afraid of someone overhearing. She did not want this wariness upon her heart.

"I confessed the truth, Lady Charlotte, because I do not wish another young lady to die like my sister. Viscount Hawley is a powerful and connected man. If you are to escape him, you need every advantage. I hope you can do what my sister and I could not. Bring that monster to justice."

Chapter Nine

The monkey on Matthew's shoulder had grown ominously quiet. The little capuchin possessed a temperamental streak, and long periods of silence often presaged temper tantrums. Given that Matthew was currently strolling through Covent Garden, he strongly preferred Banshee not start shrieking. He certainly didn't want her to leap to the ground and lead him through the twisting, fog-filled alleyways.

If he tried placing the cheeky Simia in a handheld cage, she would only injure herself on the bars, and Matthew didn't want that. She was safer on her perch. Banshee might like to play chase, but she'd spent almost the entirety of her life on ships, and she would not stray far. Hopefully.

"We're almost there, Banshee," Matthew said in a cajoling voice before he hummed the tune to a rather bawdy ditty that the monkey's old owner used to croon. She shifted and gave a purr-like sound that she emitted when content. The poor girl needed more space and another capuchin companion now that she'd reached adulthood. Thankfully, Matthew knew just who could provide that, even in Jolly Old England.

Matthew began to wish he had just told Tavish to send a carriage around rather than meet him at the Black Sheep. But he'd thought a walk would benefit Banshee before she was trundled off to Tavish's estate on the outskirts of London.

An annoyed chittering sounded from the cage Matthew held in his left hand. "Not you too, Cyrene. Patience."

The weight in the covered cage shifted, and Matthew knew the small raccoon was pacing on her three good legs. He increased his own gait, ignoring the curious looks cast his way as Banshee began to bounce in time to the vulgar song. He was in bloody Covent Garden, not Hyde Park. Couldn't a man walk in peace with a New World monkey dancing on his shoulder and a washer dog scolding him like an irate schoolmaster?

Thankfully, the wooden Black Sheep sign denoting the coffeehouse appeared in Matthew's line of sight. Hurrying even faster, he rushed past a group of startled rakehells. Unfortunately, the sudden change in speed caused Banshee to hurl what he assumed to be Simian insults at the fops. Most of the carousing rich rascals—who seemed always predisposed to recognize taunts in any language—reddened in anger.

One young man, however, grinned broadly. He elbowed his closest companion in the ribs. "I say, Hayfield, I do believe that creature just insulted your wardrobe."

Hayfield's face darkened into a dangerous shade of puce. His rather voluminous wig bobbed, and Matthew could see the man's tight-fitting Continental-style clothing stretch and bunch as his muscles tightened. "I doubt that ape has any taste."

Matthew knew better than to correct the man that Banshee was actually a monkey, not an ape. Life with his older brother had taught him discretion. It had also taught him when to retreat. Unfortunately, Banshee was not so inclined.

She screeched out several hideous noises that definitely sounded like a stream of disparaging invectives. Hayfield's jovial friend nearly doubled over in laughter. Between guffaws, he managed to huff out, "The so-called ape has a better sense of fashion than you, Hayfield."

Matthew tried to scoot into the Black Sheep before the situation deteriorated further. Unfortunately, before he could reach for the door, Hayfield made a shooing motion toward Banshee. The monkey screamed and catapulted onto the wooden sign. The hinges squeaked as the capuchin swung back and forth, hollering her grievances.

By now, a rather egalitarian throng had begun to gather—from the lowest beggar boy to a couple more toffs. Hayfield clearly did not appreciate the audience. Banshee, however, did. Her cries grew even louder.

"Sir, control that creature!" Hayfield advanced on Matthew, his formerly pleasant features twisted by barely controlled anger. The man was clearly spoiling for a fight, and a nervous energy pulsated through Matthew as his own muscles tightened. Tavish had taught Matthew how to defend himself, but Matthew preferred avoiding fisticuffs.

Slowly, Matthew placed the raccoon's cage on the ground. As he straightened, he held out both of his hands, showing his palms. "I shall endeavor to calm her, my lord. But the monkey is fairly overset."

Hayfield's friends burst into laughter, and the mirth quickly spread to the rest of the ragtag assembly. Hayfield's fist bunched, and his arm began to pull back. Matthew prepared to dodge the blow.

"You manage that vermin, or I'll manage you!" Hayfield threatened. "If not here, then on the field. Who is your second?"

"My goodness, what is all this fuss?" A woman in widow's weeds glided through the throng to stand beside Matthew. Despite the black crepe hiding her features, he recognized her voice at once: Lady Charlotte.

A murmur rose from the crowd at the sudden appearance of an aristocratic lady—one of the few types of souls not commonly found wandering freely through this particular section of London. However, Lady Charlotte ignored the rumbling as she made a show of lifting her veiled face to regard Banshee. Seemingly as startled as the rest of the group by this darkly garbed newcomer, Banshee peered down at Lady Charlotte, her black eyes alight with curiosity.

Lady Charlotte glanced first at Hayfield and then at Matthew. Even with her features obscured, she exuded the perfect degree of elegant censure with a simple tilt of her chin. She was, Matthew thought with a burst of heat, an utterly amazing woman.

Obviously recognizing Lady Charlotte as a woman of quality, Hayfield's taut body uncoiled, and a hint of chagrin washed over his face.

"That abomination was insulting me," Hayfield said defensively.

For a moment, Lady Charlotte did not say a word, and her silence made Hayfield squirm. When she did speak, her melodic voice was calibrated to perfect neutrality. "And you responded to the supposed insult by challenging a monkey to a duel?"

The crowd roared with laughter. Hayfield looked torn between anger and amusement at his own folly. When he spoke, he sounded less assured of his rightful indignation. "I asked his owner to name his second, not the ape."

"I am sure this sweet creature meant no harm. Isn't that right…" Lady Charlotte paused and turned expectantly to Matthew, clearly wanting to know the monkey's name.

"She is called Banshee," Matthew said, wishing the capuchin had a more dignified appellation given the circumstances.

Lady Charlotte swiveled back toward the monkey. "Correct, Banshee? You did not mean to insult the nice man."

Banshee blew Lady Charlotte a kiss—a trick her old owner had taught her to charm tavern wenches while in port. This time the crowd laughed good-naturedly, and Banshee seemed rather pleased with herself.

"Now will you come down off that sign?" Lady Charlotte asked, first placing the wicker basket that she held on the ground and then holding out her arms. Banshee immediately dropped from her perch and wrapped her arms around Lady Charlotte's neck. Fortunately, Banshee did not dislodge Lady Charlotte's veil but pulled it tighter.

Looking regal despite a monkey clinging to her, Lady Charlotte turned to Hayfield again. "See, my lord, it was all a misunderstanding. Banshee, show the finely dressed gentleman that you are sorry."

Banshee blew another kiss. A smile blossomed over even Hayfield's face. With a light grin, he bowed low. "Apology accepted."

"Now send him a kiss goodbye," Lady Charlotte instructed. Obviously enjoying her little performance, Banshee complied with dramatic relish. Lord Hayfield tipped his cocked hat to both monkey and woman. "Banshee. Milady."

His friends followed suit, and soon the group of young toffs were continuing their way up the street. The rest of the crowd dispersed, leaving only Matthew and Lady Charlotte with Banshee wrapped around her like an oversized furry necklace. Matthew's heart clattered against his chest...and not because he'd nearly been forced into a duel.

His pulse was thundering for Lady Charlotte.

It was always for Charlotte.

A wildness erupted inside Matthew, and he yearned to push back Charlotte's veil and press his lips against hers in a fierce kiss.

Of course, he'd never even attempt it.

For one, Banshee was a better chaperone than any dragon of a matron. If he tried to dislodge the capuchin now, she'd spit, scratch, or most likely do both. Nor would he risk revealing Lady Charlotte and ruining her reputation.

But even if there had been no Banshee and no onlookers, Matthew still would not have taken such liberties. It wasn't his place. She was the sister of his best friend. Lady Charlotte, if she regarded him at all, saw him at best as an acquaintance. Nothing more.

"We best hurry inside before Banshee causes another scene."

Lady Charlotte nodded. While she opened the door, Matthew retrieved her basket and the racoon's cage from the ground. The regulars looked up at their entrance but then immediately went back to talking. They'd become accustomed to seeing "widows" slip through the front room, and all sorts of creatures visited the Black Sheep at one point or another.

Banshee began to chatter, but Lady Charlotte spoke softly. Immediately, the little monkey rested its white fluffy cheek against Lady Charlotte's shoulder. An absurd jealousy toward the creature slipped through Matthew, and he ruefully shook his head at his own folly.

As soon as Lady Charlotte reached the inner sanctuary, she attempted to remove her veil. Banshee, however, would not budge. Matthew didn't blame her. He wouldn't have wanted to stop embracing Lady Charlotte either.

"Come here, Banshee," Matthew cajoled, extending his arms. Banshee emitted an emphatic screech and clung tighter.

"Go back to Dr. Talbot, sweetheart." Lady Charlotte managed to disengage one furry arm from around her neck, but as soon as she started to pry away the second, Banshee relatched the first.

"That's an interesting necklace you've got there, Lottie!" Alexander called from across the room. Before either Matthew or Lady Charlotte could respond, a seemingly disembodied gravelly voice shouted.

"Hollaaaa."

A sharp whistle followed the greeting. At the sound, Banshee pointed her chin toward the ceiling, and Matthew followed the monkey's gaze.

Pan stared down at them from his favorite beam. As soon as the parrot noticed that he'd attracted the monkey's attention, he stopped moving and puffed out his lime-green chest feathers. He trained his one amber eye on Banshee, and Matthew swore the old bird actually winked.

Banshee immediately released Lady Charlotte and leapt to a shelf on the wall. A few of the new male and female patrons gasped at the sight of a monkey in their midst. This time, Banshee ignored her audience. With single-minded intent, Banshee climbed to a joist close to Pan.

The two creatures froze, staring at each other intently. Pan's pupil began to dilate and then rapidly shrink as his tail feathers fanned out. Banshee smiled, baring her front teeth and emitting a whine. Fascinated, Matthew debated about pulling out a notebook to record the behaviors.

"My goodness, I don't know if I should be insulted or relieved that I was replaced so easily in Banshee's affections," Lady Charlotte said, drawing Matthew's attention away from the bizarre overhead courtship.

"I fear she can be quite fickle," Matthew said. "You should not feel the least bit offended."

Lady Charlotte laughed merrily, and Matthew's heart trilled like a songbird in spring. She finally removed her veil, revealing her rose-tinted cheeks and parted pink lips.

Aye, Lady Charlotte was a shining beauty, inside and out.

"How ever did you acquire Banshee?" she asked.

"From a sailor during my last travels. He'd purchased her as a baby from a port in the New World. He couldn't recall the exact one," Matthew explained.

"I am surprised he was willing to part with a pet as sweet as Banshee."

Matthew barked out a huff of laughter as he glanced at the capuchin who was making funny faces at Pan. "She flung her dung in her owner's face, and the old salt was about to toss her overboard. I intervened and purchased the little minx for two shillings. From what I've learned about capuchins, they are too freewill to live contentedly as a mere companion to a human being."

Lady Charlotte's expressive green eyes darkened, reminding him of the deep jungles from which Banshee had likely been stolen as a babe. "What are your plans for Banshee then? If she was not happy on a ship, surely she will not enjoy living in London?"

"She will be able to live in relative peace on my estate on the outskirts of the city." Tavish's deep brogue broke into the conversation.

Matthew turned to greet his benefactor. Over a decade older than Matthew, Tavish Stewart was slightly shorter and a bit broader. His dark hair had started to gray at the temples, a silvery contrast against his sun-browned skin. His even features always remained placid and unreadable, his lips curved upward in an ever-present half smile. He exuded a pleasant but distant coolness—a living male Mona Lisa.

But given the secrets Tavish kept, it was no wonder that he chose to remain enigmatic.

"Lady Charlotte, this is my employer, Mr. Tavish Stewart. Mr. Stewart, this is Lady Charlotte, Lord Heathford's sister and Miss Hannah Wick's cousin."

Despite his humble beginnings, Mr. Stewart had become more of an ingrained gentleman than Matthew. He greeted Lady Charlotte with the aplomb of a royal courtier. "Your wonderful reputation precedes you, my lady. I am very impressed by the changes you have made to the Black Sheep."

"Thank you, Mr. Stewart." Lady Charlotte dipped a little as if meeting a man of her own class. Her respect toward Tavish triggered a warm glow within Matthew. "I have also heard much of you and your enterprises. I am told you possess a very keen mind."

Tavish's half smile did not change, but his blue eyes twinkled warmly. "As do you. From what I have gleaned, you have all the makings of a wise proprietress with an instinct for profitable decisions."

Lady Charlotte's elegant mien faltered, and she turned toward Matthew. Panic danced over her features, along with hurt. Matthew's gut clenched as he realized she blamed him for spilling a secret that he hadn't even known. Matthew had been aware that Lady Charlotte had helped her cousin and Sophia design the new room, but not that she'd actually invested in the coffeehouse.

"I do apologize, Lady Charlotte. By your face, I see it is not common knowledge. The Misses Wick told me, and I was not aware that it was in confidence."

"I was not privy to your ownership interest until now, Lady Charlotte," Matthew added hastily, "but I think it is both exceedingly bold and clever. You never cease to amaze me."

A pleased smile replaced Lady Charlotte's wounded look. Once again, Matthew's stomach dipped, but this time for an entirely different reason. The fluttering excitement she evoked still stunned him despite weeks of experiencing this buoyant rush.

He'd meant the words he'd uttered. Society would condemn her for scandalously owning a portion of a coffeehouse, but it could give her an independence otherwise unobtainable for most women. But the price she could pay might be total ostracization, much worse than what he'd endured after becoming a physician.

"Thank you," she said. The words were simple, but an underlying emotion rumbled through them. It sounded so much like affection, and Matthew wanted to bask in it. But before the warmth in her voice could fully envelop his heart, she turned sharply.

Her expression smoothed into the regalness she wore like finely wrought chain mail.

"Are you close to my cousin Hannah Wick then?" Lady Charlotte asked. Her voice was light and pleasant, and nothing about her stance seemed amiss. Yet Matthew sensed a change, an increased alertness, perhaps. She reminded him of her brother right before a race.

"I have been a patron at the Black Sheep since its inception." Tavish answered the question as smoothly as Lady Charlotte asked it, but a sense of unease slithered through Matthew. Lady Charlotte had always been perceptive, and he wondered if even Tavish's talents for subterfuge would withstand her inspection. Tavish had made a rare misstep and, for some reason, had triggered Lady Charlotte's interest.

"Are you a friend of Hannah's parents? I must admit that I do not know my cousin's side of the family well or their acquaintances."

Nervous energy coursed through Matthew. Why was Lady Charlotte so intrigued by the connection between Tavish and Hannah? Alexander had never questioned it, but then again, Matthew, Tavish, and the Wick cousins had been careful not to reveal too much. If only Tavish had realized how much a highborn lady would wish to keep her part ownership in a coffeehouse a secret.

"I am always eager to find a place that offers stimulating conversation and an invigorating beverage." Tavish spoke with a calm, magnanimous assertiveness that normally distracted his audience from the fact he had failed to address a direct inquiry.

Lady Charlotte, however, was not bamboozled.

"But why this establishment in particular? You cannot throw a stone without hitting a coffeehouse in Covent Garden." Lady Charlotte's conversational tone belied the prying nature of her inquiries. "Surely something must have drawn you to my cousin's?"

"It was the name," Tavish answered with equal smoothness.

"Truly?" Lady Charlotte asked, her melodic voice tinged ever so slightly with polite interest, nothing more. "Do you feel a particular kinship with the appellation?"

"Are we not all black sheep in one way or another?" Tavish lightly tossed the question back toward Charlotte.

Matthew found his eyes flickering between Tavish and Lady Charlotte as if he were watching a tennis match at the French court between two unparalleled players. The more the underlying tension grew, the more pleasant and offhanded their voices became. Normally, Matthew would predict that Tavish would emerge the winner, but Lady Charlotte was slowly forcing the Scot into a corner with each new volley. If Tavish wasn't careful, he might teeter out of bounds…a dangerous misstep for all involved, including Lady Charlotte.

"Speaking of black sheep…" Matthew interjected with perhaps a touch more cheer than necessary. He was not a master at oblique discourse, but his statement caused both Tavish and Lady Charlotte to swivel in his direction. As they stared at him expectantly, he forced a game smile and lifted the cage in his hand.

"This is Cyrene."

"The water nymph huntress?" Lady Charlotte asked in confusion as she stared at the blanket hiding the raccoon.

"What better name for a creature that is called a 'washer' or 'washer dog' or 'washer bear' in many languages?" Matthew asked as he removed the covering. Cyrene pressed against the back of her cage and began to chitter nervously. Matthew carefully reached a finger between the wooden slats to give a few comforting scratches. Although Cyrene displayed a degree of affection for him, the little kit was still liable to bite, especially in this state.

"My goodness!" Lady Charlotte exclaimed as she bent slightly at her knees to get a better view of Cyrene. To Matthew's delight, he noticed that she did not move closer to the cage, which he assumed was in an attempt to keep from further startling Cyrene. "It looks like she is wearing a little mask!"

Cyrene peeked at Lady Charlotte from behind her thick striped tail. When her curious, sparkling black gaze met Lady Charlotte's, Lady Charlotte clasped her hands together. "She is adorable. What do we call her kind in English?"

"A raccoon," Matthew said. "It is derived from the word used by the Algonquian tribe."

"Where is she from?" Lady Charlotte asked.

"I was exploring the woods in the New World, and I happened across a set of beaver traps. Cyrene was ensnared, her front paw crushed beyond my abilities to repair it. Her mother was nowhere to be seen, and I doubted Cyrene would live long in the wild. I knew she would be perfect for Tavish's menagerie, so I took her with me on my adventures. I'll miss the little mite, but she'll be much happier in the large outdoor enclosure that Tavish can provide."

"You have a menagerie, Mr. Stewart?" Lady Charlotte asked.

"An ever expanding one thanks to the efforts of Dr. Talbot." Tavish patted Matthew's shoulder, and Matthew couldn't help a shy grin. Although they were not even twenty years apart, Tavish had become something of a father figure to Matthew.

"He's collected even more kinds of animals than can be found at the Tower of London." Hannah joined the conversation, a tray filled with steaming mugs of coffee in her hands. "It is a true marvel."

"You've been there?" Lady Charlotte asked her cousin, her voice once again as light as a silkworm's gossamer.

Over the back of Lady Charlotte's head, Matthew widened his eyes in warning, while Tavish gave a quick jerk of his head. Hannah, who was perhaps the best secret keeper of them all, showed no external reaction. She shrugged nonchalantly. "Mr. Stewart is very generous in allowing the hardworking people of London entrance to the grounds of his home. He does not charge a single shilling. A lot of us Covent Garden folks have managed to make a trip to his property once or twice."

Lady Charlotte shot a sweet, seemingly artless smile in Tavish's direction. "Is your menagerie open to the nobility as well? I have always loved seeing the exotic animals at the Tower."

"I am afraid you will find smaller, more pedestrian fare at mine," Tavish responded with his standard casual charm as he dramatically undersold his collection. "Scottish wildcats, a few badgers, a family of hedgehogs—that sort of thing."

"It sounds absolutely wonderful," Lady Charlotte said. "I would love to see Banshee arrive at her new home. You are taking her there today, aren't you? And Cyrene too?"

Matthew exchanged a look with Tavish. A visit from someone as astute as Lady Charlotte might be managed...if allowed ample time to prepare and warn the lads. An unexpected one, however, could result in unmitigated disaster.

"Wouldn't it be a risk to your reputation, Lady Charlotte?" Matthew asked. When she spun toward him, her eyes sparking green fire, he rather wished he hadn't spoken. Despite the intensity of her gaze, the rest of her countenance remained relaxed and jovial.

"That's why I possess this." Lady Charlotte lifted the gauze in her hand, sending the flimsy fabric fluttering like a raven's wings.

Before Matthew could respond, Alexander joined them. He peered quickly at Hannah's tray of coffees and plucked the center one. "I do believe this one is mine. I can see flecks of nutmeg floating on top."

Hannah rolled her eyes. "I was on my way over to you."

Alexander took a large sip of the drink despite the steam rising off it. He sighed contentedly. "What can I say? I am an impatient sort. I also have questions as to why a monkey is wooing Pan."

"It is Pan who is romancing the capuchin," Hannah contradicted, pride at her pet coloring her voice.

"I believe the budding courtship is mutual." Lady Charlotte tilted her chin toward the ceiling.

Matthew looked in the direction she indicated, and sure enough, the two animals were huddled against each other on the same beam. Banshee was using her slender fingers to search through Pan's feathers, while Pan had craned his neck in order to run his beak through Banshee's fur.

"Aw, they're petting each other." Lady Charlotte clasped her hands against the upper bow of her stomacher.

"Not precisely," Matthew explained. "They are finding and eating insects."

"Ew, Dr. Talbot." Hannah wrinkled her freckled nose. "Must we speak of bugs?"

"It is still a sign of affection, to be sure," Matthew added quickly as he felt heat scorch his cheeks. Sometimes, he wished he'd think before he allowed scientific facts to pour from his mouth.

"A very odd one." Hannah squinched half her face as she regarded the unconventional sweethearts preening each other.

Matthew almost opened his mouth to explain the value of ridding a partner of lice and other pests, but this time he had the forethought to stop. He, however, still itched to speak.

"But practical," Lady Charlotte observed, and Matthew once again found himself battling down the ill-advised urge to kiss her at her remarkably sensible insight. "It is a form of caring for each other—is it not? I find it endearing."

Hannah squinted at her cousin as if encountering her for the first time. "You possess an odd streak that I did not expect."

"Lottie has always been a peculiar sort. She just does a better job of hiding it than the rest of us," Alexander said between sips of his coffee.

Lady Charlotte pretended to shove her elbow into her twin's ribs. Of course, with Alexander holding the hot brew, she did not actually make contact. Alexander, however, still emitted an exaggerated *oof.* It was a tableau that Matthew had seen acted out a thousand times during the childhood summers that the three of them had spent together. Yet he still could not stop himself from finding their behavior as fascinating as a newly discovered species. It was so different to the suspicion, tension, and outright animosity in his own family.

"I prefer the term *Original,*" Lady Charlotte said, her tone just as teasing as her brother's.

"That you certainly are." The solemnly spoken words slipped from Matthew's mouth before he could stop them. A deucedly awkward silence descended as everyone stared at him. Tavish's gray eyes were especially piercing, and Matthew shifted his weight from one leg to another.

Thankfully, Lady Charlotte ended the horrid hush with one of her magnanimous smiles. "Why thank you, Dr. Talbot. Whether oddity, peculiarity, or originality, it is clear that one of my unique traits is the ability to soothe Banshee. If you are to separate her from her newly beloved Pan, my presence might make the carriage ride to Mr. Stewart's estate much less alarming for the poor dear."

Devil take it, Matthew had thought the intervening conversation had managed to distract Lady Charlotte from her sudden, intractable desire to visit Tavish's home. Instead, she had just manipulated the discussion back to her benefit.

Alexander straightened, pushing downward on his cane. "Are you going to visit Mr. Stewart's menagerie? It has been ages since I've visited. It sounds like grand fun."

With a triumphant grin, Lady Charlotte hooked her elbow through her brother's free arm. Matthew's heart plummeted, and he tried to catch Tavish's gaze in some hope that they could divert the powerful force that was Lady Charlotte. But he was too late.

"Mr. Stewart and Dr. Talbot were worried about my accompanying them without a chaperone, but now that you are here, I see no reason why we cannot join them."

"It sounds like a marvelous plan. What say you, Mr. Stewart, Dr. Talbot? Shall we depart for Ravenshall as soon as we can pry apart the sweethearts?" Alexander asked as he glanced significantly toward Banshee and Pan.

Matthew barely suppressed a groan. They had no excuse now. If he and Tavish denied the twins' request, not only would they increase Lady Charlotte's suspicion but they would trigger Alexander's as well. As much as Alexander bounced from passion to passion, once he had set his mind upon something, he was terribly tenacious. He and Lady Charlotte would be liable to show up completely unannounced at Tavish's home, which would be even more catastrophic than a hastily planned visit.

"I would be delighted to host you and your sister," Tavish said, somehow managing to sound truly honored. Matthew could never have managed such a welcoming tone without even a hint of frustration or panic.

"I best deliver the rest of this coffee," Hannah said cheerfully. Matthew did not miss the silent exchange between her and Tavish. Sure enough, after dropping off the mugs to the patrons, she disappeared into her private quarters…most likely to dispatch a messenger to warn Tavish's staff of their impending arrival.

Matthew still could not escape a sense of doom. Not for the first time, he swore he could feel the rough rope of the hangman's noose about his neck. Some days it felt looser, and some days it grew tighter. And right now, it was damn near to choking him.

Chapter Ten

Mr. Stewart, Hannah, and Matthew were all hiding something. Charlotte was certain of it. Whether it also involved Viscount Hawley was less clear—or maybe Charlotte just wanted it to be less clear. As much as she needed proof of Hawley's villainous nature, she found herself hoping that neither her cousin nor Matthew were involved. Over the past handful of weeks, Charlotte hadn't exactly begun a friendship with Hannah, but she'd observed her co-proprietresses enough to admire both Hannah and Sophia for their industriousness.

Matthew had begun to occupy Charlotte's mind since her conversation with Lady Greenvale...and not just because Charlotte was trying to untangle his motivations for warning the countess to quit talking about the mysterious choker. The mere thought of Matthew had started to send a giddy sensation spiraling through her.

It certainly made sitting across from him in Mr. Stewart's carriage an interesting experience. Charlotte wished she could attribute the odd ripples in her heart to the monkey currently curled up on her lap or to the masked three-legged creature staring at her with bright black eyes. Her palpitations, however, had everything to do with sharing tight quarters with someone who elicited so many conflicting feelings. Matthew was a shy yet bold adventurer. When he spoke, his voice was always soft and low, but it held her attention like no other. And most of all, her soul instinctually trusted Matthew, even while her brain churned with reasons to distrust him. He was the brother of the man she was being forced to wed—an attraction to him could only cause them both pain, yet still, desire kept bubbling up inside her.

A tiny hand patted Charlotte's cheek, pulling her from her reverie. Banshee tilted her head curiously and curled back her lips into a grimace-smile that showed both teeth and gums. The little monkey looked so ridiculous with her furry cheeks puffed out that Charlotte laughed.

"Banshee is indeed smitten with you," Matthew said, his voice that lovely mix of deep and mellow.

Charlotte glanced at him, and once again wondered how gray eyes could simmer with such delicious fire. The heat settled in her chest, and for a moment, she found her breath gone. *Smitten.* The word seemed to hang in the very air between them, like a tempting sweet that neither of them were ready to taste.

"There is Ravenshall in all its glory!" Alexander—oblivious as always to the undercurrent that he was interrupting—nudged Charlotte and pointed out her window. Banshee scolded him for jostling them, but Charlotte barely registered the sound. She was too busy staring at the looming edifice.

It was grand and new, with Corinthian columns and large sash windows that caught the light and tossed it back as if in defiance of the dreaded window tax. Built of stone with a faint yellow-brown cast, it exuded a warmth despite its perfect geometric precision. It was at once austere yet welcoming—a bit like its owner.

"It does make me think of the ancient buildings that I saw during my Grand Tour on the Continent," Alexander said, mentioning one of the few luxuries his parents had allowed and only because it was necessary to keep up social appearances. "Yet there is something undeniably English about it."

"Scottish," Mr. Stewart corrected mildly.

"Ah, yes," Alexander said. "It was designed by the late William Adam from Edinburgh, was it not?"

"Aye," Mr. Stewart said, his voice pleasant, yet betraying nothing. What made the gentleman so inclined to secretiveness?

Charlotte leaned toward the window, as if examining the exterior of the man's residence would somehow reveal his innermost life. Not wanting to be caught gawking, she lifted Banshee in her arms and made a show of pointing out the Palladian structure. "What do you think of your new home?"

Banshee curled back her upper lip and made a decidedly unimpressed chitter. It was most likely due to Charlotte adjusting her position, but Mr. Stewart, Matthew, and Alexander laughed heartily. Charlotte gave a perfunctory titter, but her focus was on the curious array of outbuildings, almost obscured by giant oaks. The rest of the mansion and the manicured lawn with its symmetrical plantings adhered to current fashion, but courts ringed with edifices were becoming a relic of the past. Even more unusual, the side structures—although pleasing to the eye—did not mirror each other. They were orderly arranged, but in the way of buildings at Oxford or Cambridge. One seemed almost as grand as Ravenshall, with smaller yet more prolific windows. It was certainly not a typical mews. Very few of the constructions looked like stables, and one even reminded her a bit of a utilitarian factory of sorts.

Charlotte leaned back against the squabs, making sure to assume a perfectly pleasant mien that displayed only a hint of polite curiosity. "Despite Banshee's commentary, you have a wonderful home, Mr. Stewart. You have done a good job of blending new with old. You have the most unique collection of structures around the back. I see you are not chained to the current trend of perfect symmetry."

"Thank you." Mr. Stewart's smile was as frustratingly prosaic as her own. "Although I enjoy the simplicity of repetition in current architecture, I do not feel bound by restraints when it does not suit my purposes."

Mr. Stewart's lips remained tilted in that annoyingly vague half grin, but Charlotte did not miss the flinty undercurrent. Interesting. He might think a stony tone would cause her to shy away like a startled rabbit, but then again, he didn't realize that he wasn't the predator who frightened her the most.

"What is that peculiar building?" Charlotte pointed in the direction of a comparatively low-roofed structure with a rosy brick exterior rather than a stone facade. "It does not seem to fit with the others."

Mr. Stewart exchanged a look with Matthew. Again. Wordless conversation appeared to pass between the men. Neither betrayed a single emotion.

"That is the printshop," Mr. Stewart said both casually and resolutely.

"Oh, I would love to see inside! I have recently purchased a book from your press. Dr. Talbot's illustrations make it an absolutely gorgeous volume." Charlotte punctuated her only partially feigned excitement with a bounce. Banshee scolded her, but Mr. Stewart's face remained placid.

"I am afraid it will not be possible," Mr. Stewart replied evenly. "We are in the midst of a very complex print that I have promised to a client who demands punctuality."

"Mr. Stewart never allows visitors to view the presses," Alexander joined the conversation, his voice theatrically wistful. "Goodness knows, I've tried. It would be grand hearing the machines thump and the metal type clang together—a bit like the sounds of a good horse race, don't you think?"

Matthew ignored Alexander's comment and instead leaned in

Charlotte's direction, his gray eyes searching hers. "Which volume did you buy?"

"*The Curious Animalia and Flora of the New World.*" It had been an expensive purchase that had taken several months' pin money, but Charlotte had thought it worth the price. She'd tried telling herself that she'd acquired the book to better understand Matthew for purposes of her inquiries into Hawley. But after reading *Ferus Cattus of Caledonia*, she'd picked up another work by Matthew because of his stunning drawings and descriptions. He had a way of sketching an animal that infused the ink strokes with life, and the creature seemed to peer out of the pages and stare down the reader.

"I am, quite simply, enthralled by your illustrations," Charlotte added.

As a soft smile stretched across Matthew's face, an echoing emotion swelled in Charlotte's bosom. But before it could wash over her, Mr. Stewart's brogue yanked her attention back to where it should be: the Scotsman's and Matthew's secrets.

"You will meet several of the animals that he drew today," Mr. Stewart said. "I have arranged for the coachman to bring us directly to the enclosures."

Sure enough, the carriage rumbled past Ravenshall. They headed up the manicured lawn toward an impressive fountain with sculptures of nymphs frolicking with fantastical sea creatures. The fine gravel of the path crunched under the heavy wheels of the conveyance as they traversed through the expanse of neatly trimmed grass peppered with perfectly positioned ornamental trees. Mr. Stewart clearly had funds…and plenty of them. His wealth must rival that of Charlotte's family or perhaps even exceed it.

Yet Charlotte's eyes remained mostly trained on the collection of mismatched edifices still visible behind the main mansion. It was clear Mr. Stewart wanted her nowhere near them. But why? Between the sprawling manor and the oaks, she could see little of the grounds near the structures. Here and there, though, she could spy the hustle and bustle of people. Although an estate like this employed an army of servants, there appeared to be more individuals milling about than one would expect at a country property, even one so near London.

All too soon, the carriage turned sharply, and a well-pruned hedge blocked Charlotte's view. Suppressing a sigh, she turned to look out Alexander's window but saw nothing other than flashes of the Thames River. Mr. Stewart was certainly situated on choice land. He was within easy access of the capital either by land or by water. Even the long driveway to his estate was directly off the main thoroughfare to the city, which would make Ravenshall a good place for illicit activity.

A glimpse of a well-established quay caught Charlotte's attention. She pressed against her brother to peer at it. The broad flagstone strip not only boasted a winch but even a treadwheel meant to lift goods from barges. There were also a few buildings built near the platform, presumably for storage. This was no mere landing for a pleasure yacht.

Alexander swung his head in the same direction. "It is impressive, isn't it? A little bit of the London dockyards so far inland."

"I prefer to build working monuments to trade, rather than follies romanticizing the distant past," Mr. Stewart stated. Charlotte noticed with interest that the self-made man once again appeared to give an answer without really doing so. He made prevarication an art form, but Charlotte had spent her womanhood with her mother and the ladies of the salon. She too knew how to weaponize the most prosaic of discourse.

"I must admit to naivete when it comes to machines. I would not have thought such massive hoists were necessary for a publishing house," she said, injecting the perfect amount of polite interest into her voice.

"It is not just books that we are shipping out, but the presses and other supplies arriving." Mr. Stewart answered smoothly.

"The wheel has come in handy when I have rescued larger animals from peers who could no longer keep them," Matthew added.

"Is that how you acquired the lion?" Alexander asked.

"There is a lion on this property?" Charlotte stared at Matthew. She really should not allow anything to distract her from discovering what Mr. Stewart and Matthew were hiding, but really, the king of the jungle?

Matthew's mouth twisted downward, his voice scathing. "Nemea's previous owner had purchased him at a market in Spain during the toff's Grand Tour. Nemea was only a cub, and the fop thought he would make a jolly pet. Of course, he put the poor cat in a cage smaller than even those at the Tower. Nemea became temperamental, and no one would go near him, even to feed him. His ribs were sticking out of his mange-ridden fur by the time I heard about his predicament through the Amica Fauna Society."

Charlotte's heart squeezed—both from the description of the unfortunate lion and Matthew's compassion. "How is Nemea now?"

"Why don't you see for yourself?" Mr. Stewart asked as he opened the door to the carriage.

Charlotte realized that she'd been so engrossed by Matthew's tale that she hadn't noticed that they'd stopped moving. She gave an enthusiastic nod, and Matthew immediately scrambled to the gravel path. He turned and held out his gloved palm. Scooching Banshee to her shoulder, Charlotte prepared to exit the vehicle.

As soon as Charlotte's fingers touched Matthew's, warmth crept through her despite the kid leather separating their flesh. The heat flowed up her arm with surprising force and settled in her chest.

After Matthew handed her down, their hands remained clasped a moment too long. Mr. Stewart paused in the open coach door. An actual sentiment flitted across his face, and that bemused half smile slipped for a fraction of an instant. The true emotion disappeared before Charlotte could categorize it.

"Dr. Talbot, why don't you show Lady Charlotte the menagerie yourself? That way she can ask all the questions she desires without Lord Heathford and me interrupting. Lord Heathford and I can take a different route around the grounds. He and I can release Cyrene into her new home, while you and Lady Charlotte conduct Banshee to hers."

It was a rather poor excuse to split them into pairs, especially since propriety dictated that Charlotte stay with her brother. Clearly, Mr. Stewart wished to separate from her, but was he escaping her prying questions or playing matchmaker?

Alexander's head appeared behind Mr. Stewart's bent shoulder. He raised one quizzical eyebrow. "Is that acceptable, Lottie?"

Charlotte knew her brother was checking if she was concerned about etiquette, but she was safe from chin-wags here. Mr. Stewart and even Matthew shared very little social connections with her, and Alexander would never say anything that could jeopardize her reputation. Charlotte even felt free enough to trade her widow's veil for the shepherdess hat. If it hadn't been for the fact she couldn't very well change in a carriage with three men, she would have donned the rest of the clothes stashed in her basket.

But she still hesitated. If Mr. Stewart was trying to rid himself of her presence, perhaps it meant that she was close to uncovering a secret.

On the other hand, Mr. Stewart was obviously not inclined to divulge anything. Matthew, however, was not as skilled at evasion. And she wanted to stroll alone with him to hear more of his stories and to watch his features soften as he spoke of the animals he so clearly loved.

"It sounds like a wonderful idea," Charlotte said cheerily as she linked her arm companionably through Matthew's. One of his shy smiles blossomed over his lips.

"It might be best for Banshee to have just the two of us nearby when we introduce her to the capuchin troop," Matthew said as he began to lead her down a side path. "Fortunately, we will pass Nemea first."

"Do you come often to Mr. Stewart's estate?" Charlotte asked as a warm spring breeze ruffled the silk sleeve of her sack-back gown. It was a rather pleasant day to take a sojourn in the country, and Charlotte suddenly wished that she and Matthew were just a man and woman taking a lovely stroll through a pleasure garden without any mystery or impending engagements pressing down upon them. What a fool she'd been during those long-ago summer days at Falcondale Hall when she could have been discovering more about the quiet Matthew Talbot.

"Aye," Matthew answered, "I am often here when I am not giving lectures at the university or seeing patients. I assist with the animals and work on my contributions to Tavish's publications."

"Does Mr. Stewart employ many servants to care for his menagerie?" Charlotte asked.

Matthew glanced away, his face in the wind now. The pieces of hair that were always escaping from his queue blew loose from the leather thong at his nape. He did not appear to notice the tendrils as they danced around his face. Instead, his gaze wandered over the slight rise and fall of the landscape before them.

"Look there." Matthew jabbed his finger in the direction of a tawny shape stretched out on a large smooth rock with no fence or wall between them and it.

Forgetting that Matthew had entirely ignored her question, Charlotte blinked and then blinked again. When the form drew back its head to emit a terrific roar, she froze.

Banshee was less composed. She screeched and scurried to the top of Charlotte's broad shepherdess hat. Dimly, Charlotte heard Banshee's feet rip and crack the straw of the fashionable bergère. The silk ribbon under her chin tightened, but she could only focus on the large predator.

"Why is it not in a cage?" Charlotte asked hoarsely. She considered herself a rather brave woman, but bearding a lion—whether inside or outside of its den—was clearly beyond the stretching point of her courage.

Matthew hurriedly laid his gloved hand over hers. "We are very safe, Lady Charlotte. My apologies for not warning you that we enclose the animals very differently than at the Tower or any other menagerie. We give the animals the maximum amount of possible space to roam. There is a ha-ha separating us from Nemea. He cannot climb the sunk fence."

Steadying her breath, Charlotte took better stock of her surroundings. At the edge of the gravel path stood a rather ineffective looking hedgerow. She assumed that the recessed stone wall was right behind the shrubbery.

"Shall we move closer?" Matthew asked gently.

"You are certain we will not be in harm's way?" Charlotte asked, wishing her voice did not sound so terribly ragged.

"I would never imperil you, Lady Charlotte." Matthew's already low voice dropped in timbre. It seemed to rumble through Charlotte, leaving delicious ripples in its wake. She wanted to believe him.

But she couldn't trust him implicitly, not in all things. Yet in this moment, right now, she knew that she could put her faith in him. He would not place her or the animals in danger.

She pressed her fingers lightly against his arm. "Show me what you wish me to see."

Matthew led them slowly to the boxwood, and Charlotte realized he'd set the snail-like pace to allow her a chance to turn if she wanted. But she didn't. She matched him step for step until they'd reached the edge of the bush.

"Look over it and down," Matthew instructed.

Charlotte peered past the shrubbery and discovered a surprisingly deep chasm. Bending over the low-lying hedge, Charlotte peered up and down the moat-like structure. The ground on the lion's side sloped downward to meet a sheer stone wall that even the big cat could not hope to climb. Although she had seen ha-has before at other estates, she had never come across such an impressive one.

"How clever!" Charlotte said.

"Seamus and John are brilliant when it comes to designing enclosures," Matthew said. "They both have the makings to become extraordinary engineers."

"Seamus and John?" Charlotte asked, glancing back at Matthew. She turned just in time to catch a panicked look cross his face before his expression blanked.

"Just a few of Mr. Stewart's servants who assist with the animals," Matthew told her. He sounded offhanded on the surface, but his voice seemed tighter than usual. Why would the mention of two workers cause such a reaction?

"What are some of their duties?" Charlotte asked. She kept her voice nonchalant as she fixed her eyes on the lion. Nemea was rolling in the grass now like a big kitty. Even at this distance, his paws appeared massive as they waggled in the air. He was a magnificent animal—all powerful sinew. But the creature's grace could not distract Charlotte from Matthew's nervousness. She only pretended that it did.

"Oh, what you would expect, really. Nothing thrilling, to be sure," Matthew answered in a rush before he tilted his head back to address Banshee. "What do you think of the lion? Bigger than a jaguar, isn't it?"

Banshee moved fretfully on Charlotte's broad hat. She could hear more of the straw breaking. It seemed like she would need to pay the milliner a visit tomorrow before her mother could catch sight of the damage.

"Perhaps we should move on," Matthew said. "Nemea's presence seems to be upsetting Banshee."

Matthew was trying to distract her again, but Charlotte had no intention of forgetting about Seamus and John. As she stepped back from the sunken wall, she feigned allowing the change in topic.

"What is a jaguar?" Charlotte asked, stumbling slightly over the unfamiliar word.

"It is the largest cat of the New World," Matthew said. "It is spotted like the leopards you have seen at the Tower but more muscular and with incredibly strong jaws."

"Are they as naughty as the Tower's leopards?" Charlotte asked. The felines had a reputation for stealing and chewing hats and other articles of clothing.

"More dangerous according to the locals in South America," Matthew said. "They say that jaguars hunt by crushing their victim's skulls and piercing the brain with their teeth. I analyzed bones during my travels there several years ago, which lends veracity to the tales."

An unbidden chill slipped through Charlotte. What a dastardly creature! It sounded as merciless as Hawley. It was a distressingly unwelcome reminder of just the kind of villain Charlotte was attempting to trap. Yet she'd find herself pulverized between the viscount's jaws for certain if she did nothing.

"Mr. Stewart is not in a possession of a jaguar?" Charlotte asked.

Matthew shook his head. "I did glimpse one while in South

America, but I only sketched it. Neither Mr. Stewart nor I wish to capture an animal that is thriving in the wild. It seems a cruelty."

A powerful surge of emotion erupted inside Charlotte as she imagined Matthew crouched in the leafy, dark jungle, furiously trying to portray the predator's power with deft strokes in graphite. Yet she could not afford to picture him as the quiet adventurer, not when she was practically engaged to his brother and unsure of his involvement with Hawley's rumored crimes. Pushing away the image of Matthew in the New World, she asked, "If you were to acquire a jaguar, then Seamus and John would design its pen?"

Matthew's jaw twitched, but other than that his expression remained steady. "Aye. That would be the way of it."

Before Charlotte could decide if she could make another inquiry without bringing too much suspicion upon herself, the chittering of monkeys wafted toward them. With an air of relief, Matthew returned the conversation to the capuchin on her hat. "Do you hear that, Banshee? That's your new family."

Charlotte could no longer feel little feet frolicking on the bergère's straw, and worry for the monkey stripped away her resolve to question Matthew further. She cast her eyes upward but could only see the wide brim. Several pieces haphazardly hung down—evidence of Banshee's previous dancing—but there was no sign of the actual capuchin.

"What is she doing?" Charlotte asked.

"She's frozen stiff and just listening," Matthew said, worry lowering his voice even more. "I am not sure if it is in anticipation or fear. She has not been around others of her kind since she was a wee bairn."

"Banshee?" Charlotte called in a singsong voice.

Immediately, a tiny, worried faced peeked below Charlotte's hat. The entire brim sagged under the monkey's weight, and soon her concerned black eyes were level with Charlotte's.

"Come here, darling," Charlotte crooned as she held out the arm not holding Matthew's elbow. Banshee immediately jumped on her shoulder and cuddled against her neck.

"You certainly do have a connection with Banshee. She is rarely this calm," Matthew said, his beautifully resonate voice catching and then reverberating in Charlotte's chest.

"Oh, she is a little sweetheart." Charlotte gazed at the adoring white face trimmed in brown and black. She had better sense than to glance at Matthew. If the look in his gray eyes matched his tone, she was sorely afraid all her resolve against the man would melt away.

The sound of the other monkeys grew louder, and Banshee trembled.

"Are you certain she will be happy with the rest of the troop?" Charlotte asked quickly. "What if they hurt her?"

Matthew laid his hand over hers again. This time, Charlotte was startled by the strength she drew from the simple gesture.

"I would not put a new chicken into a coop without introducing it properly to the flock first. Rest assured I will treat Banshee with equal care." Matthew pressed the tips of his fingers ever so slightly against her knuckles. "See how the outdoor cage is divided?"

Charlotte, who had practically tucked her chin against her chest to snuggle Banshee, looked up to find an intricate wooden structure that reminded her of a giant birdcage. It was connected to an elegantly appointed stone building with wide south-facing windows. Through the glass, Charlotte caught sight of exotic-looking fronds. The north end of the structure was built into a sturdy wall, likely to provide insulation.

"Is that an orangery?" Charlotte asked excitedly. She simply adored hothouses and their unique array of flora from far-flung lands.

"Aye," Matthew said. "It is full of trees and plants that are native to the monkeys' homeland. The capuchins are free to go in and out as they please through the upper transoms."

Charlotte glanced up and saw two tiny faces almost identical to Banshee's peering out of one of the narrow horizontal windows. The white tuffs on their cheeks seemed to flare as they cried out in excited gibberish. Two other monkeys huddled together on the limb of an ash tree, their dark bodies contrasting with the bright spring-green leaves. All four capuchins stared intently at Banshee, who was alternating between peeking at her brethren and hiding her eyes against Charlotte's neck.

"Come," Matthew said, opening the door to the orangery.

A blast of sweetly scented humid heat crashed into Charlotte. In only two steps, she traveled from familiar England to a distant land filled with tantalizing smells and wonderous pigments. The heat should have been oppressive, but it had the opposite effect. She felt as if it lifted her up and spun her around in a whirl of spiced scents. The broad-leaved trees with their narrow bare trunks cast dark shadows on the floor, so different from the dappled effect of the native English foliage. Orchids and other flowers brought splashes of color to the otherwise green world.

"Is this what the jungle is like?" Charlotte asked, her voice a solemn whisper. She had been in orangeries before, but they had always been tidy, organized affairs. This was a jumble of fronds and posies spilling everywhere.

"A fairy-tale version." Matthew's quiet words danced across Charlotte's heated skin, and she could not stop the shiver. The movement caused Banshee to cling tighter to her as the capuchin stared with deep, bottomless eyes at her surroundings. The fur on her cheeks bristled in anticipation, trepidation, or perhaps both.

"You look as nervous as Banshee," Matthew said. "Do not fret. Banshee might take a bit to adjust, but she will love it here."

Charlotte did not wish to admit that it was an altogether

different emotion that had triggered her quiver. Instead, she distracted herself by turning toward a wooden, lattice-like screen that walled off a substantial chunk of the room.

"The monkeys' portion of the hothouse?" Charlotte asked as she began walking over to the divider. Banshee, however, objected with a shriek. Clearly, the capuchin did not want to go any closer to her new companions. At least not yet.

"Aye," Matthew said. "That partition is permanent. The one that the lads erected in the outdoor cage is only temporary."

Matthew reached for Banshee, and the capuchin screamed with a range impressive enough to make an opera singer absolutely green with jealousy. How the creature managed such a piercingly loud sound with such a tiny body, Charlotte had no idea.

Matthew took a step backward, but still Banshee howled. Charlotte reached up to pet her, but the monkey shrank away. With a show of teeth, she nimbly scaled Charlotte's head as if ascending a tree. Howling the entire time, she settled on the crown of the shepherdess hat.

Charlotte helplessly lifted her hands to her ears, but that did little to block the earsplitting stream of complaints. Over the indignant cries, Charlotte shouted, "Is there a way to calm her?"

The question caused Matthew to turn a deep shade of red. He nodded reluctantly. "Aye. There is."

"What?" Charlotte asked desperately as Banshee began to jump in a tight circle. Although Charlotte could not hear the straw crackling over the shrieks, bits of it dug into her scalp.

"It is a, er, a song." Matthew shuffled his feet sheepishly.

"Then sing it!" Charlotte demanded as golden flecks cascaded from her brim.

"It is, well, rather inappropriate, given the current company. It was sung by her former owner who was an old salt…"

"There is a monkey destroying my hat and possibly my hearing. I do not believe we need to concern ourselves with propriety."

"Very well," Matthew said. Then he paused, swallowed, and paused again.

"Go on." Charlotte fluttered her hands.

Matthew spluttered out a sound that seemed somewhere between a choke and a groan. Then in a smooth, almost tender baritone, he began to croon one of the bawdiest ditties that Charlotte had ever heard—not that she had listened to many. They weren't exactly staples in the musicales that she attended.

"A lusty young smith at his vice stood a-filing, With a rub rub rub, rub rub rub, in and out, in and out, ho!" Matthew intoned. "When to him a buxom young damsel came smiling, And asked if to work at her forge he would go…"

Banshee, however, continued to screech. When Matthew reached the second "With a rub rub rub, rub rub rub, in and out, in and out, ho!" Banshee finally lowered the volume of her yowls but only by a mere fraction. Instead of jumping frightfully in a circle, Banshee's feet now landed on Charlotte's head in a distinct pattern…a pattern that mimicked the tune.

"Why isn't it working properly?" Charlotte asked, barely listening to the words as a small foot broke through the bergère's wide brim before the appendage disappeared back up the hole it had created.

"I don't know," Matthew said, his voice a bit strained. Red stained every visible inch of his upper body, reaching his hairline and disappearing into his cravat.

"Do you think I should try to sing it with you?" Charlotte called over Banshee's yowls.

"Ergh" was the only response she received from Matthew.

For the first time, Charlotte began to pay close attention to the lyrics. When Matthew sang about, "Red hot grew his iron, as both did desire," she suddenly understood exactly what "iron" the song was referring to, and it wasn't metal that the smithy was working with. The realization made her want to giggle.

When she joined Matthew singing the repetitive verse—"With a rub rub rub, rub rub rub, in and out, in and out, ho!"—she could barely stop her laughter from bubbling out too. This was the song that calmed Banshee? No wonder poor Matthew had turned the color of a scarlet ruby.

Unfortunately, the entire next stanza spoke of nothing but the blacksmith's vigorous and apparently prodigious "iron." As poor Matthew sang, "Six times did his iron, by vigorous heating, grow soft in the forge in a minute, a minute or so. As often, 'twas hardened, still beating and beating, but the more it was softened, it hardened more slow," Charlotte kept snickering. Even Matthew's voice began to quake with mirth, but somehow, they both managed to sing "rub rub rub" without losing the rather salaciously suggestive rhythm.

Matthew began the ditty anew, and Banshee finally started to calm. Charlotte, however, felt enlivened. Mirth and something even sweeter and fiercer burst through her very veins. In the middle of the next stanza, Matthew lifted Banshee from Charlotte's hat. His chest brushed against Charlotte's breasts just when they reached the line about, "They stripped to go to't, 'twas hot work and hot weather, she kindled a fire and soon made him blow..."

Matthew's voice cracked, and Charlotte's went high, but they did not miss a single word, even if a few of Charlotte's warbles ended with a snort or two, or three. While they both continued to croon, Matthew placed Banshee in the crook of one of the exotic trees. The capuchin hugged the trunk and watched them with bright black eyes. Whenever either of them tried to step back, she shrieked.

So Matthew and Charlotte stood shoulder to shoulder singing in the middle of the lush orangery about an enthusiastically copulating couple. Amid Charlotte's giggles, another sensation percolated, filling her with something she could only describe as an urge. It left her prickly and wanting more, craving more.

And whatever the more was, it had everything to do with Matthew Talbot. But she couldn't risk wanting any kind of *more* with him. Not here. Not now. Perhaps not ever.

Chapter Eleven

⸙

Matthew never realized exactly how small the confines of a coach really were until he found himself sitting across from Charlotte and her brother with the lyrics of "The Lusty Young Smith" spinning around and around in his head. Every few seconds, his lips would twitch, and he'd almost begin humming. Alexander was starting to shoot him curious looks, but it was Lady Charlotte who was practically his undoing.

She kept emitting truncated giggles and glancing his way. Mirth sparkled in her grass-green eyes, and he swore he could hear strains of the salacious ditty.

With a rub rub rub, rub rub rub, in and out, in and out, ho!

Warmth suffused Matthew, and he wished it was limited to the flush creeping over his skin. Unfortunately, a healthy portion of the flames were directed to his particular "iron," which, like the eponymous lusty smith's, was now most vigorously heated.

It was deuced embarrassing, especially considering the present company. Thankfully, his frock coat hid the evidence of his unfortunately forged and currently unwanted steel.

"What happened between you two? Lottie has turned into a veritable laughing hyena, and Matthew looks like a nervous stag—or

I suppose antelope if we're keeping the metaphor straight." Alexander swiveled his head suspiciously between them.

Devil take the sportsman for choosing now of all times to be keenly observant.

Guilt joined the already uncomfortable mix of sensations brewing inside Matthew. He should not be hungering after his best friend's sister, especially right in front of said best friend.

"We sang a rather interesting ditty," Charlotte freely admitted. "Evidently, it calms Banshee."

Matthew wanted to turn into dust and slip through the floorboards of Tavish's coach. Frantically, he tried to catch Charlotte's eyes to signal her to stop. She, however, was looking at her brother, not at him.

"Which one is it?" Alexander asked.

"I'm not familiar with its title," Charlotte said, "but the lyrics are—"

"Don't!" Matthew croaked out, his voice a rough bellow that was really much too loud for the smallness of the conveyance. He tried again at a lower volume, but he only ended up sounding more panicked, even to his own ears. "Please do not sing the lines. I beg you."

Alexander raised both his eyebrows. "Now I really want to hear them."

"No," Matthew groaned out. "Just no."

"Matthew, did you teach my sister an inappropriate song?" Alexander was chuckling too.

"A most scandalous one," Charlotte added brightly.

"It's like a lullaby to Banshee." Matthew tried to explain as he desperately scanned the carriage roof as if a trapdoor would miraculously appear. None, of course, did. He had no escape route that wasn't flinging himself out of a moving coach.

"I didn't know human skin could turn so red." Alexander cocked his head as he made a show of inspecting Matthew's complexion.

"A deep scarlet, wouldn't you say?" Now Charlotte had begun to peer at him as well.

Matthew resisted the urge to cover his face with both his hands. He couldn't stop himself from squirming though.

"More a maroon," Alexander countered, "but I wonder if we could make him turn magenta. That would truly be a marvel to see."

"You do realize that I am sitting right here?" Matthew protested.

"Oh, we know." Alexander winked at him. "That's what makes it so fun."

"Hmm," Charlotte said as she leaned forward to inspect him closely. "I may see shades of mauve beginning to blossom."

Matthew had no choice. He really was going to have to obscure his face. Perhaps he could use his cocked hat. Just as he reached for it, the carriage lurched to the right. Charlotte, who was still bent forward, was caught off-balance. To Matthew's horror, she pitched forward straight toward his still vigorously heated piece of iron. He yelped and made a move to shield himself before he realized that the carriage was not just swaying but crashing.

Years of physical training had made him quick. Matthew launched himself forward, wrapping his body around Charlotte's. She squeaked as they slammed against the wooden shell of the coach when it hit the ground. Matthew grunted as his shoulder and back absorbed most of the collision. Charlotte curled against his chest, and Alexander thudded against them, his boot accidentally catching Matthew's shin.

Panicked equine whinnies filled the air, and Matthew felt the upended coach jerk dangerously. He had no idea what had happened to the driver and the tiger, but no one was controlling the team. The horses were bolting, and that could easily mean death for them all.

Matthew's back, which was positioned in a broken window, scraped against the rutted path. He pushed Charlotte into her brother's arms and shoved them both down to the relative safety beneath the shattered glass. Wood creaked and groaned as the carriage began to rip apart. Matthew sank his fingers into the plush cushion as he fought to stand upright. Despite the jostling of the conveyance, he managed to scramble to his feet. Balancing in the curve of the carriage's right side, Matthew reached for the secured left door hanging above his head. It thunked open and flapped like an angry bird's wing. Once again digging into the thick fabric of the seat back, Matthew hoisted himself through the opening. As he reached the top, the horses bolted to the left, almost sending him flying. He clung to the frame as his feet skidded along the lacquered surface.

He finally found purchase. Using the lantern hooks for leverage, he hauled himself over to the now-vertical driver's box. He hooked his knees through the side of the seat and then swung his body down. It took two tries, but he managed to grab the reins and pull the horses to a halt.

When the carriage finally skidded to a stop, Matthew executed a flip, freeing his legs and landing neatly on the ground. No sooner had he unhitched the horses than something hit him hard. Unprepared for the blow, Matthew plummeted to the ground. When the first punch hit his head, he realized that he'd been felled by a human.

"Damn it. How are you still alive?" The voice was coarse and had definitely been cultivated in the London stews. By the smell of the man, he still resided there. "You were supposed to be a duke of limbs."

Fury and guilt pulsated through Matthew as he realized that he'd been ambushed while traveling with Charlotte and Alexander. He wasn't shocked that someone was trying to kill him. It came with his secret life. The man's choice of insult sounded like something his brothers would say, though, and not his other enemies. But Matthew had no time to unravel who had sent the assassin.

The steel of a blade caught the waning rays of the evening sun. The weapon slashed down, heading straight for his neck. Matthew caught the masked man's wrist and twisted. The knife fell from the attacker's hand and hit the dirt.

"Sorry to disappoint." Matthew swung out his foot and hooked the assailant's right knee, bringing the beefy man crashing to the ground.

Unfortunately, just as Matthew leapt to his feet, another ruffian grabbed him from behind, pressing a wickedly sharp dagger against his throat. "I've got him, Charley. You check his pockets."

Interesting. When people put blades to Matthew's jugular, that wasn't their normal response. It was something a common footpad might say, but these men wouldn't have set up an elaborate carriage crash just to steal a man's purse. This didn't feel like a highway robbery either. No one appeared to be attacking the carriage. The focus was only on Matthew.

Curious as to what the men were after, he allowed Charley to stick his large hands into the pockets of his frock coat. Sure enough, the brigand ignored his coins.

"The nob doesn't have it on him," Charley grunted as he stepped back.

"What are you looking for?" Matthew asked conversationally.

The knifepoint pricked his neck. "Shut your bloody mouth."

"Isn't that at odds with your goal? Don't you wish for me to speak?" Matthew kept his voice genial despite the tension pumping through him. Surreptitiously, he scanned the road. No other reprobates seemed to be present. Both the coachman and tiger, who must have been thrown off, were beginning to stir from their prone positions.

Charley scratched his head as he glanced over his mask at his accomplice. "The toff has a point, Eddie."

"I try," Matthew responded lightly. "I often give lectures at universities. I suppose it is my habit to give instructions."

"Are you trying to school us on how to do our job?" Eddie demanded, pressing the dagger more fully against Matthew's skin, not enough to slice but enough for Matthew to feel the weapon's sharpness. Matthew tensed, ready to disarm Eddie.

Charley signaled for his companion to stop. "Let's see what he's got to say."

"Well, it would make sense to ask if I had any hidden pockets. You do after all have a weapon against my neck, which is incentive for me to answer," Matthew said. He would be amused at how easily he was manipulating this duo if the danger to Charlotte, Alexander, and Tavish's employees was not so great.

Matthew was growing more and more convinced that these men had been sent by Hawley, but he wanted to know for certain. If it was the choker they were after, then he'd have his answer. Of course, if they were indeed Hawley's minions, then once they saw the jewelry and reported back to his brother, Hawley would realize beyond a doubt that Matthew had taken it.

But Matthew didn't care. Investigating and following Hawley hadn't done any good in the past. Matthew had decided to become the bait after all, and already it was working. He now knew the names and physiques of two of Hawley's underlings.

"Do. You. Have. A. Hidden. Pocket?" Eddie asked between gritted teeth. This time Matthew felt a slight burning as the blade scraped his flesh.

"Why, yes. I do. It is sewn into the inside of my waistcoat," Matthew said. He'd placed the choker there to show Tavish, but he hadn't had the chance. He'd debated about revealing it to Alexander, but he didn't want to put his best friend in any more danger. Alexander had faced enough of Hawley's cruelty during their school days. Matthew hadn't been able to protect him then, but maybe he could now.

Charley ripped open Matthew's frock coat, sending buttons flying. The ruffian also made quick work of opening Matthew's waistcoat. When the brigand began to poke around for the hidden compartment, Matthew laughed and squirmed. Let these men think him the ticklish fool.

"Stop moving!" Eddie roared. "Do you want to slice your own throat?"

"I can't help it," Matthew forced out between the most ridiculous giggles that he could muster.

"Addlepate," Eddie hissed, but he did pull back his weapon.

Charley found the pocket and began to yank on the jewelry. His light blue eyes widened over his mask. "This is it!"

Matthew had his answer. Before Charley could steal the choker, Matthew reached up and twisted the dagger away from Eddie while simultaneously using the man's beefy arm for leverage. Kicking up his legs, he latched them around Charley's neck. Twisting his whole body, he brought Charley down first. When his feet returned to the ground, he flipped a stunned Eddie over his shoulder. Matthew started to reach for his knife hidden in the inner lining of his frock coat, but a shot rang out.

Eddie screeched as his hat went flying. Matthew looked over his shoulder to find Alexander standing in the overturned coach, his head popping out from one of the windows. He had a pistol trained on Charley with one hand as he handed his used weapon presumably down to Lady Charlotte for reloading. She used to accompany them during their boyhood target practices at Falcondale Hall, but Alexander had always been the best shot out of the three of them.

"Should I aim to kill or to maim?" Alexander called out.

"Wound," Matthew answered. "You can't get answers from corpses."

Charley swore and yanked a scrambling Eddie to his feet. The two men immediately took off at a run. Shoving two fingers into his mouth, Eddie gave a sharp whistle. Two large horses thundered from the trees—fine mounts that men of Eddie and Charley's ilk shouldn't be able to afford. The duo from the London stews had definitely been taught to ride as they easily swung onto the warmbloods.

Matthew raced a few steps after them, but they disappeared around the bend. Even if he unhitched one of Tavish's drafts and tried riding it, he'd never catch them. Shaking his head in frustration, Matthew turned back to the carriage intent on helping Lady Charlotte escape from its ruined confines.

It seemed, however, that the intrepid woman had other plans. Just as she'd nimbly climbed trees as a child, she descended the overturned carriage, using the ornamental crenellation around the roof as hand- and footholds. When she reached the bottom, she immediately turned to grab Alexander's cane as he handed it to her. Her twin clambered down easily enough, relying on his arm muscles and good leg. Lady Charlotte helped steady him on his final step to the ground.

Matthew wanted to run to Lady Charlotte and throw his arms about her as he surveyed her for wounds. But despite their shared moment in Tavish's orangery, Matthew knew it wasn't his place. Even if she hadn't been his best friend's sister, he wasn't bridegroom material for a diamond of the ton.

"Are you okay, my lady?" Matthew called out, somehow managing to keep his emotions from his voice. "Alexander?"

"Yes," the twins called out in unison.

"I'll check on the coachman and the tiger."

"I'm fine!" The young footman, Will, called out, stumbling to his feet. "I had the wind knocked out of me. Sorry I wasn't of more assistance, sir."

Both of Tavish's employees were well aware of Matthew's fighting prowess and the need to keep it secret. But how much had Lady Charlotte and Alexander witnessed? Even his best friend didn't comprehend the true reasons for Matthew's sojourns to the New World.

But with the driver still groaning in the dirt, Matthew had no time to worry about what the siblings may have observed. Instead, he ran over to the prone man, ready to offer whatever medical treatment was necessary.

"Richard?" Matthew called the fellow's name as he drew near. "How badly are you hurt?"

"My side!" The man forced out between labored breaths as he gripped his rib cage with both hands.

"Did you injure it in the fall?" Matthew asked as he withdrew a knife from its hidden sheath in his boot. Quickly, he sliced through the man's livery, revealing a horrible welt on his left side that had already begun to turn a deep red.

"No." Richard huffed out the word as if he barely had enough air to speak. "Logs…like…battering rams…came…swinging…from the trees…on the curve…Hit me…Spooked…the horses."

As Matthew scanned Richard's injury, he thought of the surgeon's report from the inquest into the late Lady Hawley's carriage accident. The man of medicine had mentioned that the deceased driver had a large bruise on his chest, which had been attributed to being thrown from the coach. No one had survived, and it was a mystery why the vehicle had overturned on a sunny day upon a relatively well-maintained road. There had been no obvious damage such as a broken wheel or axle, and the coroner had ultimately found that the horses must have bolted. But Matthew was now certain that Charley and Eddie had helped Hawley cover up the strangulation of his second wife. They'd placed her body in a carriage driven by an unsuspecting coachman and staged an accident just like this attack. Proving their guilt and linking it to his brother, though, was a different matter.

"We were ambushed?" Alexander asked as he and Lady Charlotte joined Matthew by Richard's side.

Matthew exchanged a look with his best friend. Even without knowing about the necklace, Alexander probably suspected the viscount's involvement. The fact that Alexander wasn't bombarding Matthew with questions about his fighting skills proved his concern.

"Aye. The coach was definitely forced to overturn," Matthew said as he turned his attention back to Richard, whose breathing had grown both more shallow and rapid. Concern whipped through Matthew as he noticed the man's lips starting to turn a pale, almost bluish color.

"What is wrong with the coachman?" Charlotte asked, kneeling beside Mathew in the grass.

As Will joined them, Matthew grabbed Richard's hand to take his pulse. The man's skin felt cool and clammy, and his blood throbbed rapidly beneath Matthew's fingers. "He may have bleeding in his lung cavity. I've seen this before. I'll need to cut an incision in between his ribs and drain it to release the pressure. I'll get my bag from the carriage."

Matthew had learned the techniques of surgeons precisely for circumstances like these. In the New World, there was much less of a distinction between physicians and those who wielded scalpels. As long as Matthew could save people, he didn't care if his knowledge came from the allegedly more learned side or from rough-hewn experience.

"I'll get your tools." Will volunteered as he struggled to stand. Obviously, the young footman was still shaken.

"You rest," Alexander laid his hand on Will's shoulder. "I can manage."

"No need!" Lady Charlotte called out.

Matthew looked up to see her scaling the overturned carriage, her black widow's skirt billowing in the spring breeze. Admiration and concern warred inside him as she hoisted herself onto the skyward-facing side.

"Lottie!" Alexander hollered, grabbing his cane for leverage as he lurched to his feet. Matthew grabbed his wrist, staying him. If Alexander pursued his sister, he could startle her or push her into moving faster and less cautiously. They needed to trust Charlotte's decision.

"Be careful!" Matthew warned, still holding Alexander back. "It could be unstable."

"I will!" Charlotte promised as she dropped through the open door and disappeared.

Matthew finally felt Alexander's muscles relax under his fingers, and he released his best friend. Although he wanted to anxiously monitor Charlotte's progress, Matthew knew she'd entered the coach so that he could stay with his patient. Shoving the anxiousness deep inside, Matthew turned to Richard. He pushed back the man's clothing, making sure that the surgery site was completely exposed. As he worked, he explained the procedure in his most confident tone to the driver.

To Matthew's utter relief, Charlotte appeared in his vision. She'd long since abandoned her ruined straw hat, and her normally perfectly curled hair hung in uneven clumps. Gone was the perfect

Society miss, and back again was the girl he'd known long ago. She was breathing hard but triumphantly. A smile stretched across her face as she thrust his converted shot pouch in his direction.

As he grasped the leather straps, her grin faltered. When her green eyes widened too, Matthew followed her gaze. Icy fists of shock pummeled him as he realized that the choker was still dangling from the secret pocket in his waistcoat and clearly visible. Quickly, he shoved it inside. When he glanced back up, her expression seemed normal, without a trace of suspicion.

"Are you really able to drain the blood from his lungs?" Charlotte asked.

The question made sense and even explained her reaction to handing him his tools. Had she even seen the necklace? He sorely hoped she hadn't, because any knowledge of the choker's existence placed her in extreme danger.

Chapter Twelve

Charlotte did not know what to make of Matthew Talbot. The mild-mannered fellow had suddenly transformed into a swashbuckling hero...or villain. Judging by the surprised exclamations Alexander had made when he'd witnessed Matthew's battle against the masked men, he hadn't realized the extent of his best friend's skills either. Why would Matthew hide such talents, especially from Alexander?

When Charlotte had first popped her head through the door of the coach alongside her brother, horror had blasted through her at the sight of Matthew with a dagger to his throat. Despite her heart feeling caught in a sharp, jagged-edged trap, she'd helped her twin ready his pistols. Then she stood silently next to Alexander as he waited for an opening to shoot.

A thrill shuddered through Charlotte as she remembered how Matthew had transformed his body into a weapon. He brought down both men with ruthless proficiency. How had the scholarly Matthew become so lethal?

Charlotte wanted to believe that he'd come by his fighting prowess honestly, but she couldn't forget the necklace that she'd glimpsed dangling from his pocket. The jewelry had definitely been a chain of pearl daisies with ruby centers. Charlotte had no doubt it was the choker that Lady Greenvale had described to her...and also to Matthew.

How had it come to be in his possession? Why were the miscreants after it, and who sent them? Was Matthew keeping it safe for his brother or had he stolen it from Hawley?

Even as questions about Matthew's trustworthiness swirled in Charlotte's head, she was watching him save a man's life. She had thought of medicine as something staid, with powders administered, bed rest taken, and cool compresses laid on foreheads. She hadn't considered the blood or the heart-wrenching sound of someone struggling to breathe.

Yet just as Matthew had with the horrible ruffians, he remained calm as he opened his bag. He withdrew a narrow rectangular case with silver-plated sides and a mother-of-pearl motif of wild animals carved in abalone on the front. Pushing back the lid, he retrieved a thumb lancet. Freeing the blade from its hinged tortoiseshell cover that also functioned as a handle, Matthew confidently gripped the instrument.

"Richard, I am going to make a cut between your ribs," Matthew said, his voice competent and soothing. The coachman's chin jerked slightly in assent. Matthew's eyes flickered over to Alexander. "Hold him down in case he flinches. Lady Charlotte, do you see that silver tube peeking from my bag? Would you be so kind as to hand it to me when I request?"

"Yes." She moved instantly into position, pleased that he'd included her without once questioning if her nerves could handle the sight of gore. Of course, with the young footman gone to fetch a wagon and a carriage, she was the only option. Still, she liked that Matthew automatically assumed her capable.

As soon as he drew his blade across the coachman's flesh, blood began to well. Richard gritted his teeth, but Alexander held him firm. When Matthew asked for the metal implement, she immediately handed it to him. With supremely steady hands, Matthew pressed the tip into the wound he'd created and used the syringe at the end to pump out the pooled blood.

"Richard, I'm removing the build-up inside your chest," Matthew continued to explain in a reassuring voice. "This particular device was invented in 1707, so there is no need to fear it. When I finish, I'll insert a tube called a cannula that will continue to drain the fluids collecting around your lungs. It will make breathing easier, I promise."

"Do you want me to find the can-cannula?" Charlotte asked as she stumbled over the unfamiliar word.

Matthew glanced quickly at her, surprised pleasure evident on his face. "Yes. That would be exceedingly helpful, Lady Charlotte. It will be flexible, not stiff like the apparatus I'm currently using."

She beamed. She couldn't help it. Even with her suspicions, she liked working beside Matthew, helping him in whatever small way to save a life.

It only took her a few moments to find the cannula in his neatly organized satchel. Gripping it in her hands, she moved near Matthew as she watched in rapt fascination as he worked. When he seemed satisfied with the amount of blood he'd extracted, he removed the silver tube.

"I'll take it and clean it," Charlotte offered.

"You do know it is dripping with blood, Lottie?" Alexander pointed out.

"If Dr. Talbot isn't bothered by it, then neither am I," Charlotte said.

Matthew said nothing. He just handed her the little pump and plucked the cannula from her hand. As he inserted it, Charlotte observed carefully. His fingers moved with such deliberate confidence that she felt spellbound.

"Here," Alexander said, drawing her reluctant attention. Her brother held out his boot flask and a handkerchief. Waggling the alcohol, he next pressed it into her free hand along with the cloth. "Use these to clean the tool. I still can do it if you'd rather not."

"No. I'm fine," Charlotte said, busying herself with the task. By the time she'd finished, Richard's breathing had returned to normal. Matthew was holding the man's wrist, carefully checking his pulse. A satisfied expression crossed Matthew's countenance as he eased back on his haunches. He looked around the road, as if reorientating himself to his surroundings.

"I can no longer wait," Alexander suddenly announced. "How did you learn to fight like that?"

Charlotte stiffened. Carefully, she studied Matthew, watching if his expression betrayed anything. His facial muscles appeared to have frozen into almost comical stiffness.

He shrugged, but even that gesture seemed terribly wooden. "Here and there."

"Here and there!" Alexander thudded his cane against the ground to punctuate each word. "You were like a legendary warrior in a folktale! You don't just pick up those skills like collecting pieces of lint on your coat."

"I'm extremely good at woolgathering." Matthew accompanied his attempt at a joke with a small smile.

"Your puns need to improve if you expect to distract me with them." Alexander crossed his arms. "Tell me—"

"Oh, look!" Matthew jumped to his feet. "Tavish's other coach and the wagon for Richard are arriving. While I see to my patient, you and your sister should return to London posthaste. It's getting late, and highway robberies along the major thoroughfares leading into the city are getting worse. You don't want to be ambushed twice in one day."

"That's another thing," Alexander called after his friend who was racing toward the arriving conveyances. "What were those men after? They didn't operate like typical brigands."

Matthew ignored Alexander and began barking orders to Tavish's servants. Charlotte rose and wandered over to her brother. "You noticed how unusual the situation was too? It didn't seem like a holdup to me."

Alexander's expression smoothed into a smile as he avoided her inquiries. "Matthew is right. We better head back to the city now that the second coach is here. We're in luck that Mr. Stewart has more than one."

Charlotte narrowed her eyes. "You do realize that I am more astute than you at detecting deliberate shifts in the conversation? What are you trying to protect me from? Do you think that this attack has anything to do with Hawley?"

Alexander sighed. "I'm honestly not sure, but we can talk in the carriage."

"You promise?"

Alexander rubbed his fingers across the Nemean lion's mane on his cane and dipped his chin in consent. "Yes."

"Then let's be off."

As they walked to the unmarked coach, Matthew turned in their direction. A now-familiar warm smile stretched across his features as he waved goodbye. Cupping his hands around his mouth, he hollered, "Thank you both for assisting with Richard's surgery."

"You're welcome," Charlotte called back.

For a moment, the heaviness that had begun to resettle on her chest lifted again. But as soon as she climbed into the carriage and leaned against the squabs, the sense of darkness returned. She needed to confront what she'd witnessed, not bury it in hopes that Matthew was a good man.

"Alexander, do you think Matthew is covering up his brother's sins?" Charlotte asked, her tone soft, as if voicing the inquiry loudly would have somehow made it true.

Her brother jerked. He couldn't be feigning his utter astonishment as he stared at her in palpable disbelief. "Whatever caused you to consider such a thing? You know how Hawley treated Matthew and me whilst we were boys."

Charlotte swallowed, the old stories striking another blow against her heart, especially now that she'd begun to spend time with the adult Matthew. Yet they weren't dealing with the past but the all-too-dangerous present.

"I spoke with the sister of the second Lady Hawley," Charlotte began.

Worry flashed in her brother's hazel eyes. Immediately, he opened his mouth to speak.

Charlotte held up her hand to stay him. "Let me impart what I need to, Alexander, without interruption. It is important."

Thankfully, Alexander listened. He sat quietly, his hands gripping the head of his cane, as she told him everything she knew about the choker, including how she'd spied it in Matthew's pocket.

"I believe that's what those men were after," Charlotte finished. "That's why we were attacked."

"If that's the case, then Matthew probably liberated the choker from Hawley after he'd learned of its existence from Lady Greenvale." Alexander was gripping Hercules so tightly that his knuckles had gone white. "I didn't want to tell you this, but Matthew and I have been discreetly looking into the deaths of Hawley's wives—even before you were betrothed to him."

Relief should have flooded Charlotte, but she only felt a trickle. Alexander's explanation didn't completely address all the odd factors she'd noticed about Matthew. "But why did he keep the necklace a secret from you? Are you certain he's not just telling you that he's investigating his brother, but in reality, he's only fooling you and thwarting your inquiries?"

"Perhaps he said nothing about the choker because he wished to protect me—the same way that I want to keep you safe, Charlotte," Alexander said. "I've told you not to go sniffing after Hawley's sins. I am making discreet inquiries like we discussed. There is no need for us both to endanger ourselves."

"I don't want you hurt either, Alexander," Charlotte said, as a mixture of pain and worry pierced her. "This is my predicament."

"Not one of your own making." Alexander stabbed the end of his walking stick against the carriage floor as if it were the villain instead of Hawley. "It is more my fault than yours. Father would not be so keen on seeing you married to an heir of a dukedom if he thought me suitable of carrying on his family's legacy."

"Father's ridiculousness is hardly your fault." Charlotte reached for her brother's hand again, trying to make him understand he was not to blame—he was never to blame. "The reason for the betrothal does not matter. Only stopping it does."

Alexander bobbed his head curtly and swallowed before he began speaking again. "If you think Matthew would have anything to do with helping Hawley commit crimes, then you're wrong. He's not that sort, and he detests his brother more than anyone."

"You told me once that Matthew's relationship with his siblings was nothing like our friendship. You said they terrorized him, especially Hawley." Charlotte hated saying the words, despising what they meant, the pain they embodied. But if she was to save herself, she had to confront horrible truths, no matter how they could burn a person raw. "What if the viscount has coerced Matthew into participating in his crimes because it amuses Hawley? Wouldn't that be just the kind of torment Hawley would enjoy inflicting, knowing that Matthew would loathe himself for any treachery, even if forced?"

Alexander moved his head roughly as if he could shake off

Charlotte's words. "No. Matthew wouldn't. Even if he had, he would have confided in me."

"Would he have had the strength to resist when he was younger and still living in the familial home? Can you say without a single, solitary misgiving that Matthew has told you his every secret?"

Alexander paused and then suddenly shifted his jaw to the left. Something was clearly bothering him.

"What is it?" Charlotte asked, feeling not triumph but a heavy morass deep in her soul.

Alexander ground out a sigh. "I must admit that I've felt he's been keeping something from me for years. And then today—the way he disarmed those ruffians. He couldn't fight like that when we were lads. But even if I have no way of explaining what we witnessed today, I still can't believe that Matthew would ever hide a crime that Hawley committed—let alone participate himself."

"But you can't be sure, can you?" Charlotte asked. She knew the words cost her brother, but she was surprised how much they also weighed on her. She did not like to think ill of the man who just saved another human being…or the man who had recently developed a tendency to inspire delight inside her.

"No. Not entirely. Not after what happened today, especially if what you say about the necklace is true." Alexander sighed as he stared into the deepening twilight. Then he turned sharply and fixed Charlotte with his greenish-gold gaze. "But treat Matthew with care, Charlotte. I do believe in my heart that he's innocent, and I don't want to cause him more unnecessary agony than he's already endured."

"I do not want to bring pain upon any of our heads." But even as Charlotte spoke the words, she could not escape the premonition that, before her search into Matthew's past was over, they would all bleed one way or another.

"Do—do you have feelings for Matthew?" Alexander asked, his voice hesitant at first and then stronger.

Charlotte drew back, stunned by the question. "I—I . . . Whyever would you say that?"

"I've observed you both in the Black Sheep, and I couldn't miss the looks you gave him in the carriage before the attack. Then there was the way you watched him when he performed the surgery." For once, Alexander was completely somber.

Charlotte glanced away, knowing her twin always saw too much of her soul. "Aren't you supposed to be warning me away from any romance with your friends?"

"Not Matthew. Despite what happened today, I still would place my life in his hands without any hesitation. I even trust him with you. If we can find no other way to free you from Hawley, maybe you could marry him. He'd treat you well, Charlotte, and he's already shown his willingness to defy Society's wishes."

To Charlotte's horror, tears sprang into her eyes, and she had to battle against the hopelessness in her heart. "How could any of us be safe from Hawley if I threw him over to wed his brother? He would certainly retaliate. Don't offer me hope of the impossible, Alexander."

Chapter Thirteen

L ovey!?"

The screech, both an imperative and an inquiry, pulled Matthew's attention to the rafters as he entered the Black Sheep. He discovered a rather puffed-up Pan glowering down at him.

"Lov—EEEEY!" Somehow, the parrot managed an even greater—and certainly more piercing—demand.

From the corner of his eye, Matthew noticed that every soul in the front room of the coffeehouse had swiveled in his and the bird's direction. Embarrassment scorched Matthew.

"Banshee is happy. She went to a new home yesterday," Matthew whispered as quietly and quickly as he could. He gave the wretched avian a beseeching look, begging for understanding even as he felt like a fool.

His pleas didn't work.

Pan rose in a fury of feathers. He swooped thrice around the long, narrow room before he roosted firmly on Matthew's head. Tiny pinpricks of talons dug into Matthew's scalp as the bird leaned his long body ominously over Matthew's forehead. One amber eye burned into Matthew's left one.

"Lovey." The parrot managed to make the word short and most definitely threatening.

"Perhaps I can bring Banshee for a visit," Matthew hurriedly told the parrot, his desperation winning over his sense of absurdity.

Pan might be an intelligent rascal, but Matthew had no idea if the canny creature could cull meaning from entire sentences, especially ones that weren't literal observations.

Pan only gazed menacingly. Matthew swallowed as he scrambled for a way to extricate himself gracefully. Yet how could one be poised with a parrot perched on one's head? It was, of course, precisely why the aggravating avian performed the trick so often.

"Tuesday," Matthew blurted out, wondering how he had become a love emissary between a parrot and a monkey. "I'll fetch Banshee, and you can spend time in each other's company."

Pan only inched his glittering eye closer to Matthew's left one.

"Two featherbrains conversing. How utterly un-novel." Disdain dripped from the familiar rich bass.

Blades of ice pierced Matthew's spine as he turned to face his eldest brother. Even Pan lifted his head as if his latent wild side sensed a true predator.

Hawley lounged at the end of one of the long tables. Contrary to the viscount's preference for prominence, he'd tucked himself into a corner. Three ruffians with muscles pressing at the seams of their worn coats flanked him. Matthew tried to steady his breath, tried to remember all his training, but he seemed to revert back to the lad he'd been, cowering before his older sibling.

Somehow, he managed to retain enough presence of mind to scan Hawley's companions. By their builds, any of the trio could have been the ones who'd attacked the coach yesterday.

As everyone in the Black Sheep turned at Hawley's loud voice, he stood, his broad chest puffing out just as Pan's had moments before. He reveled in the attention, turning to all sides of the room and tipping his hat like an actor about to begin narrating a farce.

"I must make apologies for my baby brother," Hawley said with cruel joviality as he stalked toward Matthew. "He has always preferred the company of vermin to humans."

As Pan was highly regarded in the Black Sheep, the gathered company did not laugh. Instead, they shifted in their seats. The right side of Hawley's mouth dipped, and he focused his entire attention on Matthew. Matthew waited for his extremities to go numb as they had when Hawley had waylaid him as a child. To his surprise, he felt a calm steadiness instead.

"Why are you playing whoremonger to a parrot?" Hawley sneered.

"I prefer the title of Cupid to the star-crossed of the animal kingdom." The flippant words escaped from Matthew before he thought to curb them. Evidently, he wasn't entirely the quaking younger brother anymore.

Hearty chuckles rose up from the customers at Matthew's quip, and an alien feeling swept through him. For the first time, he was the one surrounded by comrades. It was odd not being the laughingstock, a position Hawley had assigned him since birth. Only here, in this magical place where paupers and princelings debated, could he, the awkward, unwanted third son best the vaunted heir apparent.

"Maybe Father is right. Maybe you are a changeling. Communicating with the beasts of the earth like the fae folk."

There it was. The old stab of shame, of knowing he didn't belong, that he never would. Matthew hadn't believed he was a fae for years, but he'd always felt he'd been born in the wrong sphere.

"Remember the 'tests' we used to conduct to see if you were a winged fairy? We never could coerce you to fly, though, now could we?" Hawley's voice had turned into a vicious sneer.

Old, half-buried memories doused Matthew, and sweat broke over his skin. The upper dormer of his old boarding school. The open window. His brothers dangling him from his feet. The gusts of wind buffeting his face. The laughter of the boys drifting through the bitter air. Taunts for him to sprout feathers and free himself.

"There's no reason to conduct trials to determine if one is a fairy." Sophia's bright voice broke into the suddenly charged stillness. Matthew turned to see her strolling through the back door, a tray of steaming coffees in her hand. Well accustomed to settling frays, she walked blithely through the room. "All you have to do is check for wings."

Placing the drinks on a nearby table, Sophia made a show of checking Matthew's back. Pan hopped onto Matthew's shoulder and joined her exaggerated inspection. From the peripheries of his vision, Matthew could see the parrot twist his head this way and that. The patrons of the Black Sheep roared with laughter at Hawley's expense. But Matthew could not feel their glee this time. He felt frozen by the past...and the future. For this brute, this terrible, foul brute was to marry Charlotte. And Hawley would try to destroy her like he did everything that was beautiful and good.

"See, no wings." Sophia patted Matthew's back for good measure. "Alas, not a fairy prince come to sweep me away from a life of drudgery. Just a mere mortal, although I agree a rather comely one."

Sophia winked at Matthew, but her friendly teasing could not even begin to erase all the old and new dread that had settled upon his heart. Despite the frost sluicing through his blood, he managed a smile.

"No wings!" Pan seconded. When his observation was greeted with chuckles, Pan repeated the words, stretching out his own wings with each utterance. "No WINGS. No WINGS. No WIIIIIIINGS!"

"There is the truth of it," Sophia said. "The matter is settled by Pan. Now who wishes to partake of my latest brew? It's a new recipe and is free of charge."

Instantly, Sophia pulled attention away from Matthew and, more dangerously, from Hawley. Worse, she had caused a group of men to laugh at the viscount. Matthew could hear his brother draw in breath. His hard gray eyes had fastened on Sophia like a white-tailed eagle on a rabbit. Sophia was no bunny, though, but a raptor in her own right. She could handle the likes of the viscount, yet Matthew could not countenance vile taunts heaped upon his friend, especially when she had come to his aid.

"What brings you to the Black Sheep?" Matthew asked Hawley, even though he knew the answer too well. It burned inside the inner pocket of his waistcoat as if its rubies were actual flames of fire.

His brother's flinty gaze fell on Matthew once more. "Why, you, of course."

"It is not like you to seek me out." Matthew kept his voice calm despite the blizzard swirling inside his chest.

"You have forgotten your place, Mat. I did not appreciate your behavior at my fiancée's salon. You invaded my realm, so I am here to conquer yours." Hawley stepped closer. He notably didn't mention the choker, but Matthew read that accusation in his brother's eyes.

Hawley must have given some signal to his roughly dressed companions. The brawny trio rose from their seats and joined Hawley. His minions literally flexed their absurdly massive muscles like a troop of baboons circling a weaker rival.

Even though Matthew could now hold his own against Hawley, fisticuffs would only imperil everyone inside the Black Sheep, especially if it degenerated into an outright brawl. He had to think of a way to quiet the simmering tensions as peaceably as possible.

"Dash it all! Here you've come to overthrow me, and I seem to have left my scepter and sword at home." Matthew desperately tried for levity. Unfortunately, humor not borne of mockery was lost on Hawley.

"That is best for you as I just would have shoved them up your—"

"Silly ol' bird!" Pan suddenly shrieked. His wings beat against Matthew's cheek before he flew directly at Hawley. Worried the bird's actions would ignite the already charged situation, Matthew tried to grab the parrot. He missed.

Caught off guard, Hawley emitted a startled yelp. Pan raked the viscount's head with his talons, sending the man's hat rolling across the floorboards. On the second pass, Pan ripped off Hawley's wig and gleefully flew off with it. Hawley's ruffians dashed around the viscount in an attempt to catch the parrot but only managed to slam into each other. When Pan changed course and swept toward them, they ducked. One man even dropped to his knees and rolled alongside Hawley's hat.

Guffaws and a smattering of clapping bounced off the white-plastered walls of the long, narrow building. Matthew had imagined a scene like this for years—where his bullying brother was brought low—but he could derive no amusement now. Not when he knew his brother would retaliate against the Black Sheep, the haunt of not just of Matthew's dearest friends but of Charlotte. Matthew's muscles tightened, and his chest constricted as he prepared to defend Pan and the coffeehouse.

Visibly pleased at the chaos, Pan plopped unceremoniously onto the viscount's bare head, dangling Hawley's hairpiece over his face. Pan leaned over to deliver his classic one-eyed stare.

"Why, you flea-bitten bag of rotting feathers!" Hawley roared as he lifted his meaty hands to snatch the parrot. Pan dropped the wig on the viscount's foot and delivered a mighty blow to Hawley's left palm with his beak. Hawley's fingers curled into a punishing fist, and Matthew, his heart thrumming madly, bent his knees as he prepared to leap for the bird.

"Nobody touches the parrot!" Sophia's voice ripped through the din with such natural authority that even Hawley instinctively followed her command.

"Nobody touches!" Pan shrieked happily as he began to strut on Hawley's head, ruffling the lord's short-cropped mane. The parrot marched like a little general, his chest puffed out, his gray claws kicking high into the air, his wings pulled back, and his spine straight.

"Do you know who I am?" Hawley shouted at Sophia. "I am Viscount—"

"I don't care if you are the bloody king, himself, or the defeated Pretender. I am the proprietress of the Black Sheep and the ruler of this domain. We have no care for titles here. Only for intelligence, which you, sir, seem to be sorely lacking."

"I will not be molested by a bird or addressed in such a manner by a—"

Every man in the coffeeshop, from cutpurse to marquess, rose in unison. Blades and pistols appeared at the ready. Hawley's ruffian still cowering on the floor slowly rose to his feet. He joined his comrades who were nervously flanking the viscount. Unlike Hawley, who was a mass of seething rage, they appeared to recognize the perilousness of their situation. They might be brutes, but so were many of the Black Sheep's patrons.

"It is past time for you to make your departure, Viscount." Sophia spoke evenly, except the last word, which dripped with disdain. Matthew felt torn between pride for his friend's cool command and fear for what trouble Hawley would heap upon her head.

"Past time!" Pan screeched as he halted his swaggering long enough to once again stick his amber eye in Hawley's line of sight.

"I have no intention of leav—" Hawley began with an imperious tone that was marred by the parrot on his head. Before Hawley could finish, his men inched so close to him that the viscount stumbled backward toward the exit. Matthew watched the forced retreat as if outside of his own body, outside the bloody room even.

"We best leave, my lord." One of Hawley's oafs bit out when

Hawley locked his legs and refused to budge any further. Matthew didn't recognize the voice as one of the men who'd ambushed Tavish's carriage.

Hawley opened his mouth, but every single customer stepped forward. Seeming to finally comprehend his own peril, Hawley glanced about him. The Black Sheep's customers simultaneously moved forward as a unit.

Matthew should have felt like part of the crowd forcing Hawley out the door. But instead, guilt and worry bombarded him. He'd brought this monster into their midst. It should be Matthew alone facing Hawley, not his compatriots and friends. An old memory of Matthew's father accusing him of being an unworldly harbinger of misfortune resurfaced with a biting sting. Old, familiar nausea sloshed inside Matthew's stomach.

Before Hawley was shuffled over the threshold, he threw back his head and shouted, "You haven't seen the last of me. You cannot bar a man of my standing from your establishment! I'll be back on the morrow. You'll see! You'll all see!"

"Fare thee well!" Pan cackled before he finally flew from Hawley's head. He landed on Sophia's shoulder and watched Hawley's retreating form with one amber eye.

When Hawley and his men had disappeared, Matthew turned to Sophia, his body still coiled for battle, his blood frozen. As much as he appreciated Sophia's support, worry filled him like a swollen creek dammed up by an ice flow. "He's a dangerous man, Sophia. You may wish to take extra precautions over the next few weeks."

Sophia merely shrugged. "What's one more enemy?"

Matthew forced a smile, but he could dredge up no good humor. Only coldness. "We have got a lot of those, haven't we?"

"It just makes life more interesting," Sophia said lightly, but Matthew knew she would take the threat seriously. Then she turned with a broad grin and faced the patrons of the Black Sheep. "Who likes the new recipe for my brew?"

An appreciative roar rose as mugs were banged. Good-natured chatter returned, and a jovial atmosphere descended once again.

But not for Matthew. Amid the comradery and laughter, Matthew felt separate. It wasn't just that he could experience no mirth. His brother had come here, to Matthew's sanctuary. It wasn't just Matthew's internal peace that Hawley had breached but his very sense of belonging. He'd felt at home at the Black Sheep, Matthew realized. But now . . . he sensed his difference. His presence, his pursuit of his brother, had placed all these people in danger.

Chapter Fourteen

Precisely a day later, Charlotte marched into the Black Sheep determined to make real progress on her search into Lord Hawley's misdeeds. Well, she didn't so much march as she strolled. But she rather thought she did it more forcefully than gracefully, which should account for something.

Instead of heading for the secret back room, Charlotte stopped just a few feet inside the main doorway. She perused the regulars from behind her veil, trying to locate any unsavory-looking fellows. She had no time left to wait for the rougher customers to venture into the clandestine side of the Black Sheep. Today marked exactly two weeks until Hawley's father returned from Scotland and three weeks until the impending betrothal ball.

She had a partial sketch of the daisy-chain choker in her reticule. She'd already shown it to Hannah and Sophia under the guise that she was helping a friend locate lost jewels. Both women had claimed never to have seen anything like it. Although Charlotte planned on asking her Society friends if they recognized it, she knew Lady Greenvale had already made inquiries in their circle. Charlotte needed a less respectable source, the kind rife with rumors of illicit jewels. What better place could she find than the main room of a coffeehouse run by two daughters of pirates?

Fiddlesticks. None of the assembled patrons looked like proper villains. Although, really, what was she expecting? A man with a peg leg, as if he'd emerged from the pages of a storybook? Perhaps a wild, burning beard that the infamous Blackbeard had allegedly sported? Absurd, right?

"If you're looking for company, lass, we're as fine as any."

A deep, resonant voice boomed, drawing Charlotte's attention to a classically handsome young man…with an eye patch. She tried not to blink. She swore she hadn't noticed any patron wearing one in her recent survey of the room. Yet here a man sat with his left eye obscured by a swatch of leather and a devil of a smile on his fine face. His wicked grin only increased when he saw that he'd secured her attention.

Although Charlotte noted his pleasing features, they did not trigger a single stirring inside her heart, not even a little swish. His visible eye was a piercing blue, but it wasn't gray. His square chin was…well…a bit too square. Lately, Charlotte had found herself drawn to a more scholarly build.

"You have nothing to fear by joining us. I know I have a reputation for giving no quarter, but I'll make an exception for a lass as comely as you."

Charlotte's heart flipped in her chest, like a button on a child's string toy. The man had just used a phrase commonly uttered by pirates.

"Why thank you, good sir," she said, keeping her tone bright but definitely not too inquisitive. She was afraid any undue interest might cause the handsome devil to curb his tongue. And she needed it to wag. If the Black Sheep had served alcohol, she would have plied him with all he could drink.

"Take this seat." The rogue pulled back the chair next to him despite the fact that one of his companions currently occupied it. The other fellow nearly toppled to the ground, but he didn't complain as he stumbled to his feet. He only tipped his hat like a subordinate might do to a superior.

Excitement became a billowing gale inside Charlotte, pushing her toward the table.

"I swear upon all me earthly treasure that true gentlemen we be and not the embodiment of Davy Jones hisself." The handsome devil swung his cup, making a gesture as grand and sweeping as his words.

Charlotte faltered, and the pulsing thrill inside her slowed. The grinning rascal seemed more like a caricature of a swashbuckler straight from a stage performance of Charles Johnson's *The Successful Pyrate*. But even if the man was toying with her, this was an opening to meet the front-room patrons.

Despite her doubts, Charlotte continued to sit. The narrow chair did little to accommodate the extra fabric of her sack-back robe à la française, but at least the black mourning dress did not have the absurdly wide panniers of her betrothal gown. After smoothing her skirts in the most compact arrangement she could manage, Charlotte turned toward the men. With her face still covered by the veil, she used the tilt of her chin to convey welcoming warmth in lieu of her normal genteel smile.

"It is wonderful to properly meet you, gentlemen." Charlotte made sure to infuse her voice with just the right tinge of graciousness. "I had been hoping more of the original patrons of the Black Sheep would, on occasion, join us newcomers in the back room."

"We were not sure that you'd welcome the likes of old sea dogs such as us, but I see we have misjudged your kind charity."

"You are sailors, then?" Charlotte asked, keeping her voice casual despite the maelstrom pounding against her chest. Unfortunately, she still could not decide if she should take the rogue seriously. Glancing around at his companions, she found their expressions wooden. The owners of the studiously blank faces were hiding something—but whether it was their comrade's balderdash or their own criminality, Charlotte was not certain.

If they were pirates, they were relatively successful. Although their earth-toned jackets and waistcoats were made of practical wool and linen rather than fine silk or velvet, the material was still of fine quality. Charlotte spied several close-cropped haircuts, which indicated habitual wig wearing. Oddly enough, none of them wore one—almost as if they had hastily stashed them beneath the table.

There were seven fellows crowded near their bonny leader, while two other men huddled together at the far end of the long table. That pair had their faces averted and seemed in conversation solely with each other. As she studied the eight closest to her, she realized they were a suspiciously uniform lot of hale lads in their twenties. She would have expected a more motley crew of varying ages.

"Aye, we are jack-tars but not of the high seas, lass." The original speaker winked at Charlotte. "We are free agents who seek our fortunes closer to home."

River pirates, then. A chill slivered through Charlotte. If this man was not trifling with her, he would have direct connections to London's seamy trade of ill-gotten goods. It would make him exactly who she was looking for . . . and extremely dangerous.

"Avast, Captain Hart," the man who Charlotte had displaced cried out in an exaggerated Devonshire accent. "You always say too much around the pretty wenches."

Charlotte had to force her eyebrows to stay in their proper place instead of arching at the man's simultaneously wooden and over-dramatic delivery. The excitement in her fizzled as she realized that the so-called pirate and his men were only bamboozling her.

"Don't be so lily-livered, me hearty." The "captain" slapped his friend on the shoulder. "The lass here would ne'er betray us. She is, after all, a patron of the Black Sheep. She'll be fair-minded and not quick to judge us by the misfortunes that have driven us to the life that we lead. And she will be true to the coffeehouse's code of silence."

"I will indeed keep your secret, if you can just tell me one truth," Charlotte said in her sweetest voice and then paused for dramatic effect. "Are you actually river pirates or are you just bamming me?"

"Oh no. They're one of the fiercest crews of brigands to sail the Thames." Hannah suddenly broke into the conversation both literally and figuratively as she reached between Captain Hart and Mr. Devonshire Accent to lay a tray of coffees on the table.

"Ach, Miss Wick, don't be spilling our secrets." Mr. Devonshire Accent slipped into a terribly fake Scottish brogue as he stretched out the "don't" into a comically long "dinna" for several excruciating beats.

Charlotte crossed her arms over her stomacher, ignoring her mother's voice in her head scolding her that ladies did not assume such vulgar, aggressive positions. She was becoming better and better at squelching those admonishments.

"Moments ago, wasn't your intonation from the southwest English coast, not the Highlands?" Charlotte narrowed her eyes at Mr. Devon-Scots Accent.

"You'll have to forgive Mr. Smith." Hannah lightly bumped the shoulder of Mr. Devon-Scots Accent as she smiled broadly at Charlotte. "He's sailed to so many ports that his inflection is as malleable as melted wax."

"On the Thames!" Charlotte added a raised eyebrow to her crossed arms, and for once, she didn't hear any internal chiding.

"Shiver me top sail and blow me down," Hart said. "Do you think, lass, that we got our start here in London? We're an experienced lot of sailors."

"Of that, I have my doubts," Charlotte said with more humor than censure. Although she was not willing to play the fool, she did not wish to alienate them either.

"Avast, my lady. You wound me." Hart grasped his chest as if she'd stabbed him with a knife. Repeatedly.

Charlotte couldn't stop herself. She rolled her eyes. Luckily, no one could see the motion behind the black gauze draped over her face.

"Truly, *Captain* Hart, I have been around the Wick cousins enough to know that real pirates don't talk as if they'd just stepped from the pages of a poorly written sensational novel!" Charlotte paused before turning to Mr. Smith. "Not to mention your decidedly fickle accent."

Deep, jolly laughter boomed through the room, and everyone jerked toward the sound. When Charlotte caught sight of the fellow who had been shielding his face when she'd first observed the table's occupants, she gasped. The man was none other than the infamous actor and playwright, Alun Powys. All the young women fantasized about him behind their fans. According to the gossips, several wealthy widows had done more than just dream.

The ribald comedies that Mr. Powys penned skewered everyone from the king to the lord chamberlain. According to rumors, he'd begun his life in the sewers and maintained extensive ties with that world. His singular male beauty had propelled him into popularity, but his sharp, biting wit had kept him there.

Charlotte had watched him perform countless times. His unpowdered raven hair always gleamed like polished jet, while his violet-blue eyes seared every heart in the theater, including hers. But even her vantage point in her parent's expensive, well-positioned box had not truly allowed her to take a full accounting of the man's physical beauty. His unusual irises twinkled with life and charm; an intriguing, thin white scar bisected his left eyebrow; his sinful lips seemed designed by Aphrodite herself; and even the dark, unfashionable stubble shadowing his face blessed him with a roguish charm. But just like with Hart, Charlotte felt no thrill.

Because he wasn't Matthew Talbot.

Had quiet, previously unassuming, scholarly Matthew ruined her for all other men?

If so, Charlotte had no idea how she felt about that. Given she was practically engaged to Matthew's villainous brother, she could not consider it. Not now, at least.

"You may as well give up the ghost," Mr. Powys said to Hart and his friends, his voice effortlessly filling the room. "The lass is cleverer than all eight of you combined."

"I am right, then?" Charlotte asked triumphantly. "These men are not pirates?"

Mr. Powys snorted. "Hardly. Billy Hart is a clerk at a counting house, and Bob Smith is a scrivener for a rather hapless solicitor. The closest either of them have come to adventure is crossing a busy thoroughfare at midday."

"That is a mighty uncharitable description, Powys," Mr. Smith complained in an accent that most assuredly had sprung from a London upbringing.

"Smith fancies himself an actor," Mr. Powys told Charlotte sotto voce, "as does Hart, but you'll not catch either of them treading the boards at any real theater. They 'put' on plays for their friends, which is probably why Hart had the eye patch in his pocket."

"Must you give all our secrets away?" Mr. Hart grumbled as he removed the piece of leather to reveal an uninjured blue eye.

"You clearly weren't fooling the lady. If you think performances like that will persuade me to cast you in one of my upcoming productions, you are sorely mistaken," Mr. Powys said.

"You're sharper than I'd given you credit for," Hannah told Charlotte, her tone surprisingly respectful.

Shocked, Charlotte glanced at her cousin, who shot her a smile that was tinged with real warmth. A spark of joy lit in Charlotte's heart. Even though Hannah couldn't see through Charlotte's veil, she grinned back. For the first time, Charlotte felt the tug of true kinship between them.

"I knew actual buccaneers wouldn't act so obvious, spouting off about treasure and saying things like 'give no quarter!'" Charlotte said.

"Very true. River pirates tend to fade into the woodwork, like Jenks, here." Powys waved his hand in the direction of the fellow he'd been conversing with earlier. The gesture was somehow both theatrical and natural. On or offstage, the actor's timing was impeccable.

"Fuck you, Powys." The nondescript man in poorly tailored clothes said as he accompanied his words with an equally obscene gesture. Then he slouched back down and returned to sipping his coffee, clearly not wanting to engage in the farce surrounding him.

Charlotte wasn't sure if Jenks was an actual brigand, or just a better actor than Smith and Hart, but she found it didn't matter. Alun Powys was a powerful man with connections to every stratum of London society except highborn ladies like her. He didn't just know secrets but how to ferret them out.

"Don't be so melancholy, Jenks," Mr. Powys said heartily. "After listening to Hart and Smith's balderdash for so long, the lady deserves a proper introduction to a real river pirate. She hardly has the look of a thieftaker. Besides, the paltry bounty on your head isn't worth the time to drum up the dragoons."

Jenks made another profane motion with one hand as he kept drinking coffee with the other. Mr. Powys only laughed louder, the mirth making his already arresting irises an even deeper purple-blue.

"My lady, would you wish to adjourn to the back room where we can have a more proper discussion among your friends?" Mr. Powys said. "I promise to regale you with true stories of derring-do."

"I would like that very much," Charlotte said, somehow managing to make her voice sound merely polite, rather than triumphant.

Together, Charlotte and Mr. Powys walked toward the back room. Just as she was about to move through the doorway, she heard more patrons enter the front of the shop. Glancing over her shoulder, she nearly stumbled when she caught sight of Hawley himself sauntering inside with three rough-looking companions. Both fear and victory slammed into Charlotte. Here was the very prize himself strolling into the Black Sheep with a sneer on his handsome visage. But if he recognized her, not only Charlotte's plans, but she, herself, would be doomed.

Quickly, she glanced at the ruffians accompanying him, memorizing the sweep of their noses, the curl of their mouths, and each and every identifying scar. As she did so, she vaguely heard the scrape of chair after chair being pushed back. The sudden stillness that had fallen over the room caused her to glance away from Hawley and his cohorts.

Every patron of the Black Sheep had stood. More than one man had his hand on his knife or sword. Before Charlotte could observe more, Mr. Powys positioned himself between her and the room. Hurriedly, he shepherded her through the passageway and shut the door behind them without ceremony.

Neither of them spoke as they walked through the hallway to the inner sanctum. Charlotte quietly debated how to bring up what she had just witnessed. She did not want to appear too eager for information, especially if Mr. Powys was friendly with Viscount Hawley. Still, anyone would be intrigued by the scene they had just witnessed. And she needed to make sure that Hawley would not burst into the back room. Although judging by the reaction of the other Black Sheep patrons, it appeared that he was not even welcome to enter the front of the establishment.

Before Charlotte could devise the perfectly worded question, she and Mr. Powys reached the inner sanctuary. With an appreciative grunt, he scanned the sumptuous space that she and her cousins had created. Men and women lounged in the comfortable furniture as they sipped coffee, the conversation buzzing.

"Clearly, I've been remiss in assuming the new venue would be as boring as a drawing room tea party," Mr. Powys said in his rather musical accent.

Charlotte longed to immediately ask him if he recognized any of the men with Hawley, but she could not just blurt out the question. Instead, she lifted her veil, careful not to remove it entirely in case the viscount did come sallying in. "The cousins Wick have done a marvelous job making this space as inviting as possible. It is a shame not all of the regular patrons have taken advantage of its comforts."

A surprised expression crossed Mr. Powys's countenance when he saw her face. "It is indeed, Lady Charlotte."

"You recognize me?" Charlotte asked, not entirely surprised. She was well-known in the literary world, even if Mr. Powys was too much of an incendiary playwright to be included in her mother's particular circle. But he must frequent more liberal salons.

"Some of my friends have attended the Duchess of Falcondale's events. They all speak very highly of your welcoming nature," Mr. Powys said.

Charlotte wondered if he had purposefully not included her mother in his second statement. The duchess was exactly the kind of hypocritical stickler whom Mr. Powys loved to lampoon. But no matter Mr. Powys's intent, his statement provided Charlotte with an excellent opening.

"I try to be hospitable to all. It was why I was trying to meet more of the front-room patrons. I noticed a few more men enter while we were leaving. I recognized one as Lord Hawley but not the other three." Charlotte moved to a set of comfortable chairs and was exceedingly glad that this was one place where she did not need to concern herself with propriety. Outside of these walls, she could never simply sit down alone with a man, especially one to whom she had not been properly introduced.

Mr. Powys shook his head as he took his seat. "I've never seen them before, but if they're with Lord Hawley, I would give them a wide berth. Men like Jenks are harmless enough as long as you don't cross them, but any fellows from the stews who associate with the viscount and his ilk are a different matter. There's never a moment they're not dangerous."

"Why do you say that?" Charlotte could not help but inch forward. Her heart began pirouetting in a mad dance against her chest.

Mr. Powys looked at her curiously, and Charlotte realized she had just shown a bit too much enthusiasm. When Mr. Powys spoke, his words seemed measured. "There are rumors that whoever crosses the viscount comes to misfortune. It only stands to reason that, if Lord Hawley is associating with men from the streets, they are the fellows bringing about such unlucky fates."

"Oh," Charlotte said, hoping that she sounded merely uninterested and not deflated. She had already surmised that on her own.

"I heard Hawley stopped by the Black Sheep yesterday and kicked up a dust. He was chased away after threatening Pan. He promised to return today, and I assume he's about to learn that he won't be able to bully his way into at least one establishment in London. Hopefully, this will be the last of him showing up here."

"Did he ever frequent the Black Sheep before?" Charlotte asked, as unease seeped through her. Had Hawley discovered her part ownership? But how?

"Not that I am aware."

The disquiet in Charlotte burgeoned into something approaching fear, but she could not back down. The only way to escape Hawley was forward. Part of her hoped that he'd never darken the doors of the Black Sheep again, but she conversely needed him too. Or at least his ruffians.

"Do you think his companions will return even if Hawley does not?" Charlotte asked.

Mr. Powys's expression stilled, and his gaze grew hard. "I generally never repeat myself, as I find it a dull habit, but do not approach those men. They are not the kind who frequent coffee-houses for intellectual banter."

"Oh, I wouldn't dream of it," Charlotte lied. "I was just seeking assurances that they wouldn't reappear and cause trouble. I would hate to find myself in the middle of any sort of brawl."

Luckily, the rogues weren't her only clue. She still had the drawing. Mr. Powys clearly would not divulge more about Hawley's men, but he might know something about the necklace.

"There was another reason that I was in the front room this morning." Charlotte reached into her reticule and pulled out the sketch. "A good friend of mine has misplaced a necklace. It is a family heirloom that her husband gifted her, and she's afraid it may have been stolen. She doesn't want to admit to him that she's lost it, and she's willing to pay to recover it. I promised to help, but I am afraid I have little idea where one finds the kind of brokers who deal in purloined goods."

"And you think I do?" Offense drenched Mr. Powys's face and voice.

Guilt horrified Charlotte as she scrambled to apologize. Then she glimpsed the amused twinkle deep in his violet-blue eyes. Her shoulders relaxed as she realized the thespian was simply teasing.

"Well, don't you?" she asked. "You are rumored to be a man of many talents, and you are certainly a far better actor than both Captain Hart and his accent-changing first mate combined."

"But I still didn't fool you, did I?" Mr. Powys said.

"You didn't let me be tricked," Charlotte laughed. "You could have masked that gleam, but you left it there for me to see."

"You are indeed clever," Mr. Powys said as he pushed the paper toward her, "and full of surprises. First, you inquire after ruffians and then you ask where you can purchase stolen merchandise. Are you purposely seeking danger for thrills, Lady Charlotte?"

Disappointment flooded Charlotte. He wouldn't give her information, not when he believed her to be a bored aristocrat looking for dangerous amusements.

"I am truly trying to help a friend," Charlotte said, hoping he could hear her sincerity. But he was accustomed to living with actors and actresses. How much stock would Mr. Powys place in tone and expression?

With a sigh, Mr. Powys picked up her sketch. "Judging by the look of it, your acquaintance may have reason to be concerned about her husband's reaction."

"Why?" Charlotte asked, as a jolt of excitement blazed through her. "Do you recognize the piece?"

"Only that it must be old. If it were paste, it would be something I'd use as a set piece for a Tudor-era play. It must have been in the family a long time." Mr. Powys flipped the drawing in her direction, and Charlotte caught it against her chest. "I won't introduce you to any dealers, but if I see the choker myself, I'll inform you."

Charlotte settled against the back of her chair, trying to fight the letdown. Mr. Powys hadn't known the secrets of the necklace after all, but he'd still given Charlotte new information. She'd realized that the piece was old-fashioned, but she hadn't guessed it was over a hundred years old. Such an object was indeed an heirloom. It wasn't from Lady Greenvale's family or she would have recognized it. Was it part of the ancestral history of the Talbots? Was there some nastiness even greater than Hawley's that his family was attempting to hide? Was Matthew involved in the subterfuge?

Chapter Fifteen

Matthew was expecting to receive a very important but very clandestine message from the Wick cousins today, so it was important not to draw attention to himself as he entered the back room of the Black Sheep. It was a little hard to be inconspicuous with Banshee on his shoulder, but fortunately the monkey immediately ascended to the rafters to join Pan. When Matthew sat down across from Alexander, his best friend did not greet him with his customary jovial grin. Instead, Alexander crossed his arms and fixed Matthew with an unyielding stare. Guilt rammed into Matthew as he tried not to shift like a truant schoolboy.

"Care to explain why just three days ago, I watched you fight like the legendary Fianna?" Alexander demanded without preamble.

Matthew forced his body to relax. "As I told you, I learned during my travels."

Alexander shot him a disbelieving look that quickly turned into a challenging one. "I also discovered through Charlotte that you are in possession of a necklace that Lady Greenvale saw the late Lady Hawley hide before her death."

Matthew could no longer feign nonchalance, not even with his history of subterfuge. He practically launched himself over the table. Furtively, he glanced around to make sure no one was listening. "Lower your voice."

"You're not going to deny it?" Alexander's voice was as soft as his hazel eyes were sharp.

"No." Worry pulsed through Matthew.

"Why didn't you tell me?" Alexander insisted, and Matthew had no trouble detecting his friend's hurt.

"I want to keep you safe," Matthew hissed. "I couldn't defend you from my siblings when we were children, but I can stop dragging you into the most dangerous parts of this mess now."

"I'm not weak because of my leg, Matthew." Alexander clenched his jaw, and Matthew knew his best friend was staunching a lifetime of pain and rejection.

The sight sliced him, and he had to set Alexander straight. "This has nothing to do with that, and everything to do with the fact that you are my true brother. I want to protect you, protect my real family from the horrible one that I was born into."

Alexander's chin visibly unclenched, and he gave a stiff nod. "I—I understand that need, Matthew. But don't bar me from this. You're a sibling to me too, and Charlotte's involved. I need to be part of this."

"I'll show it to you. Not here but when we're alone."

Alexander held Matthew's gaze just as he'd done when they were young and they'd promised to stick together against their tormentors. Relief flooded Matthew as he realized that Alexander trusted his word.

"How did Charlotte recognize the necklace?" Matthew asked.

Alexander frowned. "She's attempting to investigate Hawley herself, and she spoke to Lady Greenvale when she visited the Black Sheep."

"What?" Fear bit into Matthew and didn't release. He wanted Charlotte as far away as possible from his brother, but she'd been secretly pursuing him these past few weeks?

Alexander rubbed his temples. "I cannot entirely blame her. She needs to escape this betrothal, and your father will be in London in less than a fortnight."

"Wedding your sister to Hawley is like offering Persephone to Hades," Matthew said darkly.

"Agreed, which is why I think she needs another groom."

"You want me to help you figure out who should marry your sister?" The question came out in a string of strangled croaks, and Matthew barely stopped from physically wincing at the tortured sounds. He must demonstrate some degree of decorum. After all, Alexander didn't know about Matthew and Charlotte's relationship. Not that Matthew had a relationship with Charlotte. Necessarily. Or at all. Or at least one with any future.

Swounds. He was as distracted as a red squirrel in autumn, dashing after every thought of Charlotte as if they were acorns he needed to store away for winter.

"In a manner of speaking, yes. Why, does that fluster you?" Alexander sprawled back in his chair as he regarded Matthew quizzically.

Matthew couldn't help it. He shifted guiltily, although he really did not have anything to feel remorseful about. It was not as if he'd been engaged in torrid daydreams about Charlotte...*Deuce take it.* Of course, now his mind was merrily skipping along that hazardous but damnably beckoning route. It was a road paved not with good intentions but with fantasies of slipping silks and even more satiny skin beneath.

"Any man would be lucky to marry her," Matthew blurted before he could imagine undoing the lacings of Charlotte's stomacher and sliding his hand to cup her...*Damn.* He was still tumbling down that tantalizing path.

"I wasn't referring to any man, but to you in particular," Alexander said, his grin downright mischievous.

"To me!" Matthew delivered this as a string of mangled bleats instead of croaks. He doubted it was an improvement.

"You seem to be having an inordinate amount of difficulty conversing today." The green flecks in Alexander's hazel eyes sparkled with humor.

"It is just the thought of your sister and, well, me. Together. In that capacity." Matthew stumbled over his words, but he could not seem to stop himself from blundering on and on.

"And what capacity would that be?" Alexander's voice was extremely measured, and Matthew knew his friend was trying desperately not to laugh.

"You know!" Matthew cried in exasperation.

"No, I really do not." Alexander's mouth twitched tellingly despite his protestations.

"A romantic one!" Matthew blurted out, realizing that Alexander would not stop prodding him until he said it. In Matthew's duress, he'd spoken louder than he'd intended, and he swept his eyes around the room. Luckily, the rest of the occupants were engaged in their own conversations.

"Why are you so opposed to the idea of wedding Lottie?" Alexander leaned forward in his chair. The emerald specks in his irises were practically dancing the hornpipe now, they were so full of mirth. "Don't you esteem her?"

"Of course, I esteem her," Matthew, who generally prided himself on keeping an even tone, ground out and then immediately snapped his jaw shut. Why, oh why, was he allowing Alexander to goad him?

Alexander collapsed against the stuffed cushion of his seat with a look of supreme satisfaction. "I knew it. Have for years, actually. You've always been a trifle obvious. At least to me. Charlotte never had an inkling about your feelings."

Trying to ignore a gnawing sense of vulnerability, Matthew

defensively snapped, "I don't see why you're so bloody jolly about it. Aren't I breaking some cardinal code of friendship by fancying your sister, your *twin* sister?"

"As long as the friend in question possesses honorable intent, I find the rule ludicrous. Why would a fellow not wish for his best friend to form a union with his sibling? It is not as if you are a philandering rogue. You are a good, honest man, and more than a sight better than any of the fools that Father has chosen for Lottie. Even if we succeed in getting Hawley arrested for murder, they'll just turn around and betroth her to another unsuitable scoundrel. That is why I think the best solution is for you to elope with Lottie."

Rather thunderstruck by everything Alexander had just stated, Matthew reached for his long-neglected cup of coffee. Lifting it to his lips, he took a sip as he worked to compose himself. He still felt rather like a red squirrel dashing through a mountainous Highland forest. The only problem was that Matthew didn't know if he was running toward something or away from it.

Softly placing the mug back on the low table between them, Matthew said very carefully, "Your parents would never countenance that. I'm a mere third son. More importantly, I would not otherwise be Lady Charlotte's choice in a bridegroom."

Saying the words aloud hurt more than Matthew would have expected. After all, he knew the truth of them. But correct or not, they still scraped against his heart like a tanning knife.

Alexander leaned forward once more, his expression uncharacteristically earnest. "You are a steadfast and kind fellow."

"Which is what makes me a good physician but not necessarily the dashing husband."

"My sister has more sense than you give her credit for." Alexander frowned as his tone turned protective. "She is not dreaming of reforming some rakehell."

Matthew swiped his thumb over the condensation on his mug, wishing he could wipe away this conversation as easily. Alexander meant well. He really did. But somehow his earnestness only made the prickles of pain inside Matthew grow worse. "She needs a man of her class and of similar standing in Society. That is not me."

He noticed that Alexander didn't bother to point out that Matthew was technically the son of a duke. After all, his best friend, like Matthew, understood better than anyone that a noble birth was not a safeguard against ostracization. Instead, Alexander said, "England would do better to focus more on marriages of compatible temperaments than of status. Humans should not be treated like racing horses where bloodlines are paramount."

"This isn't about breeding," Matthew said and immediately flushed at the implication. Quickly, he added, "I am talking about disposition. Lady Charlotte is vivacious and beloved by all. I am...not." The last word soured his mouth with bitterness, but there was no escaping that untransmutable fact.

"Now you are doing yourself a disservice." Alexander's hazel eyes appeared browner now, as they always did when he was solemn. "You may be more reticent in nature than my sister, but I believe you two would complement each other. Besides, Lottie is more introspective than she reveals to the outside world."

"I am decidedly dull," Matthew said, wishing that Alexander would cease this nonsense.

"I disagree, and so, I believe, does Charlotte. Something happened between the two of you at Tavish's estate. I am sure of it. Before we were attacked, each of you kept sneaking looks at each other in the carriage. Thankfully, you never caught each other's gaze because that would have been deuced awkward for me."

A blast of euphoric excitement bolted through Matthew. But ruthlessly, he squelched it. For his sake. And most importantly for Charlotte's.

"I admit that, against all reason, I seem to have attracted your sister's attention as of late," Matthew said slowly, each word a hammer stroke against his soul. "But it is just a passing fancy for her, if even that. As they say, a bird cannot love a fish. Your sister is meant to fly among the songbirds of the tropics, not scrounge the bottom of the ocean with a colorless flounder. Rather than elevate me to her sphere, I very much fear I would drag her down to mine."

"Look to the rafters if you want proof of the impossible turned possible. Is there not a parrot courting his monkey love?" Alexander asked.

Matthew quirked the left corner of his lips, but his amusement was sardonic rather than jolly. "In this scenario, are you casting your sister as the ill-tempered, one-eyed bird with delusions of being a pirate or the feces-flinging capuchin?"

Alexander gave Matthew a hard stare. "You're prevaricating."

Matthew gave his mug of coffee a slight push—just enough to send it skidding a half-inch but not enough to upset its contents. "You want the unvarnished truth, Alexander? You are right to compare us to a monkey and a parrot. We are that dissimilar, and a union with me would remove Charlotte from her rightful world—the world in which she reigns."

Alexander's gaze grew even sharper. "Is this about that changeling balderdash your family tormented you with?"

"You know I find their claims absurd. There are no such things as fairies or fae folk." Matthew practically barked the words.

"But then—"

"This is not a discussion I wish to have." Matthew barely managed to make his voice flat instead of a growl.

Alexander immediately snapped back in his seat and gave an understanding nod. "Very well. Let's change it back to how you became so proficient at fighting. And please do not mention the New World again."

"I traveled to ports all over the Americas. It only makes sense that I picked up some skills," Matthew lied. There would never be a good time for Alexander to probe into Matthew's hidden life, but now was especially fraught, with the Wick cousins about to hand Matthew instructions detailing his next illicit mission.

Alexander started to speak, but before Matthew could listen to his friend, he noticed Sophia signaling with a twist of her hand. The movement was slight, but Matthew had been looking for just such a sign. Alexander's voice faded into the background as Matthew concentrated on Sophia, who was across the room preparing coffees.

Damn. The message Matthew was waiting for must have arrived, and Sophia meant to deliver it to him straightaway.

Matthew tried to shake his head to indicate that now was not the time to covertly transfer the missive into his possession, but Sophia missed his gesture.

"Is that a no then?" Alexander demanded, his body now on the edge of his chair, his voice louder than usual.

"A no to what?" Matthew asked, realizing that Alexander must have asked an important question that Matthew had inadvertently answered when trying to silently communicate with Sophia.

"Were you not listening to me?" Alexander practically roared.

Given that Matthew kept avoiding Alexander's questions with half-truths, Matthew could understand his friend's frustration. Unfortunately, now Hannah was trying to attract his attention. As she walked by him carrying trays, she brushed against his shoulder and then pointed surreptitiously in her cousin's direction on the other side of the coffeehouse. Matthew tried to focus on Alexander, but Hannah bumped his arm again. Matthew glanced over at Sophia and saw her slip a wadded-up piece of vellum between a cup and saucer.

"Talbot!" Alexander practically shouted, and Matthew swiveled in his friend's direction so fast that he almost upset his own coffee.

"Yes?" Matthew asked, hoping he sounded both focused and contrite.

"Are you or are you not hiding more things from me than just the necklace?" Alexander crossed his muscular arms over his chest and was now looking considerably bellicose.

"What?" Matthew asked in alarm. Surely his moments of distraction shouldn't have led Alexander to that particular conclusion. Had Alexander realized that Sophia was in the process of passing Matthew a secret missive? Alexander's back had been toward her, and he'd never noticed any similar clandestine exchanges in the past. Or at least Matthew thought Alexander hadn't.

"You just indicated that you were keeping truths from me," Alexander said.

"I did?" *Bollocks.* Matthew's voice had actually risen an octave. One would think him a green lad at subterfuge.

"Yes, you did. I asked, 'We have no more secrets between us, right?' Then you shook your head no. Is it 'No, there are secrets between us,' or, 'No, you are correct. There are no additional secrets'?"

"I wasn't shaking my head at you," Matthew said in a panic.

"Then who were you shaking it at?" Alexander asked.

Just then Hannah appeared with a tray of coffees, including the one that contained Sophia's hidden message. Hannah slid a steaming cup on a plate down before both of them. "Sophia is trying another new recipe, so they're yours for the taking."

She whirled away. Alexander, who was generally distracted by any small thing and who never passed up free refreshments, ignored the drinks. His eyes were locked on Matthew.

"Are you or are you not keeping something of import from me?" Alexander asked.

Matthew eyed the corner of vellum sticking out from underneath his new coffee. If Alexander saw the details in the missive, he would discover the clandestine life that Matthew had been hiding for years. Sweat dripped down his back, running straight between his shoulder blades. "I…." He stopped and cleared his throat, "I—"

"Alexander! Matthew!" Charlotte's voice rang out brightly, and Matthew nearly collapsed in his chair in utter relief. He turned to find Charlotte standing next to Lady Calliope.

Alexander grabbed his cane and pushed himself to his feet to warmly greet them. Matthew followed as a wave of awkwardness swept over him. Despite having seen the poet at the Black Sheep over the past few weeks, Matthew had not officially met Charlotte's best friend.

"My dear Lady Calliope, it is always a pleasure to see you." Alexander bowed deeply.

Lady Calliope's smile was as ethereal as her pale, pixie-like appearance. "It's friendly faces like yours that make this dreary city bearable."

Matthew tried not to fidget as the Society beauty's eyes landed upon him. Vaguely, he heard Charlotte introduce him, but he could barely manage to grunt out a response as shyness crushed him. He couldn't spout flowery phrases like Alexander. Swounds, Matthew struggled to simply say his name. Yet Alexander thought him a suitable life partner for the vibrant Lady Charlotte?

"Dr. Talbot is an old schoolmate of Alexander's," Charlotte breezily told Lady Calliope. "He's traveled to the New World on many occasions as a ship's surgeon."

"How adventurous! You must tell me all about it. I am always looking for inspiration for my ballads. What do the Colonies look like?" Lady Calliope beamed at him. But even the warm enthusiasm in her voice couldn't melt Matthew's frozen brain and mouth.

"Uh…trees," Matthew managed to choke out. "Green. Very green. And leafy."

Lady Calliope's eyes widened a bit, but she did not smirk. Instead, she said brightly, "Seas of green, my eye doth spy. The rustling tops, a verdant wave below the sky."

Matthew jerked his chin sharply. "Aye."

Charlotte's arm wrapped around his, and immediately the simple gesture injected him with a semblance of calm. She smiled at him and then turned to her friend. "You must read one of Matthew's books. His descriptions are very detailed, and his drawings are simply divine."

"Lady Charlotte!" A rich, resonant male voice flowed through the back room of the Black Sheep.

Every occupant turned to watch the entrance of the infamous Alun Powys. Even Matthew, who rarely had the opportunity to attend the theater, had watched the famous actor perform. Although born to a Welsh mother in the London stews, the man had become a social force in the more libertine spheres of Society. Matthew and Mr. Powys had been members of the same coffeehouse for years, but Matthew had never spoken to the man, even when they'd shared the same long table. How the deuce had Charlotte become acquainted with him? As far as Matthew knew, Mr. Powys had never ventured into the back room of the Black Sheep until now.

"Mr. Powys!" Charlotte cried out happily, as if greeting a dear companion. Matthew tried hard to mask his surprise. He should not be shocked. Charlotte possessed the wonderful ability to build strong friendships even when starting with the barest of foundations.

"I have kept my promise to return to the new room." Mr. Powys delivered one of his dashing grins that made all the ladies at the theater swoon as he joined their group. "I have not only come back, but I have brought along my good friend, Mr. George Belle."

Matthew hurriedly glanced at the tall, lean man walking behind Powys. Given George's assistance in Tavish's secret operations, it was no surprise that he'd come to the Black Sheep today. But until now, he'd always stuck to the front room. Normally, Matthew would be happy to see his comrade, but his presence only made Matthew feel even more deuced uncomfortable after Alexander's probing questions.

"You're most likely acquainted with Belle's Livery," Powys was saying to Charlotte.

"Why, yes!" Charlotte said. "Belle's offers the fastest hackneys in the city and the most nicely appointed."

"Well-sprung and sprightly—even in London traffic." George grinned broadly. Matthew knew the Black Londoner had designed the light, maneuverable carriages himself just as he personally selected each horse. In a mere decade, he'd grown his business from a single vehicle that he alone had driven to a veritable fleet of equipage and drivers. According to rumor, he held a significant portion of the hackney licenses for the city.

"The swiftness of your carriages has saved me from the embarrassment of a late arrival more than once," Alexander said as he greeted George warmly. "I am very much in your debt."

"Continue to sing the praises of my livery, and it will be paid in full," George answered cheerfully.

After the group finished the introductions, all of them sat down. Despite George Belle and Alun Powys being self-made men, they had no difficulties chatting with the noble-born Lady Charlotte, Lady Calliope, and Alexander. Mr. Powys was even so bold as to exchange increasingly barbed quips with Lady Calliope over the merits of ribald political comedies, which were Mr. Powys's standard fare, versus the romantic plays that Lady Calliope occasionally penned.

Yet Matthew sat there. Quiet. Part of it. But not part of it. While Charlotte was the glowing center of it all. She was the reason Calliope was here and even Mr. Powys. How could anyone think that Matthew belonged in the same sphere as she did?

Chapter Sixteen

A day later, Charlotte's veil hid the triumphant Cheshire cat smile stretching across her face as she spied two of the hulking men she'd seen with Lord Hawley two days prior. The brutes were leaving the Black Sheep as she was walking to the entrance after being dropped off by the Estbrook coachman. Even more promising, she could not spot the viscount's fashionable form anywhere in the vicinity.

Charlotte slipped into an alley and peered around the corner to watch the two men. They swaggered leisurely along the street, one of them whistling a tune she didn't recognize. Her mouth quirked up as she guessed that Banshee might recognize the ditty, especially since it was likely a dirty one.

As the two came closer, Charlotte retreated into the shadows. She waited until their footsteps receded, and then she popped her head out again. She was just in time to see the men disappear down another street.

She paused, debating whether to follow. Mr. Powys had called these men dangerous, and she was not fool enough to think she could trifle with them. She would be venturing further from the tightly woven fabric of society into its frayed edges, where she could easily get twisted in the stray unwieldy strands. Her heart fluttered with almost painful quickness, but outwardly she remained serene.

Making up her mind, Charlotte scurried out of the alley, her furtive movements earning her more than one curious glance. She realized what a fool she was being. By trying to be stealthy, she was actually standing out. She straightened and almost dashed back to the Black Sheep. But something in her rebelled. The Duke of Lansberry was returning in ten days, and Charlotte needed more than an incomplete drawing of a necklace to stop the betrothal.

Her veil obscured her features even if her widow's weeds otherwise attracted attention. She'd already learned one lesson in subterfuge. She could manage.

Resolutely, she strolled forward. When she turned down the same thoroughfare that the two reprobates had taken, she could spy their hulking forms ahead. Staying a good distance behind, she trailed them. At the slightest twitch of their bodies in her direction, she immediately tried to obscure herself behind either a heap of refuse piled in front of an abandoned building, the entrance to a narrow passage, a cart stopped to make a delivery, or anything else that looked capable of hiding her and her voluminous skirts.

As the men drew her deeper and deeper into Covent Garden, an uneasy feeling washed over Charlotte. She was beginning to sense that she was not so much chasing the ruffians as they were luring her. Just before she scurried up the stoop of a locked business, she noticed the two exchange a sneering look, their massive shoulders heaving with laughter.

Trying to steady her breathing, Charlotte pressed her back against the closed door. She could not pursue these men any deeper into the bowels of London. She'd been foolhardy to come even this far.

Peeking down the crooked passage lined with ramshackle coffeehouses and drinking establishments, Charlotte let the two brutes vanish around a sharp jog in the road. Sighing, she turned in the opposite direction. No longer caring to be stealthy, she picked up her skirts and ran. Men stared, but she did not care.

She had only made two turns when she became acutely aware she was being followed. Laughter, cruel and mean, drifted toward her. It seemed to wrap around her heart, threatening to hold her in place.

Frantic, Charlotte scanned her derelict surroundings. The run-down buildings and sour smells matched the wane cast to people's weathered faces. No one would come to her rescue. They were all too steeped in their own misery. The sad-looking coffeeshops wouldn't offer any better shelter.

"The chit knows we're after her, Eddie." The rough voice was meant to carry to Charlotte's ears, and she realized with increasing terror that she'd heard it before…during the ambush on the way back to London from Ravenshall.

Clasping her hand over her mouth, Charlotte refused to give these men the pleasure of hearing her scream. She could not let fear overtake her. If she were to survive, she needed her wits.

"Makes it more fun, don't it, Charley?" Eddie laughed, the sound incongruously high despite the fiend's muscle-laden body.

Tears of fear streamed down Charlotte's face. They sounded so close. Frantic, she glanced over her shoulder. Charley and Eddie were only a few steps behind her. The taller man's hard blue eyes were latched on to her body, not her veil-covered face. He must have noticed her looking, and his expression darkened into sala-cious interest.

Charlotte acted on instinct. She turned sharply and sped across the street, even though there was really no place to flee. Suddenly, the thud of wheels filled the narrow thoroughfare. Charlotte smashed herself against the crumbling plaster of a half–tumbled down building as a black hackney coach careened between her and the ruffians.

The door to the conveyance slammed open, and Hannah stood there, her hand outstretched, her face as fierce as the legendary Boudicca. "Get inside now. Be quick about it."

Charlotte didn't hesitate. She immediately grabbed her cousin's hand and leapt. When she awkwardly half landed in Hannah's arms, she saw anger and not welcome on her relative's face. Surprised by the fierceness of Hannah's countenance, Charlotte took an awkward step to the side and tumbled onto the seat across from Sophia. Like a predator, Hannah sprang forward and practically pounced into a sitting position beside Charlotte.

"What in the bloody hell were you attempting back there?" Hannah didn't even raise her voice. She didn't need to. Not with the ferocious whisper that snapped from her lips like the snick of a riding crop whistling through the air.

"I—I was, uh, lost," Charlotte said in a hurried rush. Nervously, she licked her lips, hoping Hannah and Sophia would accept the rather thin explanation.

"You were following two customers of the Black Sheep, likely to your death! You promised us that your ownership in the Black Sheep wasn't a thrill-seeking lark." Hannah shoved her face into Charlotte's, but this time Charlotte held her ground despite her limbs trembling with suppressed emotions. Anticipation. Frustration. Anger. Delayed fear. All those sentiments pounded at her, threatening to shake her apart.

"Helping run the Black Sheep is not a game to me!" Charlotte's voice had become as hoarse and as harsh as her cousin's. "Haven't I proven that? I've helped make the back room a success. You know I've brought in my share of patrons. We're already making a profit—and a nice one too."

"Yet you chased our customers!" Hannah protested.

Charlotte could feel her cousin's hot, angry breath sweep across her own flushed skin.

"Are you worried I've scared them away? I promise that I had good reas—"

"I'm afraid you're going to get yourself attacked or murdered!" Hannah did shout this time, and her words took Charlotte aback. Not because of the content but because of the note of actual concern in Hannah's voice.

"I—" Charlotte had no earthly idea how to respond, and she hazarded a glance at Sophia. The other Wick cousin sat watching them, her expression intense but otherwise betraying nothing.

"Does it excite you to flirt with the seamy underbelly of life?" Hannah demanded, her rage returned. "Stay in your gilt sphere, Cousin. Stop consorting with thieves and killers."

Hannah's rapidly shifting emotions had sent Charlotte's careening too. The acceptance she'd felt at Hannah's show of concern burned away in the flames of renewed fury. "If I don't make the acquaintances of criminals, then I am going to end up married to a homicidal husband who has already murdered two wives. I need to prove one of Lord Hawley's crimes. That's why I was following those ruffians. I saw the viscount with them two days ago."

Hannah's entire body jerked. "Hawley is not a man to be trifled with. What you are attempting is more than dangerous. It is foolishly deadly."

"Then what am I to do? Marry him?"

"Refuse," Hannah said. "Refuse just as my mother did when her parents arranged her marriage."

Charlotte rubbed her temples, wishing it could all be so simple. "I have no dashing pirate waiting to whisk me to safety. I may live in a world of gilt, but that is all that it is—a gilded, glittering surface masking the iron bars keeping me caged."

"Do not speak to us of being confined by the circumstances of your birth," Hannah snapped. "Especially not to Sophia. Both of our families have had to fight for their place in the world but none more than hers."

"Power is something taken from my people, not given to us," Sophia said, her voice quiet but ardent. "The countries of Europe murdered my mother's Taíno ancestors and claimed their lands, which the invaders cleared using the forced labor of my mother's African forebearers. My people's work, their lives, their very essence, are what fuel much of the lavish existence of the British upper and middling classes. That ill-begotten wealth comes from New World plantations and merchant vessels with their human cargo and goods wrought by blood. And my people are left with ashes. Yet, somehow, we still manage to create, to produce, to live, to dream. If we can survive with nothing, you can too with the power that you possess."

Pain and guilt ripped through Charlotte. She had not meant to discount the Wick cousins' experiences, especially Sophia's. For all her philosophical reading about the human condition, she had never truly wrestled with the horrors of the slave trade or its connection to the luxuries of coffee, spices, tobacco, and so many of the aristocratic pleasures.

"By no means do I think my cosseted existence can begin to compare with what the peoples of the New World and Africa have suffered. I am fortunate in so many ways—ways that I am just now considering. Yet I am also like a treasured doll—told what clothes to wear, the posture to assume, the words to say. Above all, I am seen as incapable of making my own decisions. What power do you think I have?" Charlotte asked in genuine confusion.

"Plenty." Sophia's brown eyes flashed with a commanding golden light. "Society's perception of your fragility is your very strength."

"Pardon?" Charlotte asked.

"If you swoon, what happens?" Hannah asked hotly.

"People would coming running over to help, I suppose," Charlotte surmised. "A doctor might be summoned."

"What if Sophia fainted?" Hannah asked.

Charlotte lifted her chin to meet the other women's gazes. She didn't speak the answer—that Sophia might be wrongly accused of imbibing too much gin or just being lazy. Things that weren't right or fair. Charlotte wasn't meant to say the words aloud but to herself, to internalize them.

"I see your point," Charlotte murmured as she rubbed her finger against a chip in the bench's battle-scarred veneer. "I can use my ladylike sensibilities to command a great deal of attention, but I am afraid that even an extremely theatrical collapse won't dissuade my parents from marrying me off to Hawley. I invested in the Black Sheep so that eventually I would have the financial independence to support myself. But I also hoped that the coffeehouse could help me discover tangible evidence of Lord Hawley's misdeeds. I am afraid that, even if I defied my parents and threw the viscount over, he would still come after me. I need to prove his villainy in a way that stops him from not only hurting me but all his future victims."

Sophia frowned in concern. "Verifying rumors about a man like Hawley is like pinning down a wispy phantom. Even a seasoned thieftaker would fail."

"But I must try! I truly do not wish to court danger, but…"

"Trailing brigands is not the soundest plan." Hannah's voice gentled again. "You are no match for subterfuge against seasoned criminals. You're fortunate that Sophia and I happened to be departing in a hackney carriage when Sophia spotted you trailing those men like a flightless crow. If we hadn't ordered the driver to follow you, well… I think you are worldly enough to understand what we saved you from."

Charlotte glanced at her cousin and spotted a hint of understanding in her gem-like gaze. Perhaps Hannah was beginning to understand that Charlotte's need to escape Lord Hawley was not just some spoiled tantrum.

"Is that how you came to rescue me?" Charlotte asked. She'd been so caught up in first fear and then in the discussion that she hadn't stopped to consider how fortuitous the women's arrival had been.

"Aye," Sophia said.

"Are we headed back to the Black Sheep?" Charlotte asked.

The two cousins exchanged one of their infamous looks. Charlotte glanced outside and realized that they were traveling near the wharves of the Pool of London where the tall-masted seafaring vessels docked.

"There isn't time," Sophia said, her tone as matter-of-fact as always. "We unfortunately wasted too much of it watching over you, and others are relying on us."

"You may see things, Charlotte, that you can tell no one about, not even Alexander," Hannah said sharply.

Something in her cousin's face caused new concerns to whip through Charlotte. "See things? What sort of things?"

"You will understand when you witness them," Sophia said cryptically.

Charlotte swiveled her body to look from one Wick cousin to another. Their miens were completely serious, their jaws set in the resolute way of soldiers. Still, Charlotte hoped to see one of them crack a smile—just a little one—to assure her that this was all a joke.

"You're teasing me," Charlotte said and then waited a beat. Neither of the women's expressions changed. "Right?" Still nothing. "Correct?" Charlotte's voice went high on the last question.

Slowly, both of the Wick cousins shook their heads. Sophia was the one to speak. "We would not have dragged you along unless it was absolutely necessary. But we must be in place and ready to assist if something goes wrong tonight."

Upon those ominous words, the carriage pulled to a stop. No sooner did it cease swaying than a fierce knocking sounded on the door. Hannah swung it open to reveal a young, pale-faced boy with a terrified expression on his face. His clothes were rough but not ragged. His wide blue eyes first latched on to Hannah's face and then Sophia's.

"Belle sent me," the lad huffed out. "Dragoons all over. He's worried Dr. Talbot is walking into an ambush."

Matthew? Soldiers? A trap? A devastating agony scoured Charlotte's insides, and the pain almost caused her to pitch forward. But she managed to stand despite her shaking legs.

Matthew was in danger. Her stunned mind wasn't even attempting to determine what the peril could be. Charlotte's heart only knew that she had to save him.

Chapter Seventeen

⁓

The water of the Thames slapped against the wharf's pilings, the sound echoing in Matthew's empty chest. No matter how many rescue missions he'd undertaken, dread always carved a gaping hollow inside him. Soon, purpose and energy would fill that void, but right now, Matthew waited in the shadows, his eyes scanning his target.

The *Valiant* looked like any other merchantman, its hull a solid black silhouette against the moonlit sky, with its masts stabbing into the starry firmament. It was neither a particularly large vessel nor a noticeably small one. It did not appear powerful nor rundown, menacing nor ghostly. It was no different than any of the hundred other barques lining the London quay.

Yet Matthew had learned that the most innocuous exteriors could obscure indescribable horrors within. The *Valiant* wasn't a barbarous slaver, the most inhumane vessels that had ever set sail. It did, however, contain white British prisoners who were about to be shipped to the New World and then sold as indentured servants for work in the tobacco fields of Virginia and Maryland. Ten criminals on board were only boys. A few had been found poaching to feed their families. Others were pickpockets who had only filched items of low value from rich, powerful men. All the boys had broken a law and were not innocent victims of kidnapping like Black Africans, but the severity of their punishment far outweighed any harm they had wrought. Desperation and starvation had driven the children to commit the acts in the first place.

Matthew watched the decks of the ship as he took stock of the men on watch. Since this was a merchantman and not a Royal Navy vessel, sneaking aboard wasn't as dangerous as when Matthew freed street urchins who'd been forcibly pressed into His Majesty's service. Yet military guards assigned to the vessel would be armed and prepared to defend their goods…and human cargo. Worse, Matthew had heard rumors that the government was considering sending dragoons to watch the docks after his successful raids on other ships transporting child prisoners.

An impatient amber eye suddenly appeared in Matthew's line of vision. Although Pan did not utter a sound, he made his irritation evident by digging his talons into Matthew's scalp. The bloodthirsty bird always hated waiting.

Matthew reached up to calm the parrot but received a sharp peck instead. Pan fluttered and fluffed his wings against Matthew's temples. Matthew ignored the tickle of feathers as he scanned his target one last time. With his plan formulated and each guard accounted for, he pointed toward the ship's mizzenmast.

Pan immediately recognized the signal. Without a sound other than his wings beating against the air, he soared into position. In the moonlight, Matthew could see Pan's shadow against the white of the furled sail, but the men below would never think to look for it.

"Hollaaaa!" Pan cried out enthusiastically. Unlike Matthew, the old rascal loved their nighttime adventures.

Every man on deck swiveled in the direction of the voice. With no one looking down at the docks, Matthew stepped out from the barrels he'd been hiding behind. Keeping to the darkness as much as possible, he quickly slunk to the ship.

"Where's a fine mort? Where's a fine mort?" Pan croaked out, sounding exactly like a drunken sailor searching for a dockside whore.

"Is that voice coming from this ship?" One of the soldiers called to another in confusion.

Bollocks! Matthew prayed that no one would check the wharf. Hurriedly, he ducked behind a barrel.

"Aye," another answered.

"Murder on board! Murder on board! Murder on board!" Pan shrieked.

Matthew heard the scurrying of feet as the guards tried to locate the disembodied cackle. Taking advantage of the confusion, Matthew left his second hiding place and grabbed ahold of the ship's mooring line, first with his gloved hands and then with his feet. After years of practice, it didn't take him long to inch his way up the rope. Still, his muscles burned by the time he reached the main deck, but he didn't dare climb over the rail. Instead, he clung tight and listened first.

"It's a ghost!" A young ensign with an incongruously deep, booming voice shouted.

"Don't be a ninnyhammer." An officer with a deep Scottish brogue chortled. "A jack-tar is just soused."

"Sounds like that old toothless salt when he's in his cups. Old Akerman, is it?" another man offered.

Matthew reached for the railing. The guards seemed in deep debate now and not liable to notice his ascent. As Matthew swung one leg over the wooden structure, Pan cried out again. "Where's a fine mort? Where's a fine mort?"

Matthew spared a grin for the parrot's perfectly timed theatrics. The cries hid the thump his boots made when they hit the main deck. Creeping behind the small stowed boats, Matthew secreted his movements the best he could. Luckily, he'd learned how to make good use of shadows. The men were so busy arguing with the young ensign, however, that Matthew may not have needed any subterfuge.

"It is most assuredly a phantom!" the ensign cried out.

"What? One who died with his poker in the fire?" Another soldier sneered.

"Banshee. Love. Banshee. Love." Pan's cackle had turned mournful and rather haunting.

"Now, doesn't that sound like the devil himself?" the ensign demanded. "And it is coming from above us!"

Peering over one of the small craft, Matthew saw all the guards gathered on the quarterdeck. The ensign was jabbing his finger in the direction of the towering masts, and all of the soldiers stared into the night sky.

With everyone distracted, Matthew slithered on his belly and left his hiding place to advance into the open. Moving as quickly as an adder after its prey, he wriggled to the hatch. As soon as his hands touched the cover, Pan began to wail. It sounded like the groans of a drunkard...or the moans of an apparition. Either way, it covered the noise Matthew made as he lifted the wood just far enough to make an opening to squeeze through. Stepping onto the rungs of the narrow ladder, he surreptitiously lowered the cover back into position. Quietly, he climbed down one level, careful not to wake the sailors sleeping in their hammocks.

The snores of the crew members were thankfully loud enough to obscure any sound Matthew made as he descended into the bowels of the ship. A stench rose from the hold. According to Matthew's intelligence, the prisoners had been stuck in the dark, cramped quarters for over a week. The stink of sweat mixed with the stale, fishy odor of the sea. A chill seized Matthew as he allowed his eyes to adjust to the inky darkness. Heading deeper into the blackness, he felt his way behind a large crate. Using it as a shield, he untied the dark lantern secured to his belt and lit it.

Matthew only permitted a sliver of illumination as he crept through the warren of barrels, chests, and wooden boxes. Finally, he saw the heavy locked wooden door closing off a small compartment tucked into the bow of the ship. The narrow opening for passing food—or pans of human waste—confirmed that Matthew had found the cell.

He adjusted his lantern so that it shined upon the padlock and then grabbed his tools from the bag at his hip. The mechanism was not sophisticated, and it easily sprang apart in his hands.

Slowly, he pulled back the heavy door. The thin glow from Matthew's lamp reflected off pale, wan faces. Brutish and scrawny, old and young, sickly and hale, they were pressed into a space so small that there was not even room to shuffle more than five inches in either direction. The children had been tossed into this abominable pen with violent criminals.

As appalling as the conditions were for the prisoners, they were not even close to the horrors Matthew had witnessed on a slaver that Sophia's mother, Brave Mary, and her pirate crew had seized to rescue African hostages. Matthew had helped Brave Mary's physician, Dr. Diaz—an escaped slave himself—treat the sick and injured.

But he couldn't think of that suffering now, not with Royal Guards circling above his head and ten young charges to bring to safety.

A few of the healthier-looking men inside the small cabin shifted at the sight of Matthew, but the clanking of their leg irons was the only sound they made. The more alert ones scanned him, observing his mask and solid black attire. They did not raise an alarm, probably in hopes that he'd come to rescue them all.

But Matthew had come specifically for the children, not to release the violent offenders. Prison reform was necessary, but the youths would face the most immediate harm from illness, the jailors, and the men they were shackled together with. The Colonies could offer the adults a new start, a far better chance than they would face if they stayed rotting in a gaol in England.

"I've come for the youngsters. If you don't make a sound, the guards won't know they're gone until after the ship has sailed. You'll have more room, and I've brought food and silver in return for your silence." Matthew spoke in a low voice. "If you raise an alarm, the guards will seize what I've brought before you have a chance to squirrel it away."

The men did not speak but silently shifted to let him enter. Their legs might be chained, but they could still attack. Keeping his mind blank to the danger he faced, Matthew instead focused his almost painfully heightened senses on picking the locks on the boys' chains. He started, as he always did, with the smallest. He'd done this so many times, it was almost as if he possessed a key. When he'd freed the biggest youth, Matthew moved swiftly to the hatch, his feet moving in time to the rapid beat of his heart. Only when he stood on the threshold did he reach inside his bag and press bundles of dried cod, biscuits, and coins into the outstretched hands. Then Matthew quickly shut and relocked the door, but he felt no relief. The danger was hardly over.

He turned to find ten pairs of eyes shining in the low light of his lamp. Each gaze displayed a different mixture of fear, desperate hope, and disbelief.

"I mean you no harm. I'm taking you to a new home—a place full of boys like yourselves. You'll be kept safe from those looking for you. If you bolt when we are off this ship, you will be on your own to avoid the thieftakers," Matthew quietly explained, knowing that no words would earn these boys' trust. Only time would do that. They would need to see for themselves the dormitories that Tavish had built for the young men to live in while they learned trades.

"Keep quiet," Matthew instructed as he waved for the ten lads to follow him. Slowly, he led them up the ladder as he forced his breathing to stay measured. The boys were already fearful enough without adding his own tension to the mix.

When Matthew reached the hatch to the upper deck, he paused to listen. Good old Pan was still shrieking about murder and fine morts.

"We've looked everywhere," one of the soldiers was saying.

"Maybe Jenkins is right about it being a ghost," one of the other men said, his tone half-serious and half-joking.

"See! I was right, wasn't I?" Jenkins crowed proudly.

"Not you too, Davis," another fellow groaned.

Matthew counted the voices in his head. All the guards were accounted for, and from the direction of the sound, they were still gathered on the quarterdeck. Cautiously, his heartstrings drawn as tightly as a hunter's bow, Matthew lifted the cover to the hatch just far enough to peer out. Sure enough, he could see the shadowy figures milling above him.

Gesturing for the boys to stay put, Matthew once again snaked across the deck on his belly—this time in the direction of the water rather than the wharf. Finding a barrel he could lift, he heaved it overboard and ducked behind one of the small boats. At the splash, Pan did as he'd been carefully trained to do. He flew out over the water and started screaming.

"Man overboard! Man overboard! Man overboard! Drowning! Drowning! Drowning!"

At the sound, the guards ran to the edge of the ship and stared into the inky darkness. Walking swiftly in a crouched position, his muscles filled with what felt like an energy separate from his own, Matthew slipped back to the hatch. Opening it, he waved to the boys to head to the side of the ship facing the wharf. Already trained as pickpockets and poachers, the lads moved with silent quickness, allowing the shadows to swallow them up.

He indicated for the tallest escapee to shimmy down the rope to safety. The youth moved quickly, and the next eight followed. The second to last, though, began to shake halfway down, causing the rope to bob. Matthew glanced at the smallest child standing beside him, as he debated whether he should leave the boy momentarily behind to assist the one stuck over the water. Luckily, one of the adolescents shimmied up to the frightened lad and guided him down. Taking no chances, Matthew crouched and used his hands to signal that the last waif should climb on his back. With the urchin clinging fiercely to his neck, Matthew made his way to shore as quickly as possible.

When they were all on the ground, Matthew felt his muscles uncoil a fraction. His breathing more naturally steady than forced, he led the lads through the jumble of the dockyards toward the rendezvous spot where two of George Belle's carriages waited. Pan had just resettled on Matthew's shoulder when he heard it.

The steady clop of hooves.

Not from one horse but many. An entire company of them.

The area was filled with dragoons.

Ice sluiced through Matthew's veins, and the breath whooshed from his body. He felt like he had as a lad, when his brothers had dumped him in a frosty lough and held him under.

But Matthew shoved back the freezing panic and forced himself to calmly consider his next move. He needed to draw the soldiers away from the boys, but without him as a guide, how could they reach safety?

"Dr. Talbot!" A voice with a familiar Irish accent hissed.

Matthew turned to spy Seamus and John emerging from the shadows of a massive warehouse. A mix of irritation and relief spiraled through Matthew at the sight of Tavish's best engineers. Both the young men insisted on accompanying either the carriages or the boats during rescues, but Matthew and Tavish had strictly forbidden them from leaving the safety of the conveyances. Neither was properly trained yet.

In the moonlight, Seamus's freckles stood out against his white skin. He was even paler than usual. John hid his fear better, but Matthew could sense his nervousness as the two younger men hurried to Matthew's side.

"Dragoons are everywhere," John whispered, his voice tinged with a Caribbean accent. Through the help of Brave Mary, his family had escaped a sugar plantation when he was a baby. Although he'd grown up on the island that Brave Mary had settled for escaped slaves, he'd chosen to emigrate to London a few years ago to pursue an education.

"I noticed the influx," Matthew observed drily as he scanned the area for approaching soldiers.

"We thought we would distract the dragoons while you bring the boys to safety." John, who had a thin build like Matthew, pushed back his shoulders. Beside him, Seamus did the same.

"No," Matthew said instantly, not wanting to put the young engineers at any more risk. "I'll provide the diversion. You two lead the lads to the carriages."

"But—" Seamus began to protest before Matthew cut him off.

"We do not have time to argue." As if to punctuate Matthew's words, five men on horseback rounded the corner of the warehouse where John and Seamus had been hiding only moments before. The brass buttons on the dragoons' coats shimmered in the moonlight, but even without their uniforms, their stiff bearing would have marked them as military men.

Before John or Seamus could act, Matthew dashed from their

hiding spot among crates lined up on the wharf next to the street. He paused long enough for the soldiers to not only see him but to take an account of his physique. Matthew had been spotted by dragoons and military guards before, and he was certain the men were on the lookout for someone matching his build.

Sure enough, two of the dragoons gave a shout.

"That's him!"

"There he is!"

Still masked, Matthew tore off in the opposite direction from where Belle's carriages were waiting. Pan dug his talons into Matthew's coat for purchase before squawking back to their pursuers. "Hang in chains! Hang in chains!"

"Must you pick an insult that gives them ideas on what to do with my corpse?" Matthew huffed out in a low voice as he swerved into a narrow alley that would prevent the men from riding even two abreast.

Pan, however, ignored him and shrieked. "Hang in chains! Hang in chains!"

"You do know you could just fly back to the others?" Matthew growled under his breath but loud enough for Pan to hear. The bird did not listen to Matthew and only increased the volume of the same insult. Pan had always taken perverse delight in accompanying Matthew on midnight chases through London town.

Although Matthew was fleet of foot—courtesy of years of trying to escape his older brothers—he could not outrun a horse, especially not a military-trained one. But he had learned how to use London's twisting alleys against the massive warmbloods. Unfortunately, barreling into London's rabbit warren of closes meant risking blundering into a dead-end. But racing down the alleys was better than taking to the rooftops.

Matthew hated fleeing on top of buildings. First, there was the jumping through empty air—not the most calming of pursuits.

Worse, one never knew the condition of the structure one was about to land upon. Furthermore, landing face-first into thatch was deuced uncomfortable, and dried vegetation made for a poor running surface.

The narrow passage suddenly dumped Matthew onto a large street. More dragoons spotted him as he dashed across the cobblestones.

"Hang in chains! Hang in chains! Hang in chains!" Pan sounded downright gleeful.

His blood thumping even faster than the hooves behind him, Matthew flew into another alleyway next to a noisy tavern. An…erm…*embracing* couple looked up from their lovemaking. Both made hasty efforts to cover their nakedness as Matthew dashed past them.

"My sincerest apologies!" Matthew shouted as he did his best to avert his eyes. Pan, however, had no shame.

"Beast with two backs! Beast with two backs!"

"Sophia never should have taught you Shakespeare," Matthew scolded Pan.

Unchastened, Pan gaily yelled, "Beast with two backs! Hang in chains! Beast with two backs! Where's a fine mort?"

"I truly am sorry," Matthew called back to the couple just as the dragoons came stampeding into the alley. Quickly, Matthew slipped into another narrow passageway and then another. He'd gone about a hundred yards when he realized he'd blundered into a dead-end.

His heart, already pounding from exertion, slammed against his rib cage with what felt like enough force to crack his sternum. Matthew did not give in to panic, though, for in uncontrolled fear lay death. Instead, he harnessed his heightened senses as he madly looked for an escape.

"Roof! Roof! Roof!" Pan called happily. He loved when Matthew jumped from one building to the next.

Matthew ignored the parrot. Thankfully, Matthew's gaze landed upon a low-lying structure that appeared to be a stable of sorts, jammed between the taller structures. It might make a good passage to another alley or, at least, a place of temporary shelter.

Matthew threw back the rickety half door and bolted inside… only to come skidding to an ignoble stop. Bits of straw flew everywhere as Matthew found himself face-to-face with a goat. An angry, thoroughly disgruntled billy goat.

Matthew froze. The goat did not. It simply kept chewing the straw in its mouth as if daring Matthew to take another step. Its already unholy eyes glowed in the moonlight streaming in the windows behind Matthew. He could only pray that the animal didn't start screaming.

The goat continued to watch Matthew—a long piece of dried grass slowly disappearing between its crooked teeth. The tuft at the end of the blade switched back and forth in an almost mesmerizing and oddly intimidating sway.

Matthew moved to the left, hoping to squeeze past the cloven-footed sentry. The animal casually scuttled in the same direction. Matthew bobbed to the right. The creature blocked him again. Matthew feinted to the left and then dove right. He didn't fool the capra. The goat shuffled into Matthew's path, not even breaking the rhythm of its mastication.

The head of the straw disappeared between the goat's lips. The horned beast immediately lowered its head as if it had been waiting to finish its snack before charging. One hoof struck the ground. Then the next. The creature's sides puffed out before it emitted a displeased huff.

Matthew didn't wait for the goat to lift another leg. He jumped onto the three-foot wooden partition bisecting the stable. He dashed across the narrow surface, spreading out his arms in an attempt to maintain his balance.

It didn't work.

He fell headfirst into a pile of straw of questionable freshness. As he worked to extricate himself from the malodorous mound, he told himself that he should at least be grateful that he'd landed on the non-goat side of the dilapidated structure.

"Fiend!" Pan cried out.

Matthew jerked his head toward the wooden divider, and to his horror, he saw the tips of horns. Slowly but steadily, more of the spikes appeared. Next, eerie, snake-like reddish-gold eyes eased into view.

The deuced devil must have found a crate or another object to scale.

When Matthew spied the tip of the creature's pink nose, he clamored for purchase in the shifting pile of pungent straw. Somehow, Matthew managed to grip the sill of a rather narrow window. He did not have time to properly calculate if he could squeeze through.

When Matthew heard the ominous thud of a hoof on top of the partition, he heaved his body upward. Pan flew into the air and stayed behind in the stable. Matthew could hear the bird's wings beating in the air as he cackled, "Stop, fiend! Stop, fiend!"

Matthew's broad shoulders stuck in the frame. He wriggled back and tried to jam one shoulder followed by the other.

Then he felt it. A pull on the seat of his breeches. The damnable goat had Matthew's attire caught between its teeth!

"Stop, fiend! Stop, fiend!" Pan shouted. Matthew realized that the parrot was literally protecting his flank, even if his call would likely attract the dragoons' attention.

With renewed urgency, Matthew jammed his shoulders through

the opening. He could feel his upper arms burn as a good layer of skin was scraped away. Matthew didn't hesitate though. He popped into the moonlit night with enough force to tear his clothing from the beast's mouth.

He crashed to the ground but managed to tuck and roll his body just in time to avoid smashing his head on the cobblestones. Bouncing to his feet, he turned to see Pan fly from the stable. The goat's head appeared next, its eyes gleaming even more brightly than before. This time, though, instead of chewing a long piece of straw, it deliberately munched on a swatch of Matthew's breeches. Inch by inch, the material slowly disappeared into the creature's maw.

Matthew had no time to watch the consumption of the fabric. He had only started to scan the new alleyway when dragoons appeared at both ends. Above Matthew's head, the goat continued to eat, its horns poking through the open window like twin blades. Even if Matthew wanted to battle the cloven-footed devil, he couldn't squeeze himself back through the window quickly enough.

"Roof! Roof! Roof!" Pan chortled above Matthew's head.

"You always have to be right, don't you?" Matthew asked the parrot. He gripped the window frame under the goat's hairy chin and sprang so quickly onto the sill that the goat screamed, dropping what remained of the saliva-covered wool. Before the creature could react further, Matthew had already hoisted himself onto the relatively low roof of the stable. He scrambled up the eaves of a neighboring building and then was off, leaping through the air with Pan as his faithful shadow.

He'd only gone three blocks when rotting timbers over an abandoned building gave way beneath his feet. Matthew landed, quite painfully, on a large beam. Gritting his teeth against the blazing hot agony, he managed to grip the cruck before he toppled off and plummeted twenty feet to the ground.

Pan landed a few feet away and cocked his head inquisitively at Matthew. "Oof?"

"I...hate...rooftops." Matthew forced out between his gritted teeth. Pan seemed amused. Matthew was not.

He could hear the dragoons on the streets outside the building. Each clip-clop sounded closer and closer. Horror and fear mingled with the aches coursing through Matthew. He needed to gather his strength to flee once more...but would it be too late?

Chapter Eighteen

⁂

T his is not good," Sophia spoke, her voice low as she pulled back the curtain to the window of the Belle carriage.

Hannah looked out her side and swore a low oath. "No, it isn't."

"The number of dragoons?" Charlotte asked, unable to keep her voice from being pitched too high. Worry thudded through her like a plodding, endless funeral dirge that promised only more horror at the end.

"Not just the amount of troops, but how they are fanning out. They're methodically checking streets, houses, and businesses. They must be trying to corner Matthew."

"If they haven't already," Hannah added darkly.

Charlotte suppressed the stab of pain that her cousin's words triggered. She had to remain alert, stay fierce. For Matthew's sake.

"We're at least close to the hideout that Tavish owns." Sophia looked over at Charlotte.

But they knew Matthew wasn't there. The three of them had already checked the ramshackle building and had climbed back into the coach only minutes earlier. Charlotte was not certain of all the details, but Matthew was involved in liberating children sentenced to years of forced labor in the Colonies. Hannah and Sophia occasionally lent aid to him and Mr. Stewart.

"We need to create a distraction." Hannah drummed her fingers against the wooden seat. "One that will give Matthew a chance to slip to safety."

Her heart a massive, swollen lump of terror, Charlotte glanced at the men on horseback. With the moonlight glinting off the rows of buttons on their uniforms, they were regal looking. Despite their deadly intent, they reminded her of footmen bustling about before a ball. Both were accustomed to taking commands and protecting the strictures of Society. An idea formed, and Charlotte instantly spoke before fear could silence her.

"I can distract the soldiers." The words sounded so calm, so-matter-of-fact, that it was almost as if another speaker had uttered them. But the voice was Charlotte's and, moreover, so was the intent.

"You?" Hannah looked at her skeptically. "This isn't a gilded ballroom to swan about in."

Charlotte glanced toward Sophia, always finding her the more calmly rational of the two. "Did you not tell me that as a noble white woman I have certain power in my perceived weaknesses?"

"I think I understand what you're planning, but explain more," Sophia said.

"I'll play the classic damsel in distress, and all of those fine military men are going to clamor to slay dragons for me."

"Her suggestion does possess some merit." Sophia turned toward Hannah. "It is less dangerous than most options."

Hannah leaned forward in her seat as she studied Charlotte. "Your acting is sufficient?"

"My entire life has been playing the role of an elegant but guileless Society miss." Charlotte kept her voice steady despite the trembling in her extremities.

Something flashed in Hannah's eyes, but Charlotte had no wherewithal to identify the emotion. Her cousin glanced away and rapped sharply on the ceiling of the coach. The vehicle turned into a dark alley opposite from where the dragoons were congregating. As soon as the conveyance rolled to a shuddering stop, the women quickly debarked.

"Do you have a believable story concocted?" Sophia asked softly as they marched toward the clomp of horses and shouts of the dragoons. "This is not the usual haunt of a lady."

"Hence the distress," Charlotte replied with a coolness she did not feel. She had a plan, but she could only pray it would not collapse under scrutiny.

"Perhaps we should discuss it more," Hannah said nervously as she slacked her pace.

Charlotte did not slow down. "There is no time. If you are afraid that I will make a muck of things, you are welcome to stay behind. There is no need for us all to risk being accused of assisting a fugitive."

Neither Hannah nor Sophia answered Charlotte verbally. They just flanked her.

Charlotte drew strength from their silent support as the three of them strode from the darkness. They entered the street where the dragoons seemed to have set up a command from which to search the alleyways to the south. One man shouted most of the instructions.

Charlotte hurried in his direction, pretending not to notice the milling horses and uniformed men. A few gave her startled looks, but because she was not their quarry, they otherwise paid her little heed. When she was within earshot of the commanding officer, she cried out in her most dramatic voice, "We are saved! Oh, good sir, I cannot tell you how relieved I am to discover an upstanding gentleman in this dreadful area of London!"

The captain turned his steed in Charlotte's direction. At the sight of her finely made gown, his mouth drooped in astonishment.

He recovered quickly, but Charlotte knew she had unsettled him. Good. She needed his thoughts scattered.

"I have been betrayed!" Charlotte cried theatrically. The pitch of her voice drew the attention of the nearest soldiers. Even more importantly, with their leader's attention diverted, the clockwork motions of the search had become disrupted. Charlotte thought she might be overdoing her feigned alarm, but her plan was succeeding...for now.

"Pardon me, madame, but this scarcely seems the place for you and your companions." The captain's deep voice rumbled with irritation. Clearly, he did not appreciate an unknown woman—even a well-spoken one—blundering into his carefully orchestrated maneuvers. However, since his posture remain relaxed, he didn't appear to regard her as a threat.

"How well I know that, good sir." Charlotte wailed. She practically threw herself at his horse as if to embrace the man's boot. As she'd intended, the sudden movement caused even the well-trained equine to shy away. The captain, who had loosened his grip on the reins, had difficulty getting his mount under control. One of the hoofs kicked near Charlotte. She theatrically fell to the ground and began to cry in loud sobs.

Both Hannah and Sophia made clucks of distress, but instead of helping her, they literally wrung their hands. With audible sighs, several soldiers dismounted to help Charlotte to her feet. The whole episode felt like a farce, yet the men seemed to accept the women's weeping as a true display—a bothersome display, but real.

"How solicitous you are!" Charlotte said and then sniffed very loudly. "It is the most kindness I have received in days! You are true gentlemen."

The dragoons' buttons nearly popped off their puffed chests as some of their annoyance transformed into pride. Their captain, however, was not so easily placated.

"What is the meaning of this? How have you come to be here?" The man's tone was sharp, but Charlotte could tell that he was making a feeble effort to soften it.

Charlotte pulled a handkerchief from her reticule and began twisting it in her gloved hands. "It all began with my dear husband's death. He was a wealthy man, a merchant—Mr. Thomas Smith—certainly you have heard of him?"

Charlotte paused as if she expected a positive response to the innocuous name she had entirely fabricated. The poor captain uttered a helpless, noncommittal grunt. He seemed unsure of how to deal with her, but her profusion of tears had apparently allayed his suspicions.

"His partner tidying up his affairs was acting oddly, and my inheritance was not what my husband told me it would be." Charlotte worked her delicate handkerchief so fiercely she felt some of the threads rip. The officer's gaze darted to her fingers, and his frustration visibly melted into pity. Clearly, he thought her overset. She was barely keeping her sharp panic for Matthew at bay, so it wasn't hard to act emotional.

"I am but a woman with little knowledge of financial affairs. I had no one to turn to as my father is also dead, and I have no brothers. I hoped to accompany my husband's partner to his office so that I might inquire more from the clerks. When he proposed such a late appointment, I had my suspicions, but there was no choice. I even brought two of my companions for safety." Charlotte sobbed out the long-winded tale, purposely getting louder and louder. More and more of the soldiers had gathered around, either to hear her story or to try to determine what the devil was going on.

"But then he dumped us here in the streets near the wharves!" Charlotte belted out the last sentence before dissolving into an utter puddle of tears. The captain dismounted with a resigned grunt. Awkwardly, he thumped, more than patted, Charlotte on the back. She turned and clung to him, blubbering profusely.

"He clearly meant for the cutpurses to do what he could not!" Hannah took up the cry next, her wail utterly piercing.

"Murder us!" Sophia added, her voice a tragic whisper that hung ominously in the air.

"Now, now. You are safe. All three of you." The captain softened his voice, his tone for small children.

Normally, the patronization would secretly grate, but Charlotte could only feel relief. Her ploy was working! Maybe, just maybe, Matthew could take advantage of the distraction and make his way to Mr. Stewart's property.

"It's him—the man who's been freeing the convicts!" A cry went up, obliterating Charlotte's nascent hope. "Look! On the rooftops!"

White-hot dismay stabbed Charlotte, ripping through her innards. Everything suddenly moved at a slowed down speed. As if outside her own corporal body, Charlotte watched a shadowy figure leap from rooftop to rooftop. The dragoon captain's arm brushed hers as he began to raise his flintlock pistol.

She had to stop the slug from hitting Matthew. A shot—even a nonfatal one—would be deadly. It would either cause him to plummet to his death or slow him down enough to be caught and hung.

Even if Charlotte's mind felt frozen, her instincts were not. Her muscles acted of their own accord. With an airy cry, she thrust her hand up as if she meant to lay it on her forehead. Although a true swoon would result in her crumpling to the ground, Charlotte instead sprang into the air just as the dragoon captain raised his weapon. Her dramatic arcing leap positioned her right in the path of the ball.

A spark. A blast. A searing pain in Charlotte's arm.

She tumbled into a heap, no longer playacting. She clutched her arm, feeling the hot, stickiness flow onto her trembling fingers. It hurt. Oh, did it hurt.

But she couldn't allow the pain to hold her captive. The rest of the soldiers still had their Brown Bess flintlock muskets raised…and all pointed at Matthew's retreating form.

"Oooooooooooooooooooooow!" She made the howl as earsplitting as possible. Her own agony fueled her cry. It echoed over the narrow street, bouncing off the buildings and echoing back in an amplified shriek.

"You wounded me!" Charlotte accused in an equally high yet booming wail. "Grievously! Most grievously indeed! Villains! Villains all of you!"

Her purposefully melodramatic words sparked confusion in the men, and the captain paled in the moonlight. "Madame! I did not mean—"

"Put down your weapons!" She cried hysterically. "Put them down! You're all frightening me! Owwwwwwwww! You were supposed to keep me safe! Blackguards! Scoundrels! Miscreants!"

As she writhed on the ground, Charlotte surreptitiously looked for Matthew. She saw nothing. He had blended into the shadows again.

The captain must have noticed the same for he jerkily signaled for the men to lower their muskets as he ripped off his sash. He dashed to Charlotte's side while his men complied with his command. The now-silent alley rippled with nervousness as the soldiers watched their captain fall to his knees by a lady of obvious wealth, whom their leader had accidentally shot at close range with a pistol.

"Madame, let me assist you," the captain began, his voice hesitant as he wrapped his sash around her arm to staunch the bleeding.

Daggers of pain radiated down Charlotte's arm and up toward

her shoulder. When the captain cinched the material, she gritted her teeth against the new onslaught of agony. She could not afford to actually faint…or even to lose focus.

"Get away from me!" Charlotte let the words explode from her lips like a firework over Spring Gardens. As much as her arm burned, she needed to get herself, Hannah, and Sophia to safety. She couldn't stop to think about what had almost happened until the three of them were away from the dragoons. "You have all done enough! I want to go home. Now! Find me a carriage!"

The men hesitated, and the harried captain waved his hand as he bent over Charlotte. "Go! Do as the lady commands! Find a hackney and bring it here." When the soldiers still paused, he added hoarsely, "Now!"

The dragoons scattered in all directions. Hannah and Sophia crowded around her. They pushed the captain aside as they examined her arm.

"There's so much blood!" Real shock threaded through Hannah's voice, and Charlotte realized her cousin had thought she'd been feigning injury.

"The makeshift bandage should stop it for now, but she must see a surgeon immediately. I insist on accompanying…" The captain started to say.

"Get. Away. From. Me. Now!" Charlotte screamed. Although she knew she was risking more damage to her arm, she began to thrash.

"You best back away, sir," Hannah said with calm authority. "Your presence is doing my mistress more harm than good."

The captain reluctantly scuttled backward, his worried eyes still on them. Charlotte calmed, and Sophia rested her palm against Charlotte's fingers on the uninjured side of her body. Charlotte gripped Sophia's hand, drawing strength from her. Real tears smarted her eyes, and Charlotte desperately tried not to concentrate on the awful burning sensation in the fleshy part of her upper left arm.

Thankfully, one of Belle's carriages—the very one they'd just traveled in—emerged into the street, shepherded by the dragoons. Charlotte had suspected this would be the first hackney located. The coachman, obviously well-versed in subterfuge, gave no indication that he knew Charlotte and the Wick cousins.

Hannah and Sophia helped Charlotte to her feet. The captain tried to assist, but every time he came close, Charlotte began to twist and moan. Finally, Hannah convinced him to leave them be. The leader of the dragoons instead turned his focus to the carriage driver as he barked out strict instructions for Charlotte to be delivered to the nearest reputable surgeon.

Hannah and Sophia quickly bundled Charlotte into the vehicle. She sank against the squabs, wincing as the movement jarred her wound.

"Here. Let me put pressure on it. It's going to hurt, but we must make sure the bleeding is stopped." Hannah produced a handkerchief and held it against Charlotte's injury.

She yelped and then bit her lip before she made another sound. Now that she no longer had a military audience, she wanted to appear brave in front of Hannah and Sophia. Deep, excruciating throbs pulsated through her entire limb. The sensation only worsened as the carriage lurched forward.

No one spoke for several long minutes. Even though it was improbable that the dragoons could hear them, they all seemed loath to talk until they had traveled several blocks. With each creak of the carriage, more and more of Charlotte's muscles uncoiled. Yet the tension did not decrease. Instead, her body trembled as the enormity of what she had done slammed into her.

"No dragoons are tailing us." Sophia spoke first as she stared out of the small opening she'd made in the otherwise drawn curtains.

"I do not believe the captain was skeptical of Charlotte's story. He is just glad to be rid of our presence."

"G—g-g—ooo-d-d," Charlotte managed through chattering teeth.

"What were you thinking?" Hannah suddenly blurted out. Her tone sounded harsh on the surface, but Charlotte could detect real concern. "Do you know how much damage a ball can wreak on the human body at close range? If it had hit your chest, you'd have a hole where your heart had been."

Charlotte's shaking worsened, and her stomach twisted. Her jaw wobbled uncontrollably as she tried to answer. "I h-h-h-a-d to sa-ave Matt-hew."

"Why didn't you just grab the captain's arm?" Hannah asked.

"D-d-didn't wa-ant t-to raise suspicion about u-ssss." Charlotte really wished she could force her limbs to cooperate, but the shivers were throughout her body now.

"But your arm could have been blown apart! If it hadn't just grazed you…" Hannah trailed off, and the emotion drenching her voice seemed to sweep through Charlotte too. Hannah cared about her. And that…that was worth any scolding.

"I know." Charlotte whispered, resting her good hand on her left. The feel of her wounded arm—still there, still attached, still warm—gave her comfort. She'd acted foolishly. Heroically, but foolishly. She was lucky she had managed to escape with only a deep gouge.

"You're upsetting her, Hannah," Sophia interjected quietly.

Her cousin's sharp gaze raked over Charlotte. She sighed, a sharp but accepting sound. "You won't try something like that again?"

"Not wi-thout think-ing of alter-natives." Charlotte still spoke jerkily, but she was beginning to learn how to accommodate the quivers still sweeping through her.

"Good," Hannah said, apparently satisfied.

"We're at Tavish's building," Sophia announced. "With any luck, Matthew will be inside and can take care of Charlotte's wound."

"You are su-ure no one fol-lowed us?" Charlotte asked as panic once again washed over her. Her wound needed tending, but she would hate to lead the dragoons straight to Matthew.

"Not with Belle's men driving," Hannah answered confidently. "Even if they had, Sophia would have noticed. You can't outfox her."

"Let's get you out of this carriage and inside." Sophia left her seat and gently grabbed Charlotte's elbow on her uninjured side.

With both Hannah and Sophia supporting her, Charlotte succeeded in forcing her quaking body to rise and descend from the carriage. The coachman started to climb down from his box to assist, but Sophia waved for him to sit down. "We are fine. Thank you."

Together, the three of them walked up the steps leading to a nondescript building on an equally nondescript street. Hannah fished a key from her pocket and opened the door. No one lit a single taper as they slipped into the darkness. Using touch rather than words, the Wick cousins guided Charlotte to a moonlit upper room. Sophia released Charlotte and headed over to press against the stones of an unlit fireplace. Almost immediately, a hidden panel sprang open, and a warm light emanated from a dark, secret staircase.

Sophia disappeared up the extremely narrow steps. Charlotte assumed the middle position with Hannah gripping her right elbow to support her from behind. Even though Charlotte's legs felt limp and uncooperative, she did not slip. It did, however, require so much focus to steady herself that sweat dotted her brow. At least all the concentration diverted her attention from the excruciating throbbing.

"Sophia! I knew you and Hannah were the women who started

that commotion! I can't thank you both enough…" Matthew's excited voice immediately trailed off when Charlotte stumbled into the small, windowless room wedged against the fireplace.

"Charlotte!" Her name was a hoarse, guttural whisper on Matthew's lips. He moved to her side so quickly it was as if he'd simply manifested there. Charlotte felt his strong arms band around her as he lifted her gently but swiftly into the air. His dear face, so pale and worried, hovered above hers as he carried her to a narrow cot tucked against the wall.

Charlotte studied every detail of his countenance—the countenance that she'd feared she'd never see again. For the first time, she noticed silvery-white streaks in his gray irises. How had she missed the way that they glowed? And there was a black burst around his pupil. Her already overexercised heart began pumping furiously once more. But this time it was not from fear…but from a very different emotion.

"How are you here—?" Matthew asked, his gravelly voice a harsh contrast to the gentle way he laid Charlotte on the straw tick. Cutting off his own question, he shook his head as if chiding himself. When he spoke again, his voice changed to soft efficiency—his physician tone. "Time for that later. Where are you injured? This blood is yours, correct?"

"It is," Hannah answered for Charlotte as she peered over Matthew's shoulder. "She was hit by a musket ball when she jumped to protect you."

"What?" Matthew's gray eyes became steeped in horror and disbelief. She thought his hand on hers began to shake, but it could have been her own trembling. "Charlotte, you shouldn't have done that—"

"Hannah has already lectured her," Sophia broke in. "The captain placed a tourniquet around her arm, but blood is starting to seep through."

Charlotte watched as Matthew undid the makeshift bandage. Whether or not his fingers had quavered before, they were completely steady now. When he revealed the injury, he made a harsh sound in the back of his throat. "Your wound may require stitches. Hannah, can you get my bag? I keep one in the chest over there for emergencies."

Matthew returned his attention to Charlotte. "I must cut your sleeve and remove it. I apologize, but I am afraid I have no choice."

Despite her pain, Charlotte laughed at the interjection of propriety into a situation that was anything but. "I daresay it's ruined already."

Matthew gave her a half grin, which did more to calm Charlotte than words ever could. Hannah reappeared at Matthew's side, and he rummaged in a leather case. Withdrawing a pair of scissors, he carefully snipped through the layers of material. Charlotte wondered if she should look away, so as not to see the wound, but she found herself wanting to watch Matthew work again.

His long, tanned fingers moved competently. The steadiness, the certainty in which he performed each small action fascinated Charlotte . . . as did the sight of his masculine hand against the pale, slightly rounded flesh of her upper arm. There was nothing sexual in his actions, yet no man had ever touched Charlotte so intimately. Even through the hot, radiating pain from the gash, she could feel the tender glide of his touch.

"It is indeed deep," Matthew said, his voice placid, but she could detect a well-hidden undercurrent of concern. "Stitches are definitely necessary."

That sounded unpleasant, but Charlotte didn't protest. She tightened her mouth and nodded. She hoped she wouldn't make a fool of herself and scream like one of Banshee's namesakes.

"Here." Hannah thrust a flask under Charlotte's lips. The strong pungent smell slammed into her.

"What is that?" Charlotte asked.

"Whiskey," Hannah said.

Charlotte tried very hard not to wrinkle her nose at the proffered drink. "I'm afraid I am not accustomed to anything stronger than sherry. I would become very inebriated, very quickly."

"That is the point." Hannah wiggled the container impatiently, causing more of the vapors to escape.

Sophia popped into Charlotte's vision. "What Hannah is so inelegantly trying to say is that drinking alcohol will help dull the pain when Matthew jabs your skin with a needle."

"'Jabs' is not a very comforting word," Hannah protested.

Sophia shot her cousin an irritated look. "You're the one who started plying her with hard spirits without explaining why."

"It's a wonderful, peated elixir from the Highlands." Hannah waggled the flask for emphasis. "Who wouldn't wish for some?"

"It might be best if you both weren't arguing," Matthew interjected quietly. "Charlotte is losing more blood than I would like, and I must work fast."

"I'll take a sip," Charlotte said hastily as she reached for the whiskey with her uninjured arm. If the liquor would alleviate some of the pain, she'd gladly down it, no matter how pungent.

Her first swallow triggered a coughing fit. The liquid burned down her throat, and her upper arm stung from the involuntary movement of her body. The second sip went down a trifle better, as did the third.

"How do you like it?" Hannah asked cheerfully, as if they were in the coffeehouse trying one of Sophia's creations instead of jammed into a secret room with Charlotte's blood dripping onto the rough-hewn floor. "Isn't whiskey fiercely delicious?"

"Would you like my honest opinion?" Charlotte asked after she managed another fiery swig.

"Oh, most definitely," Sophia said.

Charlotte still tried to answer as diplomatically as possible. "I must admit to preferring champagne."

Sophia grinned. "Don't we all?"

"Not me," Hannah shook her head. "I don't want ethereal drinks. The bolder the better."

Charlotte took another mouthful, and it caused her to splutter. "Bold is one description for it."

"The more you drink, the more you'll like it," Hannah said sagely.

A pleasant warmth kindled in Charlotte's stomach and slowly spread through her body, making her think of immersing herself in a hot, freshly drawn bath. A sweet haze descended, and despite the circumstances, Charlotte giggled suddenly. "I do believe you are right, Hannah. Whiskey can be exceedingly delightful."

Chapter Nineteen

For the entire carriage ride to Tavish's estate, Charlotte had been staring at Matthew with what he could only describe as dreamy eyes. She was, of course, entirely pickled by the whiskey Hannah had given her. But still...

Her gaze moved languidly over his face, lingering first on his eyes. Next, it traced his jawline, looped around what he assumed were his ears, bounced over the flyaway pieces of his queue, and finally returned to his eyes.

As Charlotte thoroughly studied his irises, her lips spread into a soft, beckoning smile that caused the most vibrant sensations to riot through Matthew. The iridescent sparks only intensified when her lavish attention latched on to his mouth, because then she pursed hers as if in preparation for a kiss.

Matthew's body had grown from warm to burning hot, and he was sorely afraid it might begin reacting in other, more inappropriate, ways. His heart quickened into a rhythm so sweet that it almost pained him with its honeyed force. Hope too—the fickle mirage—bloomed inside him as he dared to imagine that Charlotte's reaction was not some passing, spirit-induced fancy, but a true affection.

The fact that Charlotte had risked her life to save his only compounded Matthew's wishful longing and further muddled his feelings. He hated that she had been wounded saving him, but he also felt immensely grateful. He was more than a little in awe over Charlotte's bravery—and the fact her courage had protected him. Her fierce strength, hidden under so many layers of refinement, had been one of the things that had always drawn him to her.

And now his want had transformed into raw need.

Unfortunately, or maybe fortunately, they were not alone. The tipsy Charlotte was wedged between the Wick cousins while Matthew, with Pan perched on his shoulder, sat on the opposite bench. Beside him lounged Tavish, who had rushed to London after receiving a message about the trouble with the dragoons. Tavish had decided that the safest course of action was to travel to his estate rather than deposit a drunken, injured Charlotte at her parents' home in the middle of the night. Hannah had sent a message to Alexander, telling him to arrange things so it appeared that Charlotte was staying at Lady Calliope's.

Judging by the amused look on Hannah's face and the curious one on Sophia's, the Wick cousins were clearly aware of Charlotte's keen interest. Matthew hadn't hazarded a glance at Tavish in a long while, but his mentor was holding himself stiffly…as if he was desperately trying not to laugh.

Suddenly, without warning, Charlotte leaned forward…or rather she swayed vaguely in Matthew's direction and then tipped over. Luckily, Hannah and Sophia caught her. Charlotte seemed oblivious to the fact she had almost tumbled onto the floor of Tavish's well-sprung carriage. Instead, she stared up at Matthew, her expression like that of a blissful sprite.

"Your eyes are a marvel, Matthew." She slurred her words slightly as she unsteadily jabbed a finger in his direction. Even though she mashed some syllables together and hung on to others too long, her overall elocution was remarkably clear.

Heat, embarrassment, and concern rushed through Matthew. Although a part of him felt flattered, Matthew worried that

Charlotte would have been mortified if she had been fully cognizant of what she was saying.

"That is very kind of you, Lady Charlotte." Matthew made his voice polite and exceedingly neutral. "Yours are marvelous as well, but you might wish to shut them. You should rest after your injury and stitches."

Charlotte, however, did not seem to hear. Still pointing at him, or at least in his general direction, she continued, "I have no earthly idea how gray eyes can seem so, so, so very warm. Sparkly warm. Yuletide warm…"

Charlotte trailed off as if searching for the right word. Suddenly, she gave a silly grin and said triumphantly, "Just warm."

"Warm!" Pan squawked in a loud cackle.

Tavish's shoulder scraped against Matthew's as the man tried to smother his laughter. He was not successful. A strangled chortle escaped him.

Charlotte bobbled in his direction, her face scrunched, her voice slightly cross. "But aren't his eyes snuggly? Just look at them!"

Sophia gently patted Charlotte's shoulder. "Perhaps you should sleep. Matthew is right. You've had an eventful day, and he is a physician. It is wise to listen."

"All right," Charlotte agreed with a grin. She yawned like a Scottish kit before burrowing back into the squabs. Her eyelids fluttered closed. Within seconds, her head lolled against Hannah's shoulder, and a tiny snore escaped her.

At first, Matthew did his best to look anywhere but at Charlotte, especially with every other occupant of the carriage scrutinizing him. Pan resettled on Matthew's head and bent to stick his amber eye in front of Matthew's. Despite the parrot and the unwanted attention, Matthew could not help but occasionally glance at Charlotte—quick peeks that only caused his heart to swell more.

Thankfully, no one spoke, giving Matthew time to unravel why

Charlotte had chosen to fling herself between him and a lead ball. Both his heart and his brain seemed too afraid to hope for what the answer could be.

Matthew was still shying away from the obvious but impossible conclusion when the carriage pulled up at Tavish's estate. Hannah signaled for him to carry Charlotte, who remained fast asleep. It might not be entirely proper, but both Hannah and Sophia were there as some sort of chaperones. Besides, Tavish and the people he employed would never even whisper about this night.

Even with Matthew's forearms burning from where he'd scraped them during his escape from the goat, Charlotte felt deceptively fragile, a weight much less than some of the animals that he hauled in crates. She was not delicate, though, but fiercer than the wildest panther.

Charlotte curled against his chest. Every muscle lining Matthew's rib cage seized with tenderness and the need to protect— nay, not just to protect but to shelter. To care for her. Not just physically, but in a way much, much more encompassing.

They made an odd procession as they trooped through the stately manor. Tavish took the lead while Matthew followed with Charlotte in his arms and Pan still perched like an absurd feathered cap on his head. Hannah and Sophia made up the rear.

After two sets of stairs, Matthew was feeling a slight strain in his back when they finally reached a well-appointed guest bedroom. Matthew turned sideways and inched through the open door, careful not to bump Charlotte's head or feet. Pan whistled in annoyance as his lime-green crown passed under the frame. Hannah and Sophia bustled behind them. Tavish, however, lingered in the hallway, presumably to give Charlotte a semblance of privacy.

Just as Matthew gingerly lowered Charlotte onto the featherbed, Pan shrieked, "Banshee!"

Charlotte's eyelids snapped open. She blinked several times, clearly trying to gather her senses. The light from the Wick cousins' candles illuminated her irises, revealing that a semblance of lucidity had returned.

"Oh, we've arrived at Mr. Stewart's." Charlotte stretched like a lynx.

Matthew tried exceedingly hard not to notice how the action pulled down her already fashionably low-cut bodice. When she hissed in pain, though, all other thoughts but concern fled his mind.

"You must be careful not to move your arm too much," Matthew instructed. "It is best not to take off the sling I've placed it in."

"How are you feeling?" Sophia asked Charlotte.

"Sore…and also fuzzy—like my head is encased in wonderfully springy cotton fluff," Charlotte reported.

"The latter would be from the whiskey," Hannah said matter-of-factly.

"Banshee!" Pan screamed.

Charlotte carefully turned her head in the direction of the bird, and her mouth stretched into a silly grin. "Ooooooh, are you escorting Pan to see his monkey-love?"

"Ban-sheeeeee!" Pan bellowed even louder than before.

Matthew could feel the parrot bobbing up and down on his head. His talons seemed to dig a wee bit deeper with each demanding bounce.

"I am afraid I don't have a choice," Matthew sighed.

"I want to come and see their reunion," Charlotte announced as if this were the most obvious decision to make after being shot and then becoming inebriated…or, upon further consideration, the intoxication might be the reason for her sudden unbridled enthusiasm.

"You should rest," Matthew told her. "You can see them in the morning."

Charlotte pouted, an expression he had never witnessed on her face even during their childhood. Clearly, she was still more than a little tipsy. "But I witnessed the very beginning of their courtship. I wish to observe the next chapter."

"Banshee. My love!" Pan crowed, not improving the situation.

With the air of a military commander, Hannah patted the mattress. "Lie down, Cousin. I promise Pan and Banshee's ardor will not have cooled by the morrow. Listen to Matthew. He is well versed in injuries like yours and how to care for them."

"But—"

Hannah gave the eiderdown padding another much more fearsome whack. Wide-eyed, Charlotte glanced at her cousin and studied her unyielding expression. Charlotte heaved out a childish sigh and dramatically flopped back before emitting a squeak of pain.

Matthew immediately inspected her bandage for signs of bleeding, but Hannah was not so solicitous. "That is exactly why you need to stay abed."

Charlotte wrinkled her nose, but she did not otherwise protest. Instead, she wiggled down into the soft bedding.

When Matthew was certain that Charlotte had not ripped a stitch, he quickly made his goodbyes. There was so much he wanted to say to her but not in front of an audience and definitely not when her decision-making was impaired by alcohol. He certainly did not wish to pry secrets from her that she would not otherwise tell.

"Ban-sheeee!" Pan cried out irritably, digging his talons into Matthew's scalp.

"We're going to her. I promise!" Matthew pushed open the front door of Tavish's mansion and headed down the gravel path to the orangery.

"Banshee!" Pan shouted into the night, clearly not satisfied with Matthew's promises.

"Shhh! You'll not only wake up the entire household but all the students in the dormitories."

The parrot, however, would not be guilted. He maintained his ridiculous screeching even when Matthew entered the glasshouse. Only after Matthew began lighting the tapers set in the corners of the building did Pan's tone change from demanding to adoring. A rustle of leaves overhead indicated that Banshee heard them. Matthew turned in the direction of the noise, and sure enough, the soft candlelight illuminated the monkey's pale little face peeking out from behind a large frond.

Banshee's lips curled back to show her toothy, loving grimace. Pan made an appreciative sound. Then with a flap of lime-colored wings, the avian joined his monkey sweetheart.

Matthew's matchmaking duties complete for the evening, he turned back to the candles with the intent of extinguishing them. It had been a long, long, long day and night. He wanted nothing more than to head to the bedchamber that he used whenever staying on Tavish's estate. He had just started to blow on the first flame when a soft voice stopped him.

"Don't snuff out the candles. Not yet."

Matthew's body somehow simultaneously froze and warmed. He spun on his heels and then stood rooted to the heated floor.

Charlotte.

She still wore the dress he'd had to cut, the sliced-off sleeve a visceral reminder of her bravery. The raw-edged sable fabric contrasted with her pale flesh, making the delicate skin appear almost luminescent in the flickering candlelight.

Matthew's breath stuck in his windpipe, creating a painful pressure. He tried to swallow it, but the slide of his muscles only made the lump worse.

Charlotte glided in his direction, her gait not as elegant as usual and perhaps even a wee wobbly but not dangerously unsteady. When she reached his side, she smiled at him. Matthew's heart pitched.

"We should not be here, Charlotte," Matthew said softly. "You need rest."

"Pish!" Charlotte waggled her hand as she swayed. Fortunately, she righted herself before he had to touch her tempting form. "My arm is wounded, not my leg."

"You've also imbibed hard spirits, which I have a feeling is a first for you," Matthew pointed out, hoping that he didn't sound like a complete ass, explaining things she was capable of deducing on her own.

"Whiskey is a new drink for me," she admitted. "It does inspire a pleasant, buoyant feeling, doesn't it? Rather freeing. It's funny. Champagne may have bubbles, but it is whiskey that makes you bubbly."

"I do not wish to take advantage of your feelings of liberty," Matthew said solemnly.

Charlotte giggled and then immediately stopped. "I did not mean to laugh at you. It is just that you are so eminently trustworthy."

A soft emotion rushed through Matthew. Did he have Charlotte's trust? That seemed like a kind of miracle.

"Of course, I would never hurt you, Charlotte, but I don't want you to betray confidences to me that you might not otherwise wish to share." Matthew tried to make her understand.

Again, that whisp of a grin floated across her face, and it seemed to harken all his senses. The perfumed, floral air of the hothouse suddenly seemed even sweeter, heavier, and warmer. He could hear the pounding of his own heart over the chittering monkeys.

"You are not worried about the impropriety of us being together?" Charlotte asked.

"Mr. Stewart's servants are beyond discreet. If someone does notice us, they will never speak of it. Your reputation is safe."

Charlotte's expressive lips pulled downward at the last sentence. "I very much wish that I did not have to care about my reputation. It is exceedingly bothersome."

Matthew chuckled. "It was a relief when I destroyed mine by becoming a physician."

"It is not precisely the same." Charlotte scrunched her face in concentration for a few beats. Then her expression smoothed as the words apparently came to her. "My flawless 'moral' perfection is the sum and total of my worth in Society. Without it, I have utterly no value, no use. No longer suited for breeding or for motherhood. A tarnished, soiled thing."

The brutality of her words struck Matthew. He'd always understood the precariousness of a lady's position, but he had never considered it with such unvarnished harshness.

"You are not your reputation, Charlotte," Matthew said, barely realizing that he had not used 'Lady' before her name. "You are a wonderful, courageous, witty, intelligent person. Hell, you are the hero who stepped in front of a lead ball to save me!"

"All good traits." But even as Charlotte seemed to agree, her mouth twisted with irony, and she added, "For a man. His honor includes the things that you just ascribed to me, but a woman's is her meekness, humility, and above all, her virginity. Often what is seen as a virtue in a fellow is cast as a sin in a miss."

Matthew opened his mouth but nothing emerged. He scrambled to find the right words to convey the gross unfairness of it all.

"But as I have learned tonight, I am more fortunate than others of my sex," Charlotte continued before Matthew could speak. "Being born a lady, I can use my virtue as a weapon, to bend others to my will as they try to protect me. I am kept as a beautiful, caged bird with my needs provided for. I do not have to make my way in the world by performing the very actions that the world scorns women for—to take up positions that people hold as lesser simply because women typically execute those tasks. As long as I stay pretty, speak quietly upon command, and otherwise remain silent, I am esteemed and cosseted."

"Your very spirit has always captivated me." Matthew grabbed the hand of her uninjured arm and squeezed it tightly. He forgot to hide his admiration in his need to demonstrate that she was much more than her virtuous reputation. "The way you command a room with your presence, your active mind, and, yes, even your kindness impress me."

Charlotte swayed into him and almost overset them both. Matthew instinctively wrapped his free arm around her body to prevent them from crashing to the floor. Charlotte gazed at him, her green eyes drenched with a yearning he had never even hoped to imagine that he could inspire in her.

"Could you kiss me?" Charlotte asked. "Not because it is proper or improper, but simply because I want to kiss you?"

Matthew's heart seemed to still and then vibrate. Emotion broke through him in sharp but sweet shards. He wanted to say yes, to dip his mouth to hers, to taste—nay, to drink from her lips.

"I can't." The words ripped from him in a guttural groan.

Charlotte eased back, hurt flashing over her delicate features. The sight of her pain caused the splinters inside Matthew to explode into even smaller slivers.

"You do not fancy me?" Charlotte's voice was shocked and heartbreakingly unsure.

The truth tore from the depths of Matthew with a force he was powerless to stop. "I have esteemed you since I first laid eyes upon you in the foyer of your parents' house. You were wearing a pale blue silk dress, and you came racing down the stairs to embrace your brother. You were so full of life that you made something in me come alive—and that part of me has lived for you ever since."

Swounds. Had he just said that? He sounded like a besotted jester spouting some overly poetic nonsense.

Charlotte didn't laugh. Instead, her eyes widened, and her mouth formed a perfect *o.* Somehow, she managed to look even more kissable than she had just moments before, but Matthew held himself perfectly still, his heart galloping, his flesh prickling, his breathing harsh. The sensations deepened as he waited for Charlotte to fully comprehend his confession.

A brilliant, gorgeous smile bloomed over her face as the rest of her countenance brightened with an inner light. Charlotte laughed—throaty and full-bodied. Her uninjured arm looped around his neck, and she gently pulled him closer.

"Now you really must kiss me." Her voice was as rich and intoxicating as her mirth.

Matthew's lips hovered above hers, a hair's breadth apart. But he did not move. Instead, he moaned out a promise, forgetting the differences in their stations, their widely divergent social spheres, and even the ever-present threat of his brutish brother.

"Tomorrow," Matthew rasped out. "If you still want me to kiss you tomorrow, then I will."

Charlotte danced away from him, once again reminding him of an impish pixie. She paused on the threshold of the glasshouse, her emerald eyes glowing greener than any of the lush plants surrounding her. "Be here. Ten o'clock. Pray do not be tardy."

Then Charlotte disappeared into the darkness. Matthew did not follow. Tavish had men guarding the estate, and she would be safe on the walk back to the main house. Instead, he sank down onto a stone bench and stared out into the night, his body, his mind, his very soul shaken.

What had just happened? Would Charlotte even remember their encounter tomorrow? How much would she regret if she did?

One thing was certain. Matthew was going to be in this very hothouse at ten o'clock sharp—no, make that a quarter to ten.

Chapter Twenty

Charlotte awoke in an ornately carved bed that was most definitely not her own. As she lay staring up at the canopy, she tried recalling the details of the previous night. Her sore, stiff arm provided a poignant reminder of the encounter with the dragoons. Her memory began to get fuzzy, however, right at the point Hannah had placed the flask under her lips.

Flashes came slowly. The carriage ride to Tavish's. Matthew watching her with such solemn worry. Laughter. Pan screeching about Banshee. The moonlit walk to the orangery.

Suddenly, the staccato images smoothed into a harmonious, steady stream. Her conversation with Matthew, the almost kiss, his confession—they all flooded back, the edges misty and dreamlike but otherwise clear.

Charlotte waited for the hot flush of embarrassment, but it did not come. Not even the faintest whisp. She had asked a person who she desired to kiss her. It was not wicked or wanton or even forward. A man would not be faulted for making his longing known. Why should she? Charlotte was tired of false propriety, and she was done with Society dictating what her emotions should be. Instead, thrills shot through Charlotte—glorious and full of exuberant possibilities.

I have esteemed you since I first laid eyes upon you in the foyer of your parents' house. The memory of Matthew's hoarse, throaty voice caressed Charlotte. Delightful chills coursed freely down her body. Reaching behind her back with her injured arm, she snagged one of the fluffy pillows and hugged it tightly against her chest. Although Charlotte had never been one for squealing, a happy squeak erupted from her. The sound filled the quiet room, and Charlotte squeezed the eiderdown even tighter.

The enormity of Matthew's admission struck her. He didn't just fancy her now. He had. For years. Over an entire decade.

It occurred to her that ten years was a long period to desire someone. They had spent much of that time apart. A tweak of concern pricked Charlotte's bliss. She was accustomed to people only seeing the facade that she presented. They admired her outward glitter but knew nothing—and frankly cared nothing—for what lay inside. Apart from Alexander and a few friends like Calliope, no one wished to see Charlotte's true self. Had Matthew crafted her into some sort of an ideal? Had he actually fancied her for years or who he dreamed her to be?

Charlotte laughed shakily at the dismal thought. Here she was tearing apart Matthew's feelings, when she had not even had a chance to fully explore her own attraction to him. Staying abed woolgathering would resolve nothing. She needed to see him again...and soon.

Ten o'clock. Her parting words to Matthew echoed in Charlotte's mind.

Goodness, what was the time? Between the alcohol she'd imbibed, the late-night activities, and her injury, there was no telling how long she had slept.

Charlotte bolted upright and hissed at the sharp pain in her left arm. Ignoring the spasm, she tore back the bed-curtains with her right hand. Sunlight streamed into the room from a large window. Charlotte bounced to her feet looking frantically for a clock. To her surprise and relief, one with a delicate porcelain face hung on the wall, cheerfully ticking away. It was a statement to Mr. Stewart's wealth that he had a timepiece in a mere guest room.

Quickly, Charlotte padded across the floor and checked the slender copper hands. It would be ten o'clock in less than fifteen minutes.

Sweet anticipation sizzled through her. As she turned to bolt from the room, she caught sight of her reflection in a rather large mirror, another display of Mr. Stewart's riches. But Charlotte barely noticed the gilt-covered curlicues that framed the shiny surface. She was too focused on herself. She looked a terrible fright, her hair hanging in wild clumps from her sagging coiffure. Any trace of makeup had rubbed away. What little fabric remained of her left sleeve dangled above the white bandages stained a light pink near the wound. Her dress was crinkled and rumpled. At certain angles, Charlotte could even detect the sight of dried blood staining the silk.

Goodness knew what had happened to her basket of clothes. Most likely, it had been left in Mr. Belle's hackney carriage. Charlotte had no choice but to meet Matthew looking like an atrocious mess...unless she opted to stay in her appointed room until fresh attire could be provided.

Charlotte tapped her foot as she considered her reflection. Then she watched as a catlike grin spread across her otherwise wane face. Why not? Why not appear just like this and stop trying to look perfect for one *un*shining moment.

The idea felt more scandalous than even an assignation in a hothouse. A laugh—bold and merry—burst from Charlotte. Before she could change her mind, she allowed the wild feeling to sweep her forward. Pausing only to don footwear, she sallied from the room and down the elegant hallways. By the time she reached the main garden promenade, she was practically running. She hadn't moved with such unrestrained quickness since childhood. She almost felt like a girl again, pounding off to a new adventure in the woods.

As Charlotte rounded the final bend, she could spy Matthew through the large, impressive windows. He sat patiently on a stone bench with a book open in his hands. She paused for a brief moment, watching this scholarly, heroic man who set her ablaze. He was so calm, so intellectual, but last night she had watched him fly across rooftops.

Her pace slower now, she quietly resumed walking. When she opened the orangery's door, a blast of perfumed warmth enveloped her. In the room to her left, monkeys chattered. Pan fluttered in and out of the tall palm fronds as he inspected Charlotte. Although he shot a menacing one-eyed glare in her direction, he otherwise seemed to accept her presence and quickly returned to his roost beside Banshee.

Apparently absorbed by his book, Matthew did not notice her entrance. Instead, he methodically turned a page.

Charlotte was about to announce her presence, but ten chimes suddenly rang. The clear sound surprised her as she realized that Mr. Stewart must have a clock tower installed on his estate.

When Matthew lifted his eyes, Charlotte was ready. She smiled at him and simply said, "It's ten o'clock. I'm here for my kiss."

The book dropped from Matthew's fingers just as the bells stopped. The thick tome made a faint thud, but Matthew didn't look down. His gray eyes remained riveted on hers.

He rose slowly, almost as if she were a wildcat that would scamper away if he moved too quickly. She tried smiling in encouragement, but his first step remained tentative. He took one more. Then another. Then a fourth. By the fifth, he walked with more confidence.

She stood near the doorway, waiting for him to come to her. His strides were rapid now. She could see his chest rising and falling as if he'd run a long distance instead of traversing only a few feet. Suddenly, she felt winded too, in a wonderful, heady way. Her chest hurt but with utter sweetness.

Matthew stopped in front of her, the toes of his shoes almost touching hers. Their body heat mingled in the already heavy air of the orangery. For a moment, neither spoke.

They simply looked.

Charlotte had never known a mere glance could carry so much meaning. Her skin tingled with an awareness she did not entirely understand, but she fully embraced. Emotions—molten and lovely— swirled in a lovely dance. Her heartbeat and her breathing seemed delightfully erratic, flitting here and there like iridescent butterflies in a beautiful fairy-tale dream.

"You are positive this is what you desire, Charlotte?" The rich undertones in Matthew's voice seemed just as sensual as the aromatic atmosphere of the glasshouse.

She reached for him with her right arm, cupping the back of his head. Half of his hair fell loose from his queue, a silky curtain against her hand. Unable to stop herself, she brushed her fingers through the smooth strands and then against the faint, scratchy stubble on his cheek. His eyelids fluttered shut at the contact, and she heard him inhale sharply.

"Most assuredly, Matthew." Her words sounded as bold as she felt, and her heart trilled.

Matthew moved his mouth…but not to her own. Instead, he first sought the palm she'd been holding against his cheek. The feathery touch sent pleasure shimmering down her arm. When his tongue darted out, she gasped, not from shock but delight. Her body quivered but not as it had last night. This tremor was wonderful.

Matthew's teeth scraped ever so slightly against her skin as he worked his way down to her wrist. When he licked the creases there, a deep moan escaped from Charlotte. She had never made such a sound in her life—she never thought herself capable of an utterance like that. But then she'd never realized that such maddening, sparkling yearning existed.

If her left arm had not been in a sling and tightly bound to her side, she would have flung it around Matthew's neck as well for balance. Matthew wrapped his arms about her. The lean muscles of his limbs pressed against her back, and suddenly she wanted to feel even more of his coiled strength. Just as she had the first time they'd reunited at the Black Sheep, she wanted to explore him—every well-shaped, delectable, sculpted inch.

Matthew's mouth finally pressed against hers, warm and urgent, matching the billowing need inside her. She had experienced stolen kisses before but nothing like this.

Their lips rubbed against each other, but even that pressure was not enough. Remembering how Matthew's tongue had created almost magical sensations throughout her entire body, Charlotte plunged hers inside his mouth. He gasped and pulled her closer. Encouraged, she plundered his mouth. Standing on her toes, she deepened their kiss. Feelings strummed through her, every piece of her vibrating with want and delight.

But she still needed more.

So, evidently, did Matthew. He hoisted her upward, and she instinctively tried to wrap her legs around his torso. Unfortunately, her skirts and undergarments made that impossible. Their lips still melded together, he carried her to the stone bench. It should have felt awkward or at least silly to have her feet dangling in the air as if she were floating, but all of her senses were preoccupied with the taste of Matthew, the feel of his body pressed against hers, the sound of his breathing, and even the fresh, clean smell of him.

As smoothly as Matthew had carried her across the orangery, their collapse onto the seat did not proceed as gracefully. As he bent to lower her, the voluminous fabric of her sack-back gown bunched awkwardly. Instead of compressing under the weight of her body, the extra fabric turned into a spring, propelling her toward Matthew. When he adjusted his position to catch her, his feet caught in her skirts.

He released her just as he tottered to a heap. Already off-balance, Charlotte toppled face-first. She landed smack on top of Matthew but with their bodies perpendicular to each other. Her decolletage was smushed against his forearm, while her lower half was draped over his chest.

Although she used her uninjured right arm to stop her fall, the impact still caused a ripple of pain. The wound had felt worse, but she couldn't stop a hiss. Matthew instantly sat up to check her arm, but given their position, his nose nearly touched her posterior.

A giggle bubbled from Charlotte, and she didn't even try to stop her mirth. Between peals of laughter, she managed to huff out, "I…am…fine."

"Are you absolutely certain?" Matthew asked. "Perhaps I should inspect your injury."

The giddiness made Charlotte bold. "At the moment, I would prefer an entirely different kind of examination."

Matthew's eyes widened, making them appear even more silvery. He looked so stunned that she laughed even harder. Finally, he joined her, his chuckles a deep contrast to her lighter ones. But the sounds harmonized into glorious crescendos of joy.

"This was not exactly how I envisioned the ending of our first kiss," Matthew confessed, his voice crackling with amusement and happiness. "But I must say I like sharing a chuckle with you."

His words sobered Charlotte as that odd combination of excitement and concern struck once again. She could only hope that it had been the real her that he'd been fantasizing about. Charlotte did not want to live up to some perfect version of herself that would come with expectations as confining as her parents' dictates.

"Tell me about those imagined embraces," Charlotte said, making her voice low and throaty as she rearranged herself to sit next to him on the floor. Her question was part flirtation, part subtle inquiry into how he had viewed her for all those years.

Matthew's face flamed. He nervously clambered to his feet and awkwardly offered her his hand as if they hadn't been plastered to each other only moments prior. Normally, she found his shyness endearing, but now she hoped it wasn't a sign that he had imagined her to be absolutely flawless. He gestured for her to take a seat, and she complied, smoothing her skirts nervously. Her worries dimmed slightly when he joined her, the side of his body flush against hers. She leaned her head against his shoulder tentatively, and he did not pull away.

"You needn't be alarmed," Matthew told her softly, obviously misinterpreting whatever disquiet he sensed from her. "They were innocent daydreams—sweet kisses, perhaps a minuet or two."

Charlotte didn't mind sweet, but she did not want innocent. She was tired of being treated like a Meissen figurine. She wondered how Matthew would react if she did not embody the ingenuous, virtuous miss.

"Mine were not," she said as she snagged the edge of his cravat.

"Pardon?" Matthew's voice cracked a bit, and the tips of his ears turned a deep scarlet.

"My fantasies about you were not innocent." Charlotte tugged on the knots of the cloth, unloosening it.

Matthew did not stop her. He glanced down, studying her busy fingers with wide-eyed wonderment. When his gaze returned to hers, he did not appear chiding and definitely not morally outraged. In fact, he looked adorably smitten.

"You've had fantasies about me?" Matthew asked.

Charlotte gently pulled on his neckerchief. The silk unfurled slowly, just in time to reveal his deep swallow. His throat muscles convulsed. Charlotte lightly placed her fingertip on his tightened Adam's apple. She drew a faint line down to the top button of his waistcoat and gave it a light tap.

"When I saw you in the Black Sheep, I noticed your physique had changed...strengthened since I'd last laid eyes on you. I found myself wondering what was underneath all of your starchy layers." She fiddled meaningfully with the thin circle of brass. Matthew's gaze swept downward. With his throat exposed, it wasn't hard for Charlotte to detect his gulp.

Heady anticipation pressed down upon her, thicker than even the humid air of the hothouse. Charlotte held still, hoping that Matthew would not reject this side of her—that he viewed her as a woman, not as a precious prize.

"I am yours to study." Matthew's voice sounded like raw, splintered wood, and the roughness slid across Charlotte's body with a delicious friction. She shivered and fumbled with the button. Matthew did not try to assist her—he simply watched, allowing her to explore him at the pace she chose. His relinquishment of control caused a burst of tender excitement to explode inside Charlotte. Her fingers clenched around the smooth brass, and she involuntarily pulled. The threads popped. She was so startled that she jerked her arm back, sending the button sailing through the air.

It hit the floor with an inordinately loud *ping.* Charlotte followed the flashing piece of metal with her eyes as it bounced in a wild pattern over the terra-cotta tile floor. Another helpless giggle escaped as she realized she was literally tearing the clothing off Matthew.

"Don't worry," he said softly in her ear. "I am perfectly capable of sewing it back on. I am exceedingly skilled with a needle."

Delighted by his response, she turned back to him with an arched brow. "What else are you talented at?"

"My pursuits are generally scholarly, but I am hoping that may be changing." Matthew's words were an endearing combination of bashfulness and flirtatiousness.

Charlotte discovered that her hands had steadied. This time she could have made short work of unbuttoning his waistcoat, but she drew out the process. Their breathing became increasingly ragged as they closely watched more and more of the white lawn of his shirt appearing. When his waistcoat hung open, Charlotte pushed back the layers of his outer garments and spread her hand over his chest. Only the thinnest of linen separated her palm from his flesh. She could feel his heat, the contours of his muscles, and the shallow dip and swell of his rib cage as he breathed. A marvelous, hot, slick emotion spiraled through her, and she felt almost as if she were spinning. She glanced upward to find him gazing downward, her own frenetic emotions reflected in his silvery eyes. The obsidian shards around his pupils glittered with intensity.

Their mouths crashed together. Want met want with an incendiary blast. If she'd felt caught in a whirl before, she was now being spun into the air, the tempest within and without. Beneath her fingers, she could feel the thud of his heart that matched the increasingly maddening tempo of her own. Their internal rhythm drove the kiss, and their upper bodies began to move in time with the wildness of their pounding blood.

They became lost in each other, their world concentrated down to the sliding of lips, the intertwining of eager tongues, the roving of hands. Bliss and magic. Wonder and delight. Passion and need.

They kissed until a loud—very loud—throat clearing, as if the creator of the noise had been making it for a while now and increasing the volume each time.

Charlotte jerked, but poor Matthew sprang. He leapt with the might of a cat, but unfortunately, not with its grace. His left knee whacked against the stone seat with a resounding crack. He bobbled and somehow managed not to pitch over the bench entirely. He did, however, thump back down on the marble slab surface with enough force that he emitted a rather pained *ooooof.*

"Are you all right?" Charlotte asked.

"Aye." Matthew had to audibly squeeze the word out, but he did not appear to be sorely injured.

In unison, Charlotte and Matthew slowly turned to face the throat clearer. Charlotte half hoped that Pan had learned how to make the human-like sound. Unfortunately, Charlotte's gaze did not land on a certain glowering, lime-green parrot but rather on her brother, her decidedly uncomfortable-looking brother.

"I beg both of your pardons, but I tried opening and shutting the door with a good deal of enthusiasm." Alexander seemed torn between amusement and embarrassment. "It seems that even several bangs were not enough to disturb your—erm...perhaps it would be most prudent if I just end the sentence there."

"That would be for the best," Charlotte said shortly as she struggled to find her own composure. At least Alexander did not appear outraged, nor had he devolved into overprotectiveness. For her own part, she felt terribly self-conscious but not guilty.

Alexander scratched his head with the hand not holding the handle of his cane. "After Hannah's cryptic message last night, Tavish sent for me this morning. He said you'd been injured, Lottie, but that you were safe now."

"That is correct," Charlotte said primly. If Alexander wanted to skirt around any awkward conversation, she would gladly play along.

"Tavish also asked me to fetch the both of you. He thought it was best that we discuss as a group the full story of what led to last night's adventures." Alexander was still prattling, but he seemed to have regained some of his typical jovial equilibrium. "When Lottie wasn't in her room, Hannah suggested that the two of you may have gone to the orangery to see Pan and Banshee, so I came here."

"I—I…well…I—I." Matthew stumbled incoherently over his words, and Charlotte wished she could grab his hand to soothe him. But given the circumstances, she was fairly certain it would have the exact opposite effect.

Alexander became uncharacteristically grave as he regarded them. "As I have told you both on separate occasions, I could not be happier than for a match between my best friend and my sister."

The bubble of happiness that rose in Charlotte quickly burst upon his next words.

"But you must be cautious. Charlotte is as good as engaged to Lord Hawley, and until we extricate her from the impending betrothal, you must be very discreet. If the viscount learns about your mutual affection, he'll devise the cruelest punishment possible."

A chill ripped through Charlotte, shredding all the happiness dancing through her. Between the events of last night and this morning, she had somehow managed to expel Hawley from her mind. She hadn't even thought of him when she'd rushed to meet Matthew. Considering she was not technically engaged and the proposed union was not her choice, she felt no remorse. But she did worry about the peril she'd unthinkingly unleashed.

"I promise nothing like this will happen again until we have everything properly sorted," Matthew said quickly.

Although Charlotte knew that Matthew was making a prudent vow given the circumstances, she felt a keen sense of loss. She wanted to embrace Matthew again. To kiss him. To hold him. Perhaps to do even more—a more that she could not fully verbalize, but that she instinctually yearned for.

A congenial grin touched Alexander's lips, and he looked more like his usual self. "You shouldn't refrain entirely. Just do not engage in too much exploration."

Alexander paused for effect. "It would be very wise if you make sure in the future not to meet in a building comprised mostly of glass windows."

"I shall endeavor to keep that in mind," Charlotte promised, making her voice as light as her brother's.

But despite her sibling's attempt at levity, a heaviness now lay upon Charlotte's spirits. She had allowed Matthew's nighttime heroics to distract her from her own mission. Until she could irrevocably tear herself from Hawley's grasp, she must remain on guard...and not just of her person but also of her heart. Even as that warning churned through her mind, she knew she would not be able to stay away from Matthew. Prudence be damned.

Chapter Twenty~One

M atthew sat stiffly in a silk-cushioned chair in Tavish's favorite sitting room for entertaining guests. He wished he could draw some comfort from the familiar surroundings where he'd spent many agreeable hours discussing science.

Unfortunately, the insertion of Charlotte into another of Matthew's haunts reinforced his sense that everything had changed. She had thoroughly and completely upended his entire existence.

Even half an hour later, his body still felt the effects of her caresses. His skin prickled as if awakened from a long slumber. His heart had not yet settled back into its normal beat. Instead, it remained erratic and as excitable as a young hare in spring. And his mind…well…his mind kept straying back to the amorous encounter despite the current presence of not only Charlotte's brother but of Hannah, Sophia, and Tavish as well.

Matthew tried to remind himself of Alexander's warning. A romance with Charlotte, no matter how innocent, would make her a target for Hawley's vile vengeance. Even without the very real specter of his brother's violence, Matthew knew he wasn't a proper match for Charlotte. Yet in the face of these facts, Matthew still could not help but imagine taking Charlotte into his arms again. Feeling her lithe form as she…

Swounds. He needed to focus on the conversation swirling around him and not on the woman perched less than a yard away.

"Now that we are all properly assembled and provided with appropriate refreshments, does anyone care to tell me how my twin came to have her arm in a sling?" Alexander asked the question with his typical good humor, the ankle of his bad leg propped on the knee of his good one. He looked like any gentleman of leisure, but Matthew knew that his best friend was concerned beneath the veneer of joviality.

"I was shot by a dragoon when he fired at Matthew who was leaping from rooftop to rooftop." Charlotte's face did not betray even the slightest hint of impishness, but Matthew could sense that she was enjoying shocking her brother. It was exactly how Alexander would relay such a story.

Charlotte's pluck soothed some of Matthew's guilt, replacing it with warm pride. He hated that he had dragged her into danger—however inadvertently—but it seemed that Charlotte was made of stern stuff.

Alexander's mien of nonchalance dropped as he bolted upright in his chair. His raised leg thumped to the ground with a resounding bang.

This was Alexander-the-athlete, ready to defend his sister against any foe.

"What?" Alexander demanded. "You were shot! Tavish's missive said you had a minor accident."

"Well, it is only a flesh wound. Matthew stitched it up very handily. Didn't you, Matthew?" Charlotte idly took a bite of a scone and winked impishly at Matthew over the pastry. Despite the seriousness of the situation, Matthew felt a bubble of mirth.

Alexander, however, remained unamused. Glancing at each of the room's occupants, he whirled back and forth in his chair like a well-engineered Swiss automaton. "Matthew needed to sew your flesh back together! And what is this about jumping on rooftops?

Have you all gone mad? What were you truly doing last night? Any of you?"

"I believe we were helping free children being transported to the Colonies. I am a little unclear on all the details." Charlotte took a sip of coffee.

"Are you telling me that you confronted dragoons, and you don't know exactly why?" Alexander folded his arms across his chest. "Can someone please make sense of this jumble?"

"I suppose we should commence at the beginning," Hannah said, her tone just as light as Charlotte's.

"Which one?" Sophia asked. "There are so many to choose from."

"Just start somewhere," Alexander ground out.

"Tavish. The tale opens with him," Matthew said, taking pity on Alexander. He paused to glance at his mentor. "That is, if you wish to tell the story, sir."

That succeeded in quieting the room. Hannah and Sophia knew some of Tavish's background but not nearly all of it.

Tavish's questioning blue eyes solemnly regarded Matthew. After all, their pasts intertwined in ways no one suspected.

Matthew nodded, feeling a sweeping sensation of relief that he could finally reveal years of secrets. He'd longed to confide in Alexander, but he hadn't wanted to needlessly endanger his best friend. Now though, Alexander had become a part of this and so had Charlotte. Half-truths imperiled them more than the full, unabridged story.

"My family were crofters on Matthew's father's estate in Scotland," Tavish explained. "Poor ones with cursed luck at farming. My father had tried his hand at soldiering but returned from fighting in the Colonies with ill health that left him bedridden. My mother tried her best to support me, my father, and my two grandmothers, but there was never enough bread to feed us. I started poaching as a wee lad—first with snares then with a cross-bow. One day, Matthew's mother caught me setting a trap when I was about seven. Instead of telling her new husband, the duke, she offered me a job at the manor house, making sure I was paid well enough to help my family. The duchess developed a maternal interest in me, teaching me to read and write. She cared a great deal about nature, and she taught me what she knew about the woods surrounding the estate. I believe that she was preparing for how she would instruct her children but—"

Tavish paused as he looked at Matthew, obviously seeking permission to continue. The next part revealed more about Matthew's past than it did about Tavish's. Yet it was critical to both their histories.

Matthew cleared his throat. He hated talking about his family, the way he'd been raised, but he needn't expose it all...just enough to connect the pieces of the tale. "My father believed in a rigid upbringing for his heirs, so he insisted that his own nursemaid from his childhood oversee most of the care for Hawley. The same happened with my second eldest brother. My mother hoped that since I would be the third in line that she might finally be allowed to play a more active role in my care, but she died shortly after I was born."

The last words fell from Matthew's mouth with an ease that he did not feel. It sounded so dry, so divorced from the devastating loss of what her love might have meant to his awful boyhood. The sentence did not hint at how his superstitious father had immediately blamed Matthew for her death and suspected him—an undersized babe—of being a changeling.

"I was able to speak with the duchess one last time before her passing." Tavish smoothly reentered the conversation. Unlike the others, he knew exactly what Matthew had left unsaid. "She asked me that I teach Matthew all that she had shown me—how to love the beauty of the natural world. I was kept on as part of the household staff, but when my attempts to teach Matthew about flowers and songbirds were eventually brought to the attention of the duke, I was dismissed without reference. Without means to care for my family, I again resorted to poaching."

"I shall never understand the aristocracy." Hannah shook her head in disgust. "That is absurd. You would think the duke would want his son to have the broadest education possible."

"Not from the poor son of a crofter," Tavish said swiftly.

Alexander and Charlotte nodded as if they understood, and to a great extent, they did. Alexander's family had outright rejected and punished him for his clubfoot, and Charlotte had lived a strict, highly regulated existence. But unlike what the twins believed, it wasn't just societal rules that had driven the old duke to fire Tavish, but his fears that Matthew was a fae. He'd believed that exposure to the natural world would further foster Matthew's innate dark magic.

"This time when I was caught hunting, I was arrested and sentenced to exile in the Colonies. The passage over was…brutal, disease filled, not something I wish to recall." Tavish's tone became both rough and rushed as the words seemed to squeeze from deep inside him.

Matthew's father—his family—had caused this pain. The duke, Hawley, and Matthew's middle brother, Henry, still condemned poachers, mere lads, to hard labor far from their homes. The guilt of that ate at Matthew. His family's mistreatment of their crofters had festered inside him since boyhood, long before he'd even learned of Tavish's plight.

Matthew had rejected that ill-begotten wealth when he—driven to help others instead of taking from them—had become a physician. But his efforts had always felt paltry in the face of all the harm that his relatives had caused. Then Tavish had offered him a more concrete way to counteract his family's sins.

"When I arrived in the New World," Tavish continued, "I was purchased by a Marylander with a tobacco plantation—or rather, he paid for my passage and in return I was obliged to serve his whims for fourteen years. But being an indentured servant was better than what the Black people toiling alongside me faced. They were and are trapped for their entire lives, and so are their children and their children's children. Laws give some protection to white indentured servants, not that my master paid any attention to them. I managed to escape the horrors. With my education, I made my fortune and invested in my own shipping company. When I returned to London, I decided to save boys in similar situations."

"Not only did he help free them, but he set up living quarters here on his premises," Matthew explained, feeling a rush of fierce pride and affection. "The printing shop was originally started as a way to teach the lads a useful trade."

"That's why there are so many people and outbuildings!" Charlotte practically bounced in her chair—an exuberant reaction that reminded Matthew of the girl she'd been when she'd run wild on her parents' northern estate. "I knew something was unique about them!"

"I have also established a more formal school that includes university-level learning but with a focus on practical skills rather than philosophical. There is more math and science than Greek plays studied here," Tavish added.

"He also accepts students who my mother and her crew save from slaver ships," Sophia added.

"Is that how you know each other?" Charlotte asked.

"No," Tavish chuckled. "I first met Sophia and Hannah when Brave Mary captured my flagship. I was on it at the time."

"Mother quickly discovered that Tavish not only had a policy of refusing to transport slaves or indentured servants but also sugar and tobacco," Sophia added. "He had several escapees from tobacco plantations aboard whom he was taking to England for their safety."

"She immediately saw that our interests aligned. Her pirating operation focuses on freeing Africans, but she also saves white indentured servants like her husband and brother-in-law. Brave Mary settled an island for freed slaves in the Caribbean, but some of the residents wish to earn their fortunes in big cities. She was already considering establishing a place in London that could serve as a safe haven for all peoples to gather."

"The Black Sheep!" Alexander gave his cane a thump. He swung toward Matthew, his usual jovial smile replaced by perfectly straight lips that did little to mask his hurt. "I cannot believe that you never breathed a word of this to me."

Guilt wormed through Matthew. "I wanted to tell you so many times."

"I forbade him," Tavish broke in with firm surety. "It was my first condition of hiring him on as a physician."

"What exactly did you do on those voyages?" Charlotte asked.

"I was the ship's surgeon, and I did conduct scientific expeditions into the interior, but I wasn't only gathering information on flora and fauna but the plantations as well." Matthew spoke carefully, loath to paint himself as some sort of valiant Robin Hood–esque hero.

"Where he helped free slaves and abused indentured servants," Tavish said.

"There were many locals who assisted," Matthew said stiffly. "I was merely a messenger."

Sophia snorted. "That is an understatement. Charlotte witnessed you practically flying through the sky last night. She is bright enough to realize you have a great deal of experience at evading danger."

Matthew really was a scholar. His occasional forays into sub-terfuge were the aberration. He didn't want Charlotte hoodwinked into seeing him as a romantic storybook hero. Fortunately, he knew the perfect way to divert the conversation.

"Why was Lady Charlotte with you and Hannah last night?" There had been no time for Matthew to ask the question when he'd been stitching Charlotte's wound. And last evening and this morn-ing in the hothouse, there were other more tantalizing concerns occupying Matthew's mind.

Sophia and Hannah quickly launched into the tale of how they'd rescued Charlotte from ruffians. Matthew was horrified to discover that she'd been trailing two of Hawley's minions through a rough section of Covent Garden.

"Why would you do something so bloody dangerous?" The question tore from Matthew's very being before he had a chance to temper his language.

"It is the only way to stop the betrothal. Your father is due back in little over a week, and I had to act," Charlotte explained, her voice laced with desperation.

Hannah made a harsh sound. "With the way you're investigat-ing, you're more likely to avoid the wedding by being dead."

"Hannah!" Sophia admonished. "You needn't be so harsh!"

Matthew flinched as he imagined Charlotte's lifeless body. He wanted to reach for her—to hold her, to reassure himself that she hadn't been harmed by the miscreants.

"My cousin is only telling the truth—although perhaps more colorfully than my nerves would like," Alexander broke in and then addressed his sister. "You need the frankness, Lottie. I told you not to approach Hawley. I promised I would look into it."

Matthew tried to wrestle back his fear. Logic. He needed to employ logic.

"Why are either of you endangering yourselves? Alexander

knows that I've been trying to find proof of Hawley's crimes for years. He is my brother. There may not be a lot of kinship lost between us, but I did grow up with him. I have the best chance of ferreting out his secrets."

To Matthew's shock, guilt flashed over the countenances of both Lovett siblings. The two immediately shared one of those "twin" looks that Matthew recalled from his summers at their parents' estate. The exchange had never made him feel so much like an outsider as it did now.

"I wasn't sure if you were part of his criminal activities," Charlotte admitted.

Unexpected pain serrated Matthew. "You believed…" He paused, glancing from one twin to another. "You both believed me capable…of…" He trailed off, unable to conjure the right description for the level of his brother's depravity.

"Not a willing participant," Charlotte quickly amended. "I thought maybe he had forced you to do something when you were young and has been blackmailing you into silence ever since."

Matthew did not want Charlotte to falsely see him as a dashing hero, but neither did he wish her to view him as some sort of sniveling coward. "If I had any proof that my brother killed people, I would not remain silent."

"I should never have doubted your character, but I could not afford to take any chances, Matthew. You were acting suspiciously, and you were hiding something. I wasn't entirely wrong, was I?" Charlotte asked.

Matthew once again battled back his emotions in an attempt to think rationally. Charlotte had every right to protect herself against the powerful Hawley. It wasn't that far-fetched to imagine that Matthew had been coerced by his brother to carry out crimes. Instead of feeling put out, Matthew should be relieved by Charlotte's caution. She'd need it to survive the viscount.

Until recently, Charlotte had little contact with Matthew. But he had spent literal years in Alexander's company.

"Did you truly suspect me of conspiring with Hawley?" Matthew turned toward Alexander, trying to keep raw accusation from his voice.

To his surprise, Matthew heard the same underlying indictment in Alexander's tone when he answered. "I found it extremely unlikely, but there was the matter of the necklace."

"I thought we resolved that!" Matthew protested.

"You still haven't shown it to me." Alexander crossed his arms, his expression uncharacteristically grumpy. "Nor did you explain how it came to be in your possession, although I may have an inkling now that I've heard about your rooftop leaping skills."

"Wait! You talked about the choker with Matthew? Why didn't you tell me?" Charlotte dropped her scone on her plate as she turned toward her brother.

"I was going to, but you never showed up at the Black Sheep because you were following criminals through the back alleys of London!" Alexander rarely raised his voice, but he did so now, his irritation palpable.

"What piece of jewelry are the three of you talking about?" Hannah asked.

Matthew found himself getting irritated too. Frustrated with all the mistrust, he reached into his inner pocket. Withdrawing the choker, he slammed it down on the table holding the scones and seedcakes. "This one—not that it is a bloody help in proving that Hawley murdered his late wife."

"May I interject for a moment?" Sophia asked in her pragmatic way. "It appears that the three of you have been investigating Hawley separately to keep the others safe. Wouldn't it be more prudent if you worked together starting with this choker? To me, collaboration seems less dangerous than keeping secrets and inadvertently working against each other."

Matthew forced his breathing to steady, just as he did before missions. He instinctually wanted to plead with Charlotte to stop pursuing Hawley and allow him to continue to trail his brother alone. But this wasn't his struggle for freedom. It was Charlotte's.

In as few words as possible, Matthew explained how he'd discovered the choker in Hawley's house in a cleverly hidden compartment. "I am certain that he is the one behind last week's ambush."

"So am I," Charlotte said. "The men who I followed yesterday were definitely the two who you fought, Matthew."

Instead of scolding Charlotte or letting fear take hold again, Matthew forced himself to only nod in agreement. "I suspected they might be when Hawley showed up at the Black Sheep. I wasn't certain though. But we unfortunately don't have any evidence proving the men attacked us or that they did so on my brother's orders. The necklace is the only concrete clue, but of what, I don't know. I checked it for engravings to help identify it, but there aren't any."

"I showed a drawing of it to my Society friends and even to Mr. Powys. No one recognized it, but Mr. Powys did say that it looks like it is from the Tudor era," Charlotte said.

"That may explain why I cannot find a maker's mark." Matthew nudged the onyx pendant with his forefinger. "This is the most unusual part. I've stared at the creature in the cameo from all angles, but I simply cannot identify it."

"Lion?" Charlotte offered.

"Badger," Alexander said. "Most definitely a badger."

"It looks nothing like a badger." Charlotte rolled her eyes at her brother.

"A misshapen dragon?" Hannah offered as she poked at the animal's nose. "Although this would be a rather smooshed snout."

"It could even be a poorly executed squirrel with a scrawny tail," Sophia said as she lifted the cameo to study it more closely. "Or an angry monkey."

"I vote for angry monkey since my badger suggestion was so rudely vetoed." Alexander sent his twin a miffed look.

Sophia sighed and laid the piece back down. "It is almost as if the artist was intentional in the crudeness. The carving is otherwise very finely done. It is remarkable how all the white was carved away from the black onyx, except for the creature itself."

Tavish reached for the choker next. Holding it in the light streaming from the window, he frowned.

"What is it?" Matthew asked.

"It is odd. It reminds me of rock carvings in Scotland that I used to play near as a boy." Tavish clicked his tongue off the top of his mouth as he rubbed his thumb over the relief. "It wasn't this image precisely but the style."

"How old are these etchings?" Charlotte asked. "Are they from the Tudor era as well?"

Tavish chuckled and handed the choker to Matthew. "Much older, I am afraid. Ancient—perhaps even before Roman times."

Charlotte suddenly straightened, her green eyes shining. "I know of someone who might be of assistance: Miss Georgina Harrington. We were debutantes together. She was fascinated with history—Roman, Norman, Anglo-Saxon. Why, I remember her trying to talk to Lord McAllister about some Pictish stones found on his land. He was so terribly bored, but I found her conversation fascinating."

"Do you think she is trustworthy?" Matthew asked.

"I do. She hasn't left her home in Essex for years, and she was the scholarly sort, hardly the kind to attract Hawley's attentions. But it might be faster to ask her cousin, Mr. Percy Pendergrast, who is an antiquarian. He's fast friends with Alexander and is often at the Black Sheep."

Alexander cleared his throat. "I would write to Miss Georgina Harrington."

"Why? Pendergrast seems like a good chap, and he's not close with my older brothers." Matthew studied Alexander closely. "Should I be more guarded around him?"

"Don't worry. He's not in league with Hawley." Alexander waved his hand, looking decidedly uncomfortable. "It is just…well…write to Miss Harrington."

"It has always struck me as odd that Mr. Pendergrast is an expert on ancient Roman relics. His interests have always been more of a sporting nature like Alexander's." Charlotte cocked her head.

"Do you think Miss Harrington is actually the one with the knowledge?" Sophia asked, leaning forward in interest.

"She would not be the first female intellectual to seek acceptance by pretending to be a male relative," Hannah said.

"Aaaaand this is not the mystery we are here to solve." Alexander clapped his hands together. "We should focus on devising a plan to unearth Hawley's worst secrets."

"Why don't we convene a team to discuss strategy, just as Tavish and I do before a complicated rescue?" Matthew suggested.

"We could just discuss it now," Hannah pointed out. "This is one of the safest places to talk."

Matthew shook his head. "We need to involve more players. Except for Charlotte, none of us have access to Hawley's elite circle. Some of his well-heeled cronies are friends with Lady Calliope's half brother. Lady Calliope might have an idea of how we can learn more about Hawley. Then, of course, there's George Belle and his invaluable system of carriages."

"Alun Powys would be a good addition too," Sophia added. "You and Tavish have not worked with him, but he has proved useful in some of our ventures. He also has a personal interest in your brother. One of Hawley's mistresses who died in a suspicious fire was a performer at Alun's playhouse. Alun also has connections with both hedonistic elites and lowborn criminals."

Matthew turned to Charlotte. "Do you agree with this proposal?"

Despite her torn dress and simple coiffure, Charlotte looked absolutely radiant. She did not need perfection to shine but confidence alone.

"I do. Let's reconvene at the Black Sheep after we've heard back from Miss Harrington," Charlotte said, her voice resolute.

.ℒ.

"Lottie requested that just the two of you ride in the second carriage." Alexander spoke softly as he lightly grabbed Matthew's arm. They were about to climb into Tavish's coaches for the ride back to London.

Surprised, Matthew swung his body to study his best friend. "It isn't proper."

Alexander snorted. "Nothing has been proper since my sister decided to race through London after two ruffians. If the Wick cousins or Tavish are inclined to tell tales—which I doubt any of them are—Lottie's reputation will already be ruined. A carriage ride hardly makes it worse."

"But what if someone recognizes us outside of the coffeehouse?" Matthew asked as an odd sense of something akin to panic gripped him. He wanted more time alone with Charlotte, yet the strength of his emotions, their emotions, unsettled him. He'd had no time to analyze the ramifications of their encounter in the hothouse.

"You'll be arriving in one of Tavish's unmarked coaches, and

Lottie still has her veil," Alexander pointed out. "My sister is well aware of any potential danger, and this is a risk she's willing to take."

Matthew glanced at the nondescript coach that he'd watched Charlotte enter. He nervously lifted his hand to his cravat to loosen the swath of fabric. "Do you really think this wise?" Matthew asked, more to himself than to Alexander, but his best friend answered anyway.

"Today's revelations aside, I have always regarded you as eminently trustworthy," Alexander said. "My sister is perfectly safe with you if that is what she desires."

A new kind of pressure settled on Matthew as he returned his attention to his best friend. "My omissions have not entirely broken your faith in me?"

Alexander rubbed the lion on top of his cane before he spoke. "I would be prevaricating if I did not confess to some hurt that you kept an entire secret life from me. Intellectually, I know you were only doing what Tavish asked and what you believed to be best, yet there is still a sting. I shall get over it, though, in due course."

Matthew huffed out his own breath. "I sympathize with your statement of knowing something academically but not emotionally. There is nothing, though, that can dint the friendship I feel for you."

Alexander delivered one of his easy boyish grins as he straightened to his full height. "You best conserve your mawkish mutterings for my sister. After all the novels she's read, she expects pretty words from a suitor."

Alexander winked and then headed whistling to the lead carriage, which held the Wick cousins and Tavish. The jaunty tune floated back toward Matthew, and he wished he could share his friend's joviality. Although he was relieved that he and Alexander had agreed they could move beyond the secrets Matthew had kept, he felt much less certain of his relationship with Charlotte.

Battling both trepidation and excitement, Matthew entered the rear coach. Charlotte had already pulled the curtains closed, but the light from the open door framed her perfectly. The decidedly wicked smile on her angelic face momentarily paralyzed Matthew's heart before the confused muscle began jumping about.

"This is only the second time I've planned an assignation. It is a bit rushed, but I did not know when the opportunity would present itself again." Charlotte winked, her green eyes sparkling with mirth and something even more intoxicating—want. "How am I doing?"

"Argh." He sounded like a strangled goat.

Charlotte, however, did not appear to mind his inelegant response. In contrast, it appeared to delight her.

"I shall take that as a yes," she laughed brightly. She reached up and tugged at his hands just as the carriage started.

Matthew pitched forward, nearly tumbling onto Charlotte's silk-covered lap. Fortunately, she released his fingers just in time to allow him to catch himself. His arms bracketed her slim body, his palms pressing into the plush, upholstered seat back. Only a scant inch separated their lips, their eyes on level with each other. With each intake of her breath, her breasts grazed against his chest, the softness teasing him. Their legs had become a hopeless tangle of limbs with her petticoats wrapping their calves together.

"Hmm, I am perhaps more talented at trysts than I even thought," Charlotte said and then pressed her lips against his.

Matthew's mind, which always seemed to churn out thoughts even when he wished to quiet it, went blank—or rather, not blank but utterly and completely saturated with Charlotte. The faint smell of rosewater on her skin. The heat rising from her body. The friction of her mouth against his. The feel of her fingers tangling in his hair. The slight weight of her uninjured arm resting on his back.

He lost himself in her entirely just as he had in the hothouse. His doubts melted into pure need. He stopped worrying about whether he was right for Charlotte and instead reveled in how right he felt wrapped in her arms.

Matthew had spent his youth in scholarly pursuits and much of his adult life at sea or in the wilds of the Americas, which had given him little time to woo women. Yet his inexperience with the opposite sex did little to inhibit his natural response to Charlotte. His ardor, so long confined, flowed freely into hungry caresses and deep, endless kisses.

Her sighs guided him like stars, telling him where to touch, where to linger, and where to tease. It was as if his heart were an astrolabe specifically designed for the sounds of her pleasure.

He moved his mouth from hers, trailing it across the delicate skin of her jaw. Her gasp ricocheted through him, and he swore his body trembled in resonance with hers. He loved exploring her smooth skin. Whenever a spot seemed to particularly delight her, he lingered, devouring her pleasure, making it both of theirs.

Her delicate fingers drifted over him, leaving glowing trails of sparks in their wake. They teased his scalp, then his back, next his forearms, and finally, his chest. Charlotte was diligent as a surveyor, her hands appearing to map every contour of him—as if she craved him as much as he did her.

Her hand tugged at his loose cravat as he explored the intriguing juncture between her neck and shoulder. Need pulsated through him, hot and messy and more powerful than any urge he had ever experienced before. Her hand slipped beneath his clothes and skimmed across his bare shoulders. The intimacy of the touch nearly undid him. She made a sound deep in her throat, and his cock, which he thought could not swell bigger, hardened even more.

She pressed against him, and he groaned. Driven by instinct, his body began to move against hers. Despite the need fermenting inside him, Matthew remained careful not to brush against her injured arm.

Charlotte tugged insistently at his layers of garments with her good hand. In a heat-filled trance, he obligingly shed each one—frock coat…waistcoat…linen shirt. In between each removal, his lips moved farther and more intimately down her skin. His mouth drifted to her shoulders as he followed the line of her collarbone. Her breaths became sharp, uneven sounds.

Her hand moved from his chest to his back, and she pulled him toward her. Arching her body sinuously against his, her fingers slid with delicious friction along the muscles near his lower spine. He groaned and then kissed the soft, delicate flesh of her breasts, still constrained by her stomacher. He couldn't just hear her heartbeat but could feel it. His profession was the study of human bodies, but this was no clinical examination. This was beyond science, beyond mere sinew, bone, and blood. There was something deeper. Something magical. Something transforming.

A rattling bump brought Matthew tumbling back to reality. Charlotte hissed in pain. Her hand flew from his back to rest on her sling.

"Did I hurt you?" Matthew asked, aghast.

"No." Charlotte gave a quick shake of her head. "It was the jolt from the carriage."

"I should have been more careful," Matthew said as he sat down beside Charlotte. He swore his body still vibrated like a tuning fork. "I daresay I stopped thinking entirely."

"So did I." Charlotte pressed against him, resting her head on his shoulder. She shifted to gaze at him, her green eyes shining. "I know it is risky being together, but it's so intoxicatingly thrilling."

Certainly, the description applied to Charlotte, but to him? Worry slivered through Matthew, and not just because of her mention of danger. Was the peril the main reason for her excitement, her attraction? Would she want plain, boring, studious him once she discovered that his life was more about scientific theory than rooftop capers?

"I generally prefer dull pursuits," Matthew blurted out.

Charlotte blinked and lifted her head. "Pardon?"

Matthew's face flamed when he realized how terribly clumsy his words had been. "I do not mean to say...that is...I liked the kissing, and I would very much like to do it again."

Charlotte grinned, her body once more relaxing against his as she cupped his face with her hand. "As would I."

"I meant that I am a scholar by nature and habit. What you witnessed last night was an aberration. I would not want you to assume that I was some sort of dashing romantic hero."

Charlotte tapped lightly against his chest, her face flushed with excitement. She had never appeared more beautiful to him. "I find you exceedingly dashing and romantic."

Oh, how Matthew wanted to bask in her words, but he could not. For both their sakes, but mostly hers. He would not lie to her. He gently grabbed her fingers and tried to make his gaze as serious as possible. "I assure you that I am not. My outward sheen of adventure will wear off, and you may find me and my quiet life very dull indeed. I am not one for balls or operas or even literary salons or musicales—even if I would be invited to attend. Most evenings when I am in London, you will find me reading dusty tomes or attending scientific lectures."

Hurt and insult flashed in Charlotte's emerald green eyes. "Do you really find me so shallow that you believe I would not enjoy comfortable nights by the fireside just reading, or so dim-witted that I would not understand lectures of a more learned bent?"

"Not at all!" Matthew gasped out, eager to make it clear that he was not intending to belittle her. "You are wonderfully intelligent and beyond thoughtful. Those are two traits that have always drawn me to you."

The insult in her green irises dimmed but did not entirely retreat. Desperate, Matthew encircled his hand with hers. "What I mean is—"

Before he could finish, the carriage drew to a stop. Matthew frantically tried to think of the right thing to say before they would need to disembark, but he was never good with words of the heart. As he scrambled to explain his messy emotions, Charlotte withdrew her fingers from his.

"We best put ourselves to right before we open the door—or Alexander does," she said quickly as she began straightening her bodice. "Knowing my brother, he could burst in any moment. Subtlety is not his strong point."

"Uhhh, no it is not," Matthew said, rather insipidly.

His chest seemed full to bursting with sentiments he wanted to share, but he was at an entire loss on how to express them. He wanted the best for Charlotte, even if it cost him everything.

Chapter Twenty~Two

Five days later and less than a week until the Duke of Lansberry's return, Charlotte walked into the back room of the Black Sheep. The first meeting to bring down Lord Hawley was about to begin. Hannah and Sophia had closed the coffeehouse to all other patrons, and Charlotte had in her pocket Miss Georgina Harrington's response to their inquiries about the choker's pendant. She just needed to convince Calliope, Mr. Powys, and Mr. Belle to join their group of conspirators.

Charlotte discovered she was the last to arrive, and she glanced surreptitiously at Matthew. She hadn't seen him since their carriage ride back to London. He held himself even more stiffly than usual. Although his skin was not beet red, it had a slight pink flush. A responding heat flooded her.

"What happened to your arm?" Calliope's shocked voice interrupted Charlotte's study of Matthew. Her best friend clamored from a cushioned pink divan where she'd been sitting next to Alexander and across from Matthew and Mr. Stewart. "Does your injury have anything to do with why Alexander had me inform your mother that you spent a night last week at Estbrook House when you clearly did not?"

"Let's all organize before Charlotte answers that particular inquiry." Sophia took charge. "Mr. Powys and Mr. Belle, would you join us?"

Calliope's honey-brown eyes widened. Charlotte could tell that her friend wished to ask more questions, but she remained silent until everyone had gathered in a loose circle of hastily arranged chairs and sofas.

To Charlotte's surprise, she was selected to explain the situation to the newcomers. This was different from when she spoke at the salon. She wasn't hosting; she was leading.

"So it is an intrigue!" Calliope exclaimed when Charlotte finished. Always an animated woman with golden features, Calliope positively glowed at the idea of an adventure.

Mr. Powys emitted a rather rude snort. Sitting across from the shimmering Calliope, he appeared her exact opposite with his black hair and deep blue eyes. Despite leaning back in his chair, he appeared just as engaged in the conversation as Calliope, yet he approached it with a cool, deadly seriousness.

"This is your friend's life, not a sentimental romance that you're penning." Mr. Powys's Welsh accent remained as lilting as ever, but it still could slice like a newly sharpened sword.

Calliope, however, merely raised a burnished eyebrow. "Does this mean you actually read my plays before summarily rejecting them from being performed at your precious theater? Afraid to add lighter fare to your offerings of misery, doom, or sinful bawdy?"

Charlotte looked quickly between Calliope and Mr. Powys. Her friend mainly wrote epic, romantic poems, but she did dabble in the occasional play. Charlotte hadn't known that she'd tried to have one of her works performed at Mr. Powys's playhouse... or that he had refused. Calliope's writings were very popular, and any dramatizations of her stories always drew a healthy crowd. Yet they were dreamy, passionate affairs compared to the ribald yet scathing comedies or dark dramas that Mr. Powys generally championed.

"I have heard too much sugar may cause gout, so I do my best to avoid anything too sweet," Mr. Powys answered.

"Whilst vinegar may preserve you, it would be a pity to lead a sour, pickled existence, even if it tends to be a long one," Calliope shot right back.

"Have you two met previously?" Hannah broke into the verbal sparring, her own voice curt. She was clearly annoyed at the secondary conversation.

"Just briefly at the Black Sheep a week ago," Calliope answered.

"But we have corresponded," Mr. Powys added, "although Lady Calliope tends to contact the other owners of the Dionysia."

"Only because you do not respond to my letters," Calliope said breezily.

"Will you two be able to set aside your squabbles—at least until we have secured proof of Viscount Hawley's villainy?" Hannah demanded.

"My cousin is right," Charlotte said softly. Then, she added with more force, "We cannot afford any fighting among ourselves."

A sudden stillness descended upon Mr. Powys. His veneer of charm vanished. Stripped of all the roles he played, he was left with the lethality that had allowed him to rise from street urchin to co-owner of one of the most successful theaters in London, second only to Drury Lane. He brought to mind one of the Four Horsemen of the Apocalypse—angelically handsome but bent on annihilating those who had done wrong.

"Hawley is nothing but a murderer. He arranged for Althea's death, even if he didn't personally light the flame that killed her. I am certain of it," Mr. Powys spat out, referring to the actress and former mistress of the viscount who died in a mysterious fire. "Hanging is too good for Hawley—not that they'd likely execute a nob. But I'll do whatever is necessary to see his power reduced."

"And I will suffer anything to keep you safe, Charlotte," Calliope said as she reached over to give Charlotte's hand a comforting squeeze. "I can manage to be civil."

"As can I," Mr. Powys intoned.

"Where do we begin?" Charlotte looked around the room.

"Hawley is bloody good at slithering away from his crimes without leaving a trace," Mr. Powys reported bitterly. "I could find nothing to directly connect him to Althea's murder."

"Nor could I," Mr. Belle said. "Two years ago, in the wake of Althea's death, I ordered my men to trail him from his haunts in London for six months. Although he met with villains of all sorts at the time, no one in my employ witnessed him committing an actual crime."

"I've experienced the same trouble when I've shadowed him," Matthew said. "It's been over a year since I tried, though, since I was in the Colonies."

"That piece of jewelry must be the key," Charlotte said as she pulled out Miss Harrington's letter. "I'm sure of it. Miss Harrington did not recognize the necklace itself, but she did identify the creature on the pendant. Here. Let me read what she wrote:

I must admit it was a surprise to hear from you, Lady Charlotte, or that you even remembered a wallflower like myself. I do not often think of my less than illustrious debut, but your kindness toward me was always a spot of brightness during those disaster-filled days. I am delighted to be able to return your charity by answering a few simple questions. I do not recognize the choker in the drawing that you sent, but I have been always more interested in pieces worn by the long-dead than the living. You are correct that the jewelry appears to be Tudor, which is also too modern of an era for the likes of me. The cameo though, contains an ancient pagan symbol of a Scottish wildcat. The image is not Pictish as you suggested but rather from the Chatti people. They were a Teutonic tribe chased by Romans from the region that is now the

Landgraviate of Hesse-Darmstadt. Pliny the Elder and Tacitus both mention the Chatti, but I digress. Some of the tribe escaped to Scotland, and a few Highland clans claim descent from them. I would assume that the pendant is not actually a carving from antiquity but an attempt a century and a half ago to replicate the old, half-forgotten art.

"Matthew, does your family have any connection to the wildcat?" Alexander asked when Charlotte finished. "I don't recall there being any, but you do have Scottish blood."

"The only interest my family has in the predator is hastening its eradication." Matthew frowned as he pulled out the choker for everyone to examine. "You witnessed my brother's reaction to the felines when I spoke at your mother's salon. He has no love for the animal, especially not enough to value a cameo emblazoned with the beast. I'm surprised that he didn't toss it immediately."

"But it is an important symbol to certain clans, as Miss Harrington said." A nervous excitement trickled through Charlotte. The individual pieces started to form a cohesive whole, but she still couldn't make out the entire image. "At the salon, Lady Fiona Sutherland mentioned that her family's crest contains one."

Calliope picked up the necklace and frowned. "This looks nothing like the Sutherland heraldry. Their symbol clearly consists of some sort of cat. This looks like a malformed pig."

"The Keith family also says that they are Chatti," Matthew pointed out. "Remember the shy young miss who mentioned that her ancestor was saved by a wildcat?"

"Lady Margaret!" Charlotte practically shouted her name as everything slammed into place. In her eagerness, she forgot entirely to hide her familiarity with Matthew. She clung to his arm as her wild speculation fell from her lips. "Her grandmother was

Lady Chattiglen. She was an old-fashioned sort—the very kind to wear a Tudor necklace. She was killed by a highwayman. All her jewelry was taken. Do you think…it seems improbable but…it could…I mean…"

"What is it?" Hannah asked impatiently.

"Could Lord Hawley be a highwayman? Maybe the late Lady Hawley discovered the necklace in his belongings and realized its significance. When she confronted him, he had his men orchestrate the accident. It sounds absurd, but—"

"It doesn't sound far-fetched in the least. My brother takes pleasure from inflicting pain." A horrible hollowness rang through Matthew's voice, and she wondered what he had endured at his older brothers' hands. She recalled the stories Alexander had told her about Hawley, Henry, and their friends. More than once they'd stolen Alexander's cane and forced him to walk across a narrow board over an icy, fast-running stream in the dead of winter. He'd invariably fallen in when they jostled the plank. What had they done to Matthew, who'd lived with his tormentors his entire childhood until he'd escaped to Charlotte's family home for the summers?

Charlotte's insides clenched, her skin prickling with the awfulness of it all. She longed to reach for Matthew, to hold him close, but she refrained. There would be time later when they did not have an audience.

"I agree with Matthew." Alexander reached for his walking stick and fiddled with the handle. "Hawley would be more than capable of doing something like that. It would amuse him when people speculated on the highwayman's identity."

"Hawley detested Lady Chattiglen. I remember him complaining about her to our brother Henry. When Hawley was down from Oxford, she chided him at a soiree for failing to acknowledge her.

She made a witty comment about his eyesight, and his friends laughed. He never forgave her." Matthew visibly held his body with brittle stiffness. It was how he had carried himself all those years ago, a boy not just content but desperate to stay in the shadows. Pain seeped through Charlotte.

"In the past year, there has been a noticeable increase in highway robberies." Mr. Powys leaned forward. "There's gossip about it almost every night at the theater. But we'd stopped trailing Hawley a year and a half ago when our previous efforts had proved fruitless."

"We should make a list of the holdups and see if Hawley had a grudge against any of the other victims," Charlotte suggested.

"I was about to recommend the same thing," Sophia said.

For the next half hour, they did precisely that. It did not take long to confirm a distinct pattern between Hawley and many members of the nobility, gentry, and demimonde who had been victimized in the past twelve months.

"What should our next step be? We cannot simply hand over the necklace since we have no proof that it was in Lord Hawley's possession," Mr. Belle pointed out.

"Nor can I easily explain how it came to be in my hands." Matthew sighed in frustration, but he seemed less rigid than when they'd first started the conversation. "I can return it to my brother's town house, but this time Hawley will likely dispose of it, rather than keeping it as a trophy. I could search his place for other damning souvenirs, but I am afraid he will use his money to explain away their existence. He may even find a poor sot who would confess in return for a bit of blunt to help feed his family."

A sense of certainty shot through Charlotte. She knew exactly how to free herself. She just needed to be brave enough to see her plan through. "We must catch him in the act, and it starts with me becoming the bait. That way, we can manipulate the timing and location of Hawley's next attack. I have an idea for how to lay the final trap, but I need all your help to set it."

⚬

"Enjoy checking Charlotte's bandages, Matthew!" Hannah sent them a wink before she shut the door to hers and Sophia's private quarters above the coffeeshop. The whole wound inspection had been entirely Hannah's idea.

"We are not lacking in fairy godmother matchmakers at least," Charlotte said as soon as Hannah's footsteps on the stairs faded away.

Matthew snorted. "I suppose I feel a bit like Charles Perrault's Cendrillon, although I must say a glass slipper sounds deuced uncomfortable."

"Does that make me the prince?" Charlotte asked. "Because I also feel akin to Cendrillon. I may not be sweeping ashes and working as a servant, but you are saving me from a terrible fate."

"You are freeing yourself," Matthew corrected, leaning forward in his chair to frame her face with his hands. "You are neither a prince nor a princess but the ruler of your own destiny."

Emotion rushed through Charlotte like a fast-moving river. She leaned a scant two inches forward, and once again their lips met. Headiness mixed with the already powerful swell, and Charlotte lost all sense of caution. She allowed the current to carry her as eddies of lust bubbled and frothed within.

Their kiss deepened, their mouths working against each other with such fury that their breaths soon became short gasps. Brilliant sensations cascaded through Charlotte like bright musical notes. She'd never felt so alive, so connected with her own body. She had never understood before how it could be an instrument of her own pleasure.

Yet even among the glorious symphony, an off note echoed deep inside her. One of worry. Of fear. And definitely of danger.

Charlotte eased back from Matthew. "But it is not only me involved in this plan. You are all risking yourselves for my safety. Every one of you."

Matthew pushed her hair back, his fingers lingering to brush against her cheek. There was so much kindness in his touch, so much reverence that it almost brought tears springing to her eyes.

"It is a battle that I am very willing to fight," Matthew said, his voice hoarse. "With the exception of Sophia and Hannah, each of us in this skirmish had previous dealings with Hawley. It was already our separate missions to stop him from wreaking harm from the shadows. You've only brought us together. And the Wick cousins are fierce. They have made it their life's purpose to defend the weak against people like the viscount. You ask nothing of us that we do not wish to give."

Charlotte reached out with her uninjured arm and pressed her palm against Matthew's bicep. She could feel his strength, not just of his hard, unyielding muscles but of his spirit. He had the ferocity and loyalty of the fabled English lion...or maybe, more accurately, the tenacity of the Scottish wildcat. He did not flaunt his power—a power many overlooked—but it made it no less real.

Matthew gazed at her, his gray eyes awash with an intensity that scared her. He was a protector, but then, she also fought for her loved ones.

"I could never forgive myself if you are injured in this madcap plan of mine," Charlotte said.

"It is not so madcap. After all, I am generally accustomed to breaking onto ships patrolled by the Royal Guards. Any adventure that does not involve flinging oneself through the air and landing on questionably sound slate or thatch is a well-planned one in my opinion." A glimmer of a smile tugged at Matthew's lips, and that little bit of mirth swept inside Charlotte, rejuvenating her flagging courage.

"I am not sure. There may be rooftop jumping yet." Charlotte paused to kiss Matthew's cheek. "I wouldn't mind sailing through the starry skies with you."

Matthew released a soft chortle. "One rough landing on rotting reeds and grass will disabuse you of that notion."

"Hmm," Charlotte tapped her finger against Matthew's chest as she made a show of considering his words. "I do suppose there is another kind of frolicking I would prefer to do with you."

Her words triggered another splutter of laughter from Matthew. "I would vastly prefer that as well."

"When this is over, we will need to arrange it," Charlotte said, as that glorious, freeing emotion returned. Matthew made her happy in a way she had never expected to feel. She giggled. "You have turned me into a veritable minx, and I like it."

"I do too," Matthew said, his voice so wonderfully sonorous that it triggered a shiver of delight inside Charlotte.

She leaned forward and kissed him. His lips immediately softened, and within moments, she'd coaxed a deep moan from him. His arms wrapped around her, cradling her snugly against him. Their bodies began to move against each other, the rhythm echoing the pulsating need inside Charlotte. She poured her pent-up fears, longings, and even uncertainties into the embrace. For once, she didn't fight or stifle the feelings brewing inside her. She let them flow, messy and uninhibited, and she knew with absolute clarity that Matthew did the same. There was a desperation and a wildness to their embrace, yet also a depth that both excited and calmed.

When they finally broke apart, panting for air, Charlotte gasped out, "We will defeat Hawley. For me. For you. For his other victims. I won't let him hurt you again."

"Nor will I let him bring his evilness into your life," Matthew vowed.

Their mouths meshed again, their words devolving into groans of pleasure, yet still promises all the same. In the bliss surrounding them, a bright future seemed gloriously possible—even when it would appear utterly improbable in harsher light.

Chapter Twenty~Three

T ension twisted Matthew's insides into a veritable Gordian knot as he and Alexander climbed the steps to Charlotte's familial home. Matthew hazarded a glance over at his friend who looked as grim as Matthew felt.

"I cannot believe we are about to forcibly insert ourselves into a dinner party consisting of my father and brother and your parents and sister." Matthew, with Pan perched on his shoulder, paused on the top of the stairs to wait for Alexander, who was making his way more slowly as he used his cane and the railing for support.

"Neither can I, but it is integral to Charlotte's plan." Alexander joined Matthew but didn't raise the door knocker just yet.

"Did we really need to bring Pan?" Matthew glanced up at the bird who'd begun to whistle innocently.

"The goal is to irritate Hawley as much as possible. Including Pan ensures that the dinner party will end in disaster without an official betrothal." Alexander paused and then addressed the bird. "Isn't that true?"

"Beast with two backs!" Pan screamed and then cackled to himself. "Beast with two backs!"

"I wish our strategy didn't involve Charlotte risking her reputation by feigning a dalliance with me." Matthew heaved out a sigh as he prepared himself for the debacle he was about to create.

Alexander arched a single auburn eyebrow. "Feigning? I am not sure if you fully understand the meaning of that word."

"Kiss! Kiss! Kiss!" Pan screeched.

Matthew shot Alexander a glare. "This is not the time for quips. You know your sister means to provoke Hawley's wrath."

"How else do you expect to lay a trap? Nothing will infuriate Hawley more than you stealing his betrothed. His rage will make him reckless."

Before Matthew could respond, Alexander rapped to announce their presence. When the distinguished butler opened the door, he regarded them with politeness so stiff it verged on censure.

"We're here to sup with my parents and sister," Alexander proclaimed with a jovial grin.

The man's already narrow lips thinned even more. "I am afraid the duke and the duchess are not at hom—"

Alexander did not permit the servant to finish. He strategically angled his cane so that if the manservant stepped forward, he would trip over it. Alexander pushed past the tall fellow and made his way down the massive hallway as quickly as his foot and uneven stride would allow. Matthew followed as Pan screeched out hideous guffaws from his perch on Matthew's shoulder.

"My lord!" The butler managed to infuse his voice with both contrition and condescension.

"No need to show us the way. I know, even if I rarely take meals with the family." Alexander continued plowing forward, the ferrule of the cane beating a rapid tattoo against the floor.

"No need!" Pan called gleefully. "No need!"

"Your parents—" the manservant started to say, but Alexander had already pushed open the door to the dining room.

Pan decided at that moment to fly from Matthew's shoulder. Soaring straight past Alexander, he called out as if he were the host, "Welcome! Welcome! Welcome!"

The first person Matthew spotted was his brother. Looking even more cocksure than King George himself, the pompous ass lounged in a chair next to Charlotte. And why wouldn't Hawley be confident? He had the power, the money, and the unearned deference despite the nasty rumors that swirled about him like overly sweet, fetid fruit. Matthew wanted to strut up and plant a facer straight in the viscount's smiling mug.

But Matthew couldn't.

And he feared it wasn't just because it would spoil the scheme Charlotte had so cleverly crafted. His brother held a power over him that Matthew couldn't completely break.

"What are you doing here?" The Duke of Lansberry rose from his seat, his patrician face white as he looked between Pan and Matthew. He probably regarded the parrot as some sort of familiar. The man had instigated so much of Matthew's boyhood suffering, yet he was the one who was afraid. If Matthew had magical powers, wouldn't he have spirited himself away years ago?

"Oh, I am to blame for their presence," Charlotte said cheerfully as Pan landed on her head. She didn't even flinch. Instead, she merely lifted her eyes vaguely in the direction of the bird. "Why good evening, Pan. Your feathered presence is always a delight."

Hawley glared at Pan like the creature was his mortal enemy while Matthew's father not so subtly started moving his chair away. The Duke of Falcondale stared at his wife with the clear command for her to fix the situation. Even the salon hostess's legendary composure seemed shaken as abject horror cracked her ever-present half smile.

"What," the Duchess of Falcondale began to say, her voice abnormally shrill. She paused and then swallowed. Her lips smoothed into a placid line. When she spoke next, her tone matched her pleasant expression. "What do you mean, Charlotte dear?"

"You told me we were going to host the Duke of Lansberry and his esteemed son. I assumed that you meant Dr. Talbot, so I sent him a letter inviting him to supper tonight."

"Whyever." Matthew's father slid his chair farther away. "Would you." Scrape. "Think." Scrape. Scrape. "That."

Pan cocked his head, watching the Duke of Lansberry with extreme interest. Matthew inched closer to his father, hoping to divert the bird if it flew at the nobleman. Unfortunately, that only made the duke more nervous. Glancing worriedly at Matthew, he scooched his chair backward now, instead of just to the side.

"Why would I not be confused as to which offspring Mother meant?" Charlotte was the picture of guilelessness. "Your youngest son is exceedingly learned. I'm sure you must have read his books. After his lecture at the salon, I have devoured each one."

"I do not read such unnatural drivel." Matthew's father spoke distractedly, his attention solely on Pan. The parrot twisted its neck at a seemingly impossible angle and stared upside down at Lansberry.

"Your son writes about flora and fauna. I cannot think of anything more natural than that." Charlotte sounded truly confused, and Matthew could only hope that his father did not blurt out that he believed his son to be a changeling. Matthew never wanted Charlotte to know the true pain and humiliation of his childhood.

"Why does that bird keep staring at me?" Lansberry breathed out the words.

"Father, it is just a parrot." Hawley sounded annoyed. Although he'd taken advantage of the duke's fears to torment Matthew, he'd always disdained his father's weakness. Perhaps it was why he'd transformed any insecurities of his own into cruelty.

"If you stop looking at him, I'm sure Pan will lose interest in you, my lord," Charlotte offered, her voice as bright as ever.

"Alexander, please kindly remove that feathered beast." The duchess's benevolent tone was marred by a quaver of barely concealed disgust.

"Listen to your mother." Falcondale spoke with cold assurance that his words would instantly be obeyed.

Pan, however, did not give a fig for ducal commands. He fluttered down from Charlotte's head and landed on the table. His one eye boring into Matthew's father, he began a slow hop across the fine linen cloth.

"Not the fish course!" The Duchess of Falcondale shrieked, completely losing her decorum as Pan's gray talons landed smack in the middle of the expensive sturgeon.

White flecks flew everywhere, but the parrot was not deterred. He continued his march toward Matthew's father.

Lansberry gave his chair a final push and then stood. "Your Graces. My apologies but I am afraid that I must bid you both adieu. I have urgent matters that I need to attend to."

"There is no reason for you to depart," Falcondale said stiffly. "We will get rid of the unexpected guests, including the vermin. There is still much to discuss tonight."

Matthew's father did not respond. He was already bolting toward the exit. Unfortunately, he arrived at the open door just as a footman appeared carrying a huge, towering aspic. The servant tried to steady the monstrosity as he skidded to a stop. For a moment, it looked like he might succeed. But Lansberry was not so agile. He crashed into the young man. Layers of artfully arranged quail eggs and sliced vegetables quivered ominously. Then with a squelch, the entire concoction toppled over. Gelatin sprayed the room. Pan gave an excited squawk as he chased after carrot rounds that had been freed of their jelly casing. Lansberry simply fled.

The Duchess of Falcondale stood and surveyed the damage. Her stance did not seem as fluid as it normally did as she turned to Hawley. "My lord, why don't you take Lady Charlotte for a turn about the garden? It appears it will be a while before the next dish can be served."

Matthew's gut clenched as he realized the duchess's intentions. It was highly inappropriate for a man to walk alone with an unmarried miss, especially in the evening, unless he was about to offer marriage.

"I would be honored." Hawley shot Matthew a smirk as he rose to his feet.

"In that case, Matthew and I should accompany you both." Alexander smiled cheerfully. "We wouldn't want to leave my sister unchaperoned."

∞

"Thus, I returned to civilization the same way I had reached the wilderness—by canoe. When I arrived at the mouth of the river, I traded in my paddle for a berth on Mr. Stewart's ship and the power of sail." Matthew bent close to Charlotte as he spoke, acutely aware of their brothers trailing behind them.

When they'd reached the garden, Charlotte had immediately grabbed his arm, leaving an irate Hawley with Alexander. Although Matthew knew this was all part of the scheme to goad the viscount into personally attacking them in his highwayman garb, Matthew still didn't like how Charlotte was purposely courting his brother's ire. When she'd begged Matthew to tell her about his adventures in America, he had felt the rage rising from Hawley like a palpable force.

"My baby brother is weaving fantasies," Hawley huffed out.

Charlotte only pulled Matthew's arm more tightly against her body—a gesture that could not be missed by Hawley, even in the gray evening light. "Let's walk a little faster, Dr. Talbot. Hearing your stories just imbues me with vigor."

When they'd walked a little distance from their siblings, Charlotte pretended to whisper conspiratorially to Matthew, even though she fully intended his brother to hear. "You are ready for the Duke of Blackglen's ball tomorrow night, then? A certain Queen Elizabeth will be looking for her Sir Francis Drake."

This was the final part of the trap they were laying tonight. They needed to present Hawley with the perfect opportunity to attack them. At Charlotte's request, Lady Calliope had asked her half brother to host the masquerade. In doing so, Charlotte had created a lure that she could control and that Hawley would never pass up. But that didn't mean it wasn't without danger.

A burning sensation shot through Matthew's shoulder as he was unceremoniously yanked away from Charlotte and bodily spun to face Hawley. His brother's flint-gray gaze bore into him. The hate in it had long ago ceased to sear Matthew, but that didn't mean he failed to recognize the warning. He'd become his brother's target. Again.

But this time Matthew wanted the rage directed at him.

"Jesters don't play at being pirates, Mat." Hawley stuck his nose close to Matthew's and said the last *t* with such violence that spittle hit Matthew's cheeks. "You're not going to Blackglen's, especially dressed as the infamous Drake, and certainly not with my fiancée."

Bitter irony filled Matthew, almost causing him to laugh. He wasn't actually a buccaneer, but he had sailed with them. He was damn well closer to being a real pirate than Hawley was to being an actual highwayman. His brother was merely a spoiled coxcomb using a mask to terrorize.

In response to Hawley, Matthew only uttered one word. "Privateer."

"What?" Hawley huffed out, his voice low with menace.

Matthew affected a nervous throat clearing, as he would've when he'd been a child vainly attempting to use his brain against Hawley's adolescent brawn. "Sir Francis Drake had letters of marque from Queen Elizabeth, so that means he was acting within the law—English law, of course, not Spanish, yet still legal—and thus was not technically a rover—"

Hawley's meaty fist closed around Matthew's throat. "Shut up, Mat. Nobody asked for a bloody history lesson, you prig."

Charlotte and Alexander both started to step forward, but Matthew signaled with his eyes for them to stay back. Hawley must have registered the flicker but mistook it for panic. His lips twisted into a triumphant sneer. The pressure against Matthew's windpipe increased. "That's right, Jester. 'Bout time you remembered your place, right under my boot heel."

"Lord Hawley," Charlotte said nervously, and the concern in her voice nearly wrecked Matthew. "I am sure your brother meant no harm."

"He's a whelp, and I don't acknowledge him as a true sibling." Hawley turned and smiled at Charlotte as if his words not only excused his actions but made them valiant in some twisted way. His fingers remained pressed against Matthew's larynx as he continued talking to Charlotte in a conversational tone. "Father believes Mat is a changeling. A maid on our Scottish estate tried hanging iron tongs by his bed and did all sorts of things with eggshells—boiled water in them, sometimes milk, even made bread in them once. We asked Father if we could devise our own trials, and he showed us every book on changelings in the library. Those examinations were jolly good fun, weren't they, Mat? Much more interesting than watching an eggshell filled with water in the hearth. Remember when you were sleeping and Henry and I stabbed your leg with a hot poker? Or the times we'd dunk you over and over in the lough? You used to cry and beg us to stop, but your fairy brethren never came to save you, did they?"

Matthew's stomach heaved, and he was very much afraid he would vomit. Fresh, new embarrassment poured like salt over wounds that had festered for years.

He remembered the stale smell of woodsmoke, the odor of cooking meat, the stifling heat of the kitchen in summertime—a place his father had only ever ventured to oversee the results of the young maid's folk "cures." Matthew rarely saw his father except on those occasions as the man's gray eyes nervously assessed him.

But those long-ago days were almost pleasant memories compared to recollections of his brothers' tests. Their father hadn't merely allowed his near drownings or the burning of his flesh, he'd encouraged it—as if it would somehow bring back his dead wife, a woman he'd always treated like a porcelain doll instead of a living, breathing human being. Or maybe it wasn't her he wanted, but another son like his eldest two—hale, brash boys—not a quiet one who preferred sketching a flowering plant to fencing lessons.

Caught in the thrall of old memories and struggling to breathe through Hawley's chokehold, Matthew acted on instinct. He gripped his brother's hand, twisting it effortlessly away from his neck. Grappling with Hawley hadn't been part of the plan, but Matthew couldn't stop now. He subdued his brother quickly, twisting and yanking his arm behind his back. The position forced Hawley to stand on his tiptoes. Despite being several stones heavier than Matthew, the viscount could not free himself, no matter how hard he struggled. Sweat dripped from Hawley's brow, and he gritted his teeth in pain.

"I am not a changeling," Matthew said very calmly and then released his brother.

Hawley nearly crumpled but righted himself, glaring ferociously. For a moment, Matthew thought his brother would charge him. But Hawley didn't—most likely because he didn't wish to risk another humiliation. He just promised retribution with his eyes before he turned toward Charlotte.

"I should warn you not to attend Blackglen's masquerade, especially if we are to be betrothed. However, I find myself rather scintillated by the idea of dancing with my bride-to-be in such a sinful place. You are not exactly who I expected you to be, but that just makes me want to make you mine all the more."

Flexing his bruised fingers, Hawley glanced briefly at Matthew, his mouth set in a sneer. "We shall meet again, Mat, and you will remember your place."

Then he was gone.

"I'll go after him and make sure he doesn't say anything to Mother and Father," Alexander said before he disappeared after the viscount.

Breathing heavily, Matthew leaned against a tree. His body threatened to shake like a green lad's. One would think he'd never faced a hazard in his life before.

"Are you all right, Matthew?" Charlotte whispered gently.

Matthew lifted his head, his heart damn near bleeding from the effort. He didn't want her to see him like this. He didn't want anyone to. Alexander had, but that was years ago when they were mere boys, and his friend had been in terrible shape too.

He had no idea what to say to Charlotte. His brain, that marvelous center of thought, seemed to have utterly abandoned him.

Chapter Twenty-Four

Her heart a morass of pain, Charlotte gently tugged on Matthew's hand. Like a sleepwalker, he let her lead him to her favorite bench—one tucked away from prying eyes. Wordlessly, he sank down, and she sat next to him. In the silence, she searched for how to offer comfort. One wrong word could hurt Matthew further, and he had already been immeasurably wounded. It had been clear from his haunted expression that he hadn't wanted her to witness how his family had treated him like a scourge.

But she could not ignore the horrible, terrible scene either. The awful weight of it nearly crushed her, and she wondered how Matthew had borne it. Tears sprang to her eyes, but she did not let them fall. Matthew would notice. If he'd had the strength to endure years of abuse, she surely could manage to remain steady for him.

Finally, Matthew lifted his head. His countenance contained a raw vulnerability that nearly caused Charlotte to crumple.

He expected rejection. Horror roared through Charlotte as she suddenly understood how deeply and thoroughly his family had scarred him. Their relentless attacks had not just been aimed at his physical body but at his very soul.

She knew the pain of being molded into an image of perfection— of how much it hurt to be viewed as an ideal instead of a person. But Matthew's father hadn't even regarded his own son as human. He hadn't just wanted to change him but exchange him with another, his "real" child.

Charlotte simply opened her palm and laid it on the weathered boards between them. Matthew turned to stare at her hand. Each passing second brought a burst of fresh pain to Charlotte's heart. She was just about to return her fist to her lap when Matthew's fingers closed around hers. They tightened almost painfully, as if he were afraid she would vanish if he didn't hold on.

Charlotte ran her thumb over his knuckles in gentle, assuring sweeps. She hoped he understood that she would never abandon him. That she didn't want to leave him.

"Changelings don't exist," Matthew spoke suddenly, and his choice of words didn't just make her eyes smart but her heart as well.

"I know," she said quietly.

"I am not one," he added as if it needed to be said; and maybe for him, it did.

"You are not," she agreed. "Even if you were, it wouldn't alter my feelings for you."

A bark of surprised laughter escaped Matthew but bitterness mixed with the mirth. "You wouldn't be afraid of me whisking you off to a fairy hill and keeping you hostage?"

A realization that Charlotte's heart already knew finally reached her mind. Matthew didn't think her shallow. He had never thought her shallow. He viewed them as literally from different worlds.

Oh, she knew he did not actually believe himself to be a fae, but that didn't mean that his family hadn't convinced him that he didn't belong. They had forced him over and over to endure tests meant to prove that he was not merely different but entirely alien. The examinations were meant to break the so-called fairy, and they'd fractured something inside Matthew, forcing him to regard himself as less. And that...that caused Charlotte's very soul to bleed.

"I wouldn't be a hostage, Matthew. I'd willingly go to whatever sphere you inhabited."

Matthew gently untangled his fingers from hers, and Charlotte almost made a sound of protest. She knew Matthew was retreating. Not just for a moment but permanently.

Matthew scrubbed his hands over his face, his entire form drenched in weariness. "In this instance, you would be leaving the charmed world full of dancing, light, and music. It would be the opposite of a fairy tale, I am afraid."

"Matthew, I have been happier in the back room of the Black Sheep than I have ever been at any ball, musicale, or salon. I've been carefully saving my own funds for a new life, although I daresay with your talents as a doctor, writer, and illustrator, you are well equipped to keep a comfortable roof over our heads. I was always planning on leaving Society behind." Charlotte laid her hand against Matthew's shoulder, hoping he could feel her strength.

"By marrying me, you wouldn't only be burdening yourself with an outcast. You will become one yourself." Matthew let his fingers fall from his face, and his eyes burned with pain and remorse. "I know what it is like to be unwanted. I do not wish for you to suffer the same fate by association with me."

"The aristocracy is a world I am more than willing to abandon. It is nothing but a gilded cage."

"But I am afraid you will find what I can offer you is a wooden one!" Matthew blurted out. "I cannot provide you the lifestyle for which you have been born to, which you deserve. I am not a pauper but nor do I have your parents' wealth. There will be no more stately manors, no more elaborate coaches, no more—"

Anger stirred in Charlotte, but she forced the ire to settle. This wasn't really about her; it was about Matthew and what he'd suffered at the hands of the people who were supposed to love him the most.

"My parents abandoned me at our family estate until I became old enough and pretty enough to be of use to them. I have withstood a childhood of being unwelcomed, Matthew, and I have endured a young adulthood of being desired only for my external trappings. When I am with you, I feel like I belong somewhere. I like that feeling. I want that feeling. Do not deny me, deny us. I cannot comprehend what you suffered and survived, but you are worthy of a family, Matthew, of a marriage. I would be honored to join my name with yours."

Matthew swallowed, and Charlotte could hear how hard the simple movement was for him to make. She was hurting him when she meant to reassure. The realization devastated her. What else could she do or say to prove to him that he mattered, that they mattered?

"What can someone like me ever offer you, Charlotte? Truly offer?" Matthew asked.

Matthew had been taught not to accept himself. Until he could embrace who he was, Matthew was right. He and Charlotte had no future. He would always be waiting for her to tire of him and of their life together. She could not heal Matthew's deep-set wounds with words or gestures or even abiding affection. Matthew had to do that. Yes, she could help him, support him. But the work—the real work—had to be accomplished by him alone.

"You can offer me happiness and support and, most of all, love, Matthew," Charlotte told him quietly. "But you must also believe that you can, and you must be able to accept all the affection and joy I wish to shower on you. Because as incorrect as you are about what will make my life meaningful, you are right that we have no future until you trust that we can have a wonderful partnership."

Tears glinted in Matthew's eyes. "I want to have such faith, but I do not know if I can. I don't want to destroy your bliss by seizing my own happiness."

"Those two things are not mutually exclusive, and they could even be integrally entwined," Charlotte said, her voice so grave the words nearly sounded like sobs even to her own ears. "But you must see that for yourself."

Charlotte slowly rose, and Matthew stiffly joined her. They stood for a moment, the ancient smell of yew wafting over them. She sensed Matthew didn't want to leave any more than she did, but both knew no more could be said. Matthew saw himself as incompatible with Charlotte and likely with any life companion, and Charlotte could not persuade him otherwise.

"I...I suppose I shall see you at Blackglen's masquerade?" Matthew finally asked.

"Yes," Charlotte said. "I will be there. We'll bring down Hawley together. I promise you that."

Because even if she could not release Matthew from the grasp of his hideous family, she was bloody well going to free herself.

Chapter Twenty-Five

T he seafaring Dragon has arrived, I see."
Dressed as Sir Francis Drake, or El Draque, as the Spanish had dubbed the wily privateer, Matthew turned to find a Merlin in a mask adorned with paste gems and dark robes. Mr. Powys made no attempt to disguise his native accent, probably since he rarely employed it on stage. Moreover, his native intonation was perfect for the old wizard considering the myth's Welsh origins.

Mr. Powys next gazed up and down at Alexander in his tattered robes and rough-hewn staff before a smile spread across his lips below his domino. "Shakespeare's Prospero?"

"The very one." Alexander executed a slight bow.

"We make an ideal pair for summoning the perfect storm to cast down upon the viscount's unsuspecting head." Mr. Powys raised his own crook, a rather ornate affair that probably was a theater prop. The fake jewels were of good quality and seemed to wink in the generous candlelight that filled the Duke of Blackglen's glittering, mirrored ballroom.

The three of them were congregated in a sizable and comfortably appointed alcove that Calliope had described to them back at the Black Sheep. It had curtains at the entrance to the main room that could be drawn for privacy if desired. The massive hall had similar nooks and crannies throughout its entire length. They were clearly designed for convenient assignations of all sorts. More than one set of rich, velvety curtains had been closed, even though the event had barely begun.

Strains of music drifted from the balcony where an orchestra played. The melody was as bright and playful as the gathered throng. Everyone wore a mask…and some little else. Greek and Roman goddesses, nymphs, fairies, sprites, and other beautiful fae creatures flitted through the assembly in diaphanous gowns, their rouged nipples visible under sheer fabric. Shirtless men paraded around as satyrs, fauns, centaurs, Minotaurs, Greek gods, and Roman gladiators. Yet the clothes they did wear were clearly well-made from expensive fabrics. Even those dressed as peasants and yeomen had donned carefully stitched garments of delicately woven wools and linens that no actual lower-class person could afford. Sailors swaggered through the crowd in open fine lawn shirts and pantaloons of silk.

"Our quarry has, unfortunately, not yet arrived, gentlemen." A lady drifted into their midst, her face covered by a gold mask that showed just a hint of her sensuous mouth. Matthew instinctually knew the newcomer clad in the rich-blue gown was not Charlotte, even though the color of her hair was obscured by a cluster of green silks, cut and sewed to look like aquatic plants. She must be Lady Calliope, as the Wick cousins could afford neither the domino nor the ultramarine satin that could only have been dyed using crushed lapis lazuli.

When Lady Calliope caught sight of Mr. Powys, she laughed merrily and waved her fake sword marked by the word *Excalibur*. "I suppose I am the Dame du Lac to your Merlin. Beware: According to the legend, I do successfully seduce you."

Matthew nearly winced when a thunderous expression descended over the visible portion of Mr. Powys's face. Clearly, the man neither appreciated Lady Calliope dressing as the Lady of the Lake nor her calling the legendary Welsh figure by a French appellation. Considering that Calliope was the descendant of Norman nobles from France who had subjugated Mr. Powys's ancestors in Wales, Matthew understood the man's reaction. Since the Arthurian myths had been thoroughly adopted by all of England and further transformed on the Continent, Matthew doubted that Calliope was aware of the impact that her outfit had on Mr. Powys.

"This *Myrddin*," Mr. Powys said, putting stress on the original Welsh name for the great wizard, "is most canny."

Calliope drifted farther into the alcove. Her costume was more akin to an elegant night rail than a true dress. The only thing that gave the garment structure was Calliope's own body. The fine material fluttered against her ankles as she walked, giving the illusion that she really was adorned with deep-blue water. The muscles in Mr. Powys's throat worked—either from unwanted lust or irritation, or both.

Lady Calliope smiled, a wicked grin framed by her gold mask. Unlike the paste gems in Mr. Powys's, the precious metal threads appeared real. "But I am clever too."

Mr. Powys scowled. "I am hardly likely to succumb to the overly bejeweled charms of a garish Norman-usurper imitation of the true Arglwyddes y Llyn."

"Is there a reason we are engaging in a history lesson?" Hannah asked as she marched into the recess with Sophia. Both were wearing black dresses similar to Lady Calliope's ultramarine one, with fabric snakes sewn into the garments. A very smug-looking Pan perched on Sophia's shoulder with a tiny eye patch over his lost eye. The bird seemed to be enjoying the raucous atmosphere.

"History!" Pan called gleefully.

Mr. Powys ignored Hannah's question. Instead, he smoothed his glower into the handsome grin he wore when playing romantic heroes on the stage. "Furies; how appropriate."

"Lady Calliope lent us the costumes," Sophia explained.

"My oldest two sisters and I once dressed as the Erinyes for one of my brother's balls," Lady Calliope explained. "I thought they were fitting for tonight."

"I wish I could be the third." Charlotte's voice floated into their alcove, and Matthew instantly stiffened. Memories from their parting in the garden ripped through him. He wanted to wrap his arms around her and beg her to forget what he'd said. But nothing had changed. They were still from two different worlds.

"You are a Fury in spirit." Sophia slung her arm around Charlotte.

"Murder! Murder!" Pan trilled happily.

Matthew's hand tightened on his fake rapier as he gazed at Charlotte in her golden mantle and vibrant fuchsia gown. Instead of the stomacher and decorative petticoat adding color contrast, the dress sported lighter panels of pink at the sides. Leaves the hue of the dress had been embroidered on the strips, and they seemed to rustle as she walked. The gauzy material at her neck was a more fashionable take on the starchy neck ruffs of Queen Elizabeth's court. Charlotte had left her red tresses unpowdered, a fitting tribute to the auburn-haired queen.

Her mask was gold like Calliope's. A strip of pink gauze hung below the curve of the visor. It helped to obscure Charlotte's entire face, as it would be most dangerous for her reputation to be recognized by anyone but Hawley. Still, Matthew could see her red painted lips through the sheer fabric. Their sensuous, upturned tilt caused curls of heady emotion to unfurl inside him.

He wanted to caress, to taste, to worship her. But he couldn't give himself leave to do so, even if the lady herself permitted it.

"Are we certain Hawley isn't here?" Mr. Powys asked. "Perhaps we just aren't able to recognize him in his costume."

"My brother is vain," Matthew said quietly. "He wouldn't show up heavily disguised. He wants to be recognized and admired."

"Matthew is right," Lady Calliope agreed. "My brother says he prefers a half mask attached to a handle. He only occasionally uses it to obscure his features."

"How often does Blackglen host these events?" Sophia asked as she scanned the crowded ballroom.

"Regularly during the Season," Lady Calliope said. "Perhaps twice a month, maybe even thrice."

Hannah, who had no qualms discussing money, lifted the veil attached to her mask to reveal her gaped mouth. "How does he afford it? He must be burning more candles than a poor family does in several years—and they're beeswax."

"Not to mention he has crammed more posies into this ballroom than could fill the carts of every Covent Garden flower seller," Sophia added.

"Be glad for that," Mr. Powys said drily. "At least their perfume partially masks the odor of so many people under one roof. Rich or poor, all people smell the same when stuffed like pigs in a pen."

"You could at least attempt not to insult your host." Lady Calliope playfully brandished her Excalibur in Mr. Powys's direction.

He batted it away easily with his staff. Unfortunately, Lady Calliope assumed a fencing pose. Mr. Powys, who was no stranger to staged swordplay, took up an exaggerated defensive position.

Charlotte suddenly gasped, and Matthew felt like she had sucked in his very breath—for there, on the steps leading down into the ballroom, stood Hawley dressed as another Sir Francis Drake, complete with two flintlock pistols. Knowing the viscount's penchant for chaos and his disregard for anyone's safety, the weapons were very likely loaded, hopefully with only powder and no lead.

"Hawley has arrived," Alexander announced to the group.

"Oh my, he is a popinjay," Hannah said. "He fairly struts like a peacock."

"He's padded his doublet to appear more muscular," Sophia

added. "He did not cut such a fine form when I saw him in the Black Sheep."

"Fine form!" Hannah repeated, flinging one arm with enough force that the snakes appliqued onto her gown seemed to quiver in sympathetic amusement. "He is ridiculously bulgy. He looks like a walking caricature of Sir Francis Drake."

"Fool! Fool! Fool!" Pan cackled as he lifted his gray foot to his face, as if embarrassed on Hawley's behalf.

"It is a costume ball, so exaggeration is fashionable, not that I am defending the man," Mr. Powys said.

"He doesn't look satirical but more like an utter jackanapes," Calliope chimed in.

Hawley would be horrified at their reaction to his carefully cultivated costume, but Matthew could not feel even a glimmer of satisfaction at their scathing descriptions. Instead, slick fear slid through him.

"Do not mistake his absurdities for a lack of lethalness," Matthew warned. "There is nothing remotely comedic about the viscount."

"Matthew is right," Alexander said. "Hannah and Sophia may be accustomed to dealing with more deadly-looking men, but Hawley isn't a buffoon. He has power—financial and political."

"Matthew and I should join the dance to draw his attention." Charlotte's resolute statement caused fear to twist through Matthew. He wanted to protest as Charlotte handed her golden robes to Hannah, but he knew it was a necessary part of the plan. At least her arm had healed enough that she wouldn't reopen her wound during any intricate steps.

As they entered the main ballroom, Hawley spotted them. With a swagger, he also moved to join the dancing as the orchestra finished the last chords of a spirited, high-stepping rigaudon. The dark tension swirling through Matthew was in direct contrast to the sweet, delicate notes of the next country dance. He should have felt joy standing across from the woman he'd imagined as his part-ner during his long-ago lessons. Instead, suffocating dread filled Matthew.

Their palms pressed together momentarily as the dance required. Heat merged with the firestorm already raging inside him. He felt enflamed from within and without, his skin pulled tight. His entire body seemed to balk at the measured steps, so light and precise, when he just wanted to grab Charlotte and run.

But he couldn't. Wouldn't. This was Charlotte's choice, her risk.

And so they danced, their movements deceptively bright and serene as they set a trap for a monster.

Chapter Twenty-Six

Charlotte would not recommend dancing with a former sweetheart while trying to entrap an unwanted fiancé. It did terrible things to one's nerves and absolutely shredded the heart.

"You do look wonderful tonight," Matthew said awkwardly when the dance forced them to lace their arms together behind their backs and circle around each other. Charlotte wished that she wasn't acutely aware of how very dashing he appeared in his gold-trimmed coat and high boots.

"I would prefer if I were dressed as a Fury with Hannah and Sophia," Charlotte replied with a flippancy she did not entirely feel but that suited her mood. "I feel like an Erinyes, not an Elizabeth."

She wanted to flay Hawley for what he had done to Matthew. It was no longer enough for Charlotte to escape the vile excuse for a man; she planned on destroying the viscount.

"Queen Elizabeth was a bit of a Fury in her own right, was she not?" Matthew pointed out. "But she was a mortal who didn't need supernatural powers to wreak vengeance."

"No, just a navy and a convenient tempest," Charlotte shot back.

"You command a small army tonight," Matthew reminded her.

"I have precisely two dragoons who are only agreeing to stay in Mr. Belle's carriage with Mr. Stewart because Sophia has brought a growler of her best coffee creation."

"I did not mean the actual military men," Matthew said, "but the eclectic lot that you have assembled from the Black Sheep's patrons and me, your ever-humble servant."

"I don't desire an ever-humble servant," Charlotte told him tartly before she could stop the words. "I want a partner."

The choreography of the country dance allowed her to whirl away from Matthew before he could answer. He glanced back at her, but she ignored him as she focused on the next man down the line, a cheerful fellow dressed as Friar Tuck. His footwork was more than competent, and he seemed like a pleasant chap, the perfect partner before having to deal with Hawley next.

"I see you have finally found your way into the arms of your correct El Draque," Hawley whispered into Charlotte's ear as soon as the steps moved them together. He should have been looking the opposite direction, but he was hardly likely to follow the rules of a mere dance. Even if this wasn't a masque, he was a man and a bloody heir apparent to a dukedom. He could take such liberties. But she—she would be blamed for permitting a breach of etiquette.

Anger—hot and swift—swept through Charlotte. She was so blasted tired of the hypocrisies that not just protected men like Hawley but let them thrive.

She no longer wanted this glittering world of false pretenses that held her prisoner. No matter the outcome tonight, she was done with it. This was her last ball. Her last mincing dance. The last time she would hide behind a mask—any mask. She was seizing her freedom now, even if it meant living in a hovel near the Black Sheep until her interest in the coffeehouse made enough coin for a more comfortable residence.

"You're not my El Draque," Charlotte practically spat at Hawley. "In fact, you're nobody's bloody dragon. You're a lizard with illusions of grandeur."

Hawley abruptly stopped moving. The genial Friar Tuck slammed into him with enough force to make the viscount jump a half step. He did not, however, remove his eyes from Charlotte's face. "Did you compare me to a lizard?"

"I did not merely compare you to one. I called you one." Charlotte stood still herself, and a strange power pulsed through her as the other dancers ceased their twirling. She, the elegant, demure Lady Charlotte Lovett, was about to cause a scene, and she was bloody well going to enjoy it.

"I. Am. El Draque!" Hawley roared out each word.

By now, everyone in the ballroom was craning to gaze at the viscount and Charlotte. The music faded away as each musician froze. One violinist halted so abruptly that he accidently screeched his bow across his strings.

Charlotte ran her eyes over Hawley's excessively padded figure and snorted. "You are neither the mythical beast nor the privateer. You're a man in a costume with pistols likely borrowed from more illustrious ancestors."

Hawley yanked down his half mask. "I am Viscount Hawley as you well know, and I demand that you apologize immediately."

"No." Charlotte loved saying the word so much that she repeated it. "No! I will not."

"Yes, you will. I demand it," Hawley said, his voice lethal.

From the corner of her eye, Charlotte noticed that Matthew had moved to her side. She sensed that he wanted to grab her arm and pull her to safety. But he refrained, and she had never loved him more.

"This is the beginning of you not getting whatever you desire," Charlotte announced, and chuckles rose from the crowd. Hawley spun around, furious to see all the masked faces staring at him.

"Apologize," he said through gritted teeth.

"I won't," Charlotte said and then ripped off her mask. "And I won't marry you either. Consider this my official rejection of your—or rather, your father's proposal on your behalf."

Gasps filled the ballroom. Despite having just eviscerated her carefully cultivated social position, Charlotte found herself standing on remarkably steady legs. It was scandalous enough for an unmarried miss to attend a bacchanalian ball, but she had just revealed herself to all and sundry. To make it worse, she'd insulted a man of the noble class and thrown him over. Her parents would likely disown her the moment that they learned of this spectacle.

Charlotte was free.

She wasn't naive enough to think liberty would come without costs and hardships. But she was more than willing to face them. If the past two months had taught Charlotte anything, it was that she was capable of handling adversity. She might not approach every pitfall with aplomb, but she always attacked a problem with fierce doggedness.

"Charlotte." Matthew inched even closer to her as if he could ward off the social calamity that she'd brought her way.

Charlotte's mission had been to tease Hawley with some thinly, but still veiled, quips. No one had meant for her to openly antagonize the viscount, not even Charlotte herself.

Charlotte didn't regret deviating from the original scheme as she stared at Hawley, whose chest heaved with suppressed rage. The man would surely follow her now, eager to mete out his revenge. He'd have no caution left and would overlook even the most obvious trap.

Hawley moved forward, his arm raised to strike her. Surprised cries filled the room, as open violence toward a noblewoman was unacceptable. Matthew leapt to intercept any blow, but Charlotte was prepared. She quickly withdrew a gold-painted plaster scepter from her pocket. When Hawley's fist contacted with the cheap fake, the piece shattered. Glittering shards exploded onto Hawley's doublet and hose. More laughter burst through the assembly. Men, including Friar Tuck, surged forward to restrain the gold-flecked Hawley.

Charlotte had thoroughly and utterly humiliated the viscount. Already, gossips were reevaluating the vaunted status he'd enjoyed through the years. Titled young men with family fortunes did not get unceremoniously discarded. As an heir apparent to a dukedom, Hawley would not remain an outcast, but snickers might covertly follow him for years.

"Are you trying to accost one of my female guests, Hawley?" The Duke of Blackglen's drawl broke through the chaos. Blackglen was dressed in the flowing robes of Bacchus with no pretense of propriety. The belted white fabric gaped open to reveal a rather finely formed male chest. Most would look ridiculous with a wreath of wax grapes around his head, but the purple complemented the duke's dark brown curls.

"She is the one at fault!" Hawley blustered.

The Duke of Blackglen's voice was as lazy as ever as he spoke. "You cannot mean to claim that this lady tried to attack you with a plaster scepter, Hawley. Really, I don't expect much from you, but that explanation is absurdly childish."

"I—I am the—" Hawley began, but Blackglen cut him off.

"Yes, Hawley, we all know who you are. Everyone does, just like they know me. I, however, do not have the constant urge to announce my rank. But as a duke whose title is older than both your father's and your paltry courtesy one, I am telling you to leave my premises. You have broken one of the few rules I have."

"No need to toss him out, your grace. I was just leaving." Charlotte reached for Matthew's arm. They had meant to slip away quietly, but that would no longer work. Charlotte had already destroyed her reputation, and Matthew's would only improve if she boldly departed with him. Charlotte could think of no clearer way to declare that she did not give a fig about being associated with Matthew.

"You're leaving with Mat?" Hawley demanded.

"Yes," Charlotte said. "I am."

"Mat?" Lord Blackglen asked with mild interest. "Are you Hawley's brother—Dr. Matthew Talbot?"

"Yes," Matthew said carefully, slowly lowering his golden mask.

Lord Blackglen grinned. "My sister has been regaling me with stories of your exploits in the Colonies. I even went so far as to purchase your book, *The Curious Animalia and Flora of the New World*. Come again to one of my masques. I want to hear more about your adventures. And bring Lady Charlotte. She is an utter delight. I am only sorry we haven't met sooner."

With that, Blackglen strode away, his robes swishing, his comically large goblet aloft in the air. As if he were truly the Roman god of revelry, the orchestra once again began playing, and people returned to their carousing as if they had never been interrupted.

Holding on to Matthew's arm, Charlotte walked with him, unmasked, through the silk-clad throng. Her blood thundered through her veins, and a glorious power filled her. She had publicly seized authorship of her own story, and she had no intention of giving the pen back to anyone.

Chapter Twenty~Seven

⬥

Matthew really should have been concentrating on the fact that his homicidal brother was very likely stalking him and his friends through the inky night. The presence of the two dragoons in the carriage paradoxically increased the chance of violence. Hawley would do anything to avoid capture. Even the pompous arse would understand that he could never emerge unscathed from such a scandal. He might not hang, but he'd never again assume his place in Society.

Yet despite the danger literally chasing them, Matthew had trouble paying attention to the shadows as he sat on top of the carriage box with Mr. Belle. Instead, he could only remember how Charlotte looked as she stood in the middle of the well-lit ballroom and tore off her mask. She hadn't hesitated one whit, nor had the motion appeared rash. She made the deliberate choice to expose her identity and destroy her flawless reputation.

And Matthew could not be prouder. Charlotte was indeed a marvel. She'd dressed down his brother in a way that no one else had. Ever. But she'd accomplished more than that. Much more. She hadn't just made a stand against Hawley, she'd made a stand for herself.

Matthew wanted to tell Charlotte how utterly remarkable she'd been, but he'd had no chance. As soon as they'd left the ball, she'd climbed into the carriage with the dragoons. He'd joined

Mr. Belle on top to provide a first line of defense for the coach's occupants. The rest of the group had quickly changed into the attire of highwaymen and were waiting on their own mounts to tail Hawley.

Mr. Belle was driving at a pace slow enough for Hawley to easily overtake them but fast enough not to draw suspicion. Between the horses' measured gait and the rocking of the high carriage box, the journey seemed deceptively serene.

A shadow detached from the cluster of ash and hemlock. The moon was only a crescent, and little illumination fell on the landscape. Still, it was possible to make out a horse and rider.

"Steady now," Mr. Belle said. He was speaking to his horses, but Matthew needed to hear the words too. This wasn't a typical mission. It was too personal on too many overlapping levels. Matthew required his wits, not messy, ill-defined emotions.

He rubbed his thumb against the familiar smooth wood of his gunstock. Tavish had given him the expensive rifled Queen Anne pistol before his first voyage and told him to be safe. It had marked the moment when Matthew had first felt a glimmer of familial acceptance. It had been odd, that feeling of belonging. He'd awkwardly accepted the weapon and boarded the ship without a backward glance. It had taken him crossing an ocean twice to come to terms with the feelings the gift had evoked.

Hawley positioned himself squarely in the middle of the road. A pistol barrel winked in the glow from the coach lanterns. As Mr. Belle pulled back on the reins, he asked Matthew quietly, "Are you at the ready?"

"Aye," Matthew replied with a bone-deep surety that shocked him. He felt prepared to meet his brother—not just steeled for conflict but ready for it. An emotion that shockingly felt like confidence roared through Matthew. Witnessing Charlotte's self-assurance had awoken his own.

"Stand and deliv—" Hawley began before the horses even fully stopped.

"Swounds, have you always been this unimaginative?" Matthew asked as he stood up in the box as it rattled to and fro. The bays were still dancing about, but Matthew easily maintained his balance after years of breaking onto ships.

Hawley swung his gun toward Matthew. "How dare you, a mere coachman, criticize me? Do you not realize that I have a pistol?"

It actually didn't surprise Matthew that Hawley apparently hadn't recognized his voice. His brother had never allowed him to speak much in his presence, and he'd certainly never listened to Matthew.

Instead of correcting Hawley, Matthew merely lifted his own weapon. "What a shocking coincidence. I also have a weapon."

"This is a holdup! I am holding up this coach."

"You don't appear very good at it," Matthew goaded him, knowing his brother was too far away for a shot to hit near the carriage. "Are you certain you've done this before?"

Hawley pulled the trigger, but as Matthew predicted, the lead ball kicked up dirt a yard away. The horses started to shy, but Mr. Belle expertly calmed them. Matthew stayed upright, his pistol still leveled at his brother.

"That was a warning shot!" Hawley cried, although he'd clearly meant to hit Matthew.

"Was it really?" Matthew asked, judging the distance very carefully as Hawley moved his horse forward.

"Oi!" Mr. Powys, dressed as a brigand, stepped onto the road. His Welsh accent had completely vanished into a deep Cockney one. "I'd claim that 'stand and deliver' was my line, but, bugger it, the coachman is right. Only a lobcock would utter that. Do you think you're in a damn novel, you utter stinking shag bag?"

With a pistol trained on Hawley, Mr. Powys strolled boldly on foot toward the mounted viscount.

"Who are you?" Hawley asked disdainfully, not even bothering to turn around to face Mr. Powys.

"A real highwayman who is bloody tired of some shit-fire nob playing land pirate. These are my hunting grounds." Mr. Powys was clearly relishing the insults he was tossing at Hawley, perhaps too much.

"You are boring me," Hawley said drily. "Go away, or I shall have you shot."

"A real bite in the arse isn't it? Some nick ninny interfering with your business?" Powys asked.

"Silence, or I will order that you be killed!" Hawley roared. "In fact, men, just sho——."

A volley of gunfire filled the air. When no lead balls kicked up the earth near the carriage or Mr. Powys, relief flooded Matthew. The shots must be coming from the rest of their group, just as they'd planned. They had succeeded in surrounding Hawley's men and were now firing on the hidden ruffians.

"How could you bloody addlepates miss this miscreant!" Hawley shouted, whirling around to presumably address his hidden minions. "He is right there. In the middle of the bloody road."

"Your men are cowering, not firing muskets. I brought along me own mates," Mr. Powys snickered. "What you heard were warning shots. We've got your parcel of jolterheads surrounded."

"It's true, guv!" one of Hawley's men called out.

"Impossible!" Hawley had completely lost his temper now.

"Are you certain you are actually a brigand?" Matthew asked. "You seem like a novice. The other fellow is much more convincing."

"I most certainly am a highwayman!" Hawley shouted as he

urged his mount toward the coach. "I held up more than fifty coaches last year alone."

"Successfully?" Matthew queried.

"Yes!" Hawley snarled. "And I've killed at least two coachmen who refused to listen."

"Truly?" Matthew asked as he readied to pull his own trigger. Hawley was in range now—at least for Matthew's carefully crafted Queen Anne.

"Easy," Mr. Belle whispered so only Matthew could hear. "I know you want a confession, but you don't want to be the victim of the murder he ends up swinging for."

"I dispatched Lord Everett's man. Two shots to the chest—one with each pistol. He didn't have the decency to die on the first one and had the bollocks to try to fire his longarm! I also killed Lady Harscard's tiger. I simply didn't like the look of him." Hawley had always loved to brag about the violence he'd committed. It was a wonder the egotist had kept his nighttime activities clandestine for as long as he had.

Hawley grew so caught up in crowing that the wrist of his gun hand went limp. The barrel pointed vaguely toward a stone wall as it otherwise bobbled about like a duck on a choppy lake. Throughout the maniac rant, Hawley drifted closer and closer to the carriage. Matthew doubted his brother even noticed his forward momentum, but Matthew definitely took stock.

Because Hawley's next shot wouldn't miss.

Yet Matthew didn't feel the metallic bite of fear—just cool, calm vigilance and a wee dram of triumph. Matthew had goaded his misbegotten brother into confessing to two cold-blooded murders, and the dragoons secreted in the carriage had heard every word. Charlotte would be truly free of the man—and maybe, just maybe, so would Matthew.

"It is ironic, isn't it," Matthew said. "Father spent so many years thinking I was the evil, wicked creature in the family when all along you've been the twisted, diabolical one."

"Matthew?" Hawley's body—outlined by the glow of the coach's lanterns—stiffened in shock and then doubled over as a fit of cruel laughter poured from him. "Is that actually you up there, Mat? Thinking you can threaten me? Why, you piece of shite!"

Hawley straightened and started to right his floundering pistol. Before he could, a bang rang out, and the viscount's hat flew off. With the precision of the shot, it had to be the work of Alexander. Hawley's horse reared, but he managed to hold on.

"I am your brother, and for once, you need to listen to me," Matthew said in a steady voice that matched the surprising calmness inside him. "That shot—that was made by Alexander, who is very keen to put a lead ball in your black heart. But given we're in the presence of two of His Majesty's dragoons, he is showing restraint."

Hawley frantically tried to steady his horse while glancing wildly about him. The mention of the soldiers drove two frenzied mounted figures from the copse of trees, whipping their horses' flanks with their reins, while another of Hawley's minions emerged from behind the stone wall on the other side of the road. All of them fled, spurring their horses over hedges and across the field.

"Those would be your mates," Matthew said calmly as he heard the carriage door open. "Mine are the ones who aren't scampering off."

Hawley had always been surrounded by cronies. But in hindsight, all those friends immediately disappeared at the first whiff of trouble.

But Matthew knew his comrades would never abandon him, even if it meant putting themselves in danger. It wasn't because

Matthew had a title or a fortune to inherit. He'd earned their friendship and respect. And that realization gave Matthew a strength he'd never realized he possessed.

Hawley, in contrast, appeared to be discovering just how precarious his own situation was. He managed to control his mount enough to swing the beast in the direction of his retreating men. The dragoons, however, cut off his intended route, their pistols drawn. Hawley spurred his horse away from the soldiers and back toward the carriage.

Matthew's heart jumped. Although Alexander and the Wick cousins would likely stop him, his capture wasn't a certainty. While Hawley might have confessed in the presence of the dragoons, they needed to catch and unmask him now, before he could leave the scene and plead mistaken identity.

Matthew sprang from the carriage box. He flew through the air and then slammed into his brother's back. The force sent them both crashing to the ground. With a terrified whinny, the horse reared, pawing the air above their heads. Hawley shouted a stream of invectives. Although the words were defiant, his voice sounded even more frightened than the equine's shrill neighing.

Matthew clung to his brother as the viscount frantically tried to wriggle and punch his way free. It was odd, Hawley being the one who wished so desperately to escape.

"Damn you, let go of me!" Hawley raged, striking out with his fists and his feet. Matthew strategically moved his body into Hawley's flailing limbs as he subdued him. Dragging his brother to his feet, Matthew once again yanked Hawley's arm behind his back.

Matthew was the one in control now.

The dragoons hurried over, and Matthew released his brother into their custody. The men grabbed Hawley's arms, and the viscount thrashed like a caged badger. His lips below his mask curled back to show his teeth, and spittle flew from his mouth.

"Do you want the privilege of unmasking him?" one of the soldiers asked.

"No," Matthew said without hesitation. "That honor belongs to Lady Charlotte. This was her brilliant ploy. She is owed all the credit for exposing my brother's crimes."

Charlotte, who'd been standing outside the coach with the rest of their friends, moved forward, the hem of her golden robe rustling in the wind. Queen Elizabeth herself could not have walked with such purposeful grace.

Instead of making her way toward Hawley, Charlotte stopped at Matthew's side. The blazing look she bestowed upon him heated every fiber of Matthew's being—corporeal and incorporeal. He wondered how he could have been fool enough to doubt the depth of her passion. He'd done both of them a disservice, one that he was more than willing to fix.

"If you desire it, Matthew, I propose that we unmask him together, as true partners."

He did not hesitate. "Aye, as true partners."

"What in the bloody hell is that supposed to mean?" Hawley angrily demanded.

"What do you think it means, you sapskull?" Hannah asked. With Pan perched on her shoulder, she walked forward and handed Charlotte a boot knife.

"Silly ol' bird! Silly ol' bird!" the bird cackled cheerfully.

Hawley glared at Charlotte. "Are you truly throwing me—the heir to a dukedom—over for a clodpated physician?"

Charlotte gave him a dry look. "Most assuredly, yes."

Then she turned to Matthew. "Ready?"

"Aye," he said, retrieving his own dagger.

Together they sliced through the cords securing Hawley's mask, and the leather material slipped away. Sophia lifted one of the coach lanterns from its hook and held it up. The glow revealed Hawley's enraged countenance. The veins at his temples seemed engorged to near bursting, and the purple cast of his skin was evident even in the dull light. His gray eyes glittered with deadly venom.

He tossed back his head and tried to look untouchable, but for the first time, he wasn't. Jutting his chin into an imperious angle, he asked Charlotte with a sneer, "What do you think Mat can offer you? Even his own father wanted to exchange him for a less odd son."

But Hawley's taunts no longer had the power to keep echoing relentlessly in Matthew's mind. Instead, it was the memory of Charlotte's earlier earnest words that blazed through him and settled his heart.

Because as incorrect as you are about what will make my life meaningful, you are right that we have no future until you trust that we can have a wonderful partnership.

Matthew ignored his brother and gazed into Charlotte's eyes. His heart bursting with emotions he could no longer contain, Matthew repeated with complete assurance what Charlotte had earlier tried to tell him. "I can offer her happiness and support and, most of all, love."

"Matthew!" The reverence with which Charlotte uttered his name reverberated through him. Her love swamped him, and he finally allowed himself to soak in the wonder of it.

Matthew stepped away from his brother. Her face awash with joy, Charlotte did the same. They only stopped when a scant inch separated them. Their bodies did not meet, but it sure felt like an embrace. Every inch of Matthew was touched by her very presence.

"You truly believe that we can be happy together? Both of us?" Charlotte asked.

Matthew nodded. Emotion billowed inside him, causing his throat to swell closed. He managed to push only an "aye" through his constricted muscles, but it was enough. Charlotte threw her arms around his neck, and then they were kissing—right there, in the middle of the road, in front of all their friends, two random dragoons, one ill-tempered parrot, and an irate Hawley.

"Has the world gone entirely mad?" Hawley roared.

"Bedlam! Bedlam!" Pan flew to the viscount's head and began to dance in time with his own screeches. "Bedlam! Bedlam!"

Matthew gazed into Charlotte's green eyes. "If this is madness, then I gladly submit to it."

"As do I," Charlotte breathed, and their lips met again.

"This is the oddest arrest I've ever attended to," one of the dragoons said as he helped wrestle Hawley into the carriage to transport him to prison. As Hawley was forced to duck, Pan flapped his wings and soared over to Sophia's shoulder.

"Bedlam! Bedlam!"

"It is the best thieftaking I've ever witnessed," Sophia countered as she reached up to stroke the parrot's chest. "And I've been to my share."

"It is bang-up," Hannah agreed, yelling over Hawley's final shouts as the dragoons shut the door behind the three of them. Under the expert hands of Mr. Belle, the team pulled forward.

"I'll send a carriage round shortly to collect you all from this happy ending," Mr. Belle called to them, tipping his hat as he passed.

"Mr. Belle has the right of it. I couldn't have written a better story, and I daresay neither could Mr. Powys," Lady Calliope added as the dark night swallowed up the jet-black conveyance.

"On this point, I will not argue," Mr. Powys agreed.

"Perfection," Charlotte said as she pulled back from Matthew, their gazes still locked. "This moment is absolute perfection."

Matthew shook his head. "It's better than perfection, because it is a bit messy and unconventional, which makes it all the more real."

"Real," Charlotte grinned. "I like real."

"So do I," he whispered against her lips before his mouth captured hers in another scandalous but utterly delightful kiss.

✥

Empty of patrons, the back room of the Black Sheep had a cozy, even intimate appeal despite being long and narrow. Matthew knew that Charlotte had specifically designed the space to feel akin to a warm, comfortable embrace. This place—this creation of hers and the Wick cousins—embodied her more than any glittering ballroom or elegant sitting room. He fit here too, in this plush refuge for intellectual discussion and friendly banter. He'd let his insecurities obscure these connections for far too long.

He and Charlotte were utterly alone. The rest of their friends were celebrating in the front room, which was also currently closed to all other customers. Tavish and Mr. Powys had purchased a few kegs from a nearby tavern, and coffee and libations were flowing freely. No one—not even Pan—had said anything when Matthew and Charlotte had slipped away, even though they hadn't made any particular effort to be discreet. Although neither of them had barred the door, Matthew knew no one would dare disturb them. The back room was, for the moment, their own private sanctuary.

"I am thoroughly sorry," Matthew said, his hand firmly wrapped around Charlotte's.

She glanced at him, her face awash with an openness that encouraged his own vulnerability. Even though he was certain that she already grasped what he meant, more words needed to be spoken.

Drawing a ragged breath, he continued. "I should not have underestimated you, *us*. It was foolish and shortsighted. I should have listened to you when you said I could bring you happiness.

Until you showed me how, I could not escape my own past. I never thought less of you, Charlotte, not once."

Charlotte leaned her head against Matthew's shoulder, and the simple gesture of trust infused him with a sense of belonging that he'd never experienced before. He wrapped his arm around her waist and gently pulled her against him. He was more than ready to accept the strength that she offered and to share his own.

"When I saw you remove your mask at the ball and reject the role Society cast for you, that's when I realized that I'd been letting my family shape my existence for far too long. I'm not who they molded me to be—the unwanted outsider."

"No," Charlotte said thickly, "you are very much wanted, and not just by me. You have been an integral part of the Black Sheep family, even before I arrived. You save people, Matthew, with medicine and with sheer bravery. How many young men owe their lives to you?"

Matthew rubbed his thumb against her knuckles as he finally allowed himself to be proud of his own accomplishments. It was an odd but necessary emotion. It gave him a wholeness that he'd never felt before. "There are many."

"And think of the medical students whom you have taught. How many of them have gone on to heal the sick and the injured? There are your books that inspire others to care for the natural world and the animals that populate it."

Matthew almost protested, but he managed to accept the praise. Tears stung the back of his eyes, but with Charlotte in his arms, he could face anything.

"I am glad to inspire them," Matthew admitted.

Charlotte shifted suddenly, and her arms shot around his middle. Her embrace was as fierce as her indomitable spirit, and his heart rose in his chest.

"You inspire me," Charlotte whispered against his ear.

A delightful shiver slipped down Matthew's spine. Wrapping his other arm around her, he held her with equal fervor.

"As you do me, Charlotte. You may have begun this adventure to seek your freedom from Hawley, but you released me too. I love you, Charlotte Lovett."

She pulled back. Her green eyes glistened like dew-covered grass in the morning sun. "I love you too, Matthew Talbot."

"It is because of your strength that I can fully accept your affections," Matthew told her, his voice as raw and full as his heart. He paused for a moment and then, with startling clarity, realized he did not need to gird himself for his next words. Because they were right. For him. For Charlotte. For both their futures. "Will you marry me, Charlotte? Will you do me the honor of being my wife, my partner in whatever may come?"

Chapter Twenty~Eight

If Charlotte's arms hadn't already been firmly latched around Matthew's torso, she would have flung herself against him at his proposal. Instead, unable to contain the joy overflowing from her very being, she squeezed tighter. She released him for a second only because it allowed her to give him another hug.

"Yes!" Charlotte practically sang the word.

A brilliant, happy giggle bubbled up from deep within her. Matthew's chuckle joined hers in an exuberant chorus. Their curved lips met in a crescendo of delight and passion. The kiss started with a sweet innocence that matched their mirth but then transformed into something wilder, yet just as poignantly honeyed. It filled Charlotte with brilliant, unbreakable wonder.

When they finally inched apart, both panting heavily, Charlotte huffed out in excitement, "How soon?"

Looking confused, Matthew tucked a strand of her hair behind her ear. He took a few deep breaths before asking, "What do you mean?"

"How soon shall we wed?" Charlotte asked, eager to start a new life. After last night, she had no intention of returning to her old one, even if Matthew had not proposed. Now that he had, she wanted them to begin anew together.

Matthew grinned, grasping both her hands in his. "Whenever you desire, Charlotte."

"What about the Black Sheep? Are you fine with me retaining an interest in the business?" Charlotte asked.

Matthew's thumb traced her temple as he watched her with a surety that engulfed her heart. "It is a part of you, Charlotte, and a part that I very much like. If you wish a more public role in its running and Hannah and Sophia agree, then I will be the first to shout from the rooftops what you have accomplished. You have said you are glad to take a tradesman as a husband, and I shall be thrilled to have a tradeswoman as a wife."

Charlotte immediately kissed him with enthusiastic abandon. Yet the lack of finesse did nothing to dampen the passion. If anything, it ignited even more. Their mouths slid against each other, their tongues tangled, even their very breaths mingled.

"Let's marry as soon as the banns are posted!" she gasped as Matthew found a particularly sensitive juncture where her neck and right shoulder met.

With a dazed expression, Matthew raised his face toward hers. "Banns?"

"Wedding banns. They're statutory law now—not just canon," she said quickly before guiding his lips back to the spot that he'd been so lavishly attending. When his mouth touched her skin, she nearly screamed out. "Or Gretna Green! It's quicker."

She felt his smile against her neck before he whispered, "Gretna Green it is."

⚭

"Dear heavens, what are you wearing? Is that thing about your shoulders supposed to be a coronation robe? And what happened to your poor hair? Please tell me no one has seen you looking such affright." Charlotte's mother's horrified exclamations broke the utter silence that had descended upon the family drawing room.

Her father, who looked annoyed by the interruption to his morning routine, had rudely stayed seated when the butler had ushered Charlotte into the richly appointed but hideously uncomfortable space. Despite her father demanding that Charlotte adhere to every social grace, he saw no need to follow them himself.

She was pleased to finally show him the same consideration. It was odd and decidedly freeing to stand in her parents' London home and not feel obliged to assume any role. Not the obedient daughter. Not the elegant hostess. Not the refined Society miss. Not even a lady.

She was simply Charlotte.

Although, frankly, she was wearing a costume, but hadn't she always? This time, though, she wore the regalia of a ruler, which was fitting, seeing as Charlotte had decided to wrest control of her own life.

"I am Queen Elizabeth. I thought it was rather obvious." Charlotte swirled her golden robe with a dramatic flourish.

Her mother grimaced and limply raised her hand to her forehead. Charlotte only swung the material with increased enthusiasm.

"Lady Calliope lent me the costume." Charlotte paused for dramatic effect, knowing her next words would send her mother into a panic. "For a masquerade."

Mother's fingers fluttered to her bosom. "Please tell me that you did not attend one of the Duke of Blackglen's notorious parties. It is beyond the pale under normal circumstances, but you are practically engaged to Lord Hawley. What would he or his father think if they discovered that you entered such a den of debauchery?"

"Oh, I am no longer going to marry Hawley," Charlotte said, purposely leaving off the horrid man's title. "In fact, that is why I came. I am here to announce that I am betrothed to Dr. Matthew Talbot."

"What?" Charlotte's father jumped to his feet, interested for the first time in the conversation. "That is rubbish. The Duke of Lansberry and I already came to an agreement. The marriage contract is in the process of being drawn up."

"I am afraid you will need to toss the papers in the fire," Charlotte said. "Hawley won't consent to a union with me after I was instrumental in his arrest last night."

"His arrest!" Her mother also leapt up.

"For robbing coaches. He is the highwayman who has been targeting wealthy, well-connected nobles," Charlotte announced rather gleefully.

Her parents swiveled to stare at each other in consternation. As they were not a particularly close couple, the nonverbal exchange was highly unusual and indicated the depth of their disbelief.

Her father turned back toward Charlotte first, his face thunderous. "That is utter nonsense!"

"It is not balderdash," Charlotte said with an easy smile. "I literally unmasked Hawley myself with the aid of Dr. Talbot. Two dragoons were present who witnessed Hawley's attempt to hold up our carriage and heard the viscount confess to two murders."

"It cannot be true." All color drained from the duchess's face except her bright spots of rouge. "He is an heir to a dukedom."

"Which does not negate his criminality," Charlotte pointed out. "Regardless of what you believe, you'll read the truth in the pamphlets or hear it from your friends. Gossip as juicy and plump as this will quickly burst throughout London."

"If what she says is true, we cannot have our name linked with Viscount Hawley!" Charlotte's mother whirled on her husband, desperation shattering her genteel facade. "You must cease all negotiations with the Duke of Lansberry."

Charlotte's father began to pace. "He will not be pleased. Perhaps the second son will be a suitable replacemen—"

"I am marrying the third," Charlotte told them. "He is waiting outside in a carriage. We're headed to Gretna Green. I only wanted to be the one to tell you of Hawley's capture."

"You cannot espouse yourself to a mere surgeon!" her father shouted as he surged forward and accidentally tripped over a table. He managed to right himself, but his wig slipped over one ear. "If you are not to wed Lord Hawley, I have other plans for you."

"Be sensible, Charlotte," her mother chided.

"Being your type of sensible would have ended with me married to a self-confessed murderer," Charlotte pointed out. "I much prefer my kind of intelligence."

"If you leave with Dr. Talbot, you are cut off from all funds," her father yelled with such ferocity that his body jerked. His wig plopped unceremoniously to the ground.

"That is fine." Charlotte smiled. "Dr. Talbot is well off. We are to buy a house together. And I do possess my own funds. I invested my inheritance from Great-Aunt Abigail in the Black Sheep coffeehouse. I think she would be immensely pleased. Grandmother too. They definitely would be delighted that I am turning a nice enough profit that I could purchase my own cottage in the country."

"You cannot leave. It isn't proper. None of this is proper!" Her mother jammed her fists against her hips, a position that she generally abhorred since it ruined silhouettes and, in her opinion, made women appear like fishwives.

"I know it isn't proper," Charlotte grinned. "Isn't that wonderful?"

Before her parents could reply, Charlotte whirled from the room and strolled from the house that had never been a home. Her father bellowed her name, but Charlotte didn't even turn around as she stepped outside. Breathing in the warm, sunny air, she headed straight for the well-sprung coach that Mr. Stewart had gifted Matthew and her as an engagement gift.

Matthew already had the door open before Charlotte reached

the carriage. His gray gaze instantly took stock of her face. He'd offered to join her, but he'd understood that she wanted to defy her parents alone.

"Everything went well?" Matthew asked as he moved to allow her to enter.

"From my perspective, it proceeded perfectly. I am disinherited as we suspected, which I honestly find extremely freeing. All obligations are gone." Charlotte plopped down next to Matthew and arranged her royal robes.

Matthew fiddled with the soft fabric. "Isn't this costume a trifle hot for today?"

"It is," Charlotte admitted. "But I am enjoying feeling like a queen."

Matthew searched through the material until his fingers met hers. Charlotte's heart gave a now-familiar kick as he pressed their palms together. With his free hand, Matthew pulled the top of her mantle loose from the fastening—not enough to remove it, but the perfect amount to reveal her clavicle. He pressed his lips at the V above her shoulder, the gesture at once softly sweet and wildly passionate.

"You do not need a costume to be a queen, Charlotte," Matthew told her gravely. "You always were one, and you always will be."

"I do feel like I've come into my power today," Charlotte said as she ran her fingers against the soft velvet. When she returned her gaze to Matthew, she gave her sauciest wink. "But don't fret. I plan on disrobing very, very soon."

Matthew stilled. "Is that so?"

"It is so dreadfully warm in the carriage," Charlotte teased as she reached for Matthew's cravat and loosened it. "The activities that I have planned on our way north will only make us hotter, I am afraid."

"Hotter?" Matthew raised a teasing eyebrow as he traced his finger along her collarbone.

"Blazing," Charlotte whispered sotto voce as she removed his neckerchief and tossed it to the floor.

"Mmm," Matthew murmured as he bent to kiss the hollow at the base of her neck. "I am going to enjoy journeying with you."

"I promise to make the trip to Gretna Green and back exciting," Charlotte said as she began to undo his waistcoat. But she had only managed to slip one button from its hole when Matthew pulled back, his face unexpectedly somber.

"I did not just mean the sojourn north," Matthew said. "I was speaking in a broader sense. We shall make our life together an adventure, Charlotte—whether we are sailing to the New World on one of Tavish's vessels or whether we are tucked up in our home on a winter's night and reading before the fire."

Charlotte pressed a kiss against his cheek. "I like both versions of us. We shall live by no one's expectations except our own. Most of all, we will define our own happiness."

"A fine and noble goal," Matthew agreed. "You have already shown my heart how to accept joy that I did not know it could hold."

Charlotte beamed at the man who had helped her discover her own strength. "And you, Matthew, have shown me how to be brave enough to approach the world with kindness and to defend the people and the creatures whom society has not just forgotten but actively discarded."

"You humble and embolden me, Charlotte." Matthew straightened and turned so that they faced each other. He framed her face with his warm, elegant hands—a surgeon's hands, an adventurer's hands, and a lover's hands. They were strong, capable ones, just like the man himself.

"You do the same to me," she replied hoarsely as she too held his dear face in her palms.

"To mutual happiness and support and, most of all, love," Matthew whispered, once more echoing the words she had uttered in her family's garden as she'd tried to convince him that he could give her the future they both desired.

"To mutual happiness and support and, most of all, love," Charlotte repeated, those words becoming an unbreakable vow between them.

Epilogue

Her fingers interlaced with Matthew's, Charlotte used her own key to open the door to the Black Sheep with her other hand. For the first time, she'd donned nothing to obscure her identity. Her part ownership in the coffeehouse was scandalizing polite society (and many outside its "hallowed" circles as well), but Charlotte and Matthew had decided that they did not give a fig.

During their monthlong absence, the Black Sheep had become a legend. As they'd traveled south from their wedding, they'd heard more and more tales about how the infamous Wick cousins had unmasked Lord Hawley as a highwayman. Of course, Charlotte was featured in many accounts. Everyone from the lowliest tavern maid to the wealthiest noble absolutely relished recounting how a highborn lady had literally torn the mask from Hawley's face. The fact that the viscount's own brother had assisted only made the story more salacious.

Printed caricatures and cartoons about the capture abounded. Everyone was clamoring for the viscount to hang. Some discussion had even begun about stripping the title of duke from Lansberry. No matter the outcome, it seemed highly unlikely that Hawley would ever return to his position of power. Charlotte, Matthew, and their friends had not just defeated him but ensured that he could no longer hurt others as well.

"Welcome home, Dr. and Lady Matthew Talbot!" The shouted

greeting pulled Charlotte from her reverie, and she nearly stumbled through the open doorway. To her shock, she found their friends gathered around the long tables of the Black Sheep. Even Pan and Banshee watched from the rafters. Although Charlotte had sent a missive ahead to Hannah and Sophia that she and Matthew would be arriving, she had not expected a private fete.

"Oh, this is wonderful!" Charlotte cried in delight. "You even have a cake with white icing!"

"Which we defended with our lives!" Mr. Powys cried out. "We have the battle wounds to prove it."

"You're injured?" Matthew stepped into the room, scanning his friends with the eyes of a concerned physician.

"We just were mildly attacked by Pan. We have plied him and his lady love with dried fruit, and he is satisfied now." Alexander pointed toward the rafters with his eyes where parrot and capuchin were happily eating.

"Hello, Banshee! I've missed you." When Charlotte said the monkey's name, the little imp immediately began to chitter with joy.

Abandoning a miffed Pan, Banshee climbed down to give Charlotte a heart-meltingly sweet hug. With the monkey clinging to her neck, Charlotte recounted the tale of her trip with Matthew to Gretna Green and back. Matthew interjected here and there, but mostly he seemed content to sit next to her and hold her hand under the table.

"So how are things here at the Black Sheep?" Charlotte asked when she finished. As if sensing the tale had ended, Banshee released her and climbed back into the rafters to rejoin Pan.

"We've had so many new customers since Hawley's capture," Sophia said.

"And the crowd has gotten even more interesting," Mr. Powys piped up. "More swashbucklers. More political dissenters. More bloody nobs too."

"Even though no one has publicly mentioned the back room, we've had a parade of new female customers," Hannah said.

"My drivers have been asking me what is happening at the Black Sheep since they're getting so many requests to stop here," Mr. Belle added.

"I may be partially responsible for the clandestine rumors floating among interested young ladies in London's drawing rooms," Calliope said with a smile.

A scowling Mr. Powys hurried to add, "Women with connections to my theater have also made their way here. The Black Sheep shouldn't just be a refuge for the rich."

"Agreed," Charlotte interjected before Calliope and Mr. Powys started yet another spat. "In fact, Matthew and I were discussing an idea for the future of the Black Sheep. Hannah and Sophia would need to approve it, of course. And it would involve all of you."

"What is it?" Hannah asked.

"The Black Sheep has always been a haven for peoples of all backgrounds and even for misfits," Matthew explained. "It was one of the few places where I have felt truly comfortable."

"It was a welcome sanctuary for me to explore my yearning to become more than what Society and my parents had ascribed for me to be," Charlotte added. "But I required more than a physical place to explore my inner self. I needed your help to break the bonds holding me back. I could not have stopped Hawley without all of you."

"We were thinking of letting it be discretely known that the Black Sheep is not only a sanctuary but a place where people can come for assistance when they have no other alternatives," Matthew explained.

Charlotte looked at Hannah and Sophia, realizing that her request put them most at risk. They could have their license revoked, or even find themselves thrown into prison. "We understand that you two would bear the brunt of the danger."

"Peril is what we live for," Sophia said with a broad smile. "Helping others seek justice complements our original mission here in London."

"We should raise a toast to our new plans, but first, we need to lift our glasses to your nuptials," Hannah said.

"Toast! Toast! Toast!" Pan cried happily from his roost as Banshee shrieked her approval.

"That reminds me," Charlotte said, pulling dried buds from her reticule. "If we are to embark on this new endeavor, we'll need extra luck. Matthew picked wildflowers for me to hold when we wed at Gretna Green, and I brought them back with me. Should I toss them or just hand one to everyone?"

"Toss," Hannah said. "It will be ever much more fun. You and Matthew can even pretend that you're escaping to your bedchamber."

"You can use the entrance to the back room for the ruse," Sophia suggested.

"Carry Charlotte in your arms!" Mr. Powys suggested.

"Carry! Carry!" Pan cried out.

Laughing, Matthew hoisted Charlotte against his chest. She found herself giggling too, as she grabbed hold of the flowers. Peering over his shoulder, she whipped the entire handful at their friends. The delicate petals must have dried together, and they sailed together in a clump right over everyone's head. Unfortunately, the floral projectile attracted Pan and Banshee's attention. The capuchin screeched in a happy demand, extending one paw. Pan immediately shot into the air to fetch his "lovey's" desire.

As Charlotte watched both bird and bouquet, the door to the Black Sheep opened. Charlotte must have forgotten to secure it when she and Matthew had entered. A slender woman dressed in the rough linsey-woolsey clothing of the working class entered. It took a moment, but Charlotte recognized her as Miss Georgina

Harrington, the antiquarian who had helped them identify the wildcat symbol on the choker.

The woman's gaze focused on Charlotte's brother with a surprising intensity. Suddenly, Pan shrieked in triumph as his beak pierced the congealed bouquet. The clump of flowers burst apart, raining down upon the unsuspecting newcomer. A bluebell caught on the sharp point of Pan's bent beak as he squawked his dismay. Sprigs of the dainty yellow lady's bedstraw flowers, white oxeye daisies with their golden centers, and more purplish bluebells landed on Miss Harrington. Her mobcap was festooned with so many bright colors that it looked like a satire of a jeweled crown. Several dried petals stuck to her cheeks, with one leaf dangling impishly from the tip of her nose.

With his flower target destroyed, Pan decided to land on Miss Harrington's head. As he did with many new people, he bent his body down over the woman's brow so that his one amber eye locked with her brown ones.

"Silly ol' bird!" Pan cackled.

Miss Harrington remained entirely unperturbed by either the floral or feathered assault. She simply raised a finger and jabbed it in Alexander's direction.

"You! There! Who have you told about my ancient gold-plated helmet? And what have you done with my cousin Percy?"

Historical Note

When creating the Black Sheep coffeehouse, I took some artistic license. As stated in *Lady Charlotte Always Gets Her Man*, coffeehouses were solely the domain of men with the exception of female proprietresses. The customers sat at long tables and swigged a bitter brew, which was not the tasty concoctions that Starbucks and its ilk serve up today. For the cost of a penny, blokes from all walks of life could gather in these surprising equalitarian (at least for males) establishments and discuss business, politics, religion, science, and other enlightened and *un*enlightened topics. Called penny universities, coffeehouses became the center of social, political, and economic activity during the 1600s and 1700s. Lloyd's of London, the London Stock Exchange, and the Royal Society all arose from these establishments.

While plotting this book, I wondered what would happen if one lady pushed her way inside these hallowed buildings and established a haven that literally gave women a seat at the table. It would need to be secret, so I borrowed some ideas from the speakeasies of the 1920s. I also thought, why not make this place comfortable with tastier java than would be historically accurate? And, thus, the Black Sheep, with its hidden back room, comfy divans, and experimental brews, was born.

Matthew is very much an archetype of the more well-educated patrons of these penny universities. He may seem a bit of a

Renaissance man, but there's a reason that appellation exists. Scholars often pursued multiple disciplines during that period and the next era, the Enlightenment, which is when *Lady Charlotte Always Gets Her Man* takes place. Physicians were often naturalists, engineers, writers, philosophers, and more. One example is Erasmus Robert Darwin (Charles Darwin's grandfather) who was a physician by trade. He also wrote poems about natural history and invented various devices, such as a carriage steering apparatus.

Although the medical field is a highly regarded profession today, this wasn't always the case. In fact, physicians started using the term "doctor" in the Middle Ages to piggyback off the respect that learned intellectuals with high degrees received. When Matthew was practicing in England, there was still a distinction between physicians (who received formal educations at universities) and surgeons (who generally learned through apprenticeship and on-the-job training). The latter actually grew out of medieval barbers who would drain abscesses and engage in bloodletting as well as giving their customers a shave. Henry VIII merged the guild of surgeons and barbers in 1540, and the two groups were not separated until the 1740s, a decade or so before this book is set. In the English Colonies, however, these lines became blurred, and doctors were expected to embrace both disciplines, as Matthew does.

The Enlightenment was also a period where people began to turn from folklore to science to explain natural phenomena. However, some, like Matthew's father, still maintained their old beliefs, including that fae folk stole healthy human babies and replaced them with fairies disguised as infants. The trials that Matthew endured—with the exception of being held from an open window—were all, unfortunately, tests.

Also, during the seventeenth and the eighteenth centuries, white indentured servants were found throughout the original thirteen colonies. Although they faced hardships and abuse, it is important to stress that the treatment of Black slaves was much worse and should not be viewed with the same lens. While laws were enacted in an attempt to protect white indentured servants, Black people were not afforded the same protections. There were term limits to the indentures (generally four to seven years for adults and longer for children), but slavery was almost always permanent and hereditary. Some white indentured servants were hoodwinked into assuming their debts via predatory fees during their passage to the Colonies. Others were street urchins who were kidnapped from crowded cities in England, while still others were political prisoners from Ireland or Scotland. It could also be punishment for a crime or even a voluntary position in exchange for passage to the New World. Black people were innocent parties whose autonomy had been forcibly and horrifically stolen. The plantation system's increasing reliance on slave labor based on skin color led to the systemic racism that still haunts the United States today.

Brave Mary, Sophia's pirate-queen mother, is not based on a particular historical figure, but she is inspired by an amalgamation of pirates, including Laurens de Graaf, Black Caesar, Cheng I Sao, Grace O'Malley, and Anne Bonny. Although pirates weren't exactly the romanticized, equalitarian lot that Hollywood sometimes paints them as, peoples of many colors, genders, and sexes rose through the ranks and became fearsome captains and leaders of the high seas.

George Belle is an entirely fictional character whose real-life counterpart is actually not from this era. My idea of having George create a fleet of faster carriages-for-hire came from hansom cabs created in 1834 (nearly a century after this book takes place). The hansom eventually replaced the hackney carriage.

The Chatti wildcat symbol is mostly made up as well, although the Chatti people were a real tribe and both the Sutherland and Keith clans claim descent from them. The internet does have a picture of a Chatti wildcat, but I cannot find a legitimate source verifying its historical accuracy. In my fictional version of the image, it is very stylized, similar to images of dragons found in Anglo-Saxon metalwork.

Acknowledgments

Working with my editor, Alex Logan, on *Lady Charlotte Always Gets Her Man* has been a wonderful experience. Her perceptive comments allowed me to better develop the mystery while sharpening the plot and tightening the story's pacing. These changes allowed Matthew and Charlotte to become fully realized on the page. Watching my characters reach their potential is always the best part of the editing process.

Forever's art director, Daniela Medina, has designed an absolutely stunning cover. Every time I look at it, I give a little squeal. It brings Charlotte and Matthew to life with its delightful details.

I want to thank the rest of the publishing team at Forever. The copy editor and proofreader provided invaluable assistance as they caught errors that I overlooked and ensured that the manuscript was polished. This book would also not be possible without the diligent efforts of the production team. The publicity and marketing groups have ensured that *Lady Charlotte Always Gets Her Man* reaches readers.

The support of my agent, Jessica Watterson, has meant a lot to me through the years. She always champions my manuscripts and encourages my fledgling ideas. Without her behind-the-scenes efforts, my stories would just remain manuscripts sitting on my computer instead of fully formed books.

My critique partners have offered me valuable insight. Sarah

Morgenthaler is great in monitoring my pacing and ensuring that I don't fall down the rabbit hole of using too many figures of speech. (Yes, Sarah, I know that is both a cliché and a metaphor.) Scarlett Peckham was a huge help in pointing out places to strengthen my characters' motivations. For those who enjoyed the salacious humor of "The Lusty Young Smith," I discovered this seventeenth-century gem through my writer friend Grace Adams. As always, I want to thank the Rebelles for keeping me sane during the writing process.

My sister, Deeann Polakovsky, PA-C, is constantly willing to field my random medical questions. After the initial "they would die" response, she's game to help me figure out what injuries and maladies would work best with my plot and the historical time period. Any mistakes that I may have made in describing eighteenth-century medicine are mine and mine alone.

Thank you to my readers—the ones who have just taken a chance on a new author, the ones who loved my early twentieth-century women's historical fiction novels, and the ones who have followed me since my contemporary days when I wrote under the names Laurel Kerr and Erin Marsh.

As always, I want to extend my gratitude to my family. My husband has encouraged and supported my writing career from the beginning. Not only does he offer constant encouragement, but he is always willing to do extra chores and childcare while I'm on deadline. As a lover of all things transportation related, he's an excellent source when I have a random question about eighteenth-century ships or dockside hoists. My daughter is an awesome cheerleader, who is very proud that her mother writes even if she's too young to read my work. My mother, who was my first fan, is always available to lend a hand however she can, including helping me proofread with the eagle eye of an English major.

About the Author

Two-time Golden Heart finalist **Violet Marsh** is a lawyer who decided it was more fun to write witty banter than contractual terms. A romance enthusiast, she relishes the transformative power of love, especially when a seeming mismatch becomes the perfect pairing. Marsh also enjoys visiting the past—whether strolling through a castle's ruins, wandering around a stately manor, or researching her family genealogy online (where she discovered at least one alleged pirate, a female tavern owner, and several blacksmiths). She indulges in her love of history by writing period pieces filled with independent-minded women and men smart enough to fall for them. Marsh lives at home with Prince Handy (a guy who can fix things is definitely sexier than a mere charmer), a whirlwind (her daughter), and a suburban nesting dog (whose cuteness Marsh shamelessly uses to promote her books).